THE
ANTIQUITIES
HUNTER

THE
ANTIQUITIES
HUNTER

A Gina Miyoko Mystery

MAYA KAATHRYN BOHNHOFF

PEGASUS CRIME
NEW YORK LONDON

THE ANTIQUITIES HUNTER

Pegasus Books Ltd.
148 W 37th Street, 13th Floor
New York, NY 10018

First Pegasus Books cloth edition October 2018

Interior design by Maria Fernandez

ISBN: 978-1-68177-857-0

10 9 8 7 6 5 4 3 2 1

Printed in the United States of America
Distributed by W. W. Norton & Company, Inc.
www.pegasusbooks.us

To Linn Prentis who loved Gina "Tinkerbell" Miyoko almost as much as I did. Thank you, thank you, Linn, for taking me on as a client, believing in me, and introducing me to the rest of your team.

To Ursula K. Le Guin, masterful writer, inspiration and dear colleague at Book View Café, who thought Linn's agency would be a good match for me. Turns out she was right.

THE
ANTIQUITIES
HUNTER

Prologue

When you are alone in the dark, hurting and frightened—no, terrified—that the next sound you hear will be the dying scream of a friend, or a round being chambered, you find things to do.

I prayed. I checked my watch. I checked my jacket pockets.

I had a little pack of Kleenex, my compass, my camera, and a hair clip. That was on the practical side. On the arcane side, I had a jumble of good luck charms: a Hopi *tinu*, an *obereg*, and a piece of wire from an old Cadillac's taillight. And then, firmly in a class of its own—Things That Were Once Practical But Are Now Junk—was the cell phone that wasn't much of a cell phone this deep underground.

I turned it on and was immediately mesmerized by the pale luminescence of the little screen. I hoped there was enough kick left in its battery to light my tiny world for a while. I used the wan light to check my bandages. They were fairly dry. I had stopped bleeding.

Mercy.

I shut off the cell phone-cum-flashlight and mentally checked the rest of my personal inventory. Earrings, a fake engagement ring, a watch, my

Saint Boris medallion. I had a small custom tattoo on my right hip. Or at least I had before tonight. For all I knew, the bullet that had grazed my hip had cut a bypass through that neighborhood.

I prayed not. I was a bit superstitious about that tattoo. It was a Russian Orthodox "Old Believer" cross with a Buddha seated in an eight-petaled lotus in the heart of the second crossbar and surrounded by beams of light. I'd gotten it the year I obtained my private investigator's license. Other than the tattoo artist who put it there, my best friend Rose and I are the only two people in the world who know that tattoo exists. No one else has ever seen it. Not even my mom. It's probably the only secret I've ever been able to keep from her.

My reeling mind wandered to places more pleasant than the pitch-black guts of the Mayan temple, in which I was trapped like a wounded animal, aware that tons of rock pressed down on my hiding place, and that a man I had once liked and trusted pursued me with one aim—killing me.

How had I come to be here, you might wonder? Hell, *I* wondered myself. One day I'm chasing down delinquent dads in San Francisco, the next I'm trying to avoid becoming part of a South American archaeological site. All Cruz Veras's fault.

A jolt of raw terror shot from one end of my body to the other; I was falling asleep.

I *couldn't* fall asleep.

Okay, so the Wicked Witch of the West had routed me through her infernal poppy fields. I'd think of snow.

I pulled myself up off the stone stairs I'd been huddled on, wobbly and dizzy. My hip whinged. I took deep breaths and held them for three seconds, then let them out . . . quietly.

I was in my fifth rep when I heard something that woke me utterly: a gunshot.

A gunshot.

I pressed myself to the wall and moved down the stairs one shallow tread at a time, pausing to listen. Sounds found my ears—movement, shoes on stone. In the maze of tunnels under Itzamnaaj Balam, I couldn't tell where it came from. All I could do was continue to move, descending slowly to even lower levels. I paused, put my head against the cool stone, and listened. Sounds rose up from below, sounds that might have been the scurrying of mice anywhere else. But there were no mice down here.

My eyes were starved for light, yet dreaded to see it. It would be *him*, searching for me.

Keep moving, Gina. Just keep moving.

I fell into a sort of stupor, shuffling through the shadow lands, listening and watching. So when my eyes finally saw light, it didn't immediately register with my brain that it meant Something Bad. I found myself being drawn toward a strange, gray, faded spot on the left-hand wall of the corridor ahead. I was nearly on top of it when I realized that it was reflected light from a cross-passage to my right.

I flattened myself to the near wall and peered around the corner. Ambient light washed out of everywhere and nowhere to illuminate the narrow way. I could see clear through to its other end, where there was a wall as solid and opaque as the one behind me.

Where was the light coming from? Curiouser and curiouser.

I stepped cautiously out into the junction. And was turned to stone. He seemed to emerge from the very wall of the maze not four yards distant, his flashlight in one hand, his revolver in the other.

I gasped.

He swung slowly toward me, bringing the muzzle of his gun to bear. I stood and clutched my useless cell phone and waited for him to shoot me. He didn't.

"Hello, Gina," he said, sounding like Eeyore—relieved to have found me, but depressed as hell. "You don't look so good."

Chapter 1
Gina Miyoko, PI

My best friend, Rose Delgado, is an operative with the National Park Service (NPS). Occasionally, she is an undercover operative, believe it or not. Not many people know the Park Service has undercover agents, and I'll bet most people wouldn't have a clue why they should have them.

The Park Service has undercover agents because of pothunters. These are people who live to pilfer. I'm not talking about little mementos to take home to the kids. I'm talking about a seriously destructive black market business in artifacts chiseled, chopped, and wrenched from sites ranging from coast to coast and on both sides of the Mexican-American border. So a team of trained field agents armed with guns, "interviewing techniques," and archaeological expertise makes for a very effective unit.

Most pothunting takes place in the Southwest. For the last five years or so, that's where Rose has spent about five months of her year, on and off, doing undercover work aimed at taking black market artifacts and purveyors of the same out of circulation. The other seven months she spends in a "landlubber," catty-corner to my houseboat in Sausalito, California, where she lives with her husband, Dave, their two adorable children, and a dog named Hoho. At home, she works out of the NPS's San Francisco offices doing a variety of work—much of it generated by her time in the field.

Don't let anyone tell you that the work of a U.S. Park Service agent is all cloaks, daggers, and glamour. No, ma'am. My pal Rose spends an absurd amount of time in courtrooms testifying against the aforementioned pothunters and the entities who buy their ill-gotten goodies. Sometimes she gets to bag bigger game—museums, art houses, and private collectors who—shall we say—lack scruples when it comes to acquisitions.

Rose and Hoho and I jog together every morning when she is in town. Hoho is a chocolate Labrador retriever—a thoroughly ridiculous animal with no sense of dignity. And yes, he does bear a passing resemblance to a certain rolled snack cake.

All three of us are creatures of deep and abiding habit. So when I came back from tracking down a husband-gone-wild in Santa Cruz and Rose canceled our morning run, I was puzzled. On the third morning of yet another canceled run, she suggested we stop running altogether and get memberships at a local health club. Suspicious. Rose had long been of the opinion that health clubs should more accurately be called "hormone havens."

You could've knocked me over with a soba noodle when I inquired why we were doing this, and she said, "Because you need to meet men."

"And why is that?" I asked when I recovered from the shock.

Rose and Dave had just celebrated their tenth wedding anniversary with a romantic trip to Monterey—Dave has been in love with her since high school but she returned the favor in college—so I suspected this was one of those situations in which someone with a warm and fuzzy relationship wanted her best friend to be as warm and fuzzy as she was.

I have nothing against warm and fuzzy, you understand. I'm just no good at it. Lots of warm and fuzzy things bite, shred furniture, and pee on the carpet. Warm and fuzzy, I've found, is not all it's cracked up to be.

"Because," Rose answered my query, "you need to relearn how to trust people."

That was not the answer I expected. "I do trust people," I said. "I trust you and David and Mom and Dad . . . and Alvie. I even trust your two darling children and your not-so-darling dog."

"With the exception of my dog and kids, everyone on that list has been in your life for uncounted eons. And you even keep poor Alvie at arm's length."

Poor Alvie is the SFPD's assistant medical examiner. He is a few years older than me and has been a friend of my dad's since Alvie was a rookie. He flirted with me on and off, and had asked me out a couple of times after a respectful amount of time had passed since my near-brush with marriage.

This wasn't a subject I was comfortable with, which Rose well knew. I suspected I was being deked—drawn off topic with a deliberate emotional dodge. I gave her a look calculated to inspire guilt, and she blushed, her glowing copper skin turning ruddy.

"Have I said anything that isn't true?" she asked.

"I don't want to meet men," I said. "I don't do well with men. You may recall that I flunked Relationships 101."

"First of all, you weren't the one who flunked. Second, that was three years ago. It's time you . . . relaxed. Expanded your circle of friends."

Relaxed. I was convinced she'd started to say "recovered." I held up my hands in surrender. "Okay, I'll relax. I'll go to the club—to exercise. But you have to promise me you will not help my mother with any marriage divinations. If I catch you anywhere near her bathhouse between the hours of eleven-thirty and midnight, there will be a reckoning."

The "bathhouse," in this case, was the little cabana in which Mom and Dad kept their hot tub. This was where Mom liked to hold court and try to enlist my female friends in helping her marry me off. I suspected that like all good Russian Orthodox witches she also attempted to cast spells there, though she'd deny having even considered it.

Rose laughed, all too familiar with my mother's personal and professional obsession with Slavic arcana. It didn't sound right, that laugh, and when I looked into her eyes, I knew it was a tin-plated fake. I'm not saying big clanging alarms went off at this point, but there was an itch in the back of my mind. I know my best friend and I know when something is off. But I didn't call her on it, not yet.

Rose chose a club close to our respective offices, at which it was rumored Giants of the Major League Baseball variety were wont to sweat. We went to the club every morning for about two weeks. We swam; we did the walking/climbing/skiing machines; we took aerobics classes; we tried racquetball; we kept an eye out for Giants. We saw none. Possibly I saw none because I was too busy watching Rose. I found myself going automatically into surveillance mode whenever I was with her. What I observed did not comfort me. She looked perpetually exhausted; she seemed nervous; she didn't eat well. Little sounds in a quiet room unnerved her. Once she chewed out Dave for making too much noise, then ten minutes later snapped at him for sneaking up on her.

Still, we "clubbed." We met lots of men. Some of them even flirted with us. When that happened, my attempts to relax went to hell in the proverbial handbasket. When one of them came on to me in the Jacuzzi and invited me to coffee after, Rose disappeared before I had time to protest that I was with a friend, with the hope the guy would assume Rose and I were a lesbian couple.

I had a problem with self-saving lies like, "I have a husband, a boyfriend, a mean older brother, and a father who's an ex-samurai." And I'd begun to suspect there was not an *obereg* made that would ward off unwanted attentions from the random male. *Oberegi*, I should note, are the lucky charms my indomitable mother, Nadezhda Eliska Arkhangelski Miyoko, drops into my pockets, purses, and any other unguarded hiding place to keep me safe from unspecified harm. I also suspected my mother had planted marriage talismans for me under the altar at Our Lady of Kazan and that her long working relationship with the Saints gave her a leg up in that area.

Deciding that honesty was the best policy, I told the guy I was a private eye. The variety of expressions that bolted across his face filled me with frank amazement.

Finally, he did a double-take and repeated, "Private eye? As in Sherlock Holmes?" as if the thought was just too ludicrous.

I am five-foot-two and weigh ninety-four pounds in a drenched trench coat. I've been told I have a "gamine" look.

Sweet, huh?

This has been a great challenge to my efforts in making a living as a PI. I don't look like a PI, which should be an asset, professionally speaking. In reality it's a mixed blessing. But the list of credentials I've accrued—a bachelor's degree in criminal justice, graduating from the police academy with three years on the SFPD, and a level III concealed carry license, to name a few—add the extra weight to back me up that my five-foot-two, ninety-four pounds in a wet trench coat just can't.

Anyway, at that point I mentioned that I had a license to carry, and a black belt in kung fu, both of which my wannabe-pickup could see for himself if he'd like to drop around to my office. Then I lovingly described my baby-blue Taurus .357 Magnum (which has a hell of a recoil, but I've gotten used to it).

I had hopes of an immediate cooling of interest, but my pool pal wanted to know some gory details: What sort of cases had I worked on? Any gruesome murders?

I had a litany of these all lined up and ready to fire. They weren't all *my* cases, mind you. In this type of situation, I pull freely from my dad's repertoire as well. As of late, my cases have been more along the lines of providing surveillance for suspicious spouses, helping some small companies to figure out who is messing with their books, and had once been hired as a bodyguard for a female athlete with a jealous competitor. Not particularly awe inspiring.

One of my most interesting cases to date was the one that launched my career as a PI. Investigating the murder of a too-nice-to-die man in my hometown, I'd ended up locked in the trunk of an aging Caddie driven by a skinhead, pinned atop a cache of weapons intended to bulk up the arsenal of a white supremacist gang, and forced to wrench a taillight wire out by its roots in order to draw the attention of the California Highway Patrol.

Somehow I sensed that this story would only encourage the guy to believe I was some sort of Jamie Bond. He'd asked for gruesome murders; I'd give him gruesome murders.

I aim to please.

I dusted off one of my father's last cases, in which a guy on trial for embezzlement felt his lawyer wasn't representing his best interests. "So he murdered him," I explained, "with a nine iron on the eighth hole. Par four," I added, because details lent an aura of heightened reality to such sordid tales.

My new acquaintance was suitably impressed. He wanted to know what broke the case.

"There was a golf ball with a partial fingerprint that matched the defendant clutched in the dead man's hand. And the pattern impressed in his forehead perfectly matched the one on the defendant's nine iron. When the police finally found the defendant's golf bag—bingo—bone chips, blood, the works."

At this point, a whole new set of expressions went into motion as my new acquaintance processed the visual images. (*Eeew! Gross!*)

"You . . . you didn't actually *see* any of this, though, right?"

"Are you kidding? I attended the autopsy." I had too, but I didn't mention that it was part of a college-level forensics course I was taking from Alvie.

My new friend's facial expression announced that I'd lost him on that last curve. I smiled and slipped out of the whirlpool, wondering if he'd be anywhere in sight by the time I popped out of the women's locker room.

As it happened, I caught him in the corridor, clearly in flight.

"I . . . ah . . . I just remembered—I've got an early meeting . . ."

I feigned regret and produced my business card: Gina S. Miyoko, Private Investigator, license number: CA988-007-09. "That's Miyoko," I said, smiling unabashedly. "*Gina* Miyoko."

He took the card, gave it a little wave and said, "Thanks." Didn't even ask what the *S.* was for.

I watched him scurry away, wondering if he'd consign the card to the trash can in the entry or tuck it into his pocket so it would end up in the laundry.

I found Rose waiting for me in the health club lounge, twisting the end of her waist-length braid around her finger and pretending to peruse a woman's magazine that I knew for a fact held no interest for her whatsoever. What she was doing instead of reading about how to keep the sizzle in her sex life was peering out the plate glass window into the parking lot as if some hardball hunk was going to arrive any minute for his morning workout.

As I was framing a sarcastic and witty remark about wannabe match-makers, I got a good look at her face. This was not the dreamy look of someone who's just swum two miles and is still under the spell of endor-phins. This was raw anxiety.

"What's wrong, Rose?" I asked.

I'd caught her off guard—so off guard, she jumped. "Oh!" she gasped. "Oh, nothing. I was just daydreaming."

My bullshit alarm sounded loud and long. This wasn't just a brain itch anymore; this was at least a yellow alert. Rose could bullshit with the best of them when she was on duty, but never did it with me or Dave or anybody else that mattered to her.

I gave her a "look," letting her read the suspicion in my narrowed eyes and giving her every opportunity to open up to me about the turmoil I could see rolling off of her in waves. But she merely ducked her head and started fumbling with her purse and workout bag. She knew I didn't believe her, but this wasn't the time or place to push it.

It was time to start digging, and I was going to start with her other half.

That evening, I went to Dave. I didn't beat around the bush either. "What's wrong with Rose?" I asked, the moment the two of us were alone.

We were barbecuing swordfish steaks on the seaward deck of my parents' houseboat, which is two slips down from mine. Rose and my mom and dad had gone out on deck to set the table and lay out the spread. The kids, Luis and Letty, had gone with them, which meant at least twenty minutes of futzing, munching, and general chaos. My mom is very particular about food placement. I believe it is a Russian form of feng shui. As I had ulterior motives I'd elected to help Dave marinate the steaks.

He looked up from his bowl of marinade with a puzzled frown wrinkling his forehead. I half expected him to say, "Nothing." What he said was, "I don't know. She won't talk to me about it."

I could hear the Devil strapping on his ice skates. "She won't talk to *you*?"

"And before you ask, yes, I have tried to get her to open up." He poked a finger into the marinade, then tasted it, frown deepening. He added some salt.

Just when I thought I'd have to prompt him again, he said, "It's got to be something work related. I'd know if it had anything to do with me or the kids."

Probably true. I opened my mouth to say so.

"And before you ask—yes, Rose and I are fine. Better than fine. We've been *great*, you know?" He glanced up at me with what I am sure he thought was a look of supreme confidence, but which fell several miles short into the camp of confusion.

I nodded. "Yeah. I know. Any ideas?"

"I'd say maybe something went wrong with a sting, but I didn't get a sense of that. I mean, she seemed pretty pleased with the way her last sting went. Uh, could you get the capers out of the fridge?"

I opened the fridge, only half seeing the contents. "I know Rose would feel responsible for anything that went pear-shaped," I said, "whether it's within her control or not."

Dave shook his head. "They got the pothunters dead to rights—a whole family of them. They've been charged already. Maybe there's been a new development?"

I found the capers behind a glass container full of clear liquid and wearing a yellow sticky note in my mother's extravagant hand. It read: *Holy Water. DO NOT DRINK.*

"What about the deposition she's got pending?" I asked. "Could she be worried about that? You know how much she hates it when these guys

8

skate away because some big museum opens up its treasury, or assigns a low-level scapegoat."

Dave's head was still shaking. "No. This is more than that. I feel it. My gut is screaming at me that something bad has happened." He turned to look at me. "You know her job, Tink. It's like baseball: 'hours of interminable boredom punctuated with moments of sheer terror.'"

"That's war, Dave. Or flying. I forget which." I did not comment on his use of my precious (read: obnoxious) nickname, which years of surly scowls on my part have been unable to bury.

"Point is," Dave said, "sometimes her job is dangerous. I mean, when she's in the field. This family she and her team caught was armed."

"But that craziness has never followed her home."

"Maybe it has, now."

I could feel the panic I'd been trying to keep at bay starting to creep up out of my gut, and saw my own growing unease reflected in Dave's eyes. I'd been hoping he'd tell me I was imagining things. Instead, I got validation.

Shit. *Deep breath, Gina.*

"Okay. Deep breath, Dave. We know Rose can take care of herself. She's a trained agent. She's also a damn good shot and has an epic roundhouse kick."

I should know, we practice together. No holds barred.

"Look," I went on, trying to be soothing, "maybe it's something simpler. Maybe a rift within her unit?" My heart wasn't in my words. Rose's team had been together for several years in its current form, and worked like a well-oiled machine.

Dave's hands had stilled, marinade utterly forgotten. He looked at me again, his brow unfurrowing just a bit. "Maybe someone else on the team is having problems and she just can't talk about it."

I hadn't thought of that.

"And there's the new supervisor, Ellen Robb," Dave said, half to himself.

"Rose likes Ellen," I protested. "She has nothing but good things to say about her."

"Yes, but Greg doesn't like her at all. Thinks she's too much of a Washington-style bureaucrat."

Greg Sheffield was a senior member of Rose's unit. He'd been in the field almost twice as long as Rose had and very likely, I suspected, thought the supervisory job should have gone to him instead of an outsider. Meaning there were political tensions afoot.

This information was ear-tickling. Rose has a myriad sterling qualities, two of which are a strong sense of responsibility and a penchant for consensus-building. Disunity appalls her. When we were teenagers, she used to come over and smooth things out between Mom and me. I don't know how we would've gotten through my fourteenth summer if not for Rose. She's almost two years older than I am, which somehow inclined Mom to respect her as an adult.

Greg and Rose had worked together for years. The fact that he didn't care for the new boss could be significant. If this was causing so much tension that it was affecting the team—or so much that Greg asked for a transfer, it would seem to Rose as if her second family was being torn apart.

I finally handed Dave the capers, along with my insights about Greg and the effect his disenchantment with Ellen might have on the team. As he considered this, his brow smoothed out a bit more.

"You know, I'll bet you're right. I hope you're right anyway. I don't know why I didn't think of that." He grinned at me. "You should be a psychologist . . . or a psychic."

I grimaced. "I'm just my mother's daughter."

"Ah. So now, you vill admit it?" said Mom from the doorway, in her best "moose and squirrel" accent. She regarded me down the length of her impressive nose, her dark eyes glinting with wry humor.

We laughed. I relaxed (a bit). Dave relaxed. I left it at that.

Tomorrow, I'd casually ask Mom about the holy water, and Rose about Greg and Ellen and any pistol-packing pothunters her team might have encountered. Mom would stonewall me, as she always does ("Oh, just a little class project of mine."), and Rose would spill the beans. I was willing to bank on it. I was taking no more bullshit.

I lay down to sleep with the sound of water lapping at the keel of my houseboat. Far and away, there was an underscore of pounding surf, like a mother's heartbeat. Somewhere along the path to sleep, I stumbled into a world in which the heartbeat became my own, and the hiss of surf became the hiss of traffic. There were odors here too—oil, wet concrete, something frying.

Sight was slow to register. I was swaddled in moist, cool darkness that clung to my skin. My eyes finally caught up with my other senses and informed me that I was in an alley. Before me was the opening to the street. Neon flashed blue, then red on the glistening concrete, and infused the mist with color—hot then cold. On my left and right were brick walls that seemed to go up into infinity. There was graffiti on them.

Behind me was darkness; I instinctively edged away toward the untrustworthy light.

That's when a voice spoke my name. It was a man's voice, crooning sweet slime. I knew it well. It filled me with disgust and desperation.

I ran.

In dreams one always runs when desperate, usually in the wrong direction. I did that now, bolting from the spastic light into the darkness. I suddenly and inexplicably knew I was seeking something or someone. I had no idea what or whom. As soon as this goal established itself in my mind, the alley morphed into one of those games in which computer-generated scenery flashed by at surreal speed. The CG maze shunted me here and there; walls melted and coalesced and went on in the nightmare approximation of forever—which according to dream research is measured in seconds.

I grew increasingly desperate. I gasped for breath. There was a pain in my chest.

"You don't even know where you're going, do you?" asked my invisible man.

His voice came to me as if his lips were literally pressed to my ear—as they had been before in waking life. Every nerve in my body twitched in harmony and I leapt almost to wakefulness. But I couldn't seem to emerge from this world, and when I returned to the alley, it was to find a chain-link fence blocking my path.

I hooked my fingers through the cold mesh and gave the fence a shake. Anyone whose dream path has ever ended at a chain-link fence does this. Then Rose appeared on the other side of the fence, her dark eyes huge and mute.

"What's wrong, Rose?" I asked, and the invisible man mimicked: "What's wrong, Rose?"

Rose's eyes were focused on a point over my head. Her mouth opened in a soundless scream and she ran. I wanted to turn, to see what she saw, but I was afraid to look, so I instinctively felt my pockets.

No *mingei*, no obereg. Nothing.

My pockets were empty.

I turned and ran.

The alley vanished. I was running through sand, and the sound of traffic faded back into the roar of surf. I thought I was chasing Rose, but I wasn't sure. There was a shadow on the beach in front of me; that was what I pursued—a shadow.

He was here too. "You don't get it, Tinkerbell," he said. "You never do get it."

I was in the surf then, up to my ankles, my knees, my thighs, my hips, pushing against the current. The waves would soon be over my head.

Why was I doing this?

"Stupid Gina. My stupid little monkey," he said, and I could no longer see or hear or even breathe.

I woke on a single sharp gasp of air, surprised to find my clothes plastered to my body.

My mind accepted a quick succession of realities—I'd drowned; I'd sleepwalked to the beach; I'd sprung a leak; I'd awakened from a nightmare in a cold sweat. The houseboat rocked gently; water sighed beneath it and lapped comfortingly at the keel. I sighed too.

It was so tempting to rationalize—yeah, it must be tension with Greg and the new boss; she'll tell me when she's ready. Or it's someone else on the team who has a dire problem, and loyal, loyal Rose feels she can't discuss it, even with her closest companions. I knew all this was false. I had never known Rose to hold back anything. This behavior went against all the years we had known each other. Rose, a creature of habit and as much a control freak as anyone I know, had disarranged her habits, both ephemeral and deep, to accommodate *something*. She was, as my invisible taunter pointed out, in some sort of serious trouble, and I had been, once again, slow on the uptake.

I already knew how dangerous that could be.

Chapter 2

Six Honest Serving-Men

Our Monday morning routine didn't offer me any decent opportunities to force disclosure until we were treading away among the machinery on our final cooldown. Then, the improbable happened—the gym emptied out. I chose this moment to nudge.

"Rose," I said, "Dave's worried about you."

"What?" She looked up at me from where she had been staring at the empty space between the calorie display and the little TV screen.

"He's afraid there's something dire happening at work. And that that something has got you behaving strangely."

She looked down at the lights blinking rhythmically on the machine's console. "There's nothing wrong at work."

While my mind was swirling with shotgun-wielding pothunters, I tried an easier angle. "How's Greg taking the new boss?"

She gave me a weird look. "Why do you ask?"

"Dave says Greg doesn't like her."

"He's a professional. He's adjusting. Everything will be—" She broke off suddenly and looked at me. "Okay, fine. It's bothering me, okay? Probably more than it bothers Greg. You flushed me out. Happy?" Her tone had daggers in it and her body was rigid, knuckles white as they gripped the treadmill handlebar.

"I would be, if that was anywhere close to the truth."

"Tink, really."

"Don't forget who you're talking to, Rose. What's *really* bothering you?"

"I told you: I'm worried about Greg. Really, it's not even that big a deal."

"Then why did we join the local sex-and-suntan club?"

"What?"

My making a connection between the two things took her by surprise, but before I could pounce, the room filled with a gaggle of perky senior citizens and their über-perky aerobics instructor.

Damn. Cut off at the pass.

We were fresh from the shower when the locker room cleared. Time for my one-woman blitzkrieg.

"Why are we here, Rose?" I asked. "I hate these places. *You* hate these places. You miss our runs as much as I do. Why are you not talking to me about whatever it is? What are you afraid of?" Before she could wriggle away, I added, "I'll tell you what *I'm* afraid of—I'm afraid of something happening to you while I just stand around looking stupid."

Her mouth opened, but nothing came out. We just stood there—two wet, naked women staring at each other while water dripped from our hair and bodies to soak into the stained blue indoor-outdoor carpeting.

Finally, she lowered her eyes and shook her head. "It's crazy," she said, and I smelled a confession. "I think . . . I think someone's stalking me." She sat down as if the words were a physical weight she was grappling with.

My scalp tingled and I felt a cold breeze from last night's dream. "Someone? Who?"

"I don't know. I've never gotten a close look at him."

I sat down next to her, my war stance evaporating. "Him. A man? You're sure?"

She shook her head. "I'm not sure of anything, Gina. There's a car I see in my rearview mirror more often than coincidence should allow. A guy who seems to be hovering . . ."

"Have you told anybody? Your boss?"

She shook her head and stood to begin toweling her yard-o-hair. "No. I'm not *sure*, Tink. One minute I'm certain I'm being followed, the next I think I'm suggestible and paranoid and imagining everything."

I didn't point out that she had never been suggestible or paranoid before and started toweling my own collar-length mop. "And you've changed your routines for imagination's sake?"

She slumped onto one of the benches at the center of the room. "While you were working that case in Santa Cruz for two weeks, I jogged alone. It was in the first couple of days that I noticed the car. It seemed to be everywhere. Of course, it's a Honda—burgundy, mid-aughties, California plates."

"Dime a dozen," I clichéd.

"Exactly."

"Distinguishing marks?"

"None."

"Plates?"

"Never gets close enough for me to make out more than the first two letters: *KL*."

"You've never seen the guy out of the car?"

"Once. If it's the same car. One day when I was down on the beach, I looked up at the parking lot and there was a burgundy Honda with this guy sitting on the hood watching the beach through binoculars."

"What'd he look like?"

"Like I could tell from that distance?"

I kept my narrowed eyes on her face.

She closed her eyes. "Dark hair, I think. He was wearing a baseball cap and dark glasses. Uh . . . well-tanned or dark-skinned. Slender. Tallish."

"Ish?"

"Around five-ten, five-eleven."

A titan in my little universe. "If you are being stalked, you need to tell someone. Besides me. Preferably your boss . . . or the police."

"And if I'm not, I look like I'm paranoid. Not good for my professional credibility."

I suddenly felt much less impotent than I had about two minutes earlier. "All right. The first thing we need to do is establish the existence and identity of the stalker."

"And how do I do that?"

"We, Rose. *We.*"

She smiled. The first genuine Rose Delgado smile I'd seen for weeks. "How?"

I pulled my lucky Caddie wire out of the side pocket of my gym bag and twisted it around my wrist. "We turn the tables on him."

Kipling had it that he kept "six honest serving-men" who taught him all he knew. Their names were, "What and Why and When and How and Where and Who." These "names" are permanently affixed in all caps along the top of the whiteboard that is situated perfectly for my height on the wall behind the desk in my office.

Too antsy to sit down, and nursing cups of strong coffee, Rose and I moved my office chairs out of the way and stood on either side of my desk, facing the board. The chairs in my office are easily its most decorative feature, and are quintessentially Japanese black lacquer affairs with red silk cushions I'd added myself. I'd picked up a whole set at Pier 1, free of charge, because the original cushions had gotten slashed when the store was vandalized. They were a sort of thank-you gift added to my fee for tracking down the vandals when the understaffed local PD had been unable to spare the time. Their siblings were installed around the dining table on my houseboat.

I pulled a pack of sticky notes out of my desk drawer and set them on the desktop, then laid my stainless steel and gold Parker T-Ball Jotter to the right of the pad o' stickies, and my now jumbled knot of lucky Cadillac taillight wire on the left. With this ritual complete, I said, "Let's start with the initial 'who.'"

Rose perched on the edge of the desk and watched as I picked up the Parker, clicked it open and wrote *Rose Delgado, NPS agent* on the topmost sticky note. I tore it off the pack and stuck it on the whiteboard under the word *Who*.

"What?" I asked next.

"Stalking."

This went on the board too, under the appropriate heading.

People who have watched me do this exercise may employ their own serving-man: Why? Why do I use stickies on a whiteboard instead of whiteboard markers? First of all, stickies take up less room, so they allow for more ideas to be trotted out. They're also permanent—at least until you wad them up and toss them (which I never do until a case is closed). They're easily moved from one place to another when you're building a flow of ideas or a timeline, and if you remove one, you can park it to the side without losing it via hasty erasure.

Oh, and they don't smell bad and give you a headache.

I invoked the next serving-man: "Why?"

"Because of my involvement in a current or upcoming case? That's the only thing that makes any sense."

I wrote *Open case* on the next sticky in the pack and popped it up under *Why*. "What have you got open right now?"

Rose chewed the inside of her mouth contemplatively. She'd watched me go through this ritual before when brainstorming far more mundane matters and knew where this was going.

"Okay, we're looking into a theft from the Heard Museum in Phoenix."

"You're the Primary?"

"No, Greg is. I'm the Second."

"Okay." I wrote *Heard theft* on the next slip of paper and made it the third tier below *Why* and *Open case*. *Currently Investigating* went under *When,* and *Phoenix, Arizona* went under *Where*.

"Then there's the Anasazi looting case. That one's going to trial late next month."

I raised my eyebrows, and Rose continued: "A family affair. Daddy Blankenship and two sons caught pilfering from the Chaco Canyon ruins. I'm the Primary on that one. And chief witness for the prosecution."

Ah, the gun-toting miscreants. Promising. I posted *Anasazi looting* under *Open case*; *Trial Next Month* under *When*; and *Chaco Canyon, New Mexico* under *Where*.

"Any more?"

She sipped her coffee. "We're putting together a sting against a small-time fence who's been trying to raise his profile. His name's Ted Bridges. Most of his clients are small private collectors, but he got sloppy a couple of months ago and put a few things up for auction through Sommers."

"What, not eBay?" I made another series of notes and stuck them on the board.

"He's smarter than that. He knows we snoop on eBay. To their credit, Sommers contacted us immediately."

"Oh, good for them."

Sommers was a mid-echelon auction house that had had a number of stolen artifacts turn up in sale lots over the last several years. Rose and her cohorts joked that they were coming up in the world—trying to get the same kind of notoriety in black market antiquities that the more illustrious Sotheby's had acquired.

"When is the sting taking place?"

"In about two weeks."

This went up on the whiteboard too.

"Then there's the Indian cemetery desecration on the Hopi rez. Which we're no closer to solving than we were three months ago when I left Old Oraibi."

That was personal bitterness in Rose's voice, I knew. She had been the primary agent on that case, but her emotions had gotten in the way when she was unable to slam-dunk it. The desecration and looting continued, stopping when the cemeteries were being watched, picking up again as soon as everybody looked the other way—which happened whenever the Park Service decided there were simply not enough funds to keep agents on the reservation year-round.

Rose is not the overemotional type—witness how long she'd kept mum about this stalking. And she might have been able to remain objective if her great-grandmother's relics weren't among the missing.

"That it?" I asked, adding *Hopi Rez*, *Old Oraibi*, and *Three Months Ago* to the board.

"That's it."

"Okay, what about Dave?"

She gave me a quizzical look. "Dave? Dave's a school teacher."

"And that means he has no enemies? Surely you jest." I'd done some thinking about this and I was half-hoping it might be the real reason for what was going on.

"Enemies serious enough to stalk his wife?"

"We don't know how serious this is. It could be no more than a persistent prankster. If someone was trying to yank Dave's chain for some reason, they might figure that they could do that by freaking out his wife. How would they know you'd keep it all to yourself?"

Rose shook her head, sending a ripple through her long, gleaming black hair. "I'd think this was about Dave if my stalker had acne and a boom box . . . and rode a maroon Schwinn. Most of his students don't have driver's licenses."

"Stop being obtuse. Does Dave have any students whose parents he might have cheesed off? Any school board politics he's involved in?"

"No. You know Dave—at worst, his students think he's amusingly daft. Their parents think he's a saint. As far as politics go . . ." She shrugged. "You're going to have to ask him."

I wrote: *Talk to Dave* on a sticky, stuck it off to one side in my "parking lot" area, then added *To Do* above it with a dry-erase marker.

"Anything else? Any other areas where you've had difficulties?"

"Nothing. It's got to be one of my cases, but . . ." She looked at the slim pickings on my board. "Nothing here seems likely."

"What about cases you've put to bed?"

She let out a big sigh, her frustration showing. "There is the Hochob investigation. A mixed lot of artifacts from an anonymous donor went to a museum here in the Bay Area via a Sommers private auction. But you know how that goes—we've never gotten any of the major players, and we don't really expect to. We were only able to indict one of Sommers's clerks."

"You tried to get him to roll over on his superiors, though, right?"

"Sure. But he wasn't talking. I expect he'll have a tidy nest egg waiting for him when he gets out of jail. All he'd get for confessing would be the loss of his job and a vote of thanks from the U.S. Park Service and the people of Mexico and Honduras."

I looked back at the board. "With the museum located here, that's the most relevant connection we've made so far." I added *Hochob Investigation, San Francisco,* and *Sommers Clerk* to their respective columns. "How did you guys discover this?"

"We got a tip from someone at a local museum. A docent who thought the items were suspect because they were mislabeled and without any proof of provenance . . . and he recognized some of them."

Ah, the P-word—*provenance.* To a scrupulous museum or auction house, a clear record of the path an artifact had taken to get from point A to point Z was absolutely essential. "All the artifacts were from Hochob?"

"No. There were a handful from Copán as well."

I looked at the board. That case felt as if it weighed more than the others, possibly because of the six-hundred-pound-gorilla status of the major player—Sommers. Then again, maybe that was a red herring.

"Let's rank these," I suggested. "What else floats to the top?"

"I'd say it's the Blankenship trial."

I moved *Anasazi looting* to the top of the column.

"After that, the Hopi burials—although I'm not directly involved anymore, so I'd rank those at the bottom of the list. The sting . . . I don't think that can be it, unless Bridges has figured out he's under suspicion. His recent activities don't suggest he has. He's still plugging right along . . . working the greater Phoenix area and Flagstaff. I checked. And the Heard theft—hell, Tink, we don't have *any* leads on that one."

I moved *Heard theft* to a position right beneath *Anasazi looting*.

Rose clutched her coffee cup in both hands and leaned toward the board. "Why give that one such a high ranking?"

"Maybe someone is trying to make sure you *don't* find any leads."

"In San Francisco? Why would anyone follow me here? Wouldn't they just be Snoopy-dancing over the fact that I've gone back to my home office and gotten out of their way?"

I shrugged. "Okay, good point. Maybe there's more to the Hochob case than meets the eye. You know the clerk you've nailed isn't one of the major players. In fact, *everyone* knows that, including those same major players. Maybe someone freaked out that you're so close to the museum they sold the lot so that you wouldn't happen upon more information than has already been uncovered."

"So they're following me just to make sure I don't accidentally trip over them?"

"It's a thought."

I added, *Possible Discovery* under *Why* next to *Hochob Investigation*. I wrote the name of the Anasazi looters on a note and pasted it under *Who* across from the case note. While it was true that Rose hadn't been involved directly with the Hopi case for months, it was possible someone didn't know that or thought she was close to a discovery of some sort.

Taking a step back from the board, we looked at what we had so far. A quick look at *When* caused the Anasazi looters to be the most relevant since Rose was due to testify in a just over a month. The Bridges sting was happening earlier in our timeline, but that only made Ted Bridges a candidate for Stalker of the Month if he knew when he was going to be stung—and even that seemed a stretch. The third most likely reason would be the Hochob Investigation because of its direct connection to San Francisco.

We turned our attention, finally, to *How*—specifically how a stalker involved in each of those scenarios gained anything from trailing Rose Delgado around the Bay Area. Two themes floated to the surface: intimidation and surveillance.

"How do the Heard thieves gain?" I asked. "I mean look, if I were dealing in black market relics, and brought them to San Francisco only to discover a familiar NPS agent was now on the job there, I'd just fence them in a different city."

"Unless," Rose mused, "you'd struck a deal with someone for major money *before* you did the job. And that someone just happened to be in San Francisco. In which case, you'd want to keep an eye on me until the deal was complete."

"Okay." I moved the Heard theft up. I frowned, looking at both the Heard theft and the Anasazi looting case. "These are both pretty high profile, aren't they?"

She nodded. "Yes, and in both cases there's the potential for a stiff sentence. Of course, we only have suspects for Anasazi. I suppose the idea might be to intimidate me into retracting my testimony, which would leave the prosecution with nothing but circumstantial evidence." She shook her head. "On the surface that makes sense, but whoever this guy is, he hasn't made any threatening moves. I've gotten no notes, no phone calls, no text messages, no emails. Nothing to indicate anyone is lobbying for me not to testify. And I can't imagine anybody else from Arizona sending someone all the way to San Francisco to follow me around."

"What about this guy you're going to sting—Bridges? He's still in Arizona, but couldn't he have hired someone to follow you?"

"Maybe." She looked doubtful. "But like I said, he's still dealing. You'd think if the guy suspected he was under investigation, he'd lie low. Maybe even disappear completely."

I studied my stickies. "Sommers," I said. "That name keeps coming up."

Rose snorted into her coffee cup, shooting steam past her ears. "That name *always* comes up. And it always will as long as there are black marketeers who want to sell to less than scrupulous private—and public—collectors with a lot of working capital. We know Bridges has approached Sommers, but they're showing every indication of cooperating on that case, especially since losing a clerk in the Hochob case."

"So it's Ted Bridges or the Blankenship family looters."

"Looks that way."

I picked up my lucky wire and started pulling apart the knots. "Well, there's one way to find out."

The Plan was for Rose to go jogging the next morning with nothing but Hoho for protection (which, as much as I hate to say it, means no protection at all), while I followed at a distance by bicycle, providing another set of eyes and backup, if it proved necessary. She took our usual route up Liberty Ship across Bridgeway to Filbert, from there up Napa to cross Bridgeway again into Dunphy Park.

I pedaled along on my ten-speed, a bottle of Evian riding in my water bottle holder, wearing spandex everything and one of those space-age bike helmets and a pair of mirrored goggles. My lucky Caddie wire now bobbed on a silver chain around my neck—stylishly kitschy, I thought. I fancied I looked just like any young executive on her way to work. Apart from the baby blue titanium .357 Magnum tucked into my fanny pack. I hear most young female execs favor the plain, but always tasteful, stainless steel.

My eyes caught on anything that was even remotely dark red. I was pretty amped up, but no one would ever guess that to look at me. I have a way of going into a sort of Zen bubble when things get fraught or tense. One of my COs on the SFPD was from Georgia. He described it as "hesitatin'."

"Miyoko," he'd say, "I notice that whenever things get hot and heavy, you start hesitatin'. Why is that?"

It was pure instinct, I told him—or maybe something I learned by osmosis from Dad. If you look like you're twitchy, it could give everybody around you the yips. In police work, you don't want *anybody* to get the yips—good guys or bad guys.

Keeping an eye on Rose, I knew she was trying hard to act casual too, but I couldn't fail to see the stiffness in her neck and shoulders, or that her hands were balled into fists. We were both on edge.

It wasn't until Rose swung left onto Napa Street that I caught a glimpse of a burgundy car. It was coming down Napa toward us. It was a Honda. I held my breath as the car passed Rose . . . then slowed to a crawl. Could've been looking for a parking space, but I didn't think so. There was a man behind the wheel. More than that I couldn't make out—his sun visor was pulled down, covering the upper half of his face. I couldn't tell if he was watching Rose in his rearview.

When he passed me a moment later, I pretended to be checking my watch, then pedaled a little faster as if I were late for something. In my rearview mirror, I saw the Honda's license plate: KLQ 215. It took a left on Filbert.

I missed the Bonita Street intersection on my right, what with my focus on the car. More than familiar with this neighborhood, I flew down Napa as if some of Mom's favorite demons were nipping at my wheels. I took the next right on Caledonia Street with a squeal, hoping my gut was correct and I would be able to get eyes on him as he took Litho Street down to Bridgeway and into Dunphy Park. It's the quickest way back to Rose's regular route, and if this was our guy, that's what he'd be expecting her to take.

Looking both ways at the intersection with no burgundy in sight, I made my way to Bridgeway then to the entrance of Dunphy Park, from which I could see our favored footpaths clearly. I didn't have to fake thirst as I chugged Evian, eyes darting around. I appeared to have made it to the park ahead of Rose and her tail, so I pulled in under the trees. This early on a

Tuesday morning there were a few other joggers and cyclists about, but the park was mostly empty. The air was tangy with the scents of sea, eucalyptus, and cedar—a soothing combination under any other circumstances. Right now, my heart was galloping like a runaway horse and I was sweating in spite of the slight chill in the air.

Rose and Hoho sailed past me a moment later on the park drive, Rose giving a prearranged hand signal to indicate she saw me. Looking behind her and up Bridgeway, my gaze followed the traffic flow, and there it was. The same Honda Accord, roughly three car lengths away. I tried to get another look as he turned into the drive but only saw a vaguely masculine shape with sunglasses and a hat. I let him cruise by, then pedaled down behind him. He bypassed all of the empty parking spots, angling for the only shady spot by the water. Lucky for us, he had cornered himself. This was a dead end.

Rose, meanwhile, having made it off the gravel and onto the grassy parkland, saw the direction I was headed and tacked back so we could come at the car from two different angles.

Hoho regarded this change with amicable interest.

As the Honda slid into the parking space (this guy was a paragon of parallel parking), I dropped my kickstand and left the bike in the middle of the lane a few steps behind me. If our mystery man tried to back out in a hurry, he'd have to either run over the bike or take evasive action, either of which would screw up his cloak-and-dagger routine. I liberated the Taurus from my fanny pack and held it at my side, the safety still engaged, my trigger finger pointed down the barrel.

The driver's door opened and a clean black-and-white Adidas sneaker appeared. A hand a shade or two darker than my own followed, reaching for the door handle. He paused. I held my breath, suddenly and intensely aware of the weight of the Taurus in my hand. Would he get out of the car, or slam the door back in place and try to make an exit? A difficult task to accomplish without casualties, considering that Rose and Hoho were now flanking the front of the car. The dude was surrounded (by two women and a dog—right).

Surprisingly (which is to say wisely) the man got out, glancing quickly from Rose to me and back again. He was wearing straight-leg jeans and a pale yellow shirt that accented his bronze skin. A black San Francisco Giants baseball cap and narrow mirrored shades completed the stalker ensemble.

He swept off his cap and shades and leaned back against the car, folding his arms across his chest. To the untrained observer, he may have looked at ease but I could tell he was hesitatin'. His lips were pulled into a smile (an attractive smile, as it happens) that did not quite reach his brown eyes, and there was a crease of annoyance troubling his brow. Dark hair curled around his ears and overran his collar. His sleeves were rolled up almost to his elbows, showing off muscular forearms. Not bodybuilder muscular, but clearly this was someone in good physical shape.

Rose and I closed in on him, stopping when we were about a yard away— beyond the reach of arms or legs. He looked up at us through dark lashes. He was shaking his head, which made him a perfect match for Hoho, who was smiling and wagging his tail.

"Good morning, ladies," he said in very slightly accented English. "I see I am discovered."

"Hell, yes," said Rose, her fists clenching as she faced off with her shadow. "Who the hell are you and why are you following me?"

"My name is Cruz Veras. I'm a journalist. And I'm following you, Ms. Delgado, because you're part of a story I'm working on."

Did I believe him? No. Which was why I did not stable the Taurus until he showed credentials identifying him as Cruz Sacramento Veras, an investigative journalist with a magazine published by the Mexican national historical society (the *Instituto Nacional de Antropología e Historia*, for those of you who are sticklers for detail), and I had to admit it put a (tentative) mark in the "not-a-threat" column. Obviously, we'd have to verify his story.

Rose was unwilling to be impressed, credentials or no. Her fists had yet to unclench and I suspected she wanted to punch Mr. Veras in the face. "How do you even know who I am, what I look like, where I live, what I do?" she demanded.

He looked at her unabashedly. "Ms. Delgado, your work came to my attention last year when your department brought an auction house clerk up on rather substantial charges. You may not be a Mexican national heroine now, but I could write a story that would make you one."

"How did it 'come to your attention?' The identities of field agents are not public information. It is the only way we can function in the field with a semblance of safety. Now I will ask you again. How did you find me and why?"

In the face of her obvious anger, he batted not one eye. "It is said that some of the antiquities involved in that case were pilfered from a site in Mexico. I have sources, Ms. Delgado. And they pointed to you as someone who might have the information I need."

"If you're a journalist, why not just make an appointment for an interview?" I asked.

"I intended to do exactly that," he informed me, still smiling pleasantly. "But I wanted to do some research first. Sort of a 'day in the life' look at what a Park Service agent does when she's not out busting pothunters and unscrupulous museum directors. I am, after all, an *investigative* journalist. I was merely investigating Ms. Delgado's habits."

It was a struggle not to roll my eyes. "Day in the life? Habits? And for that, you scare a woman into hiring a bodyguard?"

His brows ascended. "Bodyguard? Are you speaking of yourself . . . or the dog?"

As if knowing he had been mentioned, Hoho chuffed and wagged his tail harder.

Okay, now I wanted to help Rose punch this guy in the face whether he was telling the truth or not. "I'm a licensed private detective," I said quietly. "The pretty blue gun is not just for show. I actually know how to use it."

He gave me a direct look. "I have no doubt of that."

"So," said Rose, "you want to write a story about how I've been protecting Mexican antiquities from predation? You can't believe I'd want that kind of press, can you? My profession sort of relies on secrecy for maximum effectiveness."

He had the good graces to look chagrined. "Of course not. I assumed . . . you'd assume an assumed . . . a different name." He smiled again, self-deprecatingly, while I wondered if the sudden verbal klutziness was an attempt to make himself seem nonthreatening.

Rose glanced at me. I could see it in her eyes: the raw fury was starting to ebb. In a moment, it would be replaced by relief that this wasn't what she'd feared. I wanted to warn her to reserve judgment, but Hoho had no such reservations. All during our inquisition, he had been shamelessly nuzzling Veras's hand and wagging his tail so hard his long body described a series of furry Bezier curves.

Veras seemed to sense the relaxation of Rose's angst. "So . . . can I get an interview, Ms. Park Agent?"

"I'm not sure yet," Rose said. "Give me the best number to reach you at and I will let you know if I decide to meet with you. If I do grant you an interview, I promise only that I may listen to your questions. I can't guarantee that I'll answer them. That's the most I am willing to offer."

Veras nodded. "That is the most I would expect." He reached for his back pocket; I reached for my revolver. "Wallet," he said. Turning his back to me, he pulled a wallet out of his back pocket and fished out a card, which he handed to me. "The second number is my cell. I will check out, Ms. Bodyguard. I promise." He raised his hand as if taking an oath (on Hoho's wet nose, no less). "I can also assure you that your friend does not need protection from me. Now, may I go?"

Rose and I exchanged glances, then she stepped away from the car and said, "Feel free."

I grudgingly moved my bike and, together, we watched him drive away.

Chapter 3

Cross Sacred True

Did I mention that I'm an extremely suspicious individual? This is not my nature; it's an entirely learned suspicion—something I acquired through experience. It's my nature to be trusting, to take people at face value. I began to learn not to do this in high school—or at least I learned to conceal my trusting. I guess you could say I learned to be inscrutable.

I also developed a keen sense of what other people were about. I credit my mom with much of that. She taught me empathy, along with an annoying level of persistence, and the value of nonverbal communication. From my dad, I learned compassion and the art of observation (okay, and hesitatin'). I honed all of these traits while in police academy, and while studying for my BS in criminal justice. I like to think I perfected them on the street during my stint with the SFPD.

And yet it took being engaged to the fiancé from hell to fully break me of the habit of trust. That one broken habit was enough to make me choose PI work over any partner on the force.

My suspicion of Cruz Sacramento Veras drove me to spend the rest of my Tuesday tracking him down online. What did I find? I found that he actually was a reporter for the INAH publication—*Arqueología*. More than that, he had academic creds to go with the journalistic ones. There were letters after his name on the archaeological wiki that I unearthed—P, h, and D being three of them. I went to the *Arqueología* website and found the same info.

Okay, so some guy named Cruz Sacramento Veras actually did write and research for this magazine. That didn't mean it was the same guy. So I did some further digging and found some of his work, which included photographs. Of him. At a dig or two or three. Same face—though sporting a closely trimmed beard.

Cruz Veras, I realized, had underrepresented himself. He wasn't just an investigative journalist, he was an investigative journalist *and* practicing archaeologist whose name translates into English as "True Sacred Cross" (well, okay, detail sticklers: "Cross Sacred True"). I found myself wondering why a PhD'ed professional would stick with a name like that. I'm pretty familiar with the territory that goes with an unusual moniker. My own name—Gina Suzu Miyoko—translates as "Silver Bell Temple," which is how I ended up with the oh-so-cute nickname "Tinkerbell," which everyone seems inclined to shorten to "Tink" rather than the far more melodious "Bell."

I wondered, absurdly, if Veras had had any embarrassing nicknames thrust upon him in school by frenemies. I considered getting even for the bodyguard crack ("Were you speaking of yourself or the dog?") by asking him that if Rose decided to grant him an interview.

Rose had gone to work after our encounter with Veras. When I felt that I'd exhausted the interwebs' information on the man, I called her office and gave her the rundown. She listened, asked for a list of the URLs I'd toured, then told me that she'd done a little investigating herself.

"I checked him out through AFIS and IBIS, plus a couple of other law-enforcement databases I had access to. I got nothing." (For the uninitiated,

AFIS is the Automated Fingerprint Identification System, and IBIS is the Interagency Border Inspection System, which gives government employees like Rose access to intel from every spy shop from the FBI to Interpol.)

"Yeah," I said, realizing I was almost disappointed that we hadn't outed Mr. Veras as the head of a skeevy pothunter cartel of some sort. "The information I found online goes back about eight years. He does seem legit. But the stalking bit bugs the hell out of me."

"No kidding. I still want to go on the warpath when I think of what he put me through," Rose told me. "Which is why I'd like *you* to call him and set up the interview."

"Really, Rosie? Warpath? Tsk. So archetypal."

"Oh, shut up and call the guy. Café Lucca. One P.M. tomorrow. That work for you?"

Either it worked or I'd clear my calendar to make it work. I wanted this episode over with. "Sure you want me there?" I asked just to make sure.

"Is your dad into Sherlock Holmes?"

Café Lucca offered a reasonably quiet place for Cruz Veras to conduct his interview. We got a table in the back of the room and ordered appetizers and drinks while the journalist-professor set up his state-of-the-art digital recorder. He didn't blow into the little microphone that he aimed at Rose, nor did he tap it to see if there was a signal, which is no less than I'd expect of a professional journalist.

Lest you think my findings of the previous day led me to trust the gentleman, let me assure you, they did not. I could think of a number of nefarious reasons why someone with this guy's background might want to pry privileged information out of a federal park agent. What if he was, say, running his own illicit traffic in antiquities? Who'd be in a better position to do that than a practicing archaeologist, trusted by his superiors and peers? So with all my senses, I watched Cruz Veras carefully for any "tells," or signs of duplicity—facial expressions, body language, eye movements, nervous tics. What I caught wasn't suspicious as much as it was annoying. He was relaxed, polished, and smiled at me every chance he got, as if he thought I ought to be impressed with his Hispanic good looks and his suave aplomb.

The fact of his good looks was something that Rose hadn't given a rest for a moment since our research had failed to reveal holes in Professor True's story. She seemed to think the whole thing was sorted; he was who he said he was, and I really ought to consider flirting with a guy that she'd been terrified of for weeks just because he reminded her of Antonio Banderas. Her desperate desire to see me in a happy relationship sometimes bordered on the psychopathic.

As it was, by the time Veras started the interview, I was no more kindly disposed toward the man than I'd been when he first stepped out of his car, and only the fact that Rose seemed to have recovered from her terrors kept me from growling at him.

He started by logging a series of reference notes at the beginning of the tape—date, time, subject. He even had a working title for his article: "Agents of the Park Service: Guardians of History." A little hokey, but okay, I guess. He opened with harmless general questions about the purview of the NPS, then moved to the specific expertise of a field agent.

"Now, Ms. Delgado . . ."

"You can call me Rose." She smiled and settled further into her corner of the booth.

He smiled back, unaware that this was Rose angling to put him at ease, just as he was angling to do the same to her. This, I decided, might be fun to watch: investigator and investigated trying to out-investigate each other. Rose knew the limits of what she could tell him. I sat back to watch, wishing there was popcorn to go with my peanut-butter smoothie.

"Rose," Veras said, "it sounds as if your park service has a similar mandate to our historical institute in Mexico. What sort of expertise must an American agent exercise in the field?"

"Persistence," said Rose. "Dogged, patient persistence. And an ability to blend in to the background, or stand out in the right way, depending."

"On?"

"The role he or she is playing. Is the agent a buyer, a collector, an investigator? Does she want to be seen by the subject of the investigation or not?"

"And what role have you played most recently?"

Rose shook her head. "You know I can't be specific."

"Generally, then."

"My job is to make sure that priceless antiquities don't fall into the wrong hands. Sometimes that puts me in the field investigating, sometimes it puts me behind a desk processing information, sometimes it puts me in a courtroom. I suspect you understand that much without me having to tell you."

Veras turned his head slightly and met my eyes. "I take it you checked out my credentials."

"Of course we did," I said. "Did you expect any less?"

"No." He turned his attention back to Rose. "And, the answer is 'yes.' I do know the general shape of a park agent's job. I'm curious about the cases you've worked."

"I told you, I can't—"

"The Hochob case was all over the papers and airwaves in Mexico City. Sommers was investigated for receiving illicit goods from the Hochob dig. That's on the public record."

I saw Rosie's jaw flex, and realized that my own jaw had tightened as well. "Yes, it is," she said.

"What I was curious about, as a student of archaeology—"

I snorted. "*Professor* of archaeology, don't you mean?"

He looked at me directly again. "I'm both . . . Ms. Miyoko, isn't it?"

So I wasn't the only one who'd done some checking up. I nodded.

"What's on the public record," he continued, "is that a Sommers clerk was indicted for receiving contraband. The auction house, to all appearances, was not culpable."

Rose's nostrils flared. He'd just hit her where she lived. "Yes. To all appearances," she repeated.

I caught her eye and made bubbles in my smoothie. Subtext: *Nuh-uh. Don't go there.*

She tilted her head, stirred her iced tea, and said, "That's the way these things go."

Veras lost the relaxed look and leaned forward, elbows on the table, hands clasped, dark eyes narrowed. "And you hate that, don't you?"

Rose seemed taken aback by his sudden intensity. "I . . . It's my job."

"Which you love . . . and hate when something like that happens." It was an observation—an accurate one—not a question. He followed it with another: "Your Facebook page says you're Native American—Hopi. This is personal for you, isn't it?"

They locked eyes for a moment, then Veras looked down at his clasped hands. "I understand that. I do. I'll be honest, the Hochob case and its connection to Sommers captured my attention, in part because it seemed to me to be part of a pattern. Black market antiquities are discovered moving in or out of an auction house or museum, and no one above low-level management ends up on trial. Does it seem that way to you too?"

Rose let out a bark of laughter. "Of course it does. Because it *is* a pattern. A pattern my colleagues and I can do very little about. And really, what's to say about it, Dr. Veras—"

"Cruz, please."

"Cruz, why would your readers care that it's a pattern?"

He leaned back in his seat and shrugged, a lopsided grin tugging at one corner of his mouth. "It's a sexy case. High profile. Sheds lurid light on a respected institution or two. Plus, the Mexican people deserve to know if the antiquities that belong in their country for all to admire have been returned home. Readers will eat it up."

"Sexy?" I repeated. "Who's going to be reading this article—varsity archaeological jocks?"

"It's the same audience that reads *National Geographic* and *Scientific American* in this country. What did you expect, a bunch of stuffy archaeologists?"

Rose laughed. "Dr. Veras—Cruz. You know the archaeological world and you know what it means to work for a national agency—or at least to work closely with one. You also know the part I play is not in the public narrative. I'm sorry, but I can't give you any information other than that the antiquities will be returned to the country of origin."

"Which is *my* beat. I'm Mexican, remember? Can you tell me what caused the NPS to view Sommers as a target?"

Rose regarded him deliberately for a moment, then said, "Only in general. Obviously, any auction house that moves antiquities is going to draw the attention of the Park Service. We generally keep an eye on any lots they acquire from private collectors or estate sales. That's no secret. In theory, we expect—or at least hope—that they'll be upfront with us about any items in those collections that are of doubtful provenance. Or that lack any record of provenance at all."

"In this case?" Veras prompted.

"That's not for public consumption."

The dark eyes kindled. "All right, so you can't speak on the record. What about off the record?"

"*Off* the record?" Rose repeated. "What good does information do you that's 'off the record?' You can't put it in your story."

In answer, Veras flicked off his machine. "This isn't about my story. This is about something else. You see, this is personal to me too. These . . . scavengers are sucking away the heritage of an entire people."

Oh, jeez. He'd just played the native card.

Rose glanced at me, then back at Veras. "Okay, off the record. We got a call from a student docent at a Bay Area museum who was curious about a late-night delivery from Sommers auction house. He got a look into one of the open cartons and recognized several figures as coming from Mexican and Honduran sites that had been vandalized some ten years earlier."

"A student docent?"

"His special area of study was pre-Columbian art and architecture. The Mexican site was Hochob, of course. The Honduran site was Copán." Rose smiled grimly. "To hear the kid tell it, he just about peed his pants when he peeked into a crate and realized he was looking at a piece of the Rosalila."

I'd swear half the color drained out of Veras's face. "The Rosalila? *Dios mio.*"

I raised my hand. "Uh, just pretend I have no idea what you're talking about."

"Rosalila," Rose explained, "is an Early Classic Mayan temple that archaeologists have dated to the reign of Moon Jaguar—around C.E. 571. It's unusual in that it was completely preserved inside a later temple—right down to the pigment in the paint."

"So your student docent called the NPS?" asked Veras.

Rose nodded. "Long and short of it—my partner and I were dispatched early the next morning. The museum said they had no such artifacts. We got a court order to search the premises and found nothing, but Sommers's records showed that several crates of goods had gone missing. What was in those crates, we wondered, and who'd handled them? We put those questions to Sommers, and about a month later they coughed up a mid-level clerk who had allegedly recognized the artifacts as being stolen and—knowing that the auction house would turn them over to the authorities—decided he'd deal them to the museum himself. Since he was a Sommers employee, he could easily provide falsified paperwork that presented the artifacts as legally acquired."

"You don't believe that's what really happened," Veras observed.

Rose shrugged. "It doesn't much matter what I believe, but no, none of us believed it for a moment. We knew the objects reached the museum; we have every reason to believe the museum staffers that received them knew they were illicit. Normally, they would have made a big deal out of acquiring such treasures. Heck, they would have advertised it, thrown a gala, used it as a fund-raising opportunity. But between the time we started our investigation and the time we acquired our warrants, the artifacts had been returned to a little-used storage room at Sommers, and a clerk had been selected to take the tumble."

Veras shook his head. "He probably had the misfortune of being the one to sign for the crates when they arrived from wherever they arrived from. I'm sure he was well compensated for his pains. Where did they arrive from, these artifacts?"

"Can't tell you that. Wouldn't if I could."

Veras was nodding thoughtfully, his brow furrowed. "Of course not. It's a shame. As long as the real dealers can keep sacrificing bit players, they'll just keep doing what they're doing."

Rose grimaced. "I doubt they've stopped their trafficking just because a couple of park rangers got lucky."

She growled the *r* in rangers, which made me laugh out loud. Veras wasn't laughing. In fact, he seemed not to be listening. He gathered up his machine and stowed it in a leather courier bag. Very Indiana Jones.

"Interview over?" I asked. "Don't you want to know what happened to the pre-Columbian art?"

His eyes flickered to me for a second. "The Hochob artifacts were returned to Mexico. As I said, that's my beat. That part of the story I know, as do most of my readers. It's *this* part that's still a mystery."

Rose shifted in her seat. "To the NPS too. There are few things as frustrating to me—to any agent—as watching the real operators get clean away while some poor toady takes the fall."

"Alligator lizards," murmured Veras.

"Pardon?" I said.

"You grab an alligator lizard and its tail comes off in your hand. An evolutionary adaptation."

Rose grunted. "Apparently works for other reptilian life forms too."

Veras shifted his attention back to her. "This matters to you a lot—this cultural thievery?"

"You know it matters. As you noted, Dr. Veras, I'm Hopi."

"Cruz," he corrected.

"Cruz. There's every chance my great-grandmother's bones are in some auction house or museum storage bin even as we speak."

He continued to regard her intensely a moment more, then smiled. "That's going to make a great angle for my story, Rose. Thanks."

"Didn't you tell him a bit much?" I asked Rose when Cruz Veras had gathered up his interview goo and disappeared.

"Honestly, other than sharing how I feel about it, I didn't tell him anything he couldn't glean from news stories and public court records. Notice I didn't mention any names. Most of those have been redacted from the official reports for reasons of privacy. If he tries to find out who the student docent was, for example, he's going to have to move heaven and earth to do it."

"What did you make of his whole 'this is personal for me, too' gambit?"

She gave me a particularly searching look. "Is that what you thought it was? A gambit? That he pegged me and played the right cards to make me share my deepest feelings about my work?"

I blushed to the roots of my undisciplined hair. That was exactly what I'd thought.

"If he was playing some cynical angle, what good would knowing that I have skin in the game do him? I think he was sincere. He really does hate people sucking up his national heritage and selling it on the black market. But maybe I also think there's more to the man than meets the eye." She winked at me, put down her empty glass, and said, "Let's go shopping, Tink. I feel like spending money, and there's a little gallery down on the wharf that has the neatest knickknacks."

The relief in her face—in her whole being—was palpable. She always liked to shop when she felt life was good. Me, I preferred to bomb down the coastal highway on my Harley—which is also what I preferred to do when I felt life was crappy. Right now, Rose seemed to be feeling very good indeed, and I was a complete jerk for wanting to rain on her shopping spree.

"So, you buy his story? It didn't strike you as odd that he seemed to keep having to remind himself that he was researching a magazine article?"

"Good grief, Tink, what did I just say? The man is who he claims to be. And maybe more than he claims to be. I suspect his reasons for what he's doing may be purely personal, and not professional at all."

"But the way he was squeezing for information about the Hochob case—"

"Oh, come on—have you ever known a journalist who doesn't try to squeeze 'secrets' out of his sources? That's what interviewing is all about. He handled it exactly the way I would have done. Beezus, Gina, you're a PI, *you'd* have handled it that way."

I had to admit, she had a point. "I'm just not sure I believe the 'day-in-the-life' excuse he turned up for following you."

"What—you think he's an evil agent of the Sommers board of directors? They know the answers to everything he asked. They paid their legal firm very well to keep them informed, I'm sure."

"What if he's involved in the Heard case in some way? What if he was asking all those questions about how Sommers got busted because he wants to avoid making the same mistakes?"

At last, she blinked. "Okay . . . all right . . . you have a point. But if that's the case, he's tipped his hand, right? He's done his 'interview' and now he's gone, and I gave him very little information to work with that he couldn't dig up some other way. If he's in cahoots with Sommers or the museum or the people that looted Heard, his cover is blown. And you can bet we'll be looking at Sommers under a microscope until the Heard artifacts turn up." She looked at me speculatively for a moment. "Do you seriously distrust him? You think he's got the Evil Eye or whatever your mom calls it?"

I took a deep breath and considered that, fondling the Caddie-wire *obereg*. "*Kosoi sglaz.* No actually, I don't get any *bad* vibes from him at all. He's a little arrogant, maybe. Annoyingly personable."

Rose's eyes narrowed. "But you'd like to think he's got the *kosoi sglaz*—is that it? Why? Because he's good-looking and male?"

I opened my mouth to protest but, dammit, she was not too far from the truth.

"C'mon, Tink. Let go of it. It's been three years."

"It's hard to bounce back from something like that, Rose," I told her. "It wasn't just poor, pitiful me and my busted-up little heart. If it was just that, I swear I'd be over it by now."

She glanced down at the worn wooden tabletop. "I know. But not every man is Jeremy Augustine. A lot more men are like your dad, or my Dave, or Alvie."

"You know, I try to believe that," I said. "I really do. But every time I meet a new guy, all I can think about is Jeremy. I think about what that trust almost cost me." I polished off my smoothie and stood up. "All this morbid talk is making my palms itch. Let's go shopping."

Chapter 4
A Real Case of the Yips

"Are you sure you're a detective?" The woman asked me. Her eyes made yet another skeptical assessment of my person. Up and down and up again, her gaze coming back to fix on my face.

I pointed at my license, which hung behind me on the wall of my third floor office, conveniently located above a bail bond office off Market on Hayes. "I'm pretty sure. And the state of California is pretty sure too."

She was still skeptical, still standing just inside the office door. "You look more like a detective's secretary."

I held my tongue in check without too much difficulty. I was used to this. "Mrs. Meriweather, I assure you, I am a duly licensed private investigator with all the trimmings. I have a bachelor's degree in criminal justice, a black belt in kung fu, a nice little handgun, and a wonderful relationship with the local police."

That was mostly true, though my ex–commanding officer, Ramon Mirande, still held a bit of a grudge over my leaving the force. He'd been my dad's partner back in the day, and I was pretty sure he thought I was a wimp for not hanging in there after Dad was injured.

She sat down, finally, in one of the chairs facing my desk. "I thought private detectives always had trouble with cops," my would-be client said suspiciously.

"Only on TV," I lied. Truth was, some PIs had very bad relationships with the cops because they insisted on getting in the way or withholding evidence or doing something equally stupid when involved in a criminal case. "Now, what can I do for you?"

"Well . . ."

She pulled her oversized purse up onto her lap and half-opened the front zipper pocket as if she had not quite made up her mind to show me something.

My incoming phone line began flashing silently at that moment—a ringing phone can royally screw up an interview. She saw the flashing light as competition and reacted by pulling a photo out of her purse and shoving it across the desk at me.

I decided to let voice mail pick up and studied the photo. It showed a man and a dog apparently jogging down a beach. Moving in the opposite direction was a young woman in a crop top, bike pants, and headphones—also jogging. The two seemed to be waving at each other.

"Your husband?" I surmised.

She perked up, obviously impressed even though it was the most elementary of deductions. "And our dog, Hoover. Not for Herbert Hoover. Because he likes to clean up the floor when anybody spills."

I put down the photograph, folded my hands, and regarded her questioningly, waiting for her to tell me that the husband or the dog or both were missing.

Instead, she pointed at the woman. "I want to know who she is."

"May I ask why?"

"I think my husband is having an affair with her."

I pulled a notepad out of my desk drawer and began to scribble. "And what makes you think this, Mrs. Meriweather?"

"Well, just look at them. They're *waving* at each other."

I stopped writing and looked up at her. "Mrs. Meriweather, I jog every morning and I wave at just about everybody I pass. We're complete strangers, except for the fact that we see each other jogging every day."

"But she's . . . look at the way she's *looking* at him."

She was smiling. It was a pleasant smile. It made her look about seventeen.

My incoming line flashed again. This time I considered picking up. "Do you mind if I—?" I gestured toward the phone.

"I most certainly do."

"Okay. Sorry."

I studied the photo again, trying to see it the way this woman would. Her husband—a physically fit, nice-looking middle-aged man—greeting a very young, very cute (did I mention, young?) woman on a morning run.

"She's wearing an engagement ring," I noted.

Mrs. Meriweather flushed deeply. "You think Jack might have bought it for her?"

Well, that was one interpretation. "Not at all. I just meant it looks as if she's romantically involved elsewhere. Did you take this picture?"

"No. Oh, no! I found it in our mailbox. Last Thursday."

"Someone anonymously left you a photo of your husband waving at this girl? Any idea who?"

"I assumed it was a friend or a neighbor. Someone who wanted me to . . . be aware of what was going on."

"So you've never seen your husband with this girl yourself."

"Yes I have, actually. Well, I mean, I've followed him to the beach and seen them . . . wave. Several times," she added.

"And can you describe what else happened on these occasions?"

"Well . . . nothing. They pass each other in approximately the same spot along Belvedere every morning—that I've observed—and they always wave."

"Do they speak?"

"Sometimes they say, 'good morning.'"

"But they never stop and talk?"

"Not that I've observed." She was looking distinctly uncertain at this point, and not without reason.

I jotted down a few notes. "Tell me, Mrs. Meriweather, has your husband—Jack—ever given you any reason to suppose that he's having an affair?"

"Not before this, no."

"Has something changed in your marriage? Does he go missing at odd times? Is he less attentive? More distant? Not romantically interested in you?"

She colored again, her face going a rather becoming shade of pink. She was really quite pretty, and you needn't qualify it by adding "for a woman her age." Red-gold hair, very blue eyes.

"No, as a matter of fact, he's . . . very attentive. And romantic. And he never 'goes missing,' as you put it."

"Then what . . . ?" I shook my head and shrugged.

"Well, that's not *normal* for a man his age, is it? I mean, he's fifty-six years old. He's *supposed* to be looking around, isn't he? That's what I've read. It's what everyone says. My best friend thinks I'm a hopeless ninny because I refused to believe Jack is . . . fooling around. I thought maybe she was the one who left me the photo—so I'd consider what she said."

"Then was the photo the only thing that changed your mind? Or did Jack do something?"

"No. But everybody knows about midlife crisis," she told me earnestly, almost pleadingly. "It's . . . it's common wisdom. Isn't it?"

Ah. Case closed. "Common wisdom" and the media strike again.

"Mrs. Meriweather, not all men your husband's age go through second puberty or midlife crisis, or whatever you want to call it. My father never has. The fact is, not all men are alike. And it sounds as if Jack may be a real prize. Besides, I think he'd have to have a screw loose to fool around on someone as attractive as you."

Listen to me. Defending man-kind. Wouldn't Rose get a guffaw out of that?

45

The phone was flashing again. Probably a *real* case slipping away.

"Really?" said Mrs. Meriweather. "You think I'm overreacting?"

"Yeah, I do. And you're probably right about your 'best friend' being the one who took the picture. Look, I could take your 'case' and follow your husband around and charge you for it. But it wouldn't be ethical for me to take your money when I don't honestly believe there's a case. I think these two people just wave at each other."

She looked at me with relief. "You're probably right. I was letting my friend's voice get into my head. I feel ridiculous."

My incoming light had started flashing yet again. I never get that many calls in so short a time span. It had been nearly a week since cornering Cruz Veras, but I would be lying if I said I wasn't still waiting for a shoe to fall . . . or an axe, as the case may be. I started to have a bad feeling about this.

"It's okay, Mrs. Meriweather, I completely understand your concern, but I feel one hundred percent confident that you needn't worry anymore." I watched the flashing light out of the corner of my eye.

"Thank you so much for your time, I'm sorry to have wasted it with my silly worrying."

She moved to put on her coat as I reached for the phone. It stopped ringing just as I got the handset to my ear.

Nuts.

I put it down again, and smiled at my new ex-client as she got herself ready to walk out the door.

"Thank you, Ms. Miyoko."

"Thank *you*, Mrs. Meriweather."

When she'd gone, I played back my last batch of messages. They were all from Rose and all were variations on a theme: "Gina, something's happened. Call me." When I dug my cell phone out of my fanny pack—realizing with a sting of guilt that I'd turned the ringtones off—I saw that there were texts to match.

"I'm still being followed." Those were the first words out of Rose's mouth when I reached her on her cell phone.

"Our reporter-archaeologist friend?"

"If it is, he's changed cars. This one is a metallic green Chrysler LeBaron."

I felt a shiver run through me at the mention of LeBarons. My last encounter with one did not conjure pleasant associations, mostly because I'd found a body in the trunk. I reflexively reached for my lucky Caddie wire, which was sticking jauntily out of my pencil cup. "Well, like you said—his cover was blown, so I suppose he might have changed vehicles. When did you notice this?"

"This morning, when I drove to the courthouse for the pretrial deposition with the Blankenships' defense team. Listen, Tink, this guy—whoever he is—is a little more aggressive than our professor. I mean, maybe it is him, but . . ."

"What do you mean 'more aggressive'?"

"I mean, pacing me in the left lane, pulling up, then dropping back, tailgating. Weird stuff."

More shivers. "Close enough to get a look at?"

"Except for the smoked windows, yeah. All I can see is a silhouette with shades."

"Where are you, Rose?"

"I'm still at the courthouse. I called Ellen Robb and told her about it. Tink, this has really got me spooked. I mean, the timing and everything. I'm supposed to go back down to Albuquerque for the trial in five weeks."

"And you think someone is trying to dissuade you from doing that?"

"That's what Ellen thinks. Listen, can you meet me at the NPS offices in about half an hour?"

"I'll do better than that," I told her. "I'll meet you at the courthouse in ten minutes and escort you there."

"Woo-woo!" she said gamely. "A one-Harley motorcade."

"Don't diss Boris. One Harley is better than half a dozen lesser machines."

I sounded flip, but I was seriously worried. So, it turned out, was Ellen Robb, whom I met for the first time when I delivered Rose to her office in the business district.

Ellen was a tall, trim, well-honed woman in her mid-forties with gold-spangled red hair and bright green eyes. She wore her dark, pin-striped pantsuit well, looking like a seasoned Agent Dana Scully. She inspired instant envy in one who could not don a suit without looking like a tween playing dress-up.

Ellen had a firm, warm handshake and a no-nonsense aura of silken confidence that I decided was worth study. "Thanks for riding shotgun for Rose," she told me when we'd seated ourselves around a small, round conference table in her office. "She told me about her tail. I'd like to hear your impressions—any details you can offer."

I went over what had happened with Cruz Veras, the information we found about him, described the interview at Café Lucca, and noted that we hadn't seen him for the better part of a week. Then Rose took over, narrating what had happened on her way to the deposition.

"He must have pulled up on my left flank five or six times during the drive to the courthouse. There were a couple of times he wandered pretty damn close to the side of my car. Then he got behind me and tailgated me off the ramp and all the way to the parking garage. He didn't try to enter the garage—he would've had to have a special pass. And I didn't see him when we left to come here." She looked down at her hands, clasped in her lap. "When I'd look over at him—when he'd pull up beside me—he'd turn his head *toward* me. I could see the silhouette change. And I caught the glint of light off his sunglasses. It was beyond creepy." She looked up and met her boss's eyes. "Ellen, I feel like such a coward. I'm a trained agent, for God's sake. I'm supposed to be prepared for danger."

"Don't apologize, Rose. This isn't the kind of danger you signed up for when you took the job. This is . . . personal."

Rose slumped back in her chair as if she'd been absolved of the need to hold her backbone at attention. She shook her head, "I've been in grave-yards and burial mounds at night dealing with hostile pothunters, Ellen. But this . . . this was scarier than that."

Ellen Robb was silent for a few moments, then said, "I think the timing of this is highly suspicious. The Blankenships' defense attorneys knew exactly where you'd be this morning. On the surface, it looks like a clumsy attempt to make us think twice about sending you to Albuquerque to testify."

"And will you?" I asked. "Think twice about having her testify?"

Ellen and Rose exchanged glances.

"We could just go with the depositions," Ellen said.

Rose objected. "No way. If any questions arise over my testimony and I'm not there to clarify . . ."

"I know. It gives the defense every opportunity to toy with your testi-mony. But Rose, we have no idea how far this intimidation might go."

Rose shook her head as if trying to lose a troubling thought. "Maybe it *is* just a clumsy ploy, like you said. Regardless, just because they freaked me out does not mean I am going let them stop me. I am going to Phoenix for the Bridges sting and I am going to Albuquerque and testifying."

Ellen rose and went to her desk, where she picked up the phone and placed a call.

"Mr. Crandall, please," she said when she connected. Her voice was all business. "This is Chief Agent Ellen Robb of the National Park Service in San Francisco." She was silent for a moment while something presumably happened on the other end of the line, then said, "Mr. Crandall. I have a very pointed question to ask you and I would advise you to be completely honest in your answer. This is regarding Blankenship versus the State of New Mexico, for which you deposed Agent Delgado this morning. Has your office placed my agent under surveillance?"

She listened to his response, then said, "I ask because this morning on her way to her interview with you, someone followed Ms. Delgado from her house to the courthouse. Someone who very clearly intended that she notice she was being followed. You haven't engaged anyone for this purpose?"

I heard the phone squawk from where I was sitting. Ellen held it out from her ear.

"Do not bark at me, sir. I'm concerned for my agent's well-being. Is there a possibility your client might have arranged for such surveillance?" She paced away from the desk and back again in the time it took him to consider that, then concluded the conversation with, "I think it would be in your best interests to find out, sir."

She hung up and contemplated the phone for a moment before returning to the conference table and facing Rose.

"I think Mr. Crandall is sincerely concerned about the situation. He swears his firm is completely innocent of hiring anyone to follow you. I don't think he's quite as certain of his client. I suspect he's probably talking to the Blankenships right this moment. Meanwhile, I don't want to find out the hard way that this is more than a pitiful attempt to intimidate you, Rose. I'd like to hire someone to keep an eye on you."

Rose grimaced. "A bodyguard?"

"I could assign one of the other field operatives to you."

"Oh, Ellen, I don't want that. I'd feel as if they were babysitting me. I'm a grown woman. A trained agent. I ought to be able to take care of myself. As often as I've been in the field—"

"An agent should never go into the field alone, Rose. You need backup. You have a better idea?"

If Rose caught the veiled rebuke for not speaking up sooner about her stalker(s), she gave no indication of it. Her eyes pounced on me like a pair of hungry black kitties. "Gina. Gina's a licensed private investigator. She's already helped me unhorse one undercover stalker. We could hire her to keep an eye on me. She's my best friend so we're together a lot anyway. It won't even seem suspicious to anyone watching me."

Ellen's eyes shifted slowly to me.

Oh, good. The skeptical once-over twice in one day. I kept my expression neutral and interested and my chin up.

"You're right," Ellen Robb said after surprisingly little thought. "It's the perfect solution. She's close enough to you not to draw suspicion, and—I have to say—you don't look much like a detective, Gina."

I merely raised an eyebrow.

She smiled. "That's a good thing, in my opinion. What are your rates?"

"Usually five hundred per diem, but—"

She raised a slender hand. "No 'buts.' You're a professional. Your rates are your rates. The Park Service will pay them. I'll authorize an advance to retain your services—will a week's pay be sufficient? Good, I'll have the admin cut you a check, then we'll put you on a weekly retainer. You'll be able to fly to New Mexico for the trial next month?"

"You bet." I decided I liked doing business with Ellen Robb. She didn't make me feel as if I should apologize for expecting to be paid. Fact was, I had very little going on just then. A couple of easy insurance cases, a possible exploitation of workers' compensation benefits I was checking into for a local janitorial service, and that delinquent dad I was still keeping tabs on.

"I'd like to do a little additional sleuthing, if you don't mind," I told Ellen Robb. "I'd like to see if the person who's following Rose now is the same one we skunked out in the park last week. No extra charge."

Ellen Robb chuckled. "Sounds like a good idea. But if you come up with two stalkers, I may pay a bonus."

"One more thing," Rose said, her brow creasing. "I've never had a case follow me home like this. So far, this surveillance has all been focused on me. But I'm a little nervous about Dave and the kids. It's probably not justified, but . . ."

Ellen nodded her understanding. "I'll make arrangements for them to be covered as well. Does your husband know what's been going on?"

Rose had the good graces to look embarrassed. "I sort of framed the whole Cruz Veras episode as a humorous misunderstanding. I've only told you and Gina about the new guy."

"You should probably tell him in case he happens to notice people shadowing him."

There was a sharp rap on the office door. It swung open slightly and a male head popped through. I recognized Rose's partner, Greg Sheffield.

"Hey," he said, glancing at each of us in turn. "I don't mean to interrupt, but I noticed Rose was back from the deposition and wanted to find out how it went. Good, I guess. No one looks grim."

"Actually, we should probably look grimmer than we do," said Ellen. "It seems Rose has picked up a stalker."

Greg's eyes narrowed. "A what?"

"Someone followed her to the deposition this morning. Made threatening moves with his car. Apparently someone is making unsubtle attempts to intimidate a witness in a federal case."

Greg flushed deeply red. He came into the office, closed the door behind him, and turned to face Ellen, fists parked on his hips. "Well what are we going to do about it? Have you talked to Crandall?"

"Done and done," said Ellen. "I spoke to Crandall about five minutes ago. He denied they're keeping Rose under surveillance, but he agreed with me that he ought to make sure his clients understand that intimidation of that type is illegal and may compound their crime should they be found guilty."

"That's not *enough*, Ellen, Rosie needs protection." He took a step toward Rose.

Ellen's gaze was cool. "I've handled it, Greg. I just hired someone to keep tabs on her."

"Great. Who?"

I waved at him. "Howdy. Allow me to introduce myself—Gina S. Miyoko, bodyguard."

Greg did not seem to think much of this development. "No offense, Gina, but are you really qualified for an assignment like this?"

"Greg," Rose said quietly, "she's a licensed professional. She's an ex-cop— SFPD Major Crimes Division—and mentored by one of San Francisco's finest."

"Yeah, yeah, I know all that," said Greg, who really did know all that. He grimaced. "Oh, fine. You're probably right. I'm just . . . worried." He put a hand on Rose's shoulder and squeezed it. "We've got a hot sting to pull off soon. We can't do it without Rosie."

Rose smiled up at him, patting his hand consolingly. "Don't worry, partner. I'll be there with bells on."

Greg shot Ellen Robb a sharp glance and shook his head, but he kept any further reservations to himself.

"So tell me," I said to Rose, "is Greg Sheffield sweet on you?"

"What?" She nearly choked on her shrimp salad and had to grab a drink of water. "What in heaven's name makes you ask *that*?"

We were sitting in a restaurant on Union Square, having left Ellen's office feeling a bit lighter (and hungrier) now that we had more of a plan for stalker number two. Eating a belated lunch, we watched the street with a little more than casual interest. After lunch I planned to drop Rose back at her office and do a little more checking up on Mr. Cross Sacred True until it was time to escort her home.

I shrugged. "He just seemed awfully freaked by the whole stalker scenario, that's all. I mean, I know you guys partner a lot, but he seemed . . . I dunno . . . a little proprietary."

"I honestly don't think that had as much to do with me as with Ellen. He's not thrilled that she got the job he wanted. I've talked to him about it and, frankly, he's a little embarrassed by his own hostility. I know it seems as if he doesn't think Ellen can do her job, but he knows she can. It's just . . . hard to have someone come in from outside an organization and take the lead spot. Greg and I have been friends—and teammates—a long time, but I don't think he's . . ." She dropped her fork to her plate and glared at me in exasperation. "Oh, beezus, Tink—now you've got me thinking he's got designs on me or something!"

"Ha! Serves you right for trying to set me up with your stalker."

"You think that's who it is—Cruz Veras again?"

"I don't know," I admitted, chewing thoughtfully on a ring of calamari. "It's hard for me to imagine him making threatening moves on you in a Chrysler LeBaron. A Beamer, maybe, but a LeBaron? Never."

She tossed a shrimp at me. "*Tth'izi*," she called me, Hopi for "goat."

"Mule," I corrected, and went back to my squid.

Chapter 5

Tag Team

After lunch, I began my search for further information on Cruz Veras with a visit to the website of *Arqueología* magazine. I already knew, of course, that Dr. Cruz Veras was a contributor, but a bit more sleuthing netted me the phone number of the editorial offices, which I proceeded to call, pretending to be an archaeology grad student hoping to interview Dr. Veras for a college journal.

Was Dr. Veras available to discuss the idea?

The woman I was speaking to put me on hold briefly, then returned to tell me that Dr. Veras was on assignment and that my best chance of reaching him was his email address, which she proceeded to give me. It was the same as the one on his card. She could not possibly share his cell phone number without his permission. I already had a cell phone number, but there was no way I could confirm it with this woman under the circumstances, so I tracked down a contact number for the INAH and called them.

This time I used a similar story to reach someone in the administrative offices, said I was having trouble reaching Dr. Veras, and asked if they could confirm that the phone number he'd given me was correct. I gave a number that was one digit off, the admin I spoke to corrected it, and I expressed my embarrassment at being unable to read my own handwriting. ("Oh, of *course*, that was a nine not a four!") Before I hung up, I employed one more fib in my web of pretense.

"Dr. Veras explained to me by email that he was on assignment somewhere in the U.S. I believe he said California. Is that correct?"

"I'm sorry," the admin told me, "I am not authorized to give out that information. May I ask why you want it?"

"Oh, sorry. I'm at San Francisco State University, and was hoping I might get to meet Dr. Veras in person. Thank you for your help." I hung up and sat back in my chair.

So, our Cruz Veras was *their* Cruz Veras. That was a relief, but it complicated things. For one thing, it deepened the man's mystery: why would the institute's admin not be allowed to tell me where Dr. Veras was? For another, it meant that we had yet another stalker to flush out.

I set the Cruz Veras conundrum aside and started contemplating another trap. Given how well our initial snare had worked with Veras, I decided the basic bait and switch idea was sound, but this time Rose would have more than just little old me for backup.

My first goal was to get our stalky guy out of the LeBaron I'd seen gliding in and out of traffic in the rearview mirror of Rose's car on our way back to her office from lunch. Later that evening, as I followed her across the Golden Gate up into the headlands, I didn't see him at all. It was as we passed the cutoff where Conzelman Road left 101 to wind through the Marin Headlands, that it struck me how perfect the area would be to lay a trap with multiple moving parts and redundancies. It was isolated, and would potentially deke Rose's stalker into feeling that he could be bolder, if he was so inclined. At the same time, parting him from his vehicle eliminated the possibility of a hit-and-run or a speedy getaway if he thought he'd been made. I wanted him out of his protective shell, on foot, and in unfamiliar surroundings that could hide an entire squad of watchers if necessary.

I put the idea to Rose that evening when we got home.

"I like the way you think, Tink," Rose told me when I'd laid out the basic shape of my plan. "You know it's funny, but even though what we're doing is probably more dangerous than just sitting around quivering, it makes me feel less afraid, not more. Weird, huh?"

"Not really. I think it's sort of like going to the doctor for something that ails you. You feel better just having made the decision to go to a pro. You feel as if you're *doing* something, not just curling up in a fetal position and playing victim."

The first order of business was sitting Dave down and explaining that the encounter with the Mexican journalist we'd laughingly recounted to him not that long ago was not the end of Rose's little stalking problem. No, there was a new kid in town who had so disturbed Rose, her partner, and her boss (not to mention me) that David and the kids would be getting federal protection while we and a group of Rose's cohorts smoked the guy out.

I took the additional measure of consulting with my father, who completely agreed with Ellen Robb—you should always have backup. I've always thought those sleuths you see on TV who dive into danger without saying a word to anybody are nitwits.

It was Monday, which was Dad's SASH night—that's the Society for the Appreciation of Sherlock Holmes (I kid you not). When I walked in the front door of my parents' houseboat, the place smelled of tea, scones, and cinnamon, and I could hear the teapot whistling merrily in the background as Mom reprised her role as Mrs. Hudson to Dad and his coterie of wannabe sleuths.

Dad was in the wood-paneled "parlor," tidying up the room and arranging the chairs around the gas-log fireplace. He had already donned his deerstalker hat, and a briar pipe hung jauntily from one side of his mouth. He smiled when he saw me, causing the pipe to stick straight out from his teeth.

"Gina! Are you here for the meeting tonight? Black currant scones—your favorite."

"Mom'll give me a scone just for poking my nose into the kitchen. What can you offer to sweeten the deal?"

"What d'you need?"

I sat down in a red plaid wingback chair beside the fireplace. "Advice. I've got a new case, Dad."

He stopped puttering about and came to sit opposite me, giving me his entire attention. I love that about Dad. He listens, he watches, he *gets* things. Except for the fact that he's only five-foot-seven and Japanese, he's a ringer for the "real" Sherlock Holmes.

"Good for you!" my Sherlock said now. "Tell me about it."

"A stalker . . . or two."

"Stalker? You a detective or a bodyguard?"

"A little of both, actually," I admitted. "It's Rose, Dad. She was being followed. The guy turned out to be an archaeologist and reporter for a Mexican anthropology rag, but now that we've got *him* mostly sorted out, someone else has come out of the woodwork."

"Another stalker?"

I nodded.

"Tag team?"

I blinked. Why hadn't I thought of that?

"You think?"

"Seems an awful big coincidence."

"Yeah, but this Cruz Veras guy—the journalist . . . archaeologist— turned out to be legit."

"Well, which is he—journalist or archaeologist?"

"Both, as it happens. The guy's got a PhD—*Dr.* Veras, if you please. He works for the Mexican National Historical Institute and contributes academic articles to *Arqueología* magazine."

"*Dr.* Veras, is it? Is he single?" Mom stood in the doorway with a tea tray in her hands.

"I have no clue," I said quashingly.

"Well, you should get one," she told me, with barely a hint of her Russian accent, and deposited the tray full of scones and tea cakes on the table next to my chair. "I will bring you tea. Alvin is here. He has a PhD also."

Mom has long had it in her fertile imagination that Alvie Spielman and I are perfect for each other. I have come to the conclusion that I am not "perfect" for anyone. Which is not to say that Alvie doesn't have his appeal. He's a very good friend—a nice starting point for romance, I've been told—he has a quirky and somewhat morbid sense of humor and he's good-looking in a nerdy sort of way. Imagine Harry Potter on growth hormones, but Jewish.

"Gina has come to me for advice," my father said, and gave my mother a "look."

Mom's sleek eyebrows disappeared beneath her thick auburn bangs. "I'll invite Alvie to the kitchen," she said, and left us in peace.

I knew the rest of the SASH Squad would be here shortly, so I dove right in. "Here's the thing: I'm thinking of laying a trap for this new stalker. Nothing really perilous, just draw him out so we can get a look at him."

I laid out all of the pieces to the plan that Rose and I had concocted so far, from timing and location to the super subtle communication cues we came up with.

"My question is: How can I bulletproof it? I'd like it to be fairly solid before I present it to Rose's boss."

Dad smiled. "Ah. I notice you're not asking me if this is a good idea."

"It is, isn't it? I mean, I thought it would be better to be in control of as many variables in the situation as we can. If we just play wait and see, we're at this guy's mercy. Right?"

He was nodding. Not in a *Eureka, you've found it!* way, but in an inscrutable Zen Master Yoda way. "This seems logical."

I half expected him to add, "Grasshopper." But he didn't, so it was my turn.

"But . . . ?" I prompted.

"But what? I said it seems logical. It is always best to be the master of a situation rather than its slave. How many operatives will you use?"

"I don't know. That's up to Rose's boss, Ellen Robb."

"How many would you suggest?"

I imagined the stretch of hilly beach I reckoned would be the best damned sand trap in the Bay Area. "Enough to cover escape. One on each end of the beach trail. One in the parking area. One above the trail, one below."

He was nodding, his eyes unfocused, as if he were seeing the images in my head. "Make sure some of your assets are visible but self-involved," he said. "Otherwise—"

"The mark might be suspicious if it's too quiet," I finished.

"Nothing's ever completely bulletproof, Gina," he reminded me. "You know this as well as I do."

I shivered, understanding this as a veiled reference to the case that had cost Dad his career as a detective. "I know."

He got up to cross the room to a small black lacquer hutch that I have always thought of as the Shrine. Dad calls it a curio cabinet, but it's where he keeps his ancestors, which seems a shrine-like usage to me. When he came back to the fire, he was holding something small, which he proceeded to place in the palm of my hand.

It was a mingei—a Japanese lucky charm—in the form of a *tanuki*. In other (Russian) words, an obereg.

Now, anyone who's ever become addicted to Mario Bros. video games knows that a tanuki is a cute little potbellied critter that looks a lot like a raccoon. In fact, tanuki essentially means "raccoon dog." This is not to be confused, mind you, with Mario in a raccoon suit. The tanuki is an ancient and legendary bit of Japanese culture. Mario in a raccoon suit, not so much. The tanuki is a shape-shifter, so I suspected Dad thought this was an appropriate mingei for a private detective.

I smiled and got up to kiss his cheek. "Thanks, Dad." I pocketed the tanuki and shuffled my feet.

"You're leaving? You're not staying for the SASH meeting?"

"I really should go home and feed my cat." I edged toward the parlor door.

"Your cat eats just fine without you. I've seen her—birds, fish, small seals."

"Hi, Gina."

Alvie was in the doorway, blocking my retreat. Mom and two other SASH members—appropriately dressed for the occasion—stood behind him in the hall.

"Hi, Alvie. I was just going." I angled toward the door, making "make-a-hole" motions with my shoulder.

"Can't you stay?" Dad asked. "We're doing 'The Speckled Band.'"

I snapped my fingers. "Oh, you know, I've read that one—saw the BBC episode too. The snake did it."

My father was giving me the inscrutable Zen eyeball. I couldn't bear to look at my mother to see what she was giving me.

"Didn't I offer good advice?" Dad asked ingenuously.

I stayed.

For the entire meeting.

It was more fun than I'm willing to admit. I ended up playing Watson to Alvie's Holmes in a role-playing vignette, after which Holmes asked me out for lunch.

"It's not a date, I promise," he told me when I hesitated. "Just two friends having lunch. Friends do that, I hear."

I could feel Mom's eyes on me all the way from her study at the back of the houseboat. Could hear her thinking, *Gina, don't be a* doorak.

I wriggled inside, wanting to say "yes" and "no" simultaneously.

Relief came in the form of an ice-cold epiphany: I really was a doorak, I realized, and kicked myself for allowing even a hint of discomfort to creep into my relationship with Alvie. He didn't deserve that. Hell, *I* didn't deserve that. If I gave in to the urge to hide out even from Alvin Spielman, it would be another point scored for Jeremy Augustine.

I gave Alvie my biggest, most sincere smile. "Sure," I said. "Call me tomorrow. We'll set a definite date."

"Date?" he repeated, looking rattled. His thick, brown hair was standing on end from the many times he'd swept his fingers through it, and now he pushed his glasses up his very Holmesian nose and blinked at me.

I reached up (way up) and patted his cheek. "Call me tomorrow."

God bless him, he blushed. Alvie's such an open book. Uncomplicated. Sincere. If I were smart, I'd have fallen for him long ago. But I seemed to have a natural attraction to gold-plated scoundrels.

When I finally collected my jacket from the coatrack in the hall, I found that Mom had parked yet another lucky doodad in my pocket. It was the smallest of a set of nesting babushka dolls that I knew for a fact had once reposed under the altar at Our Lady of Kazan. I put Dad's tanuki in there with it (who knew, maybe they'd reproduce) and returned to my houseboat feeling doubly blessed.

Wednesday morning at 8:50 A.M., I parked Boris the Harley behind a restroom along the headland walk, slipped into the fragrant building, and peeled off my leather jacket to reveal an oversize Spider-Man sweatshirt. Then I rolled my jeans up to mid-calf, un-hiding sneakers and tube socks. Lastly, I pulled a Penney's bag containing a short light brown wig and a Frisbee out from beneath my sweatshirt. I stuffed my collar-length hair up under the wig, the Frisbee under my arm, and my jacket into the bag. Net effect: I went into the restroom a diminutive Hells Angel and came out a suntanned person of indeterminate gender and age.

I surreptitiously returned the Penney's bag to the motorcycle's lockbox, then skipped off down the walk, tossing my Frisbee in the air. On the way, I passed by Greg Sheffield who, in cargo shorts and a white fisherman's sweater, was ostensibly painting a seascape. Yes, you can construe from this that Ellen Robb liked my sand-trap idea, fine-tuned it, and dedicated three of her agents to it.

As prearranged, Greg didn't give me the time of day. Beneath the cable-knit, I knew, was holstered a shiny, well-used Ruger GP100. Like me, Greg favored a revolver, although I'll take my little seven-shooter over his big old six-shooter any day of the week.

Just down from the trailhead, I bypassed Agent Rodney Hammermill, to all appearances having a leisurely cup of coffee atop a saltgrass ottoman between the trail and the beach. Less than one-quarter of a mile later, I was in position myself, lying on my back atop a little dune, apparently dozing in the lee of a tuft of sedge and verbena. There was a third agent—Pearl Rodriguez—at the other end of the trail where it rose to converge with a bike path.

Barely six feet below me was the jogging trail. About thirty feet below that, down a steep sand bank peppered with stunted trees, brush, and rocks, was the beach. Above and to my left the hill rose steeply to a rocky crown. I was morbidly conscious of the item my sweatshirt concealed: my Taurus, tucked into a hip holster and digging into my upper thigh.

I'd been lying there sunning my shins for about fifteen minutes when I heard the sound of footfalls and humming—a jogger coming up the trail. A moment later, I caught that the runner was singing the theme song from *Big Trouble in Little China* (which I admit, unapologetically, is my favorite film of all time).

The signal was given—Rose thought she was being followed. If she was convinced she had no tail, she was supposed to use her best Tina Turner impersonation on "We Don't Need Another Hero."

I tensed as she jogged by below me, then turned my head to peer through the waving grasses down her back trail.

There he was.

He was older than Cruz Veras, and much bigger. Beefy's a good word. He had short brown hair, wore mirror shades, a knit cap, and a jogging suit capable of hiding any number of weapons. His jacket was loosely zipped and seemed bulkier on the left than on the right. His jogging was unconvincing as well. He ran as if his feet were made of lead, dragging the toes of his Nikes so that little puffs of sand rose up to disperse on the breeze.

I put my head down as he lumbered past, then rolled onto my left side so I could watch him. He'd gotten about three yards beyond me, his right arm bent at the elbow as he reached toward his left shoulder. Either he was having a heart attack or he was going for something in his jacket.

I got to my knees and slipped a hand under my sweatshirt, wrapping my fingers around the butt of the Taurus.

He was slowing, stopping, reaching.

Damn! Where were Greg and Rodney? Should I shout, or shoot, or—?

A second later, it all became academic; a large clod of grassy turf flew out of nowhere and connected with Rose's head. She stumbled and fell to her knees, momentum carrying her right off the trail and down the steep, sandy embankment to the beach. In seconds, she'd disappeared below the lip of the trail.

Her stalker ran to where she'd fallen and stopped, scanning the rugged hillside below. He was in profile to me, so I could see that he held a gun with both hands and was apparently looking for a target.

I eased the Taurus out of its holster.

Another dirt clod landed, this time at the stalker's feet, exploding messily onto the back of his pants. He spun, eyes scouring the steep hill behind him.

I flattened myself to the ground and tried to follow his gaze. From my vantage point, I could see nothing, but he must have seen something he didn't like, because he jammed the gun into his shoulder holster and took off back the way he'd come as fast as his leaden feet would carry him. The backup team would have to take care of him; my focus was on Rose.

I let him get out of sight behind a turn in the trail before I popped up and scanned the hill myself. I saw nothing but a thin banner of breeze-borne silt fanning out from a sand-fall just below the rocks.

Damning any possible torpedoes, I slid from my perch and raced to the place where Rose had gone over the side. I could see no trace of her, so I went over myself, reasoning that if I were being observed from the hilltop (read: making a target of myself), I'd be a whole lot less visible down among the coyote brush and toyon trees.

"Rose?" I dared to call out. "Rosie? It's Gina! You all right?"

She appeared far below me, backing out of the shadow of the embankment onto the tide-wet sand of the beach. She beckoned me to where she stood and I scrambled down, using rocks and tufts of sedge as foot holds, then dropped the last four or five feet to land beside her with a soggy *scrunch*.

"I'm fine," she said, before I could ask again, and rubbed the red spot at her temple where the divot had scored. "I took the dirt clod as a sign that I should get quickly out of sight and dove for cover. Thanks, I guess."

"It wasn't me," I told her as I looked at her for any signs of a concussion. "How does your head feel? Any dizziness or nausea?"

"Tink, imagine this is your cat talking. I meant to do that. I didn't fall . . . much. I dove chaotically."

I gave her a look as close to one of Mom's skeptical squints as I could, and she took a few steps away from me and back to demonstrate her fitness for duty. Temporarily satisfied, I inspected her person. Her braid was covered in sand and tufted with toyon needles and seagull feathers, and her joggers were filthy and torn in one knee. She was wet, too, and the side she'd landed on was caked with soggy sand. She made a half-hearted swipe at her right hip then nodded toward the trail.

"Let's get going. I can't wait to meet this guy face-to-face. I think it'll be faster if we keep to the beach until we're just below the parking lot."

I started to turn up the beach, but Rose put a hand on my arm. I looked back and met her dark gaze. There was a question in it.

"That man . . . he was armed, wasn't he?"

I nodded. "Smith and Wesson nine mil."

She exhaled sharply, then started jogging back up the beach. I sprinted after her. As I reached her, she pulled a pint-sized walkie-talkie out of her jacket pocket. I could tell at a glance she wasn't going to raise anybody on that thing; the antenna was broken. She swore and ran faster.

We scrambled up the hill to the parking lot, where we were met with a jarringly unexpected sight: Greg Sheffield was still seated at his easel, dabbing paint on a canvas. The stalker was nowhere in sight. Stunned, Rose and I stopped in unison at the edge of the tarmac just as Greg glanced up and saw us. He looked just as surprised as I'm sure we did. Frowning, he put down his paintbrush and strode toward us across the parking area.

Rose broke her silence to murmur, "This is really serious now, isn't it, Tink? That guy was going to shoot me."

"It sure looked that way, although I suppose he might've just been trying to scare you. I don't understand the motivation. It's hard to imagine the Anasazi pothunters resorting to murder to keep from going to jail for a couple of years. Hell, they might get off with heavy fines and some community service. Pulling a gun is a whole other level from aggressive driving."

Greg had reached us now, concern and confusion blooming on his face. "Rose, are you okay? What happened?" His voice went up a notch or two in panic as he took in the dirt, ripped clothes, and our shaken expressions.

"A lot," I told him. "Big out-of-shape guy in brand new jogging duds made some threatening moves with a Smith & Wesson. Where were you?"

"I was waiting for . . ." He grimaced. "I was waiting for a big out-of-shape guy in brand new jogging duds."

"You didn't see him?" Rose asked.

Greg shook his head. "No. He must have found a way to bypass the parking lot. Rodney and Pearl too, apparently, although I'm not sure how."

"He didn't come back this way?"

"Nope. *Dammit.*" He pulled out a walkie-talkie and told the other two agents to come in. Then he jammed the thing back into his pocket with a gesture of pure frustration. "*Damn* it!" he repeated, then stabbed a finger at me. "Get Rose back to the office *now*. I think it's time this escalates to the police."

Couldn't argue with that.

I saw Rose to her car and retrieved Boris from behind the restroom. I know both of us were scanning for a green LeBaron or a big beefy man in or out of a tracksuit. I'd just donned my leathers and helmet and mounted up to follow Rose back to her office for the debriefing when I saw something that made my blood boil and run cold simultaneously. Sitting back under some low trees at one end of the parking area was a burgundy Honda. Even as I was squinting to make out the license number, it backed up and disappeared into the shadows.

I revved up the Harley and gave chase, but by the time I reached the trees, the car was gone. I sat motionless on my bike, thoughts rattling around the inside of my head like aimless pinballs.

None of them were nice thoughts.

Dad's surprise suggestion was the biggest, shiniest ball of the bunch. Was Dr. Cruz Veras a dedicated journalist with a cannon for an arm, or was he part of a potentially deadly tag team?

The debriefing was painful because we exited it with more questions than answers. Ellen asked, again, if Rose wouldn't rather forego the Anasazi trial, and again, Rose respectfully declined.

"I'm not a coward and I'm not a quitter," she told her boss. "I can't believe these yo-yos mean to kill me. I think they just want to frighten me, and figure a woman should be easy to intimidate. Well, they're barking up the wrong woman."

That surprised laughter from both Ellen and me and significantly lightened the mood.

Ellen grimaced. "What about the Bridges sting? No one would blame you if you wanted to opt out and let Greg head it."

"Hell, no," Rose said. "I'm looking forward to the Bridges sting. That hotdog has been thumbing his nose at the Park Service for years, but this time, I think we're going to get him. But, I am willing to accept a little extra backup."

And so I found myself temporarily assigned to the National Park Service as an agent-in-training. At least that would be my cover to all but Greg and Rose. And in the coming week, I would be in Arizona working the sting.

Chapter 6

My Lunch with Alvie

For the next two days I saw neither burgundy Hondas nor green LeBarons. I continued to poke at the INAH, hoping to make contact with whomever counted as Cruz Veras's superior. After several frustratingly brief forays, I finally played a card I wasn't sure I should; I introduced myself to the admin as an American National Park Service agent and asked if I could speak to the head of Dr. Veras's department. I was informed that Dr. Veras *was* the head of his department.

"Then who can I escalate this to?" I asked. "This is a matter of the utmost importance. I . . . I think Dr. Veras's life might be in danger." From me, if he turned out to be dirty.

"I'm sorry," the admin told me. "Could you repeat that?"

I all but ground my teeth. "I have reason to believe Dr. Veras is the target of a gang of blackmarket antiquities hunters."

"Please," the young man implored me, "leave me your name and number and I will bring this to the appropriate persons."

Well, damn. I fibbed that I couldn't leave my name and number because I was an undercover agent on assignment (sort of true) and couldn't blow my cover.

After that stinging failure, I tried a different tack. I took a photo of Cruz Veras and used Google's lovely image tracking app to ask "who is this?" Every hit I got informed me that this was Dr. Cruz Sacramento Veras, PhD, yada, yada, yada. Except for the hits that insisted it was Antonio Banderas.

Frustrated in that, I sent an email to Dr. Veras that was short, pithy, and one I hoped that would elicit a response.

Dr. Veras, I wrote, *it appears you are a man of many talents: journalism, archaeology, and espionage to name but a few. I saw you at the headlands on Wednesday, still stalking Rose Delgado. Was the man who threatened her your associate? Lack of response to the contrary will be taken as a "yes."*

I then started packing for my trip to Arizona with clothing the weather widget on my iPhone indicated was appropriate, then settled back to enjoy my Friday night.

On Saturday I had lunch with Alvie at a Chinese restaurant on Sutter. The street in front of the restaurant was in a perpetual state of repair. This did not seem to hurt business. In fact, I suspected that many lunch-goers simply took one look at the big trench just up the street from the restaurant's front door and figured they need go no further for sustenance.

"Arizona?" he asked over dim sum, his expressive, slightly nasal voice clearly conveying surprise. "Why Arizona?"

"'Cause that's where the action is," I answered. "I've been hired to do a little sleuthing for Rose's organization."

"Rose is a park ranger."

"Rose is a park service agent. There's a difference. Rangers tell people not to feed bears. Agents tell people not to dig up other people's ancestors."

He nodded. "Didn't I hear you mention that someone dug up one of Rose's ancestors not that long ago?"

"Last winter. Her great-grandmother."

"That's harsh. So her gramma might be an exhibit in a museum someplace?"

"Or in some private collector's basement."

"Wow." He shook his head, no doubt trying to clear the image of a sweet, old Hopi grandmother mounted on someone's wall like a hunting trophy. "Does it strike you as odd that you have so many friends who deal with dead people and their stuff?"

"Not until you mentioned it."

He toyed with his *baos* for a moment, pushing them around the little plate with his chopsticks, then said, "That was a close call the other day."

"Huh?"

"At the headlands. The guy with the S&W nine mil. Good thing somebody has a live arm and dead aim."

I stared at him. "Was that . . . *you*?"

He smiled. "I'm not Clark Kent, unfortunately. But I did see the whole thing go down. So did your dad. I take it he didn't say anything."

"Not a peep. What do you mean, you saw it go down?"

"I mean, Ed got it into his head that you weren't going to have adequate backup. So he made sure you were covered by a contingent of SASH operatives."

Oh, so they were "operatives" now. "I didn't see any of you."

The smile deepened, prodding a dimple into view on his left cheek. "Yeah, your dad's still got it."

I pushed my plate aside, suddenly uninterested in food. "Where were you guys positioned?"

"All over. Ed was down on the beach. Uh, Claude Trevor was just around the bend in the trail about nine or ten yards from where Rose went over the side. I was behind you on the hillside."

"Higher up?"

"Yeah."

"Did you see where the stalker came from, then? He completely bypassed Rosie's team. Although why . . ."

Alvie lowered his eyes. "Maybe they got made. I mean, I suspected the guy with the easel. But then, I *knew* he must be an agent because I knew it was a sting. The stalker wouldn't." He shrugged.

"What about the guy with the easel?" I wanted to know.

"His palette. There was no Phthalo green on it. But there was on the seascape he was puttering with."

"No Phthalo green. Seriously?"

"Well, and I could tell he was armed. It was the way his sweater hung. Most people wouldn't notice either of those things, but the stalker might notice the bulge in his sweater if he was a pro."

"You think that might've tipped him?"

"Not really. If it was me—the stalker, I mean—the presence of someone who was armed, and that I suspected might be undercover would put me off the job completely. And I sure as hell wouldn't pull a gun out in broad daylight."

"So our wannabe assailant wasn't too bright."

Alvie shrugged. "Or his real intent was to terrorize. Or he didn't think Easel Guy was suspicious. Like I said, I *knew* he had to be a plant. Also, Sherlock here." He pointed a thumb at his chest. "I'm trained to be observant *and* a detective fiction buff. I could look at anyone in this room and find something 'off' about them . . . whether it really is or not," he added, self-deprecatingly.

"Okay, I'm impressed," I told him, then asked, "From your vantage point could you see who threw down on the guy?"

"There was someone in the rocks at the top of the hill, but I didn't get a good look at him. In fact, I thought it was one of the SASH Squad, but when we did some recon, I realized it must've been one of yours." He studied my face. "Or not."

"Why'd you think it was one of the SASH guys?"

"Giants baseball cap. A couple of the guys were wearing them. Good contextual camouflage."

That didn't prove our hurler was Cruz Veras, but he'd been wearing a Giants baseball cap when I first saw him, leaning against his car all confident and cool.

I asked Alvie a few more questions about their beach surveillance, then lapsed into ruminative silence. Alvie, God bless him, is used to that. He put up with it patiently until the main dishes arrived, then drew me out with some tales from the Crypt—the coroner's office, that is. That perked me up a bit. There's nothing like a few bizarre autopsy anecdotes to pull a woman out of a funk.

We wandered down to Union Square after lunch and tooled through Macy's which, in my book, is as much fun as Disneyland. I bought a new bathing suit and a totally ridiculous pair of spike-heeled sandals for no other reason than that Alvie stopped to admire them. To reciprocate, Alvie bought a moleskin shirt in a color he never wears.

Alvie is one of those rare men who actually enjoys shopping. I can't imagine why there aren't more of them, because shopping is about as close to our hunter-gatherer roots as the urban male (or female) is going to get. The facial expression of a woman exiting Macy's during the height of the sale season is indistinguishable from that of a lioness sitting on a fat water buffalo carcass on the savanna.

When Alvie dropped me off at home, I told him I'd had a great time (which was true) and we should do it again (which I meant). This encouraged him to ask about dinner sometime next week. He was disappointed to hear I'd be in Arizona for an indeterminate amount of time but took a rain check, and gave me a friendly peck on the cheek before folding himself into his Volvo and driving away.

In my home office I discovered two things. One was that Mom had let herself into the houseboat and left me a message on a sticky note: *Come tell me.*

She meant lunch with Alvie, of course. I was expected to give a blow-by-blow account of any romantic subtext. I had two choices: make something up, or tell the truth and be roundly disbelieved.

The second thing I found was an email message from cveras@iahm.org. It said simply: *No.*

No what? No, I'm not the Cruz Veras you want? No, I'm not a man of many talents? No, I didn't throw the dirt clod? No, the stalker isn't my associate?

In the middle of my quandary, the phone rang. It was Mom. The first words out of her mouth were: "Tell me all about it."

Chapter 7
Sting

We flew to Arizona Sunday morning—Rose, Greg, Rodney, and me. We were incognito—Rose and Greg posing as a married couple on vacation; Rodney and I pretending to be college students bound for a university-sponsored dig near Sedona. I didn't see anyone who looked like the Headland Stalker; neither did I see Cruz Veras.

I was getting more paranoid too, I realized. Every aging linebacker or slender Banderas look-alike drew my immediate attention.

We touched down at Sky Harbor a little after noon, grabbed a bite of lunch, then went by the Heard Museum to pick up a satchel of "trade goods"—artifacts that would be used as part of the sting. The flat, dry air—like the flat, dry landscape—was a shock after the cool, moist atmosphere of home. Within minutes of landing, I felt as if I was being mummified.

We drove to a budget motel in the suburb of Glendale where we settled in to prepare for the upcoming meeting and wait for the arrival of two additional agents on loan from the Phoenix field office. Rose and Greg had chosen as the "sting suite" a second floor room in a wing of the rambling motel that was shielded from the main road by its fellow wings. (I'm convinced that it must've looked like a cubist octopus from the air.) While Rose and I put identifying code numbers and tracking dots on the artifacts in unobtrusive places, Greg and Rodney went to the room next door to set up their surveillance equipment.

While they were gone, agents Frakes and Padilla checked in. At first glance, I could see this was the Brute Suit Squad. Both large men were nattily dressed in the latest from Yves Saint Bernard. It was their assignment to perform the arrest and the interrogation, playing the traditional game of Good Cop/Bad Cop.

"Which is which?" I asked.

"I'm the Good Cop," Ramon Padilla told me, and smiled as if to prove it. The smile transformed his round, bulldog face into something disturbingly cherubic.

I glanced at Chuck Frakes, who looked like an ex–prize fighter—not somebody I would have dared call Chuck. "Bad cop?"

He nodded curtly. Then smiled. Not at all cherubic. Disturbing, nonetheless.

"I live for interrogations," he informed me in a monotone.

"So how does it go down?" I asked.

"Greg will escape," Padilla said. "Rose gets arrested."

I nodded. "So that the undercover agents stay undercover."

"You got it."

"Rose says you've been after this guy for a while. How come you've never stung him before?"

Padilla sighed. "It's not for lack of trying. He's gotten really good at hiding behind other dealers, for one thing. We set up a sting, but someone else shows up to take the fall. If anybody shows up at all."

"One time," Rose recalled, "the fall guy was a college journalism student who thought it would make an exciting project for the school news rag to be in on an illegal artifact sale. He got more excitement than he bargained for."

"You busted him?"

"Yep," said Padilla cheerfully.

"He got probation and community service," explained Rose, shooting the other agent a quelling glance. "And a slightly different angle on his feature story than he'd planned. Fortunately for him, the judge was inclined to reward naiveté with lenience."

Frakes snorted.

"So you've never gotten Bridges to bite?"

"Once," Rose said. "When we set up a sting, we often allow one clandestine meeting to go down without interference."

"Lulls 'em into a false sense of security," said Padilla.

Rose continued: "Since then, he's shown up at a sting exactly one time. And at that one, he took one look at the goods, said, 'Hey, this stuff is stolen!' and left."

"Something tipped him?" I asked.

Rose grimaced. "We had an overeager young newbie in on the sting. He got a little antsy. I think he made Bridges nervous."

"How do you find guys like Bridges to begin with?"

"Antiquities shows, mostly," said Padilla.

"Antiquities shows?" I repeated. "You mean like gun shows or car shows—like that?"

The idea that there might be a cadre of zealots who bonded over potsherds and bone fragments hadn't occurred to me. I suppose it should have. Since a lot of archaeological prospecting is done in village middens (aka, municipal dumps), I found the concept comical, imagining an exhibition centuries from now at which anthro-geeks oohed and aahed over Campbell's Soup cans and Budweiser bottles.

A look at the faces of my three companions indicated that the humorous element had escaped them.

"Exactly," Rose said. "We go to the shows to look for antiquities vendors who seem willing to fudge on legal issues."

"And Mr. Bridges was willing," I guessed.

"Oh, you betcha," said Rose. "I made a few plaintive noises about the paucity of Mogollon artifacts that were in circulation for purchase and he guaranteed me he could get me as many top-grade specimens as I wanted. When I asked if that wasn't a dangerous offer, Bridges was positively gleeful. He thought the idea of 'putting one over' on Uncle Sam was a 'hoot.'"

"Joy boy," said Frakes. I'd swear his jaw snapped shut the second the words were clear of his teeth.

Rose's cell phone pinged just then. It was a text from Greg telling her they were ready for the artifacts we'd been prepping. I laid them out on the bed while Rose finished the last touches on her disguise. There were about a dozen clay and wooden figurines from New Mexico, an entire wooden flute, some stone beads, a painted deer bone, and an itty-bitty little net snare that would have been hard-pressed to hold a large grasshopper.

Half an hour later, Greg was in place in the room, Rose had gone off-campus so as to make a grand entrance, and Rodney and I hunkered down amid the surveillance equipment with Padilla and Frakes. It was like some twisted reproduction of a Norman Rockwell painting—four kids gathered around the old radio, tuning into an episode of *The Lone Ranger*.

At 7:05 P.M. Greg's voice announced that Rose—aka, "Stella Vasquez"—had parked her SUV in the lot below.

"Bridges is nowhere in sight," he said dryly. "I wonder if he's even going to show."

"You want me to wait him out?" asked Rose from the parking lot.

"No," said Greg. "It's almost ten after. Come on up, just don't hurry."

The next thing we heard was Rose's voice murmuring, "Will wonders never cease?"

"What?" Rodney asked, coming to attention.

"He's *he-ere*."

"You're kidding," said Greg, then, "Sonuvabitch."

"Muzzle it, Greg," Padilla warned him. "Don't be *too* happy to see him. You'll scare him off."

"Stella Vasquez" and Ted Bridges converged on Greg's motel room at roughly the same moment. She was knocking when we heard Bridges's breezy, "Hey, baby!"

"I'm not your baby, pops," Rose responded.

"I ain't your pops, baby."

Greg answered the knock. After the obligatory introductions, the discussion turned to the items laid out on the bed.

"Huh," Bridges grunted. "Looks like a little mouse-catcher. Man, you gotta be hard up to want to trap something that small."

"What's the flute made of?" Rose asked.

Greg answered, "Willow."

"You got papers on it?"

"No, but I can get them."

"Nice," said Bridges. "But I seen better. What do you want for the whole batch?"

"Hey, wait a minute!" Rose objected. "Leave some for me, why don't you?"

"Why should I, baby? You weren't very nice to me outside just now. Maybe if you were nice to me . . ."

Rose made a rude noise.

"Fifteen hundred," said Greg over the raspberry.

"Fifteen?" echoed Bridges. "You're pullin' my leg—the whole lot's not worth more than about three hundred fifty."

"I can't let it go for any less than fifteen hundred."

"Nine hundred," said Rose.

The negotiations went on for a while with increased antagonism between Rose and Bridges. Rodney chewed his fingernails, Padilla offered him a nail file from a neat little pocket kit, Frakes checked his sidearm, and I tried to keep track of the conversation in the other room. Then Bridges won the bid by offering eight hundred in cash and an IOU for two-fifty. It was a deal Rose protested loudly and belligerently, before settling into fitful grumbles.

"It was nice doing—" Greg began the code phrase that would send Padilla and Frakes into action.

Bridges cut him off with a laugh. "Now, baby girl, let me set things right. I just happen to have something with me that I think you're both gonna love."

There was a moment of relative quiet punctuated by the sounds of a briefcase being opened, then Bridges said, "Well, what do you make of *that*, my friends?"

"That's part of a bowl or vase, isn't it?" asked Rose. "This isn't local craftsmanship."

"Right, you are. Give the girl a prize."

Greg snorted. "C'mon, Bridges, who're you trying to snow, here? This is some sort of fantasy art piece—a reproduction—"

"Nope. This sucker's old. Ask me how old, baby," he prompted Rose.

"Okay, pops, I'll play your silly game—how old?"

"Call me Ted, or I'm gonna pack up my artifacts and strut on outta here."

"Oh, for crap's sake." Greg growled.

"It's okay, let him have his moment. How old is that bowl shard, Ted, my love?"

"Much better. I figure this guy dates from about 400 C.E."

"How much do you want for it?" asked Rose.

"Five grand."

Rose uttered a sharp bark of laughter. "It's just a shard! Probably from a midden. Maybe if you had the whole bowl . . . Besides, I don't carry that kind of money on me."

"If you did," Greg told her, "you should keep it." To Bridges he said, "You're full of it. There's no way this is authentic."

"Where'd you get it?" Rose asked.

"Why don't you and I go off someplace private where I can tell you?"

"Why don't you two get a room?" Greg asked caustically. "I need to get out of here. I got another meeting in Winslow tonight."

"Sure thing," Bridges said, and the conversation flagged again amid the rustling of fabric and paper.

The briefcase snapped shut.

"Nice doing business with you," Ted said, and Padilla and Frakes went off like a couple of firecrackers. Rodney Hammermill and I were left staring at each other.

"Does it count," I asked, "if Greg doesn't say it?"

"At this point," said Rodney, "that's academic."

Several seconds passed during which Ted Bridges tried to coerce Rose into dropping by his place for a drink. Greg was silent; according to plan, he should be on his way out the bathroom window right about now.

Then our headphones exploded with the sound of the cavalry arriving in full force.

"Federal officers!" barked Frakes. "Get back inside!"

The interrogation lasted over two hours. Ted Bridges refused to tell the agents where he got the roughly six-by-seven-inch chunk of colorful paint-work that inhabited a padded well in his briefcase, but he did roll over on a handful of other small-time dealers when promised lenience if he cooperated with the authorities. In the end, he was jailed on charges of dealing in stolen property and remanded to the Phoenix PD pending a hearing.

Now you'd think that after an entire day of catching bad guys, an agent would want to get away from it all. Uh-uh. Over a late dinner in the Indian restaurant situated conveniently next door to the business hotel in which the NPS housed its agents, Rose waited only until a pair of sweet lassis arrived before pulling a photograph of the vase fragment out of her bag and propping it up against the sugar bowl. It showed a curved piece of ceramic bearing the image of a masked or painted character in a wild feathered headdress blowing into a truly bizarre-looking instrument.

"What is that thing?" I asked.

"A conch shell," Rose answered absently, her eyes on the photo. She shook her head and addressed the shard: "What were you doing in Ted Bridges's briefcase, my friend?"

Perversely, I almost expected it to answer.

"It's valuable, isn't it?" I asked. My eyes strayed to the kitchen doors through which I had high hopes of our veggie samosas appearing at any moment.

"If it's authentic, you betcha."

"What are the chances it is?"

"In all the time we've been dogging Bridges's tracks, I've never heard of him dealing fakes."

"And if it's authentic, then what? Why is it significant?"

The arrival of our dinners delayed the answer to my question, and I was glorying in the flavor of a mighty fine goat vindaloo by the time she said, "I've seen work like this before, Tink. But not in Arizona. Odds are this is from Chiapas."

"Mexico?" I mumbled around a bite of spicy heaven.

She nodded. "The question is: how did it end up in the hands of a small-time dealer like Bridges?"

"I feel another interrogation coming on."

Rose grimaced. "Well, that's the problem, isn't it? I'm supposed to be an antiquities buyer, not an undercover cop."

"So, get Agent Frakes to do it for you. Remember, he lives for interrogations."

She laughed and slipped the photo back into her bag. "Well, I'm sure it will be a subject of discussion at our debriefing tomorrow morning."

It was, in fact, the main topic of discussion at the debriefing, which was held at the Phoenix area NPS office with Ellen Robb conferenced in from San Francisco.

"I want to question Bridges again," Rose told her. "But I'm not sure I want to blow my cover to do it."

"We did talk to him again," said Frakes. "He was uncooperative."

"He was a real jackass," Padilla corrected. "Flip, arrogant—it was as if he was convinced we couldn't touch him."

"Oh, we can touch him," said Frakes. He cracked his knuckles as if in anticipation.

Greg shook his head. "Fat lot of good that will do if we can't get him to roll over on his source for this Mesoamerican piece."

Ellen's long sigh was clearly audible over the conference phone. "What are our options?"

"We take him to trial with what we've got and keep working on him, I guess," Greg said, sounding less than hopeful.

I glanced at Rose. She had tuned out, her eyes focused on something I doubted was even in the room with us. But no, wait . . . there it was, a brown spider practicing her tatting maneuvers between the vanes of the vertical blinds.

"Or," Rose said, "we could try a little bit more deception."

"Huh?" said Padilla.

Rose turned to look at him. "Maybe Bridges won't open up to a government agent. But he might wax prideful and boast of his doings to someone he wants to impress."

"Like Stella Vasquez?" I guessed.

"I don't see—" Greg began, but Rose came to her feet on a surge of palpable electrical energy, and waved him down.

"Hear me out, Greg. Right now he's sitting in a holding cell awaiting legal counsel. Great. Why shouldn't Stella Vasquez be waiting in the cell next door? Or maybe catch him for a moment at the DA's office."

Frakes perked up (it was subtle, but I'd swear I saw his nostrils flare), and Padilla said, "Not bad, Agent Delgado."

Greg frowned. "Could work. Ellen? What's your call?"

"Sounds like a plan. Figure out what approach works best, then do it."

There was only one flaw in our "do it" scenario, which was that we'd calculated without the solvency of Ted Bridges and the efficiency of his lawyer. Rose arrived in the PPD detention block to find that Bridges had been released on bail that morning.

"I swear," Rose told me as we sat in her rental car, trying to regroup, "that guy is as slippery as a weasel in axle grease."

"Nothing to be done?" I asked.

"Research the piece to see if we can establish provenance. Some collection or field cache might be missing half a vase. Other than that, all I can do is write up my deposition and wait until the hearing to testify."

"Uh, pardon me if I'm missing something, but wasn't that the outcome you were actually hoping for when we came out here?" I said. "Quick bust; good arrest; home again jiggety-jig, news at eleven?"

Rose speared me with a hunter's gaze. "It was. Before Bridges waved that potsherd under our noses. That piece of ceramic potentially elevates this case from the bush leagues to the majors."

"Potentially?"

"If he bought it off another dealer, okay—not so much. But if it's from a new hoard or if it was stolen from a major cache . . ."

"Home run?" I surmised.

"Grand slam. Stealing bits and bones within the US of A is one thing. Smuggling them across the border from Latin America is a whole new ballgame." Rose's fingers beat a war tattoo on the steering wheel. "I have an idea. As far as Ted Bridges knows, I'm just a spunky li'l ole antiquities buyer. I've already established my interest in the vase and anything like it. What if I were to pay him a visit?"

"You mean what if *we* were to pay him a visit, right?"

She started the engine and put the rented Passat wagon in gear. "If I can see what else he's got, maybe even buy something off him, it'll be easier to establish provenance and find out where these artifacts are coming from."

"Now?" I asked.

"Why not?"

"No reason. But shouldn't you let someone back at sting central know what we're up to?"

She looked both ways and pulled out of the PPD parking lot, grinning from ear to ear. "Oh, now where'd be the fun in that?"

I knew she was just yanking my chain. I took out my cell phone. "I'm calling for backup. We're going to tell 'daddy' where we're going and who's gonna be there, like good little girls."

"Honestly, Tink, you have no sense of adventure."

"I have every sense of adventure, but my daddy didn't raise an idiot— well, okay, maybe he did, but not about police work. Never go into a 'situation'—"

"Without adequate backup," she finished. "I know, I know. 555-0483. That's the agency dispatcher. Give him or her the case ID, responding agents, and location. And, just for the record, you are a responding agent."

"Woo-wee," I said dryly, and dialed the number.

The dispatcher on shift was a perky-sounding young man named Clive, who was only too happy to forward our information to all appropriate parties and who didn't even giggle when I told him he was receiving this call from agent-in-training Gina Miyoko.

"You know where to find this guy Bridges?" I asked Rose as I hung up and pocketed my cell phone.

"He's got a more or less legitimate antique business out in Surprise."

"Surprise?"

"A half-eaten little township west of Phoenix proper. It's right next door to El Mirage. Hence, the surprise, I guess."

In less time than I expected, given the sprawling nature of the Phoenix area, we arrived in Surprise and found ourselves tooling along West Santa Fe Drive, paralleling a set of railroad tracks that had an old elementary school song running through my head (*"On the Atchison, Topeka and the Santa Fe-e-e-e!"*).

Ted Bridges's antique shop was quite literally on the wrong side of the tracks from the more prosperous commercial section of town. The shop itself was an artful little adobe that would have looked much more at home in Sedona. Rose parked the Passat in the empty parking lot in front of the adobe and we got out to take a look around. The shop was closed, so we circled it to enter the sandy courtyard in back looking for any sign of Ted Bridges.

There was none. The place was quiet except for bird twitters from the cacti and the distant sound of traffic. A breeze played lazily with dust in the courtyard, making little eddies on the cobbles.

Bridges's vehicle—a custom-painted Jeep Rubicon—was parked in the detached barn-cum-garage across from the shop. The garage door was open. The two-car garage took up only half of the building. The remainder might be storage or living quarters.

I took a couple of sideways steps and laid my hand on the hood. Still warm.

"Yeah," I said, "he's around."

"Unless he has a second car," Rose observed, nodding toward the empty half of the garage.

I glanced over at the second bay. "Could be, but I doubt it. There are no tire tracks on that side and that pile of cardboard boxes is sticking right out where a car would hit it."

"Motorcycle?"

"Then there'd be an oil slick the size of Tempe. If it's a Harley anyway."

Rose nodded and pointed. A steep adobe-and-brick staircase at the rear of the antique shop led to a second floor.

Could be an apartment.

She pulled the scrunchie from her braid and fluffed the yard or so of black silk she called hair. I grinned and ran my fingers through my own shorter do, causing utter mayhem. We moved to the bottom of the staircase and mounted it single file, Rose first. There was a mission bell hanging beside the brightly painted door, which she rang. When nothing happened, she rang it a second time then banged on the door.

"Hey, Teddy Bear!" she called. "It's Stella Vasquez. Remember me?"

Still no answer.

Rose tried the door. It opened easily. "Hey, Te-ddy!" She called, poking her head in. "It's Stella! I've come up to check out your potsherds."

When no one answered, we made a quick tour of the four rooms that made up the apartment, then went down into the antique shop below. No sign of Ted Bridges.

"Let's try the barn," Rose said, peering across the yard at the other building from the backdoor of the shop.

"You know, we made enough noise coming in here to wake the deaf. Unless that little barn has incredible insulation, Bridges should have heard us."

"So he's avoiding us, or he's not here, or he's lying in wait, or . . ." I reached for my Taurus, which was in my fanny pack.

Rose stopped me. "If he's just not sure about us and is being cautious, that is not going to put his mind at ease."

"Point taken."

Instead of my gun, I pulled out a lip gloss and wetted my legitimately parched lips. Then we made our way to the little adobe barn, calling loudly for Bridges as we went. The external rear door, which was partially concealed by a stubby juniper, was closed but not locked.

We entered cautiously. There was no one lying in wait, but the large storage room with its floor-to-ceiling shelving had clearly been tossed. The floor was littered with debris that included broken pots, boxes, packing material, and splintered furniture.

We drew our weapons in wordless unison, senses at full alert. I fought the urge to rub the sudden goose bumps from my bare arms. We made a careful sweep of the room. There was still no sign of Bridges.

I was working my way along the back wall when the linoleum beneath my sandaled feet made a very peculiar sound for a concrete foundation. I stopped and leaned on the spot, feeling Rose's eyes on me.

Squork! the patch of floor repeated.

I holstered the Taurus and got down on my hands and knees. This close to the linoleum tiles, I could see that one of them wasn't quite flat and flush. I pried at it with my too-short fingernails. It came up easily and revealed—*ta-da*!—a metal bezel with an inset ring.

"Oh, you've got to be kidding," murmured Rose practically in my ear. "A trap door?"

Indeed. And a staircase steep enough to be called a ladder descending into a dimly lit lower level. The sweet perfume of cool, dank earth wafted up from below.

"I'll go down," Rose told me. "You stay topside."

"Excuse me? I believe I'm the bodyguard here."

"And I'm the government agent."

"You go down," I said. "I'll be at your back. Looking up," I added when her mouth popped open to protest.

I kept my word too, making my way down behind her, sidesaddle, hyper-aware of the Caddie wire pendant tapping against my breast bone . . . and of my utter vulnerability on this ladder. When Rose reached the bottom, she turned, sweeping her gun in a wide arc.

"Oh, damn," she said and stepped out of sight to my right.

I came the rest of the way down in a hurry and reached the bottom to see Rose heading across the underground room, which ran the full length and width of the building above. I followed, and was not surprised to find her bending over a body—Ted Bridges's body.

I slipped the gun back into my fanny pack. "Is he—?"

She nodded, her fingertips to his neck. "Dead. Gunshot to the head."

I squatted on the floor beside her, feeling strangely but predictably numb. This was not the first time I'd been party to the discovery of a corpse.

"Please tell me," I said, "this isn't something that happens often in your line of work."

Chapter 8

The Trail Goes South

While Rose called in our backup, I gave Ted Bridges's treasure cave a thorough perusal, being very careful not to touch anything. The large room was lined on two sides with metal shelving; on the wall opposite the stairs was a big double sink set into a long empty workbench. The shelves had been looted. Every box and crate had been dispossessed of its innards, and excelsior, shredded paper, and artifacts littered the floor. That there were missing items I had no doubt.

Hours later, after the coroner's van had left, Greg went off to file a report with Ellen Robb. The place had been dusted and photographed by both the PPD forensics team and agents Frakes and Padilla, and what was assumed to be the murder weapon—which we found in one of the sinks—had been bagged. Rose directed Rodney, me, and a trio of specialists from the Phoenix office in cataloguing the artifacts left behind. It was a big job and took long enough that when Greg turned up again, he'd brought dinner.

"Find anything?" he asked Rose as we supped on mushroom-linguica pizza and iced coffee served up on the gleaming, black hood of a Park Service SUV.

"The story here won't be in what we found, Greg. It'll be in what we *haven't* found—what I suspect we aren't going to find."

His mouth full of pizza, he gave her a look that clearly said, *Enough with the mystery-speak already.*

"The thieves seemed to have been highly selective. There are a lot of very fine Mimbres, Hohokam, and Mogollon pieces still here. Some of them are freshly broken. What there *aren't* are Mesoamerican artifacts. We know Bridges had them—"

"We know he had *one*. We're not even sure it's authentic—"

"*I'm* sure. That piece is Early Classical Mayan, I'd be willing to bank on it. The point is: if he had them, someone took them. All of them. Why?"

"Because they're worth a hell of a lot more than the other stuff?" Rodney guessed, wiping cheese grease from his All-American-Boy face. Even in the gathering dusk, I could make out his freckles and suspected his blond-on-blond hair would be visible long after dark.

"That would be a good guess," said Greg. "Bridges was so freakin' proud of his damned Mayan potsherd, I'd be surprised if we were the only dealers he showed it off to."

"Well, apparently he showed it off to the wrong people." Rose sighed, sliding off the hood of the truck. "We'd better get going if we're going to finish cataloguing all that loot before next week."

"Actually," Greg said, "I'd like to suggest a division of labor. You guys finish toting up the dragon's treasure while I see if the police will let me go through his files."

Rose nodded. "Good idea. No telling what we'll find in there."

It took another two hours to finish our accounting task and repack the artifacts, trying as best we could to reunite items with the boxes they'd been stored in. While the others assembled the cache in the center of the room, I made a last visual sweep for small, easily overlooked bits.

I was skulking about the workbench when I noticed that the old black rotary phone that sat on one end was tilted at a slight angle. I lifted the phone and a piece of folded glossy paper fell out from underneath.

It was a travel brochure for a resort near Cancún, Mexico: *El Playa del Pavo Réal*—Peacock Beach. On the back of the brochure a name was written in fortuitously legible script: *Revez*. Next to it was a date: *May 2*. Two weeks ago. The date was circled . . . and not because it happened to be my birthday.

There was a little map on the back too. One that highlighted several archaeological sites that had been opened to tourist traffic.

"Hey, Rosie, is this anything?"

When she looked up from her packing I handed it to her.

A slow, sly grin spread from her lips all the way to her eyes. "Oh, I sure hope so."

"Good find, Gina," Greg told me as we hung out at the airport awaiting our homeward flight. "It may not lead anywhere, but you never know."

"Yeah, I suppose chances are it's just a souvenir from Bridges's last vacation," added Rose, "but we can always hope."

It was Friday. It had taken three—count 'em—three days to tie up loose ends with the local PD and the Park Service's Phoenix field office. It seemed inter-agency encounters almost always required extra patience to make certain the aquatic avians were marching in proper cadence. I knew this well from my own interactions with the SFPD.

We were standing in the queue making bovine progress toward the jetway when Rose took out her cell phone to switch it to airplane mode. It went off in her hand. She jumped, shook her head wryly, and answered it.

"Hey, Ramon, make it quick, okay, we're just about to board. What . . . ? Could you repeat that?" She raised her eyes to mine, practically shooting off sparks of electricity. "Oh, I wish I could kiss the messenger. *Mwah!*" She made a loud smacker into the phone and hung up.

Greg, Rodney, and I were all giving her the Vulcan Eyebrow, but she made a big show of deliberately turning off and pocketing her cell phone.

"Felipe Revez," she finally said, when she was done toying with us, "is the owner of *El Playa del Pavo Réal*. Mr. Revez has a most interesting hobby. Anyone care to guess what it is?"

"Uh, amateur archaeologist?" I guessed.

"Close, my dear. Felipe Revez is into collectibles. Specifically, art and antiquities."

By the time we touched down at SFO, the "hounds," as Rodney liked to call the research team, had determined that the date on the brochure coincided with the last time Ted Bridges had visited Cancún. At least he had a round-trip airline ticket that sandwiched that date. They had also determined that he had not stayed at Peacock Beach under his real name, and were trying to establish whether he'd checked in under an alias.

When we reconvened in Ellen Robb's office bright and early on Monday morning, the initial crime report from the Phoenix PD was on her desk. She shared it with the team—Greg, Rose, Rodney, and me—during the debriefing, for which the five of us gathered around her office table with little room to spare.

"It was a spectacularly clean crime scene," she told us. "No prints, no footprints, no discernible tire treads, no DNA evidence, no fibers—nothing. The murder weapon was Bridges's own gun; the only prints on it were his. It looks as if he was surprised in his treasure room and shot once in the head."

Greg was nodding. "Why is none of this surprising? I somehow didn't think we were dealing with amateurs."

"Nor are we dealing with minor artifacts," Ellen said. "Rose was right— the piece has been confirmed by two more experts as Early Classical Period Mayan work."

"From?" Rodney asked.

Ellen deferred to Rose, who evidently had spent her weekend doing homework instead of vegetating on the seaward deck of a houseboat like some of us had.

"Possibly from a previously unknown hoard," Rose reported, and couldn't quite keep the excitement out of her voice. "The research team is checking the artifact database for matches, but so far, no hits. This could be a new piece from a recent find. The style of the art and the subject matter resembles artifacts that have come from the Chiapas area."

"So then, the site could be either Mexican or Guatemalan," said Greg, and shook his head. "That's a lot of territory."

"No kidding," said Rose. "We could be looking at Yaxchilán, Piedras Negras, or a new site that hasn't been developed yet. Even Tikal and Palenque are in the right geographical area, but I think they're too well exploited to have produced this piece."

"Unless it turns out to be from a known cache after all," added Greg, then looked to Ellen. "How long until we know for sure?"

"I'd give the research team another day or two to complete their work."

"Then what?" I asked. "What's your next step?"

"Do we even have a next step?" Greg countered. "If this thing is from Mexico or Guatemala, we may not get clearance to go any further with the investigation. It may just be a case of making a report to the appropriate government and washing our hands of the whole affair."

"Aren't you just a little ray of sunshine?" asked Rose fondly, patting Greg on the shoulder. "Realistically, as long as we don't ask them to kick in any money, either government might be quite happy to have us come in and bust a crook. Especially if it results in us unearthing another archaeological prize."

Greg grimaced. "True, they can barely afford maintenance of the sites that have already been discovered, much less further excavation."

"No," Rose agreed, "but chances are some university can. At least for a season or two. If they're willing to battle their way through all the bureaucratic crap."

Ellen was looking thoughtful, her eyes focused on something outside her office window. "Rose, assuming we could get clearance from the governments involved, what would you recommend we do?"

Rose put both elbows on the table and leaned forward, pushing electric energy before her like the bow wave from a harbor ferry.

"I'd set up a sting operation. For Felipe Revez. Try to find out if the artifacts Ted Bridges was hoarding came from him, or if Bridges was selling him stuff he'd gotten from other sources down there."

"Isn't that a bit of a long shot?" Greg asked. "We don't know if his relationship with Revez was even in that context."

"What other context could it be?" asked Rose. "Somehow I doubt Ted Bridges was a member of Revez's yacht club."

"Yacht club?" Greg's brows rose toward his thinning hairline.

"You know what I mean. Revez is loaded. He owns a popular resort, he collects expensive art. He bids at Sommers and Sotheby's. You know what his last purchase was? A Chagall. Ted Bridges's art collection consisted of framed travel posters."

"And *Hustler* pinups," I murmured.

Greg wagged his head. "Yeah, I see your point. Okay, Rosie, what's the game plan?"

The wave of electricity hit me again, and we were off into a strategy session that made me feel like a water skier behind a warp-powered speed boat.

It was enlightening.

It was intoxicating.

It was scary. I mean, wearing-a-thin-spot-in-my-obereg scary.

And I loved every second of it. I've been a major crimes cop. I've investigated and interrogated and arrested criminals. But, this was a whole different ballgame. This was international espionage that Rose was proposing take place on foreign soil. I was terrified . . . but in a very pleasant way.

Things moved with extraordinary speed after that, in a sort of cosmic domino effect. We hatched a plot (well, mostly they hatched, I oohed and aahed over the chicks); we were given personas (or is that personae?); we invented contingency plans, backup contingency plans, and disaster plans.

We would fly to Cancún, where Rose would pass as Marianna Esposito, the wealthy and spoiled fiancée of an equally wealthy and spoiled San Francisco businessman and art collector. Ostensibly, she would be shopping for a unique wedding present for her beau—Geoffrey Catalano by name—a fictitious person with an electronic and paper presence, should anyone go looking for him. Money would be no object.

I would be her personal secretary, and Greg would be the fabulously wealthy Mr. Catalano while running the behind-the-scenes backup team with Rodney as second-in-command.

This was serious stuff to Rose.

How serious? Serious enough that she got her hair cut and colored. *Cut!* A lifetime of "just take a little off the bottom" gone—*poof!*—in one salon session.

I think that freaked me more than the strategy session. Freaked her hairdresser too. I swear he said, "Oh, honey, are you *sure*?" after every snip. The poor man was traumatized.

It did not, however, rattle me enough to make me forget about our stalkers. I saw no beefy joggers; I saw no Banderasian journalists. The coincidence of their scarcity made me wonder all over again about how they connected to Rose. The Blankenships' trial for their pillaging of the Anasazi site was coming up; the Bridges sting was over with unqualified finality. Were they connected to the first and just giving up? Or were they connected to the second and no longer on duty because they'd eliminated Bridges from the equation and disappeared his Mesoamerican cache?

Had that been the idea all along—to keep Rose from taking part in the sting because she might recognize the artifacts for what they were? Had they been trying to avoid what, in fact, happened—the U.S. National Park Service turning its eagle eyes south? It was possible, I realized, that our good Dr. Veras and the most recent stalker had been running interference, trying to keep Rose Delgado and company from bunging up the works. It struck me that if someone of Veras's stature was involved in that effort, the stakes must be much higher than some Early Classical pilfered potsherds.

I broached the idea with Rose amid preparations for our Cancún trip: "In view of what we found—or didn't find—is there any reason someone would want to keep you, in particular, away from Ted Bridges?"

She stopped and gave me a very serious look. "Wow, with all that's happening with the Revez connection, I hadn't even stopped to think. . . . I suppose it could be because Mesoamerican artifacts are one of my areas of expertise. I'd be more likely than anyone else to spot them or be able to authenticate them. In fact, I have had to authenticate them in the course of my work."

"In court?"

"Yes. Frequently."

"Which is a matter of public record, right?"

Her bronze skin shifted a couple of shades up the pallor spectrum. "I see what you're getting at, but Greg—"

"Greg's expertise is in process and law enforcement and Rodney's pretty new to the team, right?"

"Well, yeah. But that seems like such a long shot, doesn't it? I mean, who'd know me from Sacagawea?"

"You don't expect an answer to that, do you?" I asked, thinking of Cruz Veras.

She grinned at me. "No, not really. I don't know, Tink. Anything's possible, I suppose."

Anything's possible.

Later events would make me wish I'd taken those words to heart.

Chapter 9

Superstition

I am not a person who believes in premonitions. Premonitions are the classic Catch-22. If you *don't* act on them the Unspecified Bad Something *might* happen and you'll be history; if you *do* act, the Unspecified Bad Something *won't* happen, and everyone will think you're a superstitious twit. Which is why I tend to ignore premonitions and pray for survival.

I leave clairvoyance to Mom, and I generally try to ignore her premonitions as well. But on this particular morning, as I prepared to escort Rose to a pretrial meeting with the NPS attorneys on the Anasazi case, Mom showed up on my foredeck.

"Gina, I had a vision," she said without preamble.

"Mom, I'm going to be late."

"Better late than dead," she assured me dramatically, and stepped into my living room. She held something out to me on the palm of her hand. "Here."

It was a medallion. A Saint Boris medallion.

"Mom, I've already got an obereg. And a mingei."

"Not like this one. It's from a saint sharing your birthday for *extra* protection."

"Mom . . ."

"I saw a road. And, sitting in it, a raven. And much water."

All the little hairs on the back of my neck stood up and shivered. Not because my mom had seen a road and a raven and water, but because I'd had a Bad Feeling about today when I rolled out of bed this morning. I'd told myself it was the natural reaction to discovering Ted Bridges's body and not yet knowing why someone had felt compelled to kill him and disappear his collection of Latin American artifacts.

As I said, I can ignore my premonitions, and I make a point of ignoring Mom's. But when we both have them, it's kind of hard not to at least mutter an Abracadabra. Still, I ignored my little hairs and said, "Mom, we are surrounded by much water. I can't look out a window without seeing much water. Rose and I have a meeting in Pacifica, where there is much water."

"Yes, and this is going with you." She pointed at Saint Boris with her considerable nose.

There are rules for dealing with Nadia Eliska Arkhangelski Miyoko. I learned these from my father. Rule One: Nadia is always right. All other rules refer back to this one. In fact, neither Dad nor I remember what the other rules are. I took the proffered obereg and tucked it into the pocket of my jeans.

"There. Happy?"

"Better you wear it," she said, then added, "Edmund says 'be careful.'"

Dad always said that, whether I was going out on a case or down the street for ice cream. But coupled with my Bad Feeling and Mom's "vision," this warning carried unwanted weight.

"Thanks," I said, shrugging into my leather jacket. I picked up my helmet from the table beside the front door and gestured Mom in the general direction of the waterfront. "Now, I've really got to go. Rose is waiting for me."

She followed me out onto the foredeck verandah. "You have backup?"

I opened the lapel of my jacket to show her my shoulder holster. The bright titanium finish of the little Taurus reflected back the blue of the sky.

"I meant an obereg."

Oh, *real* backup. Not some Mickey Mouse handgun.

"Yes, Mom. I told you: I have my lucky Caddie wire." I tugged the chain out of my shirt so she could see it.

She seemed content with that and left me with a kiss on the cheek and the observation that I needed to eat more fruit. I tucked the wire back down the front of my shirt, glad I hadn't mentioned my own premonition. Then she would probably have insisted I carry a whole set of babushkas and Dad's tanuki as well.

I locked the house, pocketed my keys, and started down the ramp to the bike pad. I was surprised to see Mom standing next to Boris, apparently in conversation with it. She saw me, gave me a wave of her hand and continued on down the dock to her place. I surveyed the bike, wondering what she'd had to say to it, and if she'd managed to conceal any additional "backup" on it somewhere. That was when I realized the candy apple red finish of the rear fender was dappled with beads of water. Mom was nothing if not thorough.

I rolled Boris across the street to Rose and Dave's landlubber, where I had Rose laughing over the scene with Mom. I said nothing about premonitions, Bad Feelings, or ravens, preferring to play Mom as a yenta and encouraging Rose's laughter. It was a welcome sound.

"Holy water? God love her. When is she going to give up the pretense and admit she's a true believer?"

"True believer? I'm waiting for her to admit she's a *witch*. Father Valery would just love that."

It was a lightly foggy spring morning as we pulled out of Rose's driveway. The chill air was permeated with that patented Bay Area perfume of brine, cedar, and eucalyptus. I kept a respectable distance behind Rose's Toyota as we buzzed down Highway 1, trying to allow some of my pent-up tension to slip away. I had a moment of icy awareness when I thought I saw a maroon

Honda pull onto the highway behind us, but as moments went by and it failed to reappear, I settled down a bit. Still, I gave the rearview mirror regular glances, feeling creepily vulnerable. Rose should have had a whole posse riding escort, not a perky little private eye (emphasis on "little") with three amulets and a holy water blessing.

As it happened, not even a posse could have spared Rose. We were just coming up on Sharp Park when Rose's Toyota suddenly swerved off the road. Before I could do more than pull off the gas, the car hit a grassy hummock and flipped over, rolling several times before sliding out of sight to the seaward side of the dunes.

I don't remember pulling over, ditching the Harley, or scrambling across the sand. I only remember seeing the cinnamon-red Corolla lying upside down against a dune, its wheels spinning in a way that might have been comical in a cartoon. I slid down the hummock to the driver's side of the car. The roof was only slightly crumpled, for which I thanked God wordlessly. The window in the driver's side door had shattered, the safety glass crazed and beaded. Through it, I could see that the airbag had deployed. Other than that I could make out only a mosaic of green, bronze, and black cherry—Rosie's sweater, skin, and hair.

I grasped the door handle with both hands, dug my feet into the sand and pulled, but the door frame was bent and the door wouldn't budge. I tried again, throwing my whole weight into it. The car rocked slightly.

Frustrated and terrified, I leapt up to aim a kick at the window and caught movement out of the corner of my eye. Cruz Veras was sliding toward me down the back of the hill, reaching into his jacket pocket as he reached the bottom.

I didn't think; I acted, pulling the Taurus out of its holster and taking aim. "I wouldn't," I told him.

He raised both hands. "I was going for my cell phone. To call 911."

"I'm sure."

"One of us needs to do it."

"Fine. Do it. Slowly."

He opened his jacket. I saw the cell phone peeking from the left inside pocket. I also saw the leather strap of a shoulder holster. The gun was cuddled up under his left arm.

Journalist, my Aunt Kazu's yazoo. I kept the gun trained on him while he called in the accident, listening intently to his words, my hands shaking like a rookie's.

Through the chaos pattern of crazed window glass, I thought I saw movement in the kaleidoscope of color that was Rose. I wavered, wanting to drop the Taurus and help her, wanting to keep Veras under the gun.

"Let me help her," he said, slipping the phone back into his pocket. He studiously kept his hands away from his firearm.

"I don't even know who the hell you are."

"I'm Cruz Veras. That's my name. Really."

"Not a journalist."

"Yes, but not at the moment. At the moment, I'm an agent of the *Instituto Nacional de Antropología e Historia* in Mexico City."

"Agent?"

The kaleidoscope shifted again. I smelled gasoline.

"I have identification." He gestured at his inside pocket.

"First ditch the sidearm."

He grimaced, then delicately removed the gun with thumb and forefinger. It was a Glock 28—.38 caliber. I nodded toward a ragged carpet of ice plant into which he reluctantly pitched the gun. Then he pulled out his wallet with equal care and flipped it open. The photo ID within proclaimed him to be just what he had told me: Dr. Cruz Sacramento Veras, INAH agent. For all I knew he had a different ID card for every occasion. At this point, I didn't care. Swearing silently, I holstered my gun and put my booted foot through the driver's side window, careful to pick a spot furthest away from Rose's head.

Before I'd pulled my foot free, Veras was on his knees, going at the pellets with his hands knotted inside his sleeves. I joined him. It took mere seconds to clear the window, then Veras reached in and felt around Rose's neck while I ground my teeth and wondered if I should intervene.

"Pulse is strong. Her neck doesn't seem to be broken. But there's some bleeding." He drew his hand back streaked with bright red.

I leapt at the good news. "How can you tell . . . it's not broken, I mean."

"I was a paramedic for a while out of college. We'll need to get her seat belt off."

I peered through the busted out window into the cab. "I can get in on the passenger side and unlatch it. Can you support her? Get her down?"

He nodded. "Go."

I scrambled around the front end of the car, noticing a curl of greasy smoke rising from the engine compartment. The passenger-side window was mostly gone. I pulled my hands up into the sleeves of my jacket and cleared the remaining glass. For once in my life, I was glad to be petite. It made getting through the window relatively easy. It was a squeeze, but I was able to crawl on my hands and knees to where Rose dangled upside down behind the steering wheel.

Cruz Veras was already in position, lying on his side, his head and arms inside the car. As I put my hands to the seat belt latch, he reached up to support Rose.

"Okay," he said. "Let it go."

I did, but not before wrapping my right hand through the strap and taking some of Rose's weight onto the webbing. She moved again, whimpering and turning her head slightly. Blood ran down the side of her face and into her hair. Where was it coming from? Had the airbag deployed late? Had something inside the car come lose and struck her?

I swallowed my fear and said, "It's okay, Rosie. I'm here. We're going to get you out."

I thought I heard her murmur my name a second before Veras said, "Okay, slowly. Bring her down onto my chest."

We lowered her as carefully as possible so that her upper body was lying in Veras's arms, then he worked his way back out through the window while I lowered and straightened her legs.

By the time I'd gotten out and around the car, he'd carried her several yards away behind a dense growth of sedge and laid her out full length in the grassy sand. I could hear the plaintive sound of sirens now; they seemed to come from every direction at once.

I stumbled to my knees beside Rose in the sand, confused and frightened by the amount of blood around her neck and head. Given the nature of the accident, it didn't make sense.

Veras had ripped a sleeve from his shirt. He wadded it and used it to apply pressure to a wound I couldn't see from my vantage point.

"What is it?" I asked. "How—?"

"It's a bullet wound," he told me. "This wasn't an accident."

Chapter 10
Undercover Agent

The Hopi word for kachina is *katsinam*. I know this because of Rose Delgado.

Katsinam are the spirits of all created things. Those little wooden dolls tourists buy are called tinu. The wood from which a tinu is carved is chosen carefully to please the spirit that will inhabit it.

The tinu in my hands—the one I held as if it were a winning lottery ticket—was made of cottonwood. Rose's granddad carved it for her when she was fourteen for the Powamuya Ceremony—the Bean Dance. That was the year we met and adopted each other, discovering in the process that we each had a bedroom shelf inhabited by lucky charms for every occasion.

I'd had a team of them on me today as I watched Rose's car veer off the road and flip over into the dunes. The oberegi had failed me. They had failed Rose. So I clung to Rosie's prayer-covered tinu. I couldn't see the prayers, but I knew they were there. I piled more on as I sat in the hospital waiting room, watching David Delgado rock their daughter Letty, while their son,

Luis, slept at the end of a sofa, and the mysterious Cruz Veras paced and murmured soft Spanish syllables into his cell phone.

I knew he was not what he seemed to be, this man, and had as many layers as one of Rose's archaeological digs. This recent knowledge was disturbing because it meant that my highly developed research skills and painfully won sensitivity to liars had failed. If I hadn't been a quivering mass of adrenaline-hyped nerves, I would have been furious with myself for buying his lies. PIs are supposed to have a sixth sense about these things.

Hospital waiting rooms are wretched places to wait, but they're great places to internally agonize over what you could have done to avoid ending up here, hopefully watching doors through which only the desperately injured pass.

That's what I was doing: clutching Rose's tinu and agonizing. At some point I realized that Cruz Veras had pocketed his cell phone and had sat down opposite me.

When I looked up, he said, "The sniper was after Rose, Miss Miyoko. There's nothing you could have done to change that."

Suddenly, I was angry—because this almost total stranger had divined my thoughts; because I'd just come to the same conclusion and it didn't ease the pain; because anger felt somehow less impotent than grief.

"I could've been in the car *with* her instead of following at a safe distance," I said, and Cruz Veras broke eye contact and looked down at his clasped hands.

"Dammit, Tink! That is one of the stupidest things I've ever heard you say." This abuse of my truncated nickname came from Dave, who was glaring at me over the top of his daughter's head. "How do you think Rose would feel if you'd been hurt too?"

I got up and moved to a corner where I could agonize in peace. I knew I should straighten up and act like a professional, but I felt less like a PI whose stint as a bodyguard had just come to a disastrous end and more like a woman who was possibly about to lose her best friend. I was torn between reexamining the past several weeks for clues or sense or meaning, and caressing remembrances of my friendship with Rose. I rejected the latter as impossibly morbid and forced the PI to rear her icy head. What I couldn't do was sit here and tick off the final hours of Rose Delgado's life, the end of my life as I knew it, the shattering of a family for Dave and Luis and Letty. What I could do was find out why this had happened and who had done it.

Dave's mom and dad arrived to take the kids down to the cafeteria. Dave and Veras and I remained in the waiting room. Dave was praying, Veras was pacing, and I was sitting numbly in my corner when Rose's surgeon appeared through that terrifying set of doors. I was on my feet before I realized I was moving, drawn to him like a chip of iron to a magnet. Dave and I—and Cruz Veras—converged on him at the same time.

He spoke; we listened, waiting for something to jump out at us and inspire hope.

"Soft tissue damage?" I repeated, trying to keep my eyes focused on the doctor. "No spinal cord damage?"

"None. Ms. Delgado was incredibly lucky. The bullet passed through her neck cleanly and left a small exit wound. There was some damage to her throat. That should heal in time. Apart from that, she sustained a hairline fracture of the collarbone and some head trauma. And that is what we need to keep our eye on. She's in a natural coma right now, but," he added when Dave uttered a sick moan, "her vital signs are strong. She's in serious condition, but I'm hopeful we can coax her body to begin repairs. She'll spend some time in the ICU and I've put her on anti-inflammatory medication."

"Prednisone?" asked Veras.

"Dexamethasone," the doctor said, and gave him a sharp glance. "Are you a doctor?"

Veras's mouth turned up at one corner. "A doctor of archaeology. I have a bit of medical training. I know prednisone has . . . issues."

The surgeon nodded. "There are some pretty nasty side effects with continued use, yes. Which is one of the reasons I chose dexamethasone."

"But how long will this last, this coma?" asked Dave.

"That depends on Rose. But it's a perfectly natural way for the brain to react to trauma. A self-preservation mechanism. She may wake suddenly or emerge into normal sleep in a matter of hours or days. The bullet missed her major arteries. Just. She's lost very little blood, really."

My mouth popped open to object to that characterization, but the doctor seemed to know where I was headed before I got there.

"I know it looked like a lot," he said, "but it wasn't, in the grand scheme of things. She's not weak. That's the good news. The bad news is the inflammation of the brain, and we're doing everything we can to control that."

Dave nodded. "Can I . . . when can I see her?"

"You can come up now and sit with her for a bit, if you'd like."

"The kids?" He gestured down the hall.

"They'll have to wait until she's out of ICU, I'm afraid."

Dave nodded and started to follow the doctor into the intensive care unit, prompting me to make a noise somewhere between the bleat of a lamb and the mew of a bereft kitten.

The doctor shook his head, his smile kind and professional at once. "I'm sorry, Ms. Miyoko. You'll have to wait too. Family only, right now."

I watched Dave walk side by side with the doctor toward the doors to the inner sanctum. *Thus far and no further.* I felt cold. Empty. Impotent. I realized I was still clenching the tinu in my fist at the same moment I felt Cruz Veras's eyes boring into the back of my head.

"Are you planning on standing there until she wakes up?" he asked me.

"I'm not planning anything," I said.

"Not even making what she's going through count?"

"What did you have in mind? I'm fresh out of ideas at the moment."

"You were a witness."

"Oh, right. I can tell the police exactly nothing. Except that I saw her car plunge suddenly off the road."

"I think you can tell them more than that. I think you may be able to give them a description of the shooter."

Now I turned to face him. "What?"

"Come on, Gina. Turn your brain back on. You can't help Rose if you're all doped up on your own sense of impotence."

It was not lost on me that he'd decided we were on first name terms. I squeezed the tinu within an inch of its life. "What the hell would you know about my sense of impotence?"

"Right now, all of your anger is going into crushing that poor, defenseless kachina. I think there are more productive places to put it."

"It's a tinu, *Doctor* Archaeologist, and—" And it suddenly hit me. "And you think this was the same guy that tracked her to the headlands."

"I think it's possible. Don't you? I didn't get as good a look at him as you did, but he was clearly targeting her."

I released my death grip on the tinu and carefully smoothed its feathered headdress. "You ready to tell me what you were doing there?"

He nodded, his eyes still on my face. "Okay. But not here. I don't think there's much we can do here at the moment. It's got to be hours since you ate. How about we find a private place to refuel and talk?"

"The police—"

"We can do that first if you want. But I think they'll seek you out for further discussion when they're ready. I already gave them my version of what happened at the headlands, including that I thought it was an NPS sting."

"You did?"

He raised both hands in surrender. "I'm out in the open now, Gina. And I'm not about to hide anything from the authorities, in any event."

"Oh, just from me and Rose."

"I felt it was necessary. I'm offering to come clean now." He turned and made a "walk this way" gesture toward the hallway beyond the semiprivate waiting room in which we stood.

"All right. But I want to go someplace public."

His lips twitched. "Fine. Public *and* private. We can do that."

The booth in the café he chose was private by virtue of the ambient noise level. We didn't have to shout to hear each other, but even if we had, the conversation would have been swallowed up by the sounds of dishes clattering, espresso makers frothing, and other voices swirling about on the caffeine-laden air.

We ordered our food and drinks, then I sat back against the high padding of the booth, pulled my jacket more tightly around me, and said, "All right, Zorro. Who are you, really, and why have you been following Rose Delgado?"

"I've already told you who I am. Cruz Sacramento Veras. I am an operative with the INAH. Like your friend Rose, I'm a trained archaeologist with a somewhat personal interest in the history of native peoples."

"Who's been an investigative reporter."

"Yes."

"And a contributor to *Arqueología* magazine."

"Yes."

"And a paramedic."

He inclined his head.

"Man of a thousand faces."

"Perhaps not quite a thousand." He said it with a straight face.

"What face were you wearing when you started tailing Rosie?"

He pointed at his chin. "This face. The face of an undercover agent. I am charged with tracing artifacts pillaged from Mexican sites for illegal sale in the United States. Artifacts such as the one you encountered during your recent sting operation in Phoenix."

I sat up straight. "What do you know about that?"

"That it occurred. That you found a Mayan piece among the Hohokam potteries. That the dealer died violently upon his release from jail."

"And you found all this out from . . . ?"

"I've been in touch with Ellen Robb." He met my gaze levelly and every defense mechanism I had went to DEFCON One.

"I'll verify that."

He smiled at me the way people smile at bristly little kittens all puffed out in Big Bad Lion Mode. "Of course you will, and you should. This is not a business that engenders trust . . . more's the pity. And that is why I was surveilling Rose Delgado. My organization knew there were artifacts from important archaeological sites being smuggled into the U.S. for sale, and I suspected Ted Bridges of being part of that process. He was a small time player and he was sloppy, but the artifacts he was fencing were authentic. I just had no idea where or how he was acquiring them. I knew the NPS had been trying to corner Bridges for some time, and I knew of Rose's role in authenticating trafficked goods. I thought she might know more than we did about what happened to the artifacts once they crossed the border."

I gave him my best evil eye. "You mean, you suspected she might be a dirty agent."

He tilted his head in agreement. "Let's say I had to eliminate that possibility. Consider it eliminated."

I shook my head. "She was just beginning to put it together when . . . this."

"So I gather." He set his elbows on the table and leaned toward me, lowering his head and his voice. "Now about those artifacts. That vase shard, any other antiquities Mr. Bridges may have had in his possession—they are, as they say, merely the tip of an iceberg. Have you heard of Bonampak?"

"No. Is that a site?"

He nodded. "In eastern Chiapas. It is the find of a lifetime. An acropolis, burial vaults, incredible murals still as vivid as the day they were painted. Like many other sites in that impoverished region, it's now being looted of major treasures the Mexican government can't afford to protect."

"Is that where you think Ted Bridge's antiquities came from? Bonampak?"

"Possibly. A little over a year ago, I came across some relics in the vaults of a San Francisco museum that I suspected had come from Bonampak." He grimaced and shook his head. "A chance discovery. I was on vacation."

I raised an eyebrow. "In a museum's vaults."

"What can I say? It's in the blood. I showed my credentials to the assistant curator; she let me wander the trove. I examined the artifacts and I questioned their provenance. When it became clear that some of the items had come from Bonampak—a site from which no antiquities should have been available on the open market—I raised the issue to higher levels."

"And nothing came of it?" I guessed.

"The museum offered proof that they had received the lot of artifacts from a reputable auction house."

"Wait—let me guess—Sommers?"

He nodded. "The museum's papers were in order, Sommers's papers were somewhat . . . cryptic. Both organizations have been less than helpful in the process of getting the items returned to Mexico. So, unable to connect the auction house to the black market from the demand side, I thought perhaps I could take a different approach."

"Find the black marketeers and follow the relics from their side."

"The link the Park Service sting forged between Ted Bridges and Felipe Revez is the best chance I've seen of beginning at the beginning."

"Yeah, well, unfortunately, the sting's been shut down pretty definitively."

Veras's dark eyes ratcheted up the intensity a few notches. "There is no other agent who can step into the sting in Ms. Delgado's guise?"

"Unfortunately, they've already established Marianna Esposito as the cover. Airline tickets, suite booked, the whole enchilada. Somehow I can't imagine Rodney Hammermill or Greg Sheffield flouncing around in drag. And no one else knows the case as well as they do."

"You do."

"Me?"

He smiled. "You'd look better in a dress than either of them."

"Thanks . . . I think." I read his eyes. He was serious. "You're not suggesting . . ."

"Why not? You've been trained. You know the case. You were even in on the sting that established the link."

"Yeah, as backup! Besides, I'm no archaeologist."

"You know how to handle casework. And you're pretty damned cool under fire." One corner of his lip curled, annoyingly. "And you don't need to be an archaeologist, Ms. Esposito. Your personal bodyguard will be an archaeologist."

"Greg Sheffield has his own assigned role, and Rodney Hammermill's the new kid on the—"

"Not Sheffield. Not Hammermill. Me."

I sat back and stared at him in silent disbelief. Good timing. The waitress had appeared with our food and was laying it out on the table. She glanced from the enigmatic-looking Veras to fish-faced me and smiled. I'm sure she thought she'd just interrupted some sort of romantic *moment*.

The second she was gone, I leaned across my plate, endangering my new lime-green Henley and my useless hunk of Caddie wire. "Look, Indiana Jones, you seem to have immense regard for your own powers of persuasion, but there is not a snowball's chance in Hell that you're going to convince Greg Sheffield you should play a part in this operation."

He took a bite of his spinach salad. "I don't have to convince Greg Sheffield of anything. I have to convince Ellen Robb."

"Oh . . . *oh!* And I suppose you think that because she's a woman, you can just bat your excessive eyelashes at her and she'll come around."

He laughed. "No. I think that because she's a professional, she'll see the logic of my proposal."

"Logic."

He speared another bite of spinach. "Gina, Greg was a visible part of the sting on Ted Bridges. There is a possibility that Bridges knew or at least suspected that Sheffield was an undercover agent. Which means that he might have communicated that suspicion to Felipe Revez or some other Mexican contact. He never saw you."

A chilling thought occurred to me. "If he did suspect Greg, he may have suspected Rose as well. Maybe the same people that killed Bridges—"

Veras nodded. "The thought had occurred to me."

My fingernails were digging into the tabletop. "To keep the trail from leading back to Revez?"

"Are you going to eat that?" he asked, flicking a glance at my chicken curry burrito.

"What—now you want to cadge food?"

"No, I want to make sure you eat."

"Yeah, yeah—keep up my strength," I growled, but did take a bite of the burrito, which immediately whispered sweet somethings to my stomach to remind it how hungry it really was. I was halfway through the darned thing before I came up for air.

"So," Veras said, watching me finish my meal. "Are you in?"

"The sting?" I hesitated. The idea was ludicrous, but there was a very large part of me that thrilled at the idea of doing something that important. And doing it for Rose. Regardless of the danger.

He saw the hesitation, of course, and went after it with terrier-like glee. "I'll make you a bet. I bet I can get Ellen Robb to go for the sting. If I do, you're in."

"Okay. Yeah. If you can sell Ellen, I'm in."

"For work, you're going to Cancún?" Mother asked. She had paused in the act of pounding out a chicken fillet, the meat mallet poised at the top of her stroke. "Who goes to Cancún for work?"

"Apparently, private investigators do, Nadia," Dad said mildly. He had tied on his black *Iron Chef* ninja apron and was hunkered over his marinade bowl like an alchemist over a crucible. Plum sauce and spices go in; liquid gold comes out.

"Are you to go alone?"

I perched on a stool at their kitchen island and studied the bottle of ginger beer in my hands. "No. I'll have backup."

Mom's eyebrows rose. Her mallet remained poised on high.

"A bodyguard, actually."

Now Dad's eyebrows ascended. A drop of plum sauce hung in the mouth of the bottle, ready to drop into the bowl.

"Another agent. He's experienced—he's been a field operative for several years and he's an archaeologist by training, so he knows the subject matter and the situation."

The plum sauce plummeted and Dad asked, "A Park Service agent?"

"Yes, but not *our* Park Service. He's from Mexico City. Working for the, uh, the INAH."

Mom lowered the mallet. "This is Dr. Veras, yes? You're going to Cancún with Dr. Veras?"

"Yes." I kept my eyes on the mallet, praying it would go back to work on the hapless chicken breast.

It did not. She set it aside, completely absorbed in my news. "Tell," she said, crossing her arms over her breasts.

Dad glanced from her to me. "Nadia . . ."

"Nadia, *vhat*? Our daughter is going to Cancún with this Dr. Veras. What is he like, this doctor?"

"He's not a *doctor*, Mom. He's an archaeologist. And a journalist. And an undercover agent for the Mexican National Institute of Anthropology and History. I can't really go into why we're going or what we're going to be doing. All I can say is that it may be related to what happened to Rosie."

At last, she uncrossed her arms, and the meat mallet resumed its steady attack on the chicken breast. I breathed a sigh of relief and caught Dad's smile as he bent back to his crucible.

"I will have to take Dave some *galobki* and red cabbage," Mom decided. "And of course, let him know he is always welcome here while you are gone. How long?"

"I'm not sure. A week. Maybe two. Probably two."

"And this archaeologist, he knows how to fire a gun?"

"Yes, Mother. He has a nice, shiny Glock 28, .38 caliber with a magazine of twelve shots. I've never seen him use it, but I'm sure he knows how."

She looked at me. "How can you be sure? You should take him to the firing range. *Make* sure." The chicken was wafer thin, but she kept after it. "This is dangerous, this Cancún trip?"

"I . . ." I glanced over at Dad, who appeared to be absorbed in his marinade. I knew better. "Not likely. We're . . . just doing some research, really. Checking out a possible lead."

The meat mallet went through the chicken into the cutting board underneath.

"Mom," I said. "I think that one's done."

She moved the chicken doily to a waiting plate and tossed another victim onto the block. "What does he look like, this Dr. Veras?"

"Actually, he looks sort of like Antonio Banderas. A little taller, maybe."

Like I could tell. To me, height is like cold. After a certain point, any differences are irrelevant.

She considered this for a moment, then said, "Alvie looks like David Duchovny."

Dad choked.

I slid off the stool. "Alvie looks like Harry Potter on growth hormones," I said. "Need me to make a salad?"

She pointed the mallet at the refrigerator. "Spinach."

I dug into the crisper and pulled out spinach, found the bacon bits, and rooted around for the dressing. It was next to the holy water, which had diminished significantly since the last time I'd seen it.

"Mom, you been blessing things again?"

"Maybe."

I closed the fridge. "Mom . . ."

She wouldn't look at me.

"Mom, what have you blessed now?"

"Only your gun," she said conversationally.

"Nadia!" Dad exclaimed. "You shouldn't put water on a gun."

She shrugged. "A sprinkling only. It doesn't take much. It was a very small prayer."

I relaxed a little. A very small prayer. That didn't sound so bad. Still, I'd make a point of taking a trip to the firing range tomorrow. Maybe I'd invite Cruz Veras along so I could give a good report on his marksmanship.

Chapter 11
The Legend of
Marianna Esposito

She was spoiled—rotten. And bored. A rich man's significant other looking for an impressive gift and a little adventure. Her just shoulder-length, artfully black-cherry hair was streaked with blond—eyebrows dyed to match. Her eyes were a liquid shade of brown calculated to mesmerize. She spoke volumes with them. She wore silk in bright colors only found in Tahiti (or any street in New Orleans on Fat Tuesday). Her makeup was just a shade extreme without being gaudy, and had been applied by an expert—I doubted she knew how to do it herself. (In fact, I was sure of it.) She worked at being mysterious. She laughed easily.

And deep down in her Gucci purse, she carried a government-issued satellite cell phone, a magnum (loaded but with the safety on), a Saint Boris medallion, and a cottonwood katsinam carved by a Hopi medicine man for his granddaughter's coming-of-age ceremony.

Just now, she looked dubiously at the stiletto-heeled sandals on her undersized feet and took a series of awkward and wobbling steps away from the mirror.

"I think you'd better stick to these." Cruz Veras stood in the bedroom doorway of Marianna Esposito's luxurious three-room suite at the Peacock Beach Resort in Cancún, dangling a pair of gold strappy sandals with thicker heels of a less suicidal two inches.

I blew a strand of Marianna's gaudy hair out of my eyes and glared at him. A small, ornery part of me wanted to tough it out and show Señor Cross Sacred True that I could *so* walk in these damn things, but common sense won out. I slipped out of the stilettos and gratefully accepted the other pair of sandals.

"I don't know how women walk in those things," he said as I put them on.

"I don't know *why* they walk in those things," I muttered, tossing the maniacal stilettos into the closet.

"You don't?"

I glanced up at him sharply, suspecting sarcasm, but his face was deadpan.

"Marianna Esposito does," he told me. "You need to remember that."

I started to retort, then caught myself and nodded. "In other words, Gina Miyoko should be neither seen nor heard." He was right, of course. I had, in point of fact, worked for the better part of a week at muzzling Gina and learning to channel Marianna. Part of that had been memorizing her (entirely fictitious) life story. Or at least the highlights reel.

We'd spent another part of our week absorbing everything the investigative team had gleaned about Felipe Revez. While the NPS folks and Cruz looked further into his business dealings and connections in the art and antiquities world, I did some work on his social life. Felipe Revez was something of a celebrity, not just locally, but nationally. This meant that articles about him turned up in venues as varied as financial and business news, tourist and travel magazines, and Mexican celebrity gossip columns and tabloids.

If you were wondering why Marianna Esposito's hair was a deep cherry red, it was because yours truly had found photo after photo of the "mark," i.e. Felipe (Don't you just love that undercover lingo?), with a petite redhead or an Asian-looking woman hanging on his arm. To be sure, there were some statuesque blondes tucked in there as well, but short of me learning how to shape-shift or trading bodies with my friend July, statuesque was not gonna happen. Getting an outrageous dye job—that I was up for. Hey, I was Asian-looking *and* a redhead. A twofer.

I'd also noted that the women Revez fancied were fellow jet-setters or celebrities in their own right. He did not collect waifs and do the whole Eliza Doolittle thing. No, my epic makeover had to happen prior to me meeting the man.

Now, psychologically speaking, having women who are beholden to you for their status and its perks is something that men in Revez's position tended to go for, so I suspected that his choice of arm ornaments had a deeper significance. Looking at the intel on his finances and business dealings that Rose's support team had come up with, I'd suspected that this "deeper" significance related to how much money they or their families controlled, and how much of it they were willing to invest in the boyfriend's business ventures.

And this was why Gina Miyoko was debuting in spycraft as a tarted-up fishing lure.

Cruz leaned against the doorjamb. "Where did you meet your fiancé, Ms. Esposito?"

I turned Gina off, tuned in to Marianna, and laughed coyly. "I ran into him at an art auction. Literally. I was admiring a Rubens when someone called my name, I turned and decorated poor Geoffrey's lovely white tuxedo with merlot. Thank God he forgave me."

"Poor Geoffrey," Veras cooed.

I took an experimental walk away from the mirror and back again. Two inches of heel I could handle. Maybe even three. I looked back at my "bodyguard." "Can I ask you something?"

He shrugged a one-shouldered "yes."

"Are all men attracted to stupidity?"

"What?"

Hah! I'd surprised him. "Well, it's stupid to wear shoes that could pass for implements of torture and end your life with one false step."

"Ye-es. I suppose it is."

"If you're wearing them to attract male approval, it's doubly stupid. It's like wearing a big placard on your forehead that says, 'I'm an idiot. And I'm flaunting my idiocy in the hope of attracting a man.' What woman in her right mind wants to attract a guy who's attracted to stupidity?"

He looked at me as if I'd lost him on that last turn. Finally, he shook his head and smiled. "Nice shoes, Ms. Esposito. What was the question again?"

Okay, I admit it—he scored points. I returned the smile and said, "How long have you been working for Ms. Esposito, Mr. Gutierrez?"

He answered without missing a beat. "Actually, I work for Geoff Catalano. Have for about five years. I was a detective on the LAPD and worked a burglary case involving the theft from Mr. Catalano's art collection. He was impressed with my work and my knowledge of art and antiquities, and made me an offer I couldn't refuse. I keep an eye on the things my employer treasures most."

I took a deep breath. "You think we're ready for this?"

"I think we have to be."

Felipe Revez was a proud man. One of the things he was most proud of was his flagship restaurant, which, having no name of its own, was known simply as The Restaurant at Peacock Beach. So proud was he of his five-star restaurant and its Michelin three-star chef that he made the rounds of the swank dining room every evening to make sure his most affluent customers (those in the luxury suites) were suitably impressed with said chef's creations.

Our plan called for me to strike up a conversation with Revez during this schmoozing opportunity, using whatever material was on hand. As it happened, there was a lot to talk about. Revez publicly displayed pieces of his collection at various points throughout his resort—a Picasso in the foyer, pre-Columbian art in the entry to the restaurant, a trio of Egyptian canopic jars in a display near the spa. (Yeah, that's what I want to be looking at while I'm getting a hot-oil rub.)

We dined at eight o'clock, dressed to the nines. My companion (Cruz Gutierrez, by name) looked too elegant to be a bodyguard. He wore a black suit with a black silk shirt and a changeable satin tie so dark it might as well have been black. I was in silk too, yards of it. Eggplant-colored—*aubergine*, among fashionistas. It wasn't until we'd been seated that I realized my dress matched Cruz's tie if you looked at it in just the right way.

"What are you staring at? Have I stained my lapel?" he whispered when the waiter had finished the litany of house specialties, handed us menus, and departed.

I smiled. "Your tie. I just noticed we're color coordinated. Is your gun baby blue, by any chance?"

"It's pewter. But I have a tie to match."

I pouted. "I don't wear pewter. Such a masculine color, don't you think?"

We ordered, chatting about things that wouldn't sound off if overheard. We also practiced speaking in "code." That sounds silly until you realize that undercover operatives may have occasion to communicate undercover-y sorts of things while in public places. We couldn't, for example, talk openly about Rose. I'd spoken to Dave just before we came down to dinner, but hadn't told Veras anything about the call.

We were just getting started on the soup course when he asked, "You call home tonight?"

"I did. Talked to Deedee. Same old, same old. Sis is still not speaking to her hubby, Geoff is working hard and says to stay in touch."

Now, what I'd just told him is that I'd talked to Dave Delgado, Rose's condition hadn't changed, and Greg was ready and waiting for us to direct his team's activities.

"He have any plans to join you down here?"

"When he can. It's always when he can."

Veras looked up and over my head. "Ah. Our illustrious host."

I turned to look. I'd seen pictures of Revez, of course, but he was more impressive in person. He was handsome in a patrician sort of way, about five-foot-eleven, I guessed, built like a catcher, and distinguished-looking in a dark blue silk suit. At forty-five he was either just beginning to go slightly gray at the temples or had a far more subtle dye job than mine.

We'd been through the drill—if he didn't make us part of his dinner-time ego-boo rounds, I was supposed to approach him and ask about his collection of wonderful pre-Columbian knickknacks. Either way, the script was basically the same.

As it happened, Revez made our table his next-to-last stop. He was a hand-kisser. Marianna found this charming. I found it creepy. It made me feel as if little ants were marching up and down my arms. I couldn't stop the shiver it brought on, but I did manage to cover it with a laugh and a wriggle and a coy look.

He raised his sleek eyebrows; I claimed to be ticklish. Then I introduced myself and gushed about his collection.

"Why thank you, Ms. Esposito." He bowed slightly from the waist. "I am rather proud of my acquisitions. Hence, I like to show them off—if only a few at a time. You have an interest in antiquities?"

"I think some of them are lovely, but it's my fiancé who's mad for them, particularly Mayan ones. And whatever interests Geoffrey interests me."

Again with the raised eyebrows—this time accompanied by a quick glance at Cruz. "Geoffrey?" His soft accent rendered the *g* as a soft *j*.

"Geoffrey Catalano. Who is hard at work in San Francisco even as we speak." I pouted very slightly. "That man works way too hard for my taste. I prefer a more . . . relaxed lifestyle. More flexibility." I shifted my shoulders in what I hoped was a suggestive manner, and glanced up at our host. He was looking back with sphinxlike inscrutability, a slight smile playing at the corners of his mouth. Breaking eye contact, I gestured to Cruz. "This is Mr. Gutierrez."

"Ah, then Mr. Gutierrez is a . . . business associate?"

"Mr. Gutierrez is a man of many faces," I said with a pointed look at the man himself. "In this context, he's my bodyguard and my art and antiquities consultant."

"Consultant?"

"My background is in archaeology," Cruz said smoothly. "Geoff retains me to advise him in matters pertaining to his collection."

"Really?" Revez pulled out a chair and canted his head toward it. "May I?"

"Of course," I said, and Cruz nodded.

"Cruz helps Geoffrey choose most of his acquisitions," I explained as Revez seated himself. "Which is why I've brought him along on this little junket. I'm on a mission of sorts, Mr. Revez. To find a wedding present for Geoffrey that will knock his socks off. Something exciting. Something he doesn't have twenty of."

"I've explained to Marianna," Cruz said, "how difficult that may be. Her fiancé is selective and has quite an expansive and unique collection."

Revez smiled. "I understand the problem. Finding something truly exciting and new is . . . rare." He offered me a glance I thought suggestive, then turned to my escort, "I would be interested in your expert opinion of some pieces I've lately acquired for my private collection, Mr. Gutierrez. Would you be willing to look at them? Tomorrow evening, perhaps?"

"Tsk, tsk," I murmured. "Sounds like a conflict of interest."

Veras ignored me. "Please, call me 'Cruz,' and I would be most interested in seeing your private collection. I assume your best pieces are not for public display."

"Naturally not."

"I understand. My employer has also acquired a number of items that are . . . best kept out of the public eye."

Revez gave my consultant a studied look, then smiled. "I take it you're not one of those stuffy archaeologists that believes everything belongs in a museum."

"What—like Indiana Jones?" Cruz asked, sending me a sly glance. "Jones was fiction, Mr. Revez. I'm a realist."

"Please, call me Felipe," said our host and reached out to shake Cruz's hand.

"Well," I said wryly, "maybe I should just excuse myself and go powder my nose."

Both men looked at me as if I'd suddenly stood on my chair and started belting out show tunes. Then Revez smiled, leaned toward Cruz, and said something so softly I couldn't make it out. Whatever it was, it inspired laughter in my "consultant." The two men exchanged significant glances before Revez turned to take up my hand once again.

"Dear Ms. Esposito, I wouldn't dream of driving you off to the powder room. Your nose, as you surely must know, is perfectly powdered as it is." The waiter appeared with our salads at this point, and Revez excused himself to attend to another table. I asked my dinner companion a single question, then sat back and ate, half tuned in to a lecture on Mayan artifacts.

Safely back in the suite sometime later, I slipped out of the strappy sandals and curled up in a suede chair to watch Cruz Veras pull a couple of Perriers out of the fridge behind the wet bar.

"I'm wasting my time batting my lashes at that guy aren't I?" I asked.

"What do you mean?" He handed me a bottle before loosening his tie and dropping onto the elegant sofa opposite.

"I mean I think maybe *you* ought to be making sheep's eyes at him. I don't think he's my type. After all, it was you he invited up to see his artifacts."

Cruz inhaled a swig of Perrier and went into a coughing fit. I watched in bemused silence until he recovered himself.

"What in God's name," he asked when he'd gotten his voice back, "makes you think that?"

"The murmured confidences, the way he went on point . . . in your direction, not mine."

That almost got him going again. "Jealous, Ms. Esposito?"

"No. Just . . . thrown for a loop. If he turns out to be immune to Marianna's charms, I may have to resort to casting spells."

"Immune to Marianna's charms?" he repeated. "What were you planning to do, lure him into bed? Get him to talk in his sleep?" He made a snoring noise then exhaled: "The map to the treasure is in the safe. (Snore.) The combination to the safe is—"

He stopped when I threw a sandal at him. I would have caught him in the shoulder if he hadn't had the reflexes of a ninja . . . or a young J. T. Snow. He snatched it cleanly out of the air.

I smote my forehead with the heel of my hand. "Oh, don't tell me— you're an ex–baseball player."

"I haven't played since college. You have a good arm." He put the shoe carefully on the floor. "Revez 'went on point' when he found out I was an archaeologist. And the whispered confidence . . . Let me see. How can I put this? He said in essence, 'Lucky bastard. Her motor's already running.'"

"In essence?"

"Well . . . there was more to it than that. I somehow doubt you'd appreciate the crude details. Although Marianna might."

I could feel my face going red and prayed he couldn't see it in the low light. "So he thinks we're an item. I hope that's not a drawback. Maybe we should stress the 'business' part of our business relationship."

"Gina, you're engaged to one man and sharing a suite in Cancún with another. And I think you made it pretty clear that you like a relaxed and flexible lifestyle."

Now there was no way he could miss my rosy glow. I changed the subject.

"D'you think he's checking out our backstory?"

"I hope so, or all that work on the part of the tech team will have been for nothing. I expect I may have to try to dazzle him further with my knowledge of antiquities while you bat your eyelashes and wax eloquent about dear Geoffrey's billions."

I didn't doubt that Revez was interested in Geoffrey's billions and my own considerable (if imaginary) wealth. I was less convinced he was interested in my—I mean, Marianna's—hyperbolic charms.

I uncurled my legs and stood. "I guess I'll turn in. I wouldn't want to wake up with circles under my eyes."

"Are you sure? You have a reputation to uphold, after all."

"Vroom, vroom," I said and retreated toward my room.

"Gina . . ."

I turned back, caught by the sober tone of his voice.

"Ted Bridges is dead and Rose Delgado is in a coma."

"You think I need reminding?"

"I think you need reminding that Revez may have something to do with one or both of those things. He may seem urbane and civilized and even charming, but . . ."

Jeremy's face flashed before my eyes—smiling, handsome, lovable. "Trust me, Dr. Veras, my experience with men who aren't what they seem is both broad and deep."

He looked down at his bottle of fizzy water, awkwardly contrite. "I'm sorry—"

"And was before I ever met you," I added.

The look he gave me was far too searching for my taste. I beat a hasty retreat before I found out he was a licensed psychologist in addition to his other talents.

Chapter 12

The Road to Ek Balam

called Dave Delgado's cell phone as early as I dared. I didn't wake him, Rose's nurse had already done that. My best friend's condition had neither improved nor worsened. Dave promised he'd let me know if there was a change either way.

"If I'm not here," I told him, "leave a message."

"In code, right?"

"I know it seems weird."

"No, really. I get it."

I knew he got it. I suspected if—no, *when*—Rosie recovered from her injuries, she and Dave were going to have a long talk about career options that didn't require aliases, bodyguards, and super-secret code words.

Over breakfast—which we ate on the Peacock restaurant's huge, fan-shaped seaward patio—Cruz suggested we take a day trip to Ek Balam, the archaeological site closest to Cancún. Well, not counting Chichen Itza, which apparently no *serious* archaeologists *do* any more, according to my expert.

"It's like Disneyland," he told me, lip curling professorially. "Tourists go to Chichen Itza; archaeologists, historians, and students thereof go to Ek Balam."

"How 'bout we go to some local galleries first? Let me get an idea of what's available on the 'white market.' I want to know how stunned and amazed to be if we see the private cache."

Cruz gave me what can only be described as a "smoldering look." "Oh, I'll tell you how stunned and amazed to be. We'll set up some signals."

He reached over and took my left hand—the one that wasn't holding something I could stab him with. Then he drew a tickle-inducing line down the back of it with his thumb.

I started to pull my hand away, then caught the minute shake of his head. His eyes flicked toward the patio doors. I lowered my head and followed his gaze, peering out from between disconcertingly red strands of hair. Felipe Revez was framed in the archway just inside the restaurant proper, apparently going over reservations with the maître d'.

"Watching?" I murmured.

"Yes."

I straightened and looked over at Revez just as he looked up at us. I smiled, disengaged my hand from Cruz's, and waved cheerily. Cruz sat back in his chair and impatiently adjusted his napkin, the very picture of a jealous boyfriend.

Revez hesitated only momentarily, then said a final word to his maître d' and came over to our table, standing close enough to me that I could smell his expensive cologne. Something citrus-y. "Buenas dias, friends, and how are you enjoying your breakfast?"

"It's glorious," I enthused. "The weather, the birdsong, the ocean rhythm, the food. Everything conspires to laziness."

"You'll find the beach is also part of the conspiracy."

Cruz reached across the table and took back my hand. "No beaches today, Mari. We are on a mission, remember?"

I smiled and kept my attention on our host. "We're going gallery-hopping today."

Revez looked dubious. "I doubt you'll find what you're looking for in a *public* gallery, Ms. Esposito."

"Marianna," I insisted.

"I've told her that myself," Cruz said, looking at me pointedly. "But she refuses to believe me. I've suggested a day trip to Ek Balam."

This pronouncement brought Revez's sleek brows (which I'd decided reminded me of a pair of acrobatic weasels) to full attention. "Ek Balam is not currently open to tourist traffic."

"I'm not a tourist. I'm an archaeologist. And I have the credentials to prove it."

Revez aimed a smile in my direction, though his eyes were still on Cruz. "So I have found. You have an impressive résumé, Mr. Gutierrez. Marianna, I believe your adviser is correct. You'll certainly see much that is unique at Ek Balam."

Good boy. He'd done his homework on us . . . or at least on Cruz Gutierrez. "Sure," I pouted, "but what good does that do me? Even if I see something unique, it's not as if I can ask the archaeologists to just wrap it up and send it to my hotel."

Revez's smile deepened. "No? Well, perhaps not. But one never knows." He traded enigmatic glances with Cruz, quite literally over my head, then said, "Cruz, I would very much like your opinion of some of the pieces I have lately acquired for my private collection. And to be honest, I am not above trying to impress a lady." He gave a nod in my direction. "I would be honored if you both could join me for dinner tonight in my penthouse."

Cruz looked to me as if asking permission. ("Please, Mom, can I go play with this nice man's artifacts?")

I smiled brightly. "We'd love to. Do you think your private collection might contain something that would make Geoffrey green with envy?"

He answered with an enigmatic smile, offered a slight bow, and wished us good hunting. "I look forward to this evening," he said, then caught up my free hand and raised it to his lips.

I thought I was prepared, but the kiss still elicited a shiver. I prayed he didn't take it in the spirit in which it was given.

"Creepy," I murmured, watching him disappear into the shadow of the restaurant.

"Really? You don't share Marianna's taste in men? Well, don't let on, please. Let him think you shiver with delight at his touch."

"Well, *duh*."

He tucked back into his breakfast. "How was your sister this morning?"

"Still incommunicado. But I'm expecting to hear from her any time. She never stays out of touch long."

"And her husband?"

"He's holding up well, I think. Just longing for the sound of her voice."

"Understandable. And how are you holding up?" he murmured.

I glanced up at him. He was looking at me as if searching for cracks in my glossy exterior.

I laughed. "I'm fine, darling. And just dying to get on with our shopping expedition."

We finished our breakfast in relative silence, then went into Cancún proper. Except for the Isla Mujeres, Cancún is one of those places where one looks for culture only to discover that there's no *there* there. There is nothing uniquely Mexican about the place: hotels strewn along white beaches, an eternity of azure water, buses, cars, shopping malls—there was even a Walmart, for Pete's sake. If it weren't for the Spanish place names and the lesser humidity, I'd think I was in Honolulu.

For Marianna Esposito's mission, the place was a total bust. We found only one or two upscale galleries and, while Cruz saw a few artifacts with suspicious provenance, none of them were of the caliber of Ted Bridges's vase shard. Before noon we'd rented an SUV and were on our way into the Yucatán outback. The climate changed as we went—from the perfumed balm of ocean breezes to the dense, moist atmosphere of the rain forest. I had the sense of being swaddled in increasing layers of invisible gauze.

The name Ek Balam meant "Black Jaguar." The signs posted about referred to it as a temple. This was misleading. Ek Balam was a fortress. At least that's the way it was built. It had several rings of defensive walls made of huge stone blocks and set with tricky entryways. Cruz called them "baffled entries." Apparently, they were intended to baffle the enemy so much that he'd hesitate long enough to make a good target.

Inside the walls were a cluster of temples—stepped pyramids all. The landscape around them was lush and verdant, but not overgrown as I'd imagined it would be. Blame it on the movies. In my imagination it had looked like a scene from *Raiders of the Lost Ark*. In reality it was more like a natural park—not groomed, but well kept. Jungle shrubbery had been thinned throughout the site, while the trees were left to grow in graceful copses. The temples arose from among them like staircases to the clouds, lofty, solid, awe-inspiring. It was tempting just to stand there with my mouth hanging open, staring at them. But Marianna would never be so nebbish, so I pretended vague interest and followed Cruz through the picture-postcard scenery.

On one end of the compound was a ball court. It was peopled at the moment with a group taking pictures. I got the feeling the Mayans would have loved American football, although they probably would have thought today's players were pretty wimpy to wear all that padding. Beyond the ball court, the roof of the largest pyramid seemed to float above the trees.

Cruz nodded at it. "The Acropolis."

It had a front porch. A long gallery with pillars upholding a sloping roof.

"Are those shingles?" I asked as we approached.

"Thatch."

"Surely the archaeologists didn't find it like that."

Cruz laughed. "Of course not. It's a reconstruction, although the temple up there was fairly well preserved. They buried it in fill."

"They?"

"The Mayans. The same sort of thing was done at other sites as well. The most famous being Rosalila."

"Okay, that one I remember. A temple inside a temple inside a temple. Reminds me of the babushka dolls my mom is always sticking in my pockets."

He turned and looked at me. "Babushka dolls? You mean those nested dolls? The Russian ones?"

I nodded, my eyes on the expanse of stone and thatch that thrust out of the lush green of the forest. I half expected someone in a feathered kilt to come out and wave to us from the balcony railing.

"Why does your mother put Russian nesting dolls in your pockets?"

"For luck. Mom likes to think of herself as a *volkhovnitsa*—a witch. Not that she'd admit it, of course. She prefers to hide behind her PhD in Russian history. Pretends she only has an academic interest in *materia magica*. Before I left on this trip, she actually sprinkled holy water on my Harley."

"You're kidding."

"Nope. She blessed my gun too."

"She sounds . . ." He hesitated.

"It's okay, you can say it. She's eccentric. So's my dad, so they're a good match."

"Your dad was a police detective."

It wasn't a question. I didn't recall having discussed it with him, so I assumed he'd done some more homework on me. I wondered how much homework. I wondered if he knew, for example, how my dad had come to retire early.

"Yeah. Now he pretends to be Sherlock Holmes. He's mostly harmless. Although . . ."

"Although what?"

We'd stopped at the foot of the Acropolis and I turned to face him. "That day at the headlands he and his Sausalito Irregulars were also providing, shall we say, covert backup for the stalker surveillance."

He was stunned. I could tell by the way he didn't move for a five count. "Those weren't NPS agents?"

"There were three NPS agents, one in the parking area, one stationed by the trailhead, the other where the walking path met the road. Anybody else you saw that seemed . . . covert was one of my dad's guys."

"Ex-cops?"

"Two ex, two off duty, and one assistant ME."

He shook his head. "Who called them in?"

"Nobody. Dad just wanted to make sure I had enough backup."

"You almost didn't."

"Which is the perfect segue to me asking why you were there, doing Madison Baumgarner impersonations."

"My job didn't end just because you caught me out. I was following Rose. Imagine my piqued interest when I realized that someone else was also following Rose, rather aggressively, in fact. As if he very much wanted her to know it. Anything else you'd like to know?"

I considered asking how much he knew about my brief career in law enforcement, then told myself it didn't matter. I gestured at the Acropolis. "Up the stairs?"

He nodded and led the way. The handful of other folks wandering the ruins looked like students. Except for the ones that looked like professors. Both were oblivious to anything but the ruins and each other, which was just fine by me.

We climbed up into the shade of the Acropolis's thatched porch. The roof protected a façade covered completely with amazingly intricate carvings.

"This is the White Temple," Cruz told me. "Inside is the tomb of Ukit Kan Le'k Tok', a king of Ek Balam."

"Huh. Easy for you to say." I squatted before a low platform the size of a California King mattress. It was supported by a row of grinning stone faces interspersed with undulating scrollwork. "And these are his subjects?"

He hunkered down next to me. "Those are the skulls of the dead in the Underworld. The Mayans conceived of the Underworld as being under water. They also believed it had nine separate Hells."

"Groovy. So the scrolly things are waves?"

"Waves and water lilies."

"Sweet."

Cruz smiled, a bit indulgently, I thought. "Different culture; different take on death. The Mayans, not unlike the Hindus, saw death, destruction, and decay as being inseparable from life."

"Brahma the Creator, Vishnu the Preserver, Shiva the Destroyer," I murmured.

"Exactly. And Kali, the embodiment of both death *and* birth. The two seeming extremes in one entity. There's a temple at Palenque that depicts maize leaves sprouting from a skull. Out of death—life."

"They must have loved compost."

"I think it's a singularly well-rounded point of view, myself. Yin and yang eternally joined in a single symbol."

I turned and found him looking at me very gravely as if it were important that I understand this concept.

"I get it," I assured him. "It's very Zen."

"You're Buddhist?"

"My father's Buddhist—more Nichiren than Zen—Mom's Russian Orthodox. So I'm sort of a Russian Orthodox Buddhist."

"Who carries babushkas in her pocket and has a blessed gun."

I reached into the pocket of my khaki capris and pulled out Dad's tanuki and Mom's Saint Boris, holding them out for inspection.

He laughed. "I've got to meet your parents."

"No you don't. Okay, Dad maybe. But Mom . . ." I shivered at the very thought. "Trust me, you don't want to meet Mom. She'll cut off pieces of your hair while you're not looking and do all sorts of bizarre things with them."

"Like?"

"Roll them in lumps of wax and drop them into hot liquid. Burn them. Toss them into the air to see where they fall."

He looked legitimately puzzled. "Why?"

"You don't wanna know," I said and got to my feet, turning my attention to the façade of Ukit's little memorial. "Wow, this is in incredibly good condition."

Okay, I admit it. It was a dodge. In part. But the place really was in amazing condition; the stonework looked as if it had been carved yesterday.

"That's because the temple is part of the burial. It was created for the purpose of preserving the king's remains and so it was buried with him under tons of rubble and limestone fill."

I stepped closer to the door. It looked like a mouth lined with ornate teeth. The platform I'd been examining, I realized, was the protruding lower jaw. "The king's inside the monster? Eaten by Death?"

Cruz nodded, then stood and pointed up at the creature's face. There were some figures perched on it—one on its right eyelid, a larger one on its muzzle. There was also a place on the left side of the huge face where it appeared a figure had been hewn away, leaving a rough patch of stone to mark its passing. And the largest figure in the group, I realized, was headless.

"Pothunters?"

"Yes. But here, they take more than pots. Here, they take the head of the king." He pointed at the headless figure atop the creature's nose. "That was an effigy of Ukit Kan Le'k Tok', himself. The tomb inside has been similarly vandalized—little bits of it carried away to be sold to the highest bidder. I sometimes wonder . . ."

"What?"

"Perhaps it is treasonous, but I've sometimes wondered if my own government might be behind, if not the looting itself, at least the laxity with which it is prosecuted. Mexico is not a wealthy nation. And these treasures command a hefty price on the black and gray markets."

I looked up at him, trying to read his face. "If you're right about that—if the pillaging is institutionalized—then what can we do here?"

He met my eyes, his own grimmer than the death's-heads poking from the limestone façade. "Whatever we can."

We continued our tour, Cruz acting as guide and lecturer, and pointing out other places where the pothunters had struck. One of the most obvious was a doorway flanked by painted figures that were almost Egyptian in style. There had apparently been three rows of them at one time. Now there were two—the lowest (and easiest to reach) had been cleanly hacked away. I could even see the smooth bore of a masonry drill along one side. In all, I figured the missing pieces must be worth hundreds of thousands of dollars—possibly millions.

"You think we're going to see some of the missing bits of Ek Balam tonight after dinner?" I asked Cruz as we wandered back to our vehicle.

He looked up through the canopy of sun-filtering green and it struck me that his ancestors had walked here. Had lived here. Had built this. It was his in a way I had no personal referent for. But I understood Rose and her quest for her grandmother's bones. Maybe that meant I understood Cruz Veras, just a little.

"It wouldn't surprise me," he said, then glanced sideways at me and laughed. "'My God,' she thought, 'I'm shackled to an anthro-geek! Shoot me now.'"

"Actually, I was trying to empathize with you. I *do* empathize with you. Because of Rose. And Mom. And I'd say you're more crusader than geek."

He bowed. "Too kind."

We climbed back into our trusty SUV to return to Cancún and our dinner date with Felipe Revez.

The concierge began signaling me the moment we entered the hotel lobby, then met me halfway to his desk, clutching a piece of paper. "An urgent message, Ms. Esposito," he told me, holding out the note. "Your brother-in-law wanted to be sure you got it the moment you came in."

I started to reach for it, but my hand froze somewhere between here and there. Cruz took it and thanked the concierge with a crisp five-dollar bill that seemed to appear out of nowhere.

My eyes on the note, I was only peripherally aware of the concierge returning to his station. I looked up at Cruz with no idea what my face was doing. Whatever it was, it prompted him to grasp my elbow firmly and steer me across the lobby and into the elevator, where we were blessedly alone.

I leaned against the wall of the elevator while he opened the note. He didn't prolong the moment. "It says: 'Your sister left a brief message. She hung up before I could talk to her, but it's something.'"

I hiccupped and burst into tears.

Chapter 13

My Dinner with Felipe

My face was a train wreck by the time we got back to the suite. What makeup I'd put on had dissolved in the salty monsoon. I disappeared into my bathroom on the pretext of cleaning up. About fifteen minutes later, I'd cried out all my angst, kissed my various oberegi for good luck, and called Dave by cell phone to verify the contents of his message.

The news wasn't as good as I'd hoped. Rose hadn't fully regained consciousness, not even momentarily, but had merely bobbed toward it for a minute or two. Still, as Dave said, it was something.

I hung up and changed into one of Marianna's silk outfits—a vivid saffron off-the-shoulder number that made me feel, perversely, like a Buddhist monk.

Cruz was standing out on the balcony admiring the sunset when I reappeared. He apparently had acute hearing, because he turned before I was even fully into the living room.

"Better?"

"Yeah. Better. Even got rid of the hiccups. Look, I'm really sorry about all that." I nodded in the general direction of the elevator.

I couldn't see his face in the shadow of the setting sun, but he sounded puzzled. "Why are you apologizing? Your best friend has been in a coma for over a week. I take it she showed a glimmer of consciousness?"

I explained what I'd gleaned from Dave, putting as cheery a face on it as possible. "I don't usually indulge in histrionics."

"I believe," he said, "that machismo is supposed to be a male affectation. An Hispanic male affectation, at that." He studied me for a moment longer, then added, "You don't have to prove yourself, Gina. I know you're capable of pulling your own weight on this sting. Rose has faith in you. Ellen has faith in you. I see no reason why I shouldn't. Now, you should probably go put on your makeup. We're due up at Revez's penthouse in about half an hour."

"I'm wearing makeup."

"Let me see."

He came fully into the room to draw me into the bedroom where the row of lights around the vanity lit my face in less lurid hues than a Cancún sunset. After an entire two seconds of scrutiny he shook his head.

"Pardon me for saying so, but you look less like Marianna and more like Gina at the moment. You need more."

"I'm afraid to try more," I admitted. "I don't wear a lot of makeup normally, and I'm afraid if I get more liberal with the brushes, I'll end up looking like a bad mime."

"Sit down." He took me by the shoulders and settled me on the vanity stool, then reached for Marianna's makeup kit, an ornate velvet box chock full of colorful hues.

I groaned. "Oh, please. Don't tell me—you worked in a beauty salon after school when you were a kid."

He bent to scrabble in my toolkit, unsuccessfully hiding a smile. "I did stage makeup for a repertory theater group. And I have three older sisters."

"You watched them do their makeup?"

"I found the process fascinating."

"And they *let* you?"

"Not exactly."

He had me tilt my head back, then began to apply makeup with deft strokes of puff and brush and pencil. His ministrations made me nervous. It was like sitting in a dentist's chair. And, as happens when I sit in a dentist's chair, my hands balled into tight fists.

"Relax," he told me. "I promise I won't poke your eye out or make you look like a cheap tart."

"Oh, please, no. Make me look like a very expensive tart."

"You empathized with me because of your mother, you said," he recalled as he worked. "Why your mother?"

I accepted the sudden change of topic as a ploy to relax me. "I mentioned that Mom's an academic."

"A doctor of history, yes?"

"Yeah. She teaches at SFSU. I think her studies—history, folklore, arcana—I think they're her way of reclaiming her personal history. She came to the U.S. when she was twelve with her parents and her paternal grandmother. Her parents wanted their family to be thoroughly American. So they changed their name from Arkhangelski to Arkham. Then they changed their daughter's name from Nadezhda to Nancy."

"That's a bit extreme, isn't it?"

"That was just the beginning. They changed her name; they changed her language—she was to speak only English at home; they sent her to an elocution coach to get rid of her accent; they had her hair styled in the latest fashion. And they took her to a Protestant church. But the worst thing, I think, was that they tried to keep her away from great-gramma. She was a bad influence, they said. Always going on about the old country, the old ways, the old beliefs."

"So naturally her grandmother became a coconspirator," Cruz guessed.

"Coconspirator and heroine. I don't know why Russian parents would try to keep their kids from doing *anything* by force. If Russia has a national virtue, it's stubbornness. That's something all the elocution coaches and hair stylists in the universe can't change. Mom hung out with great-gramma at every opportunity, listening to her tales, absorbing her sense of the religious and the magical. She did more than listen—when she was thirteen she bought a tape recorder and recorded every story great-gramma could remember. And when she'd exhausted that source, she moved on to the nearest college library. By the time she was a sophomore in college, she'd changed her name back to the Russian, but used the diminutive, Nadia, so as not to fluster the natives. And she'd read every musty tome on Russian magic she could find. She even started writing one of her own. She did her master's thesis on comparative magic and her doctoral dissertation on magic in the Christian church. But it's more than just an academic pursuit to her. The PhD is just a smoke screen to give her a reason to immerse herself in the Motherland. She never thought of herself as Nancy Arkham. Not for one second."

I chuckled, recalling something Dad had told me when I was fifteen. One of those things we tell our teenagers to embarrass the crap out of them.

"What?" Cruz asked, sweeping a brush across my right eyelid.

"When I was born, Mom folded a lock of my hair inside a piece of linen, wrote my name on it, and hid it under the altar at Our Lady of Kazan cathedral. When Dad told me that, I was mortified." I affected a teenager's petulant whine: "'Mom, how *could* you? How *embarrassing!* What if the *priest* finds it? What will he *think*?' 'He'll think I'm a witch,' she told me. 'But it's all right. There were at least five little packets of linen under his altar. One family he might expel. Five is a pogrom.'"

Cruz laughed, then said, "Keep your eyes closed." I felt the cool slip of eyeliner above my lashes. "So, how does your Buddhist father feel about all of this?"

"I think it amuses him. Heck, I think it delights him. He's got a lock of my baby hair in his household shrine."

He moved around behind me and put his hands on my shoulders. "Okay, open and look."

I did. My cheeks were softly and rosily bronze; my eyelids were washed with gold; my lips were deep copper. I smiled at the reflection in the mirror. "Well, hello Marianna!"

Cruz shook his head. "You know, the timbre of your voice even changes when you do her."

"I assure you, it's not intentional."

"Perhaps you're a natural chameleon."

"Dad says that. He said it would make me a good spy."

"Well, let's go put your dad's thesis to the test, shall we?"

Per our host's instructions, we went downstairs to the concierge who punched in the combination to Mr. Revez's private elevator and sent us up to what I expected would be a palatial suite of rooms. I wasn't disappointed. The penthouse of *El Playa del Pavo Réal* was a hacienda in the sky. The décor framed by the soft, golden adobe walls reflected Iberian, Moroccan, and Mayan designs in dark woods and rich, warm colors. I suspected a designer would say it was a man's space, but I found I liked it very much, and apparently Felipe Revez felt that it liked me.

"You are a flame," he murmured, as he bent over my hand. "Warm, vivid. You honor my home with your light."

I tried to keep myself from shivering at the touch of his lips, but it was useless. I shot Cruz a helpless look over Revez's head and crossed my eyes.

Cruz let out a chuff of laughter, just managing to make it sound as if he were clearing his throat. "Your penthouse is spectacular, Felipe. Surely, the best of all styles."

"No more spectacular than the woman who graces it," Revez said.

"Now, I'll bet you say that to all your female guests," I teased lightly.

"No. Not all."

Cruz cleared his throat yet again, and Revez straightened and made a grand gesture toward a room that was flooded with the crimson light of the waning sun.

"Please, dinner is ready to be served. I thought the western patio would afford us the most beautiful views."

And so it did. The vista included sea and shore, inland forest, and sunset. The sea was the color of red wine, the sand was copper, and the forest deepest rust. Looking at it, I forgot momentarily who I was and why I was there. Fortunately, Revez reminded me before I opened my mouth and put my foot in it.

"How was your day? Did you enjoy the galleries?"

I shrugged, rapidly collecting my thoughts. "Not as much as I'd hoped. You were right. They were tourist traps, every last one of them. It was disappointing."

"And Ek Balam? Was that also disappointing?"

"Ek Balam," I said, turning to my host and letting Marianna's enthusiasm pour over him, "was *glorious*. The carvings were so . . . *new* looking. As if they'd been chiseled yesterday. And that tomb! Now, *that* would make a great wedding present for Geoffrey."

Revez raised his brows, and Cruz said, "Really, Mari—you're planning the man's burial before the wedding?"

"Not the tomb itself, silly. That king-size platform, the dragon's tongue. Can you imagine what an amazing bedstead that would make? Sleeping in the mouth of Hell—Geoff would *love* that."

"And you?" asked Revez teasingly. "You would love sleeping in the mouth of Hell?"

I smiled coquettishly (I hoped). "It has a certain kick to it."

"You are a surprising woman, Marianna," said Revez, and I was stunned by the conviction that he meant it.

I glanced across the dinner table at Cruz as the butler or waiter—or whatever one was supposed to call him—set out our salad plates. Cruz raised his wine glass to me and smiled.

"To surprises," he said softly.

Revez seconded the toast and we began our salad course.

"I suppose I'd have to have a replica made if I wanted such a piece, wouldn't I?" I wondered wistfully a moment later.

"The dragon's mouth?" said Revez. "I think so. It would be beyond even the most inventive . . . excavator to remove the mouth of the king's tomb."

"Well, someone seems to have removed his head," said Cruz. "And part of a frieze as well."

I added, "And don't forget that cute little friend of his. The one perched on the dragon's eyelid."

Revez's eyes narrowed slightly and fixed on Cruz's face. "You're an archaeologist, Cruz. How do you feel about such vandalism?"

"Vandalism?" Cruz watched the butler set the aromatic main course before him. "I should say 'commerce.' How do I feel about it?" He smiled and shook his head. "Do you know, Felipe, what a museum does with those treasures? What archaeological institutions do with them? A museum takes a bunch of photographs, drops the treasures into plastic trays, and locks them up in an underground vault with all the accessibility of a rabbit warren. An institution, on the other hand, barricades the entire site so that it is available to no one but the scholar and the scholar's acolytes. What do I feel? I'm happy that at least *someone* is enjoying the head of the king, since he can no longer enjoy it himself."

Revez studied Cruz a moment longer, then threw back his head and laughed, the sound seeming to roll up out of his core like the beat of a drum.

I sighed, dramatically and loudly. "Do men always have to talk shop?"

Cruz slanted me a "look." "We were talking treasure, Marianna. You like treasure as well as the next person, I think."

I stuck my bottom lip out in a moue. "I like treasure I can touch. And own. And give away if I feel like it."

"Did you see anything at Ek Balam that struck your fancy?" Revez asked me. "Besides Hell's bedstead."

"The paintings were lovely," I said.

"Friezes," correct Cruz.

"Whatever. I liked the colors. Oh, and the funerary items. The masks, the vessels. All that lapis and turquoise and gold."

"Would your fiancé like that sort of thing, do you think?"

"Let me put it this way: he doesn't have anything like that now."

"My employer is a most acquisitive man," Cruz said. "Having what others do not means a great deal to him."

"That," said Revez, lifting his wine glass, "is something I understand completely."

After dinner, Revez treated us to a tour of his fabulous penthouse. It was huge. My entire houseboat could have fit into the living room. And, as showmen are wont to do, he saved the best for last.

Behind two oversized paneled and carved doors that looked as if they, themselves, were valuable antiques, was a long, beautifully lit gallery, flanked on both sides by glass cases and wall-boxes. The walls were covered in some sort of woven fabric in a shade of gold I'd always associated with the *padrone*'s adobe, Flamenco dancers, and Zorro. Each objet d'art had its own pool of sunny light to bask in and a midnight blue velvet backdrop to bask on. It was more than impressive. This man was serious about his art.

Maybe even deadly serious, I remembered.

I *oohed* and *aahed* my way down the gallery, finding that appreciation of Revez's collection required no acting ability. He lingered at my elbow, almost touching me, but not quite, while Cruz hovered watchfully behind him.

About halfway down the left-hand side of the room, I saw something that was more than a little familiar. It was a large vase—or rather, most of a large vase—and it looked quite as if it had been fashioned by the same artisan responsible for Ted Bridges's potsherd.

"It's glorious, Felipe," I said, glancing up into our host's smiling face. "Shame it's not all in one piece. Any idea where the rest of it went?"

"It hardly matters, *corazon*," Cruz answered, flanking me. The two men locked eyes over my head. "It is a large enough piece to be worth tens of thousands—perhaps more."

Revez's smile deepened, as if the other man's feigned jealousy tickled him. "Three hundred thousand, to be exact. I acquired it just this past year.

Here," he continued, taking my elbow and steering me away from Cruz across the carpeted aisle. I'd always wondered what it felt like to be popular. "I think you may find this piece familiar."

I did. I'd seen two just like it this morning at Ek Balam.

"Oh! This is from that temple we saw today, isn't it?" I turned to shower Revez with admiration. "You clever man. How did you ever—?"

He raised a finger to my lips. "Now, that would be divulging secrets, Marianna."

"Archaeological work is seasonal," said Cruz from behind us. "Even in this part of the world. Often the 'seasons' have nothing to do with the weather. When grants run out, when projects are cut, when there are no excavations, diggers still need money to feed themselves and their families. What can they do? They dig. For whoever pays them."

"Indeed," Felipe agreed.

"So, do you have the king's head too?" I asked.

"Regrettably, no. But I have something even better." He tucked my hand through his arm and drew me to the very end of the long room where a single glass enclosure was centered in the wall. The lone object in the display was a mask.

Now, for most people—including me—the word *mask* probably conjures images of Halloween costumes, bank robbers in Nixon faces, and those silly Harlequins in white tights, neck ruffles, and dominoes. This wasn't that kind of mask. Not even Bill Gates's kids had gear like this come October 31. This was a life-size faceplate of gold inlaid with turquoise, malachite, and carnelian.

It was beautiful.

It was hideous.

The Mayans, I decided, were adept with that sort of artistic schizophrenia. It was something that separated them from the Egyptians, to whom a number of theorists had tried to connect them. While the Egyptians voted in favor of making even the Gods of Really Icky Things beautiful, graceful, and elegant, the Mayans simply portrayed the horrific with flamboyant honesty, but did it in the richest, most gorgeous materials they could lay their hands on.

I found my tongue after a long moment of reaction. "That's stunning, Felipe. What *is* it? Or should I say, *who* is it?"

Felipe was a happy man. He had scored big points with the little lady. His dark eyes gleamed in boyish zeal, but did not toss a *neener-neener* glance at Cruz, which I thought was mighty big of him.

"That," he told me, "is from a newly discovered hoard. My experts tell me it depicts the eighth-century Mayan king, Shield Jaguar II."

"Then it's from Bonampak," said Cruz, "a site that has been photographed, catalogued, and even reduced to digital imagery. There hasn't been a new hoard discovered there since the late nineties."

"That is the common wisdom," Revez said. "The common wisdom is not always correct."

"Surely, that's a death mask."

There was an edge to Cruz's voice that went beyond feigned jealousy. His face was curiously still and his eyes glinted dangerously. I wondered if I was going to have to step in and do something insane and Mariannesque to keep him from bitch-slapping our host.

"It's a life mask. The hoard appears to be made up of collected objects from a number of royal caches. Possibly it represents an early attempt at grave robbing, or perhaps it was done to *protect* the memory of the kings— an attempt to foil tomb raiders. One of my . . . seasonal employees found it while doing some surveying work for a Yale University project. There is more where this came from, Cruz."

Thank God and Saint Boris, he'd apparently read Cruz's offended zeal as gold fever.

"More?" I asked, turning to fix my antiquities guy with a brilliant smile. "Did you hear that, darling?"

Darling had heard that, and apparently the warning in my voice and eyes came through loud and clear as well. He smiled. "Extraordinary."

I turned back to Revez. "Is there another one of these?"

He laughed at me—a big-chested, booming laugh so full of patronizing fondness that I was surprised he didn't ruffle my hair or give me noogies.

"Sweet Marianna," he said. "Life masks aren't like off-the-rack clothing. They are unique. As you are unique." He kissed my hand.

Ow! A one-two punch: condescension and compliment all rolled into one. I vigorously quashed the urge to snatch back my hand and wipe it on my dress, and said, "So, this is the only one? What about his death mask?"

"That is in the National Museum in Mexico City," said Cruz.

"But, this is exactly—I mean, *exactly*—what I was looking for." I turned impulsively to our host, took one of his hands in mine, looked up into his eyes and asked, "How much?"

He shook his head. "How much?"

"For the mask. What do you want for it? I want it for Geoff."

Revez grimaced ruefully. "My dear Marianna, I'm sorry, but I simply cannot sell this mask. It is, as you can see, the centerpiece of my entire collection."

"How much did you pay for it?" I asked gauchely, and Cruz murmured, "*Sagrada Maria . . .*"

"I hesitate to speak of such things—"

"Nonsense. You spoke of such things when we were looking at that vase. Why not now?"

Revez stared at me as if I'd suddenly started speaking Swahili.

That's right, el jefe, you're looking at the business end of Marianna Esposito.

After a moment of hesitation, he smiled. It was a warm, sincere smile of unadulterated admiration. The mouse had roared. And she had roared in dollar signs, which was a language Revez understood quite well.

"You are correct. I paid nine hundred thousand for the mask. A stretch, but worth it. It was also a very difficult choice for me. In order to keep it, I had to let other equally amazing artifacts go to the open market."

"The black market, you mean," said Cruz, keeping his hand in.

Revez merely nodded.

"I'll give you nine hundred and fifty thousand for it," I said.

He shook his head.

I narrowed my eyes. "One million in American dollars."

"Mari!" Cruz exclaimed.

But Revez refused to budge. "Shield Jaguar is not for sale, my dear. For any price, however . . ."

"Yes?"

"You should know that there are other, perhaps even more stunning artifacts available from . . . this site."

Bingo. We'd apparently passed some sort of means test. To cover my suddenly racing heart, I began hesitatin'. I gave the mask another lingering look, then said, "Can you show them to me? I'd love to see them."

"They are still in situ."

"In what?" I asked even though I knew what he meant.

"He means they're still at the site," Cruz volunteered, then to Revez: "Are you suggesting that Ms. Esposito and I should go there and dig them up ourselves?"

Revez gave a one-shoulder shrug. "Come, let us discuss this in the living room where we can be more comfortable. I'll have my man Edgardo bring refreshments. Wine or coffee?"

"Coffee," I said, "would be glorious."

"Despite what you see here," Revez told us once we were seated in the opulent living room before a softly glowing gas-log fire, "I do not have a significant amount in liquid assets. I am a land baron, for lack of a better word. An entrepreneur. If you tally all my properties, yes, I suppose you would call me a wealthy man. And looking at my collection of antiquities, you might make a similar pronouncement. Were I such a man, I would be honored to *give* you, if not Shield Jaguar's mask, at the very least something to equal it. But I am not such a man, and I do not have the resources to make such an offer. . . . Thank you, Edgardo."

He paused to sip his wine, waiting to speak again until "his man" had served our coffee along with a tray of very rich little confections that I felt entitled to, considering how much hiking I'd done earlier in the day.

"When I say that I paid nine hundred thousand dollars for Shield Jaguar, I speak in part of the cost of finding it, excavating it, and paying certain people not to notice its existence or wonder where it came from."

"Then the site is unknown to academia," guessed Cruz.

"It is unknown to anyone," said Revez, "but me, my experts, and select . . . associates. And we intend that it should stay that way."

"Associates . . . ?" Cruz pressed, and I held my breath.

Oh, please don't get him all jinky.

But when Revez hesitated, Cruz continued, "I'm not asking who they are, Felipe, but simply whether they can pay for excavations."

"Suffice it to say that I am not the only person with an interest in Bonampak or its sister site. But I am, perhaps, the most . . . well-placed person. My associates have reason to keep a low profile."

Cruz smiled, slowly and wickedly, the way a man might more commonly smile at a half-naked woman or a pile of garlic fries. "And what do you suppose it might cost to . . . liberate this site?"

"A more substantial amount than even I can command."

"Five million?" I asked as if I were contemplating writing him a check. "Ten?"

"A full-fledged and covert excavation of Bonampak B, as I call it, I estimate would cost in the neighborhood of twenty million dollars."

I looked at him long and searchingly as if I were estimating his gross worth. "I don't have that kind of money," I said, and watched his face tighten. I waited a beat, then added, "But I'm marrying someone who does."

Revez raised his wine glass to me and smiled. "Glorious," he said.

Chapter 14

Her Own Woman

Tink." The word popped out of Cruz's mouth as we sat before the fire in our own suite.

I had changed into a multihued jogging suit; Cruz had donned a Giants' baseball jersey over his dress slacks. We had the doors to the balcony open to let in the fresh sea air, but though it rose into the high nineties during the day in coastal Yucatán, it could get quite cool at night. A nice combination, actually.

"You exploring a career in radio sound effects?" I asked. "I'd advise you to keep your day job, whatever that is."

"Tink," he repeated. "That's what Dave Delgado called you at the hospital. Pet name?"

"Only for a pet you hated."

"Embarrassing?"

"Annoying."

"But you let friends call you that."

"Certain friends. Friends who were around in the day. Rosie was there when I . . . acquired the damned thing. She's entitled—and Dave by extension, I guess."

"But you're not going to tell me how you acquired it?"

I looked over at him where he lounged, half in and half out of a comfy leather chair, his feet on the hearth. The look in his eyes told me that if I didn't tell him at this juncture, he'd keep after me until I did.

"Okay, this is the story: When I was a sophomore in high school, I was part of a group of kids who were . . . misfits, I guess you'd say. My friend Lee and I were too short; Rosie was too chubby, and July was too tall and too buff."

"July?"

"July Petersen. Yes, it's a family pandemic. She has a brother named 'March' and a sister named 'October.'"

"I'm going to guess—the months in which they were born?"

I nodded. "It started back a generation. Their mom's name is 'Jan'—short for 'January'—and I think they have an uncle named 'Avril.'"

"I am sincerely afraid to ask about their father."

"Oh, their father is named, simply and sensibly, 'John,'" I told him. "At any rate, we were misfits who lacked the foresight to realize that hanging out together compounded our 'misfitism.' So we made a natural and easy target for those packs of guys who just love to harass the black sheep of the fold. One of the guys that used to poke fun at us was a studious sort. When he found out my full name was Gina Suzu Miyoko, he—for reasons that escape me entirely—got out a Japanese dictionary and found out that it meant 'Silver Bell Temple.' Hence, 'Tinkerbell.' Hence, 'Tink.'"

"Ah . . . it all becomes clear. And this studious fellow . . ."

"Perry. Perry Dixon."

"You honestly don't know why he went to the trouble to look up your name?"

I shook my head, then caught the expression on his face. "Oh, really. You think he had a crush on me."

He shrugged. "Seems obvious enough."

"That just . . ." That just made all sorts of sense in view of more recent overtures Perry had made the last time I visited Grass Valley, my erstwhile hometown. I laughed. "That's just too weird. Trust me not to have seen it."

"So where is this Perry Dixon now?"

"Serving a two-year sentence in Folsom for illegal sale of firearms."

"Oh."

"Yeah. Oh."

I felt his gaze on the side of my face. It was not a comfortable sensation. "You were referring to *him*, then—with that comment about your experience with men who are not what they seem."

"Actually, no. Although, now that you mention it, I guess it applies. I was thinking of . . . someone else."

Oddly, he didn't press me on that. It was as if he possessed a sixth sense about which areas of my personal territory were posted "Beware of Dog" and which ones said "Trespassers Will Be Eaten."

I decided I'd move on anyway, just in case he tried to circle back. "So tell me," I said, "when Felipe took you aside tonight just before we left, was it to talk business? He'd said he wanted your opinion on something."

Cruz turned his face toward the fire, and I had the feeling he was hiding a smile. "He wanted to get my opinion on something, but it wasn't business related. Actually, I have an appointment with him tomorrow morning quite early to look at some of his 'investments.'"

"So . . . what was the topic of discussion, Dr. Enigma?"

"You."

"Oh, I see."

"Yes. Our host asked me about the exact nature of our relationship. That was precisely the way he put it: 'Cruz, I hope you will not find me rude, but what is the exact nature of your relationship with Marianna?'"

"And you said?"

"I said, 'I am her antiquities expert.' To which he replied: 'You are more than that or I am a blind man.' 'I am her bodyguard,' I explained. 'I am paid to be attentive to her body.'"

"You *didn't*."

He grinned. "No. I didn't. Actually, I said, 'I am paid to be attentive to her safety and security.' 'You are more than attentive,' he said. 'You are protective, and not merely on Mr. Catalano's behalf, I think.'"

"Ooh," I said. "A sixth sense, that guy."

"Well, of course, I then admitted a certain . . . attraction to you—to Marianna. How could I not be attracted to such a woman?" He made a dramatic gesture and raised his eyes heavenward.

"You could be gay."

"Yes, but Cruz Gutierrez *cannot* be gay."

"Granted. Go on."

"Then he asks me: 'What is the extent of your involvement? You share a suite. What else do you share?'"

"And you said?"

"Absolutely nothing. I simply gave him a 'look' intended to tell him that he had trespassed far enough. However, he was not to be dissuaded. He asked bluntly if you were my lover."

"And you said?"

"I told him you were not 'my' anything—you are your own woman. Oh, how did I put it? It was so poetic: 'One thing I have learned, Felipe, since knowing her: a man does not have Marianna Esposito. She has him.' Something like that." He waved his hand as if to say it was of no importance.

The humorous aspect of our intrigue suddenly hit me like a pie in the face and I laughed. I couldn't stop laughing. It all seemed so absurdly funny. Gina Miyoko, private eye, was now Gina Miyoko, femme fatale? The whole idea was so out of synch with my self-image that I couldn't wrap my mind around it.

When I'd laughed myself out, I opened my eyes and was surprised to discover that Cruz had not been laughing with me. Or even at me.

"What?" I asked, wiping tears from my face.

"Yes, I thought it was funny at first too—all this cloak and dagger. But listen, Gina . . ." He leaned forward in his chair, elbows resting on his knees, and fixed me with a straight-up gaze. "Listen to the amounts of money we have been discussing. Thousands, tens of thousands, hundreds of thousands, now millions. These are amounts of money for which some will commit murder."

"Not will," I said, catching up with his sober mood. "Have."

"Yes. Have. And I think perhaps they have because they have a secret to keep."

I nodded. "The location of Bonampak B."

"Right now, Felipe Revez supposes you to be thinking about having your husband-to-be bankroll a most dangerous and lucrative excavation. And from my conversation with him this evening, I believe he is looking for ways to influence your decision."

"Ways to . . . You think he'll try to seduce me."

"I think it is possible. Hell, he may be sincerely infatuated with you, for all we know."

He flung himself out of his chair and paced away to look into the velvet night beyond the balcony. The light pollution from Cancún threw him into fuzzy silhouette.

"What—you think I can't handle myself? That I'll start giggling like a schoolgirl? I have a *little* experience with men."

He turned back to face me. "Men like Revez? Men who might kill to protect their secrets?"

I met his gaze dead on. "Yes."

Surprise! Not the answer he'd expected.

"I get that this is dangerous, Cruz," I told him. "I understand that this is only partly a piece of fiction. But we've got to see this through."

"I'm not sure we do."

"What? What are you saying?"

I rose and crossed the room to get a better look at his face. It was inscrutable.

"In the morning, after my meeting with Revez, I'm going to give Greg Sheffield a full report. We'll see what he says. We may have enough evidence that a raid now would bag us Revez."

"But we won't bag his associates or the *location of the site*. We've at least got to come out of this with *that*."

He shrugged. "We know it's near Bonampak."

"*Bozhe moy. Near* Bonampak? That covers a hell of a lot of densely forested territory. You know what that area is like. Except where they've cleared it, it's like a . . . a jungle."

His lips twitched. "It *is* a jungle."

I peered at him in the firelight. "What is this about? Why the sudden case of jitters? I thought you were an experienced undercover guy."

"I am. You're not. Not like this."

"I'm often called on to pretend to be something I'm not. While I was checking you out, I presented myself as several different people. I—"

"You told fibs about who Gina Miyoko is. This is different. As different as that is from stepping in front of a camera in an acting role."

He was right. I knew he was right, but I was not ready to admit it. "Is this about me being a woman? A *small* woman? A defenseless-looking, small woman? Because if that's what this is about, so help me I'll . . . I'll go kung fu on your ass."

I almost got him to laugh. Almost. He shook his head, then looked past me at the fire.

"Look you," I said, poking his chest with my finger. "You're the one who talked me into this. You're the reason I'm here. You and Rose. Hell, you *used* Rose to *get* me here."

His face contorted in a split second of angst, which he shook away. "Gina, the deeper we get into this, the less sanguine I am about involving you. Greg asked me to think twice about that back at the beginning. I didn't listen to him. I'm beginning to wish I had. You should be back in the States at Rose's bedside. Not here."

"Oh, that is wrong on *so* many different levels. Look, we're here to set up a sting—to get Revez to take us to the site and show us that this is worth good old Geoffrey's money. How's that going to happen without Marianna?"

"I could set it up, acting on your behalf—"

"I'm the Golden Goose, Cruz. Not you—*me*. Revez knows that. And I think we've pretty well established that Marianna doesn't send proxies in to do her bidding."

His face said he knew I was right and hated it.

I stepped back half a pace and said, "Look, when we report to Greg, you can share your concerns with him. If he wants to pull the plug, we'll pull the plug and go home, okay?"

He looked at the floor, then at me. "But you're not going to kick back and shut up, are you?"

"What do you think?"

Chapter 15

My Breakfast with Saint Boris

I went to the spa while Cruz was with Revez the next morning. While in the hot tub, I spent some time on the phone with Dave, who told me that Rose had shown no further signs of emerging from her coma. The swelling in her brain was down, though, and the doctor had cut back on her dosage of the anti-inflammatory. One of those bad news/good news scenarios.

Anyone watching or listening would have thought I was conversing with a friend about his clever new puppy dog, and I only had to pop my head underwater a couple of times to camouflage my tears.

After that, I sat and contemplated last night's head-butting match with Cruz. I was genuinely warmed by what seemed to me to be personal concern. Warmed and a little worried. I'd asked Rose half-jokingly if Greg Sheffield was sweet on her. Now I wondered if there was such a thing as an Undercover Agent Syndrome, like the old doctor-patient thing. In this case, two people thrown together into a dangerous situation, having to work closely in tandem, depending on each other, being responsible for each other's lives. The last thing in the world I needed was to get caught up in another relationship that might result in one or both parties requiring therapy. I had learned the hard way how foundational trust is to every human relationship and how devastating it can be when that trust is broken.

It's not as if I didn't know true love was a Thing. I had my mom and dad and Rose and Dave and other friends who'd been blessed with constant partners. And it's not that I didn't know that there were people I really could trust with my life, but I wasn't yet sure that Cruz Veras was one of them. It was possible that before this gig was done, that would become an issue.

And what about all that primate posturing I'd witnessed last night? I'd assumed it was all for show—for Felipe Revez's benefit—but now I had to wonder.

Oh, come off it, Gina, I told myself. *He's playacting, just like you are. You're not a jet-set floozy and he's not a testosterone-driven paramour. He's just nervous about taking an espionage newbie into what might become a combat zone.*

It sounded so reasonable, I bought it. All I needed to do, I decided, to soothe Cruz Sacramento Veras was to remind him that I was police academy–trained with several years on the force, took target practice twice a week, and really did have a black belt in kung fu.

In fact, that's exactly what I told him when he walked into the suite later that morning. "I have a black belt in kung fu."

He stopped just inside the door and stared at me. "Excuse me?"

"I'm just reminding you—I have an actual black belt in a real martial art. I've even won tournaments. And I've actually had to use kung fu to defend myself. I'm a crack shot with my little Magnum. I was a cop with the SFPD and mentored by one of the best detectives on the force. I take regular target practice. You don't have to worry about me turning into Princess Buttercup on you in the middle of the Fire Swamp."

He regarded me a moment more with a variety of expressions playing havoc with his face. Then he shook his head, grimaced, and raised his hand to show me his cell phone. "I'm glad to hear it. I just got off the phone with

Ellen Robb. She wants us to get the location. And as much incriminating evidence as we can."

"Ellen? I thought you were going to call Greg."

"Apparently Greg and Ellen are in sharp disagreement about how we should handle this. He wanted you out of the picture. He ran a scenario by Ellen yesterday in which Geoffrey Catalano shows up in person to view the site."

"She obviously turned him down."

"For the time being. That's a contingency plan if Revez doesn't agree to take us to the site. For now, Greg is still in charge of backup—if we need it—and reconnaissance once we know where the site is."

I moved over to the sofa and sat down on one arm. "Did you discuss this with Revez this morning during your 'consultation?'"

"Briefly. He asked me if you'd spoken to Geoffrey this morning. I said you were planning on it but hadn't when I left. He asked if I would recommend to my boss that he invest in the Bonampak B venture and I hinted that Geoffrey Catalano is not a man to buy something—pardon the pun—sight unseen. He suggested we email your fiancé a photo of the Shield Jaguar mask. I said I would suggest it to you."

I nodded. "But of course that won't be enough."

"Not nearly."

I stood. "Okay. I guess I'm up next. How's my makeup this morning?"

He moved in to give a closer inspection. "Not bad, actually, but I think we need to make your eyes pop a bit more."

"Make my eyes what?" I asked, following him into the bedroom.

Cruz had told Revez that I planned to take a morning swim, so that's exactly what I did. I had just hopped out of the deliciously warm water and deposited myself on the sun deck next to the spa when a shadow fell over me. I looked up, shading my eyes.

"Tell me, Marianna Esposito, are you a sea goddess?" Revez was gazing at me with an intensity that even his dark glasses didn't soften.

I laughed. "Pardon?"

"You step from the sea covered with jewels. Certainly, only a goddess of the sea dresses in this fashion."

Hoo-boy.

I glanced down the length of my body. Salt water dew sparkled all over me like a diamanté bodysuit.

"My, it is a bit ostentatious, isn't it?" I reached for my towel.

He stopped me. "Please, don't. You are stunning. I wish a moment more to drink you in."

I pulled my shades down my nose and looked at him over the rims. "Now you're flattering me. Please, Felipe. Let's not do that dance. It's Geoff's attention you want, not mine."

Sobering, he removed his sunglasses and lowered himself to the chaise next to mine. His eyes were arresting without the dark lenses to filter them. They held mine fast.

"I will admit to you that I want very badly to mount a proper excavation of this new site. And I will admit that the idea of your fiancé underwriting it is appealing. But if you recall, Marianna, I sought your attention before Mr. Catalano's possible interest in my humble affairs was even mentioned."

I shrugged. "I assumed you were simply being hospitable."

He smiled wryly. "Hospitable? To have sexual fantasies about a female guest in my home? A woman who is engaged to be married to a man I hope to do business with? . . . A woman who is traveling with her lover?"

Now, he was fishing. "How Old World of you," I said, neither confirming nor denying my relationship with Cruz.

He reached out and appropriated my hand. The one with the giant, fake diamond on it. He fingered the cubic zirconium while I prayed he wasn't a hobby gemologist.

"Marianna, I will not hide behind convention and pretend that I am not attracted to you. I would find you attractive had you come here already married and with your husband. I envy your fiancé, Marianna—and not entirely because of his impressive financial portfolio. But I envy your bodyguard more, for he, unlike your fiancé, is with you day and night."

I took off my sunglasses just to give my free hand something to do and searched my mind for a snappy comeback. I had bubkes. What the hell would Marianna Esposito say to that line?

I put on a Mona Lisa smile and said, "He's not with me every minute, you know. Like right now, for example."

Revez looked up at me through his lashes. "Is he a jealous man?"

"I honestly don't know. I suppose he can't be and work for the man I'm going to marry." I flashed him a brilliant smile.

He shifted uncomfortably on his chaise. "Have you had breakfast?"

"No, actually. I like to get in a swim first."

"Will you have breakfast with me?" He raised his eyes in the general direction of the penthouse with its rooftop patio.

My insides squirmed at the thought of being that alone with Felipe Revez. I calmed myself. Cruz would know where I was. He understood the situation. He'd be sure to interrupt any private one-on-ones. He might even turn out to be a *very* jealous man.

I kept my smile in place. "Of course."

He rose.

I rose.

He kissed my hand.

I laughed. I moved to pick up my gauzy wrap.

He got there first and helped me into it like a proper gentleman.

I thanked him over my shoulder.

He kissed the shoulder, lingeringly. *Not* like a proper gentleman.

Gooseflesh popped out across my back and down my arms. I stepped away from him and turned. "I'll just go up and change—"

"You are lovely as you are. I would like having breakfast with a goddess."

"Yes, well . . . your goddess has salt in her hair and goosebumps all over. I promise, I won't be long."

"You can shower in my suite."

"My clothes—"

"I'll have something for you to wear . . . if you insist you need it."

I blushed. Loudly. "Really, Felipe . . ."

He laughed at me. "You're blushing! How delightful! And you tried to make me believe you had no shame."

I raised my head and looked deeply, sincerely into his eyes. "Look, Felipe. You're a very attractive man. *Very* attractive. But, I have to be honest with you—and not just because we may be doing business together. Cruz and I . . . well, it took me a long time to let him in. Trusting people—trusting men—doesn't come easily to me. And you're right—I was trying to make you believe something about me that's only partly true. I'm not saying I'm straitlaced or anything like that. But when I got engaged to Geoffrey Catalano, I was prepared to be his and only his. I figured he'd reciprocate. But I pretty quickly found out that's not the way he operates. He's not a monogamous man. So, I adjusted my expectations of him . . . and of myself."

It had the sound of a great, cosmic, inner truth, which I thought—hell, he'll be flattered that I confided in him, right? But the implicit message was: *I'm available . . . maybe.*

"Then why marry him, *amor*? Why not marry Cruz? Or is, perhaps, your lover also not a monogamous man?"

"Perhaps he is. Perhaps not. But were I to try to find out, I don't know what Geoff would . . ." I pulled my hands from his and laughed, tossing my head and grabbing up my beach bag. "I'm so sorry, Felipe. Listen to me! So melodramatic! I'm engaged to a handsome, powerful, wealthy man. I should be happy, right? Now, let's have that breakfast and talk about exciting things. Like buried treasure and ancient kings."

He acquiesced and offered me his arm. I reinstated my sunglasses, took his arm, and allowed him to escort me back into the hotel. Behind my shades, I was glancing feverishly around for Cruz. Just as we entered the building I saw him seated at a table on the patio outside the restaurant's coffee bar. How long he'd been watching, I had no way of knowing. I pulled off my sunglasses at the threshold and paused to pop them into my beach bag, taking the opportunity to give Cruz a long, and I hoped eloquent, look.

He tilted his head downward, then looked the other way.

Felipe Revez was as good as his word. Once in his suite, he pulled an ankle-length sundress made of pale sea-foam green gauze from a guest bedroom closet and escorted me to a bathroom that was bigger than my living room and kitchen put together. Hell, the *shower* was as big as my kitchen, and the tub . . . I have no words.

I must have looked at it longingly, because he said, "I have some business to conduct by phone. Don't hurry yourself on my account. Breakfast will be waiting when you come out."

I decided against a bath and showered—if you can call it a shower with that many heads and coming from that many directions. I felt like a sheep getting a tick bath. I didn't hurry. I used the opportunity to comb through the spa-side conversation.

Revez had dropped an interesting remark into all that codswallop about how lucky my guys were: he'd said something about my fiancé's "impressive portfolio." I suspected that was his way of letting me know he'd done some checking up on Mr. Geoffrey Catalano and liked what he'd found.

Once dry and in the gauzy number, which I noticed wasn't quite opaque, I dragged out my emergency makeup kit and tried to hide Gina under as much Marianna as I could squeeze out of the powder foundation, blush, lip gloss, and cream eye shadow I'd included. Then I reached into the bottom of the bag for my hairbrush. It came up tangled in the chain of my Saint Boris medallion.

I stared at the probably useless metal disk for a moment, then slipped it on over my head. The neckline of the dress was low-cut and Boris lay in the valley between my breasts, offering minimal cover, and little more comfort. I lifted the pendant to my lips automatically, packed away my gear, and emerged into the hallway.

Felipe was sitting on the patio when I came out into the cavernous living room. I dropped my bag on the sofa and went out to join him in the warm Yucatán sunshine. Breakfast was indeed waiting. Fluffy eggs, fruit, breads, thin slices of rare roast beef.

He saw me, smiled, rose, and pulled out a chair. "I was right to choose that color for you," he told me. "It is perfection."

I fingered the skirt as I sat. "So who was she?" I asked.

"Who?"

"The woman you bought this for?"

His smile deepened—bright white in his bronzed face. "Why, Marianna, I bought it for you. This morning, very early, I sent Edgardo's wife, Dolores, to find certain articles of clothing that might fit you. It sounds brash, I'm sure, but it was my intention to invite you here privately when I had known you not quite five minutes."

Wow. Talk about wild assumptions.

I didn't try to hide my blushes this time. "Felipe, I . . ."

"No. I am not expectant that this means you are 'mine.' As your Cruz says, you are your own woman. I merely wished to please you."

"It's beautiful," I said, and it was—soft and cool and beautifully embroidered about the bodice. It wasn't the sort of thing I'd ever buy for myself, but might have daydreamed about buying.

Edgardo came and served us fresh coffee, then whisked himself away to wherever it is that servants go when they are not "on stage." I had a vague image of a room somewhere in the great penthouse where off duty servants stood like department store mannequins, silent and still until called forth by their master. It was an eerie thought and it made me shiver.

"Are you cold?"

"No, just thinking." I didn't elaborate. Let him think I was contemplating the jealousy of my betrothed, or some other danger. Let him think I was mysterious.

I smiled and looked at him brightly. "Now, then. We were going to talk about buried treasure."

I don't think he heard me. He was staring at my breasts. Now, my breasts are neither dainty nor prodigious. They are, in fact, thoroughly average. Okay, maybe a bit below average in the size department, but they fit my frame. They are not, by any stretch of the imagination, exceptional enough to make men sit up and take notice.

"What is that?" he asked.

I looked down into the upside-down sterling silver face of Saint Boris. "Oh, that! That's Saint Boris. Geoffrey gave it to me."

"A Catholic saint? I am not familiar with him."

"Well, there are so many." I didn't mention his Russian Orthodox connection. "I was born on his feast day."

"And you carry it with you . . ."

"Everywhere I go. Geoff likes me to wear it."

"And you wear it now, because . . . ?"

"Because he's not here. And I intend to be acting on his behalf." I hesitated, threw him a sideways glance, and added, "It will help me keep my head on straight."

"Ah. And do you need to 'keep your head on straight,' as you put it?"

I lowered my eyes. "I think I should."

We ate in silence for a bit, then I said, "I spoke to Geoffrey this morning, by the way."

"Yes?"

"I told him all about Ek Balam and the Bedstead from Hell. I also mentioned the mask and what we talked about last night."

"Did you?" His voice tried to hide the extent of his interest, but his body gave it away. His nostrils flared slightly, his eyes narrowed, his shoulders shifted. "You mean the excavation?"

I laughed merrily. "Felipe, please! I know how much you want that dig expanded. I'm with you. Really. I think it would be glorious. But I have to convince Geoff. And he's a tough man to convince. Cruz passed along your suggestion about emailing him a photo of the mask, but that's not going to be enough. Not for Geoff."

"And what would be enough for Geoff?"

"'Rumors of treasure are a dime a dozen'," I said, with the air of one quoting. "'I need more than rumors.'" I tilted my head to one side. "That's Geoffrey for you. Mr. Show-Me-the-Money."

"He wants to see the site."

"No, he wants *me* to see it. Okay, maybe he really wants Cruz to see it. He wants to know it's the 'real deal', as he put it."

"And he'll be content with that—if you see the site? See that the treasure is real . . ."

"That's what he said. If it passes our inspection, he'll spring for digging it up and protecting it from . . . whatever it needs protecting from."

"If I may be so indelicate, how much money—"

"Twenty-five million."

Revez, to his credit, merely smiled. Lesser men might have high-fived me or done a Snoopy dance, but Felipe was a cool guy. He raised his coffee cup to mine and we toasted.

I said, "You may want to assure yourself that he's good for that much money."

He smiled. "I have already done so. Your fiancé has an impressive presence in the world of high-tech, which is apparently matched by his presence in the art world."

Thanks to the NPS cyber team. "Yes. In fact, he's let part of his collection of Egyptian bronzes to the Royal Ontario Museum in Canada."

"I saw that on the Internet," he told me. "A generous man, your Mr. Catalano."

Good, we'd gotten the background check out of the way. "So," I said, "when can we go?"

"This may be more than a day trip, you know. It may be necessary to spend the night."

"Believe it or not, I've been known to sleep on something besides satin sheets."

He smiled. "I can arrange for a trip tomorrow."

I nodded. "Trains, planes, or automobiles?"

"A little of everything, Mari—may I call you Mari?"

He was asking if he was yet on a par with Cruz. I smiled at him. "Please just call me Marianna. I've always liked my name. It's so . . . Old World. Everybody else seems to want to shorten it. Make it less than it is."

"Marianna," he said, lifting his coffee cup again. "After breakfast, I would like to take you out on my sailboat."

Damn, and I'd thought I'd played the Vulnerable Card well enough to stem the tide of testosterone. Apparently not.

"I'd hoped to go to Isla Mujeres today," I said.

"Perfect. I will take you there. You will enjoy my boat. She is called *Alegria*."

"Joy," I translated. "What a lovely name for a boat. I'd love to go."

Well, really, what else was there to say?

We had finished our meal by now, and he came around to pull out my chair. I stood with words about changing for the trip to Isla Mujeres on my lips as Revez bent his head and licked the side of my neck.

I came *this close* to squealing like a ten-year-old.

Revez, typically, took my trembling for the exact opposite of what it was and nipped me lightly on the shoulder.

This time, I couldn't control myself. I ducked out of his grasp, laughing, and sidestepped toward the living room where, as if on cue, my cell phone sang Vivaldi to me from the confines of my beach bag—the opening bars of *Domine Fili Unigenite*.

"Oh!" I said, and dove for it, breathlessly mumbling something about my sister having run away from home and waiting to hear from her, meanwhile thanking Cruz silently for the interruption.

But it wasn't Cruz, it was Dave Delgado.

"Hello? Mar-Marianna?" he said.

The signal was weak. I could barely hear him. "Dave? Dave, is that you?"

"I tried your room, your—uh—your friend said to try your cell."

I covered my right ear. "Dave, what is it?"

"Are you alone?"

"No, but—"

"She *looked* at me, Tink. She *looked* at me!"

"Is she . . . is she coming home?" I asked shakily, aware that Felipe could hear everything I said.

"I don't know. She went under again. But she was here, Tink. She was *here*." He hung up.

Felipe stood in the patio arch, watching my face. "Bad news?"

I looked up at him, suddenly aware that tears were trickling down my face. And I remembered that this man—this suave, handsome, flattering man—might very well be the one who, directly or indirectly, put Rose in the hospital.

For you, maybe, I thought.

I turned off the phone and wiped the tears from my cheeks with the back of my hand. "No, good news, actually. My sister may be coming home. That was her husband. Oh, it was all a big mess. They had a fight, she left—disappeared, really. He was beside himself. But he . . . saw her today. Spoke to her for a bit. I'm hopeful they can work it out."

He came into the room, his expression one of mild bemusement. "You are an unusual woman, Marianna Esposito. All business one moment, all woman the next. A siren, then a child. A pragmatist, then a romantic. Who are you, really?"

My answer—whatever it would have been—was forestalled by my cell phone going off in my hand like a little sonic grenade. This time it was Cruz.

"You okay?"

"Oh, hi. I'm . . . I was just having breakfast with Felipe."

"Only breakfast?"

"Yes. Of course. What did you think?"

"That I'd have to call in the cavalry. Oh, wait a moment—I *am* the cavalry."

"Are you, really?" I made a face at Felipe, who seemed amused.

"Did Dave reach you?"

"As a matter of fact, yes. Did he—"

"He told me the good news. Now what?"

I tossed my head, flipping back my hair, and trying to look—oh, I don't know—carefree, high-spirited, whatever. "Actually, I was thinking of going out to Isla Mujeres. With Felipe. He wants to show me his boat."

"*Christ*, Gina! His boat?"

"Cruz, *darling*! Language."

"*No*," he said, his voice low but emphatic. "You shouldn't—"

"Oh, by the way, the three of us are going to take a little trek tomorrow out to that site we were talking about. Felipe wants to make a day of it, maybe even an overnighter. Sound like fun?"

He was silent for a long moment. "Do you have your gun?"

"No."

"Then try to come back to the suite before you go out on the boat. You can get it then."

"Oh, really? Now how would that look?"

He reeled off several Spanish expletives, then said, "Gina, don't do this. Do you want me to break it up?"

"Cruz! Honestly, I thought you'd be overjoyed. I mean, this whole excavation thing is right up your alley. You're just going to love the trip tomorrow. Promise."

"The boat—what's the name of the boat?"

"Wish me . . . joy." I hung up and turned, laughing, to Felipe. "Surprise! I guess there's a little jealousy in all of us."

"Will there be a problem?"

"No, no problem. After all, it's just a little jaunt to Isla Mujeres, right?"

Chapter 16

La Triguena

It really was just a little jaunt to Isla Mujeres, I told myself. An eight-mile jaunt, to be exact. Nonetheless, I spent a significant portion of the trip lounging in the warm breezes at the *Alegria*'s bow and trying to concoct an excuse for not taking this relationship where Felipe Revez so clearly wanted it to go. I'd already backed myself into a corner that would make any sudden bouts of conscience on good old Geoffrey's account seem pretty lame. Which meant that Cruz and his alleged jealousy were the closest thing to an out that I had.

Alegria was a lovely boat. She had a trim hull, a beautiful and efficient galley, a sumptuous if small living area, and a captain's cabin decorated in sensuous fabrics of deep teals and earth tones. I stayed as far away from that as I could, hence my trip to the bow, where I worked at impersonating a figurehead.

But alas that wore thin, and as we approached the Isla, Felipe called out to me, "Come aft, Marianna!" He patted the seat next to him in the stern, from which he handled the tiller.

Reluctantly, I got up and moved back, the sea breeze playing with my gown and plastering it against my body. I am not Venus on the Half-Shell, believe me, but you'd've thought so the way the guy was looking at me.

It's got to be the tomcat effect, I told myself. One tomcat wants what it thinks the other tomcat has.

I came demurely aft and reached for the tiller. "Let me steer, Felipe, please? I know how. Really I do. My father taught me." All true.

"Did he? And was he a fisherman from a tiny sun-washed village?"

"You're laughing at me. Geoffrey laughs at me when I want to sail his boat. He won't even let me try. He says it's not something a woman can or could or should do."

He moved over and gestured at the tiller. "It's all yours, Marianna."

He let me take the boat all the way to the dock at Isla Mujeres where we debarked and spent the afternoon exploring the colorful clutter of touristy little shops and visiting historical points of interest. I relaxed and let myself believe I really was Marianna Esposito, enjoying a day out with a gentleman friend. Felipe played his part only too well, twice buying me things I admired, and treating me to an elegant lunch.

I thought I glanced Cruz on several occasions, but a repeat glance always came up empty. Either he'd gotten better at tailing people or my imagination was playing tricks.

Over said elegant lunch, in a charming and secluded café in which my "date" acquired a table with a stunning view of the Bahia de Mujeres, I steered the conversation back to tomorrow's trip.

"So, what shall I wear for our little tour tomorrow?" I figured that was the sort of thing that would concern Marianna.

Felipe laughed. "Our 'little tour' will be a day-long excursion into the wilds of Chiapas, my dear. You should wear sturdy shoes and clothe yourself for hiking."

"I hate sturdy shoes," I lied. "So unaesthetic."

"The aesthetic depends entirely upon the woman who wears them. On you, the most unappealing footwear would seem elegant."

Oh, gag.

I wrinkled my nose, then gave my lunch date as piercingly direct a look as I could. "I asked you not to flatter me, Felipe. Despite appearances, I'm not a piece of fluff. Tell me only what you really think of me."

The surprise in his dark eyes was followed by mirth. He tilted his head toward me. "As you wish. I think, Marianna, that you are a puzzle that I would love to solve. Tell me, does your Geoffrey tell you what he really thinks of you? Does Cruz?"

I gazed out across the patio of the restaurant to where the sun sparkled on the far-off waves like sequins on a fairytale ball gown. "Geoffrey . . . flatters everyone he expects something of. Cruz flatters no one. I always know what Cruz thinks of me."

Well there was a patent lie if I ever uttered one. I reached reflexively for Saint Boris and gave him a quick rub of repentance for all the fibbing I was having to do.

"And what does he think of you?"

"That Geoff pays him barely enough to put up with me," I said, then dropped Boris and gave Felipe a bright smile. "So, tell me about this site of yours, Felipe. You said one of your employees found it? How'd he happen to do that?"

He shrugged, no doubt gauging how much to tell me. "He was engaged in surveying Bonampak for an academic team when something caused him to travel a bit further afield."

"Something? How mysterious. What did he see?"

Again the artless shrug. "I have never been quite clear. Something about the sight lines for a minor temple-cum-observatory and the Acropolis. In any event, he followed his instinct and came upon a second site."

"Which he told no one about but you?"

"Why would he? He well understands how much I value loyalty. And I've seen no evidence of anyone else having worked there."

"So you're the only one who's been digging there? What about your associates?"

"My associates?"

"The people you mentioned last night at dinner. The people you're involved with. Do they know where the site is?"

"My chief expert does, of course. He has had to assess the find. He is also completely loyal to me."

"And your investors, do they know?"

"Does it matter?"

"It may matter to Geoffrey. I've told you: he's a man who likes . . . monopolies."

His eyes met mine with sly complicity. "Except where you are concerned?"

That was a quick change of topic. Was he flirting or being evasive about the dig?

I smiled. "He believes he has a monopoly there too."

"What would he do, do you think, if he found out that were not so?"

Okay. Where was this headed?

I gave him an honestly puzzled look. "You mean Cruz? Why would he find out about Cruz?"

"He may discover you share a room . . ."

"We share a suite of rooms. And Geoff arranged for that himself. He has this wild notion that someone is likely to kidnap me for ransom or something. He's a very paranoid man. It comforts him to think that my bodyguard is so close at hand."

"Is he blind?"

Oh, what the hell. "He believes Cruz is gay."

Felipe stared at me, stunned, then threw back his head and laughed loudly enough to draw the attention of other diners. I joined him.

"Truly?"

I nodded. "Of course, he's not."

"That much is obvious from the way he watches you."

My throat felt suddenly tight. Did Cruz watch me in a particular way? Did it matter to me that Cruz watched me in a particular way? I recalled the intensity of his gaze when he'd first brought up the idea of leaving me behind on dig visitation day, and tried to tell myself it was just that he didn't want me to get taken out on his watch.

I lowered my eyes, feeling suddenly transparent. I made an effort to get the conversation back on track. "Geoff doesn't notice things like that. But he would notice if this site has been . . . worked, as you put it. If, say, your associates were also actively removing artifacts. How much has been taken out?"

"Very little so far. It is remote but close enough to the main site that it would be difficult to exploit openly without drawing attention. We have timed our activities to coincide with quiet times at Bonampak and confined our digging to areas deep within the temple. If the site should be discovered by others, it will at least be some time before they realize it has been looted."

Looted. There's honesty for you.

"So, if this place is that remote, how are we going to get there? We're not going to have to backpack in or ride all day in a jeep?"

"You'll be comfortable, I promise. A jet will take us to Palenque. From there . . . a surprise."

Oh, good. I just love surprises. "Not backpacking," I said darkly.

He took my hand, raised it to his lips and smiled. "Not backpacking."

Have I mentioned how much I hate when he does that?

"Well that's a relief. I don't mind being a little hot, but I intensely dislike being hot and dirty at the same time."

"Ah, perhaps you will not like going down into the tunnels, then. There, you cannot escape the dirt."

"But you can escape the heat," I said. "I don't mind a few dank tunnels if that's what it takes for me to see this fabulous treasure of yours."

"You could stay aboveground, while—"

I took back my hand. "While you and Cruz do all the exploring? I don't think so. I'll see it all firsthand, thanks."

He cocked his head as if assessing me yet again. "You are very competitive, aren't you? Perhaps that is the friction I sense between you and Cruz, yes?"

Well, damn. Maybe truth *is* stranger than fiction.

"Maybe it is."

After lunch we wandered the pier, stopping for flavored ices, then visited the local cemetery—a real tourist hot spot.

"So you have your own jet, do you?" I asked as we wandered among the antique stones. It seemed less a cemetery than a garden planted with dead people who sprouted evocative statuary. "I'm impressed."

"Sorry, no. A charter, only. But the surprise conveyance is mine."

I looked up at him aslant. "A surprise you keep in Palenque? That's hundreds of miles away. Across rugged terrain. Where will we land?"

"Believe it or not there's a small airport there. With a runway close to five thousand feet long."

I stopped walking and looked at him, my eyes wide. "There won't be a lot of turbulence will there? I hate turbulence."

"As much as you hate sturdy shoes?" he teased.

"More."

"There will not be much turbulence, I assure you. But . . ."

"But?" I repeated with manifest dread.

"Have you ever flown in a helicopter?"

"Once," I said truthfully. "One of those sightseeing tours of the Grand Canyon. I prefer hot-air balloons."

"Alas, I have none. But perhaps, if you were to promise to visit again, I would look into acquiring one."

I said I'd think about it.

The sun was dipping toward the horizon when Felipe turned us back toward the docks and the *Alegria*. That slender eight miles between island and mainland, I knew, was going to be the most dangerous part of the journey.

Isla Mujeres means "Island of the Women," and is so called (my host had explained to me) because of the images of Ixchel found there by explorers. Ixchel was, disappointingly, the Mayan goddess of fertility and the moon. I'd've been happier if she were the goddess of something less romantic—like death and dismemberment maybe.

Oh, then there were the pirates who purportedly left their women on the island while they sailed around having a rare old time. Felipe regaled me with legends of Henry Morgan and Jean Lafitte and buried treasure. Then came the tales of Fermin Mundaca, after whom Felipe clearly styled himself. This was a man who made his fortune selling Mayan slaves and pirating about, and who named his hacienda *Vista Alegre*.

Sound familiar?

Mundaca had a lady love, Felipe told me as we wandered back down to the docks. Her name was Martiniana Pantoja and she was the most beautiful of five beautiful sisters. This stunning brunette was called *La Triguena*—The Brunette.

Pretty snappy with nicknames, these old Spaniards.

"But a woman like that, well . . ." Felipe shrugged and lifted me aboard the *Alegria*, his hands lingering at my waist. "Poor Mundaca wasn't the only man to fall in love with her."

Oh, goodie. An allegory.

"He was so in love with her that he dedicated the arches of his hacienda's gates to her, naming them 'The Entrance of the Brunette' and 'The Pass of the Brunette,' in the vain hope that his wealth and power would win her heart."

"The vain hope?" I asked, extricating myself from what had become an embrace.

I hastened to the stern and slipped under the tiller.

He sent a teasing look after me and went on. "Ah, yes, for you see, he was older than she by some years. She married a man closer to her own age. Legend has it that Fermin Mundaca slowly went mad with loss and grief, and died alone and broken, in Merida. We walked by his empty tomb in the Isla Mujeres cemetery."

"The one with the Jolly Roger carved on it," I recalled.

"Yes. He carved the skull and crossbones with his own hands, they say, in memory of his glory days as a pirate."

"Yo-ho," I said. "The pirate's life for me."

He put his hand over his heart and pretended to collapse at the helm. "You mock my pain, *La Triguena*. For you will marry a younger man and you are the lover of a younger man, while I . . ." He let out a great sigh.

I laughed, and when he reached for me, I leapt up and said, "Oh, look! The moon."

It had risen before the sunset, a great silver ghost at the horizon, looking almost translucent in the aqua sky. I danced a couple of steps away and raised my hands so that the moon was suspended between them like a luminous ball. I looked back over my shoulder at Felipe as he steered us out onto the waters of the Bahia de Mujeres.

"What was the name of that goddess again?" I asked.

"Ixchel," he said, and shook his head.

"What?"

He opened his mouth as if to speak, then shook his head again and turned his attention to steering the boat.

I stood with my hands on the roof of the cabin, looking over the bow as we navigated the smooth waters near the island. I hoped I presented a romantic picture for him to enjoy, but knew I couldn't hold the pose forever.

Sure enough, when we got out into the open waters of the bay, the breeze picked up, the waves got choppy, and the boat began to bob like a bath toy. It was hard to keep my feet. I was contemplating climbing forward again and playing at being a figurehead when Felipe slipped up behind me and wrapped his arms around my waist.

I jumped almost out of my skin. "Felipe!" came out in a yip. "Who's driving the boat?"

"You sail a boat, Marianna. You don't drive it."

He murmured that into my ear, his hands moving over the suddenly very thin gauze that covered my torso. His lips were on my neck again, then on my shoulder, caressing.

"Ixchel," he whispered.

Great, Gina. Now what?

Unless Cruz was in one of those far-off motor launches with a harpoon, or skulking under the *Alegria* in scuba gear, I was on my own out here. Alone on a boat in a flimsy piece of gauze with an amorous pirate who enjoyed pretending that I was a Mayan fertility goddess. Under the circumstances (that I needed to keep this man on friendly terms with me) I couldn't even threaten him with my black belt.

"Don't tell me you have autopilot?"

"We're anchored, *amor.*"

Some detective I was. With all the chop and wind, I hadn't detected that we'd stopped moving.

"Come below with me," he murmured.

"Oh, but Felipe—the sunset and the moon—if we go below, we won't be able to see them any more."

He chuckled. I could feel the trembling of his diaphragm against my back. Among other things.

"Yes, but if we make love up here, everyone will see us."

"Oh, but imagine it—the setting sun, the rising moon."

His breath was hot on my ear and I could tell he was imagining it quite vividly.

"If that's what you wish . . ."

He let go of me to take off his light jacket and I leapt to the gunwale, laughing. I had one out and one out alone and I took it. I lifted my skirts, executed a pirouette, and fell overboard.

When we returned to the docks below Revez's hotel, I was wrapped in his jacket—which was thoroughly soaked—and my teeth were chattering like castanets, more from adrenaline-laced relief than cold. The romantic mood had fled, and along with it any resemblance I might have had to either the goddess Ixchel or La Triguena.

And miracle of miracles, as I set foot on the dock, there was Cruz, looking appropriately vexed. He squared off in a delicately prickly pas de deux with Revez, executing his part flawlessly.

"The trip is off," he stormed convincingly toward the end of the set-to. "Geoffrey will—"

"Geoffrey will get his wedding present," I snapped between castanet clicks. "He wants us to see this site and we're going to see the site." I turned to Revez. "I'm sorry, Felipe. I really am. But now you know. I can't dance."

He looked at me enigmatically, then took my damp hand and kissed it. "Dancing," he said, "is overrated. I will see you—both—in the morning?"

"You'll see us *both*," I repeated, glaring at Cruz.

He favored Revez with a stiff nod and brusquely steered me into the hotel, up to our suite, and into the living room. We stood there in complete silence for a good five count, just staring at each other, then simultaneously burst into laughter.

I contacted Greg as soon as my teeth stopped chattering and told him everything I'd gleaned about Revez's plans for the next day: the chartered jet, the helicopter I suspected he kept at Palenque. On the actual location of the new site I was lamentably sketchy. Felipe had been talkative, but vague. It would take an archaeologist or maybe even a cartographer to decipher what it was about the sight lines at Bonampak that would lead an experienced digger to suspect a satellite site lay beyond what had already been mapped and surveyed.

Greg decided his team would work out of Palenque, where they would contrive to look like a documentary film crew. The plan called for Cruz to record as much information as possible via the high-tech gizmos he'd packed among his shaving gear, and hand it all over to Greg when we returned to reconnect with the charter jet. Greg expected Rodney to have a flight plan for it by the next morning, and possibly even get the info on Revez's copter—good to have, in the event that he decided to use it to disappear at some point.

"It's too bad," Greg told me, "you couldn't have found out where he planned to land the helicopter. I guess Rod will have to check for a flight plan."

"Won't that arouse suspicion?"

"Possibly, but I think he can use his documentarian persona to wangle some information."

"Why? We'll have the GPS unit."

"And if something happens to it or you're forced to leave it behind for some reason?"

"Yeah. I see your point: trust in technology but tie your camel."

"What?"

"Nothing. Sorry, I couldn't get the landing coordinates, Greg, but Revez is being understandably cagey and longitude and latitude just don't make real good pillow talk."

"Excuse me?"

"Never mind. Long story."

There was a moment of hesitant silence on the other end of the line. Then Greg said, "Look, Gina, I'm not real happy about sending you out there. Neither is Cruz."

"Yeah, well, it looks like I'm going regardless."

"You don't have to. I'd understand—shit, I think any of us would understand—if you wanted to opt out. If you told Ellen—"

"I'm not a quitter, Greg. I'm going through with this. I've reminded Cruz, and I'll remind you: I'm a trained detective. I won't let you guys down."

Greg made an exasperated noise. "Gina, for the love of God! That's *not* what this is about. I'm not afraid you won't perform well. I'm afraid you'll end up in harm's way. Cruz is right—when there are large amounts of money involved, people do crazy things."

"I know that, Greg. Trust me, I know that only too well."

"Pillow talk?" Cruz repeated when I hung up my cell phone.

"It's an expression."

"Yes, this I know."

"I was joking. Believe me, I had no intention of getting anywhere near a pillow with Felipe Revez. Why do you think I dove overboard?"

"To save your virginity?"

"Bingo."

He gave me a sideways look and laughed.

Chapter 17

A Day Trip to Bonampak B

The shrill light of dawn found us dressed for a safari and wired for sound. Or at least, Cruz was wired for sound. He was also carrying a powerful GPS transponder unit that pretended to be a PDA.

After hearing my description of what had happened on Felipe's boat, Cruz had decided it wasn't safe for me to wear anything electronic. There was no telling when Revez would decide to get amorous, even with Cruz around.

In fact, I had the distinct impression that stealing nibbles from under the other tomcat's nose was a game Felipe Revez enjoyed. He had, in fact, left a noticeable nibble on my shoulder, possibly in the hope that Cruz would see it. If he had seen it, he neglected to mention it to me.

"By the way, just so we keep our stories straight," I told Cruz as we took the elevator up to Revez's penthouse for breakfast, "Revez thinks good old Geoff arranged for our shared suite and that he hasn't a clue about our affair."

"Ah, so we *are* having an affair."

"I hinted at it."

"And how are we keeping this affair secret from your paranoid fiancé?"

"He thinks you're gay."

His lips twitched. "Oh, indeed. What else should I know about myself?"

"I sort of hinted that I think you don't like me very much but just tolerate me because Geoff pays you so well. And Revez is sure the 'friction' he feels between us is competitiveness. He came up with that all by himself."

"Did he really?" Cruz kept his eyes on the elevator's digital floor readout. "Is that what you think it is?"

"Makes sense."

"If you say so."

The doors slid open with a quiet *shush* and we stepped off onto the terracotta tiles leading to the front doors of the penthouse.

"You don't think that's it?" I asked. "The friction?"

Cruz glanced toward the doors, which were opening. "I think you still don't trust me."

Felipe was now standing in the doorway and I was certain he'd heard Cruz's enigmatic parting shot. That, and the slight frisson between us as we stepped over his threshold was the perfect sauce for Felipe's interest in Marianna. If that was not glee in his eyes, I don't know what it was.

Breakfast was unenlightening. Felipe quickly got back on a more amiable footing with Cruz, trotting out some artifacts for his professional opinion. They had come from Bonampak B, of course, and they were stunning.

"I hope," Cruz said, fingering the gleaming lip of a horn-shaped drinking cup, "you are leaving something for my employer to discover."

"Trust me, Cruz. This is nothing compared to the wealth that is still there. It is a storehouse, my friend. Not a static cache created for a king's death, but a living treasure trove he surely must have added to in life."

"I thought you said there was a tomb—tunnels," I interjected.

"It was a tomb. At least it was built to be a tomb. But, at some point, it was converted to a treasure house. I am eager to see if Mr. Gutierrez agrees with this assessment."

He wasn't kidding about being eager. We took our coffee on the nifty little jet he'd chartered out of Cancún. Palenque is roughly four hundred miles from Cancún, but this was, not surprisingly, the easy leg of the trip.

There was another man on the jet with us—a stranger. Dressed in a black leather jacket and chinos, he sat in the rear of the cabin and ignored us pretty much to the same extent that Revez ignored him. I took him as a bodyguard and assumed he was armed, as were we. I'd left my Taurus behind, but had tucked a dainty Smith & Wesson .22 that Cruz had lent me into my tiny (and virtually useless) Michael Kors "backpack."

Not that I intended to indulge in any shootouts.

We set down at Palenque Airport at about 10:25 A.M. and were in the air again in Revez's private helicopter less than an hour later. It was a fairly new R44 Raven four-seater. I'd somehow expected a flashy color, knowing Revez's taste in décor, but his copter was a bilious shade somewhere between green and brown.

Its presence also effectively solved the mystery of the extra passenger on the jet. He may have been a bodyguard, but he was most definitely a helicopter pilot. He gave Cruz and me headsets and some brusque instructions on how to use them to communicate over the noise of the rotors, then he powered up and headed southwest.

I don't think Revez said more than two words to the guy, but he and Cruz chatted away in Spanish about everything from archeology to baseball. I half-dozed against Cruz's shoulder, occasionally perking up when they hit on a point of interest.

Revez, it turned out, was somewhat of a baseball aficionado, who knew a great deal about Fidel Castro's abortive attempt to break into the American major leagues. I dozed off contemplating how different history might have been had he become a starter for the Cincinnati Reds instead of a revolutionary.

The two men had seemingly drawn a truce; there was no evidence of yesterday's acrimony. If Revez thought Cruz's amiability was odd, he sure didn't show it. I've noticed that before about guys. They seem to have an unparalleled ability to compartmentalize things like jealousy, loyalty, and whatnot for the sake of mutual goals.

It was midday when we touched down again, this time in the middle of a steaming jungle. I knew we had to be somewhere near Bonampak, but I sure couldn't see it from ground level. I thought we were in the middle of a trackless waste until I saw the camouflage netting strung between the trees to one side of the "landing pad" (which was little more than a cleared spot in the surrounding greenery), and realized this was a regular stop on someone's itinerary. The pilot, who was sitting on the ground in the lee of his copter smoking a cigarette, certainly seemed to be well acquainted with it.

"How far from Bonampak are we?" Cruz asked, looking around.

"About ten miles from the main site. Far enough from the secondary site to need a vehicle." He made a broad gesture at the camouflage wrap and I realized that it was a makeshift garage beneath which hunkered a perfectly hideous Humvee in full military drab.

And that was when he got out the blindfolds.

I kid you not.

We submitted, but I could tell by the way his jaw muscles tightened up that Cruz was less than thrilled with the situation. I have to admit, when confronted with this new wrinkle, it suddenly occurred to me to wonder if there was the slightest chance Revez had made us as being something other than what we pretended to be. Dr. Cruz Veras was not invisible in the Mexican archaeology community, and though Cruz Gutierrez seemed an entirely different person, it was conceivable that Revez might have recognized him. Or that the NPS cyber team had left a chink in our armor, or . . .

I shut the voice o' doom down. The NPS team was professional. They knew their jobs. And I had not imagined that Felipe Revez found me—or rather, Marianna Esposito—very attractive. Would he have reacted that way (and most sincerely, I could tell) if he thought I was a spy?

This train of thought did not completely shield me from prickles of vulnerability or unwanted images of Rose's car diving into the dunes or Ted Bridges's lifeless body stretched out on the floor of his pirate lair. We were in the middle of the jungle where screams would not be heard any better than they would in space. And although Cruz's GPS gizmo was going to get the whole ride down on digital media, that did nothing to help us if we were, say, yanked from the car and shot.

Several truly comforting thoughts intruded on my five seconds of panic at the sight of the blindfolds. First, if Felipe Revez suspected we were not who we pretended to be, he could have no idea what sort of backup we had. For all he knew, there were U.S. government ninjas all around us, ready to pounce at the first sign of betrayal. I fervently hoped that might militate against him deciding to torture the truth out of us, if he was so inclined. Second, there were two of us and one of him, and at least one of us was trained in martial arts. Third, there were Cruz's Glock and my S&W.

So instead of tumbling down the rabbit hole into a state of panic that neither Marianna nor Gina would ever give in to, I spent part of the interminable and damned uncomfortable drive mentally rehearsing my most damaging kung fu moves—the ones my sensei objected to as being "Tiger" moves unworthy of a student of the Hung Gar school. This was, potentially, not the time for niceties or doctrinal purity. I had practiced those moves blindfolded in the dojo. I could do them blindfolded in a jungle just as well, I figured.

Having used part of the interminable drive coming up with different ways to fend off attackers, I spent the rest of the trip trying to make nice with the Hummer's *autovoi*—which is my personal term for its mechanical spirit.

Here's the theory: according to Russian lore each home has a *domovoi*—a house spirit. These guys live behind stoves or in attics and are generally charged with taking care of the homestead and ensuring domestic tranquility. They moan and groan when there's trouble on the horizon, or pull your hair to warn of potential violence. A really top-notch *domovoi* will finish chores left undone by absentminded teenagers, spouses, or roommates. A disgruntled one can severely jink up your household: books leap from shelves; keys and glasses go missing; things get put away in the wrong place; tasks you thought you'd completed come mysteriously to naught, as if someone had just discovered your personal Undo key. To keep this from happening, you're supposed to feed the *domovoi* every night. Mom always does and always has as far back as I can remember. And every night, something ate the food. I'm not sure I want to know what that something actually was.

My theory, such as it is, is that if houses have *domovoi,* then cars must have *autovoi.* And I suppose, if I'm to be consistent and logical in this irrational philosophizing, then Boris the Harley must have some sort of spirit as well. I just haven't figured out what to call it yet. Motovoi? Harleyvoi?

Whatever. As long as it's willing to answer to "Boris" and doesn't mind the occasional anointing with holy water, all is well.

I did this exercise, you understand, to keep my mind busy while I was being bounced all over Chiapas with a safety harness biting into my shoulders, and my knees being whacked against the Humvee's inadequately padded door frame. I turned a deaf inner ear to my reptilian hindbrain, which gibbered that the jig was up and we were going to have to fight our way out of the jungle. At least, I assumed that Cruz was versed in hand-to-hand combat and wouldn't be useless after he'd emptied his magazine.

Right about the time I had made peace with the *Humvoi,* we slowed to a stop. I slowed my breathing as well, the better to listen to the sounds around me. My hands were ready to jab, block, or chop, but I flattered myself that it didn't show. I tried to cover any tension in my face with a mask of Marianna-esque annoyance as I heard car doors open. A moment later, my blindfold was removed and I opened my eyes to see—surprise!—a jungle. And so far nothing else, though all of my senses were on high alert for sudden movement or unexpected sound.

I shot Revez a baleful glance. "You promised there wouldn't be any backpacking."

"A promise I intend to keep. We have arrived at our destination."

He held his hand out to me. I took it, letting him help me out of the Hummer.

"I don't see anything."

Cruz stood at the front of the vehicle with his hands in his pockets, watching Revez like your neighbor's rottweiler watches your cat. There was something almost feral in his dark eyes, as if the jungle and the journey had worn his veneer of civilization thin.

"That's because you are not a trained archaeologist, *corazon*." He pointed to his left at a riotously green hillside. "A pyramid, if I am not mistaken."

"I'm impressed," said Revez, letting his hand linger at the small of my back. "It *is* a pyramid. A temple with a tomb, as it happens. Come." He let go of my hand and led the way toward the mound of greenery.

It really was a pyramid, its lines blurred by overgrowth. As we rounded it, I saw other similar shapes nearby—at least two of them set across what might have once been a small plaza, but which was now a wild tangle of foliage.

On the front of the building, the greenery had a peculiarly lumpy look to it. Revez tugged at a bit of shrubbery and an entire section of the screening bushes and vines rolled aside. They were attached to a framework of chicken wire and PVC pipe borne on what looked like Radio Flyer wagon wheels. Behind the screen was the entrance to the temple.

This was not like the nice, neat, landscaped entrances I'd seen at Ek Balam and in photos of Bonampak. This was messy—a dark hole in the hillside choked with roots and littered with fill and crumbled rock. This was a place whose *domovoi* was on a very long sabbatical.

"We have to go in there?" asked Marianna, wrinkling her nose in distaste.

Crybaby.

Cruz looked down his nose at me and Revez laughed.

"It gets better inside," he promised. "This is here in the event someone else should prove to be as curious as the fellow who found it."

He moved ahead of us into the darkness.

Cruz put his hands on my upper arms and steered me into the black void.

"You don't have to do that," I told him.

"I wouldn't want you to fall and break something," he said, loudly enough for Revez to hear.

Beneath the hill, inside the temple, the damp earth enveloped us in its cool perfume. It's a fragrance I happen to love. I'm neither claustrophobic nor afraid of the dark, and I absolutely adore caves. I find them comforting. The walls of the passage felt like cool, damp silk; the roots we ducked beneath and around were living stalactites.

Alas, Marianna was less sanguine about these things than I.

"Oh, what was that?" she whined as something crunched beneath her soles. "This isn't going to be like one of those horrid adventure movies, is it?"

Light flared. I shoved aside a tangle of roots and stood fully upright in a long, partially cleared corridor illuminated by a battery-powered lamp set atop what looked like an old steamer trunk. The passage seemed to run for yards beneath the ersatz hill, interrupted at intervals by what I assumed were doorways. The chamber in which we stood was some sort of vestibule—wider than the corridor beyond. Its walls were covered with paintings half-obscured by dirt.

Even through the filth I could see that the colors were intact.

I turned to Revez. "You haven't cleared these off?"

"As I mentioned earlier, if anyone finds this place, we don't want them to realize the extent of our presence immediately. In fact, we've planted some items about to suggest the attentions of merely curious locals, or perhaps secretive archaeology students."

"To what purpose?" asked Cruz.

"To buy time. While archaeologists or authorities may poke about out here, trying to determine the extent of our digging—" He gestured down the corridor. "—we can continue to remove artifacts from the heart of the cache."

His smug expression said, *I'm too sneaky for my shirt. Too crafty for my pants. So cunning it hurts.*

He enjoyed our obvious puzzlement for a moment, then moved to place his hand on a slab of rock that had fallen from the ceiling to stand, cockeyed, against the wall to our right.

"Oh, don't tell me," I said. "You've got a secret doorway into the mountain."

He grinned at me and produced what looked like a walkie-talkie from his jacket pocket. "*Abierto sesamó*," he said, and pressed a button on the keypad.

There was a loud, metallic *thunk*, and the top of the slab began to lower toward us accompanied by the clatter of chain through gears. It was like a drawbridge opening. It stopped when it formed about a forty-five degree angle with the wall, revealing the mechanism behind it. It was simple, really: chains, pulleys, and an electronically controlled motor mounted on the ceiling of the passage beyond—a glorified garage door opener. Low-tech, but effective.

Revez took my hand and drew me through the V-shaped aperture. Cruz brought up the rear. The corridor in which we stood had been cleared almost completely—as had the walls. And cleared of more than fill. Entire sections of the colorful friezes that had once lined the passage had been carefully excised, leaving neat bare patches that reminded me of boarded-up windows.

"You have done much here," commented Cruz, laying subtle stress on the word "much." "Clearly you have found a market for these things."

"Clearly."

"Not as lucrative as you would like?"

"I am compelled to share my discoveries with others. And at the pace I can remove objects from the site, there is more demand than supply. Recently, I began to explore . . . alternatives to my current working arrangement."

"Which is?" Cruz asked.

"I hand over what my people find to my investors."

"Your people?"

"Diggers, who are blindfolded for the trek out here, just as you were. My experts, of course, and a handful of men who, shall we say, owe me their lives and their loyalty."

"You're not afraid one of them might divulge the location?" Cruz asked.

"Certainly, my associates—and my investors—have tried to pry the location out of my men, but, as I said, they know where their loyalties must lie. So, my investors pay me a modest retainer and allow me to keep certain items for myself. Over the last year or so, I began to investigate my own channels for releasing antiquities to the lucrative North American market. I acquired an operative—a talented individual with the ability to move between Mexico and the U.S. at will. I was able to place some pieces and gather enough capital to hire another 'agent,' then a third." He hesitated.

"I'm impressed, Felipe," I prompted. "And I have to say, I think even Geoff would be impressed with your . . . entrepreneurship. I take it you want to establish a broader conduit."

"I wish to establish a more direct conduit. One that is far more stable and certain." He glanced from me to Cruz. "Not long ago, I was informed that the newest of my American operatives had been murdered, and his . . . inventory stolen. What the murderers did not get, I assume the authorities did. I have had to cease operations. It is simply not safe to continue."

We both knew who he meant. Did he suspect that we knew? Were his eyes just a bit too sharply trained on Cruz's face? Was he fishing for a reaction? Was I being unduly paranoid?

"Do you have any idea who might have murdered your operative?" asked Cruz. "Surely you don't think it merely coincidence?"

"I fear that a certain associate might have noticed that this person was trafficking artifacts from Bonampak B and took matters into his own hands. The operative, I belatedly realized, was an unwise man and reckless. He rather liked to flout authority."

That could have been a reading of the late Ted Bridges's horoscope.

"You fear," Cruz guessed, "that this associate may connect you to the murdered operative?"

Revez turned from Cruz to me, his eyes over-bright in the glow of his lamp and said, "Marianna, with your fiancé's investment in this enterprise, I can establish direct contact with buyers in the U.S. I will no longer need my associates or, indeed, my other investors. And if Mr. Catalano is willing to finance a major excavation, we can have this place picked clean within a year."

"At which point, you will disappear?" suggested Cruz.

"Only if necessary. If my involvement in this were to become a legal issue."

"Can you hide this place from the authorities for a year with a full-scale excavation going on?" I asked.

"I have already kept it hidden for two. True, I have not brought in heavy machinery. But in a site such as this, bulldozers and backhoes are not what is needed. What is needed is manpower, small machinery, a security system, and a means of lifting larger amounts of artifacts out. Currently, I have not the resources to do a tenth of what is needed." He gestured down the corridor. "Let me show you."

The ancients weren't idiots. They had obviously intended that any vandals or robbers greedy enough to enter would die of starvation or go stark raving straitjacket long before they got to the really juicy stuff. The place was a labyrinth of close, chill passages—some of which were barely wide enough to accommodate a full-sized man. I was lost within seconds of leaving the main hall. We turned this way and that for what seemed like miles, while I tried to imagine what the maze of corridors might look like from above . . . and became increasingly aware of how much earth and stone and jungle was pressing down on us.

If this had been a natural cave, I wouldn't have cared, but the fact that it was manmade and probably held together with nothing but friction and prayers made me jinky, notwithstanding that it had withstood time and jungle vines for uncounted centuries.

I glanced repeatedly at Cruz to see how he was reacting to this. His face was grim, his eyes unreadable. Occasionally he met my gaze; mostly he watched Revez the way I imagine a mongoose watches a cobra.

Revez set the whole thing up like a true showman. At the end of a journey that had me wishing for my good old Girl Scout pocket compass, breadcrumbs, or a ball of bewitched twine, he led us to a doorway that reminded me eerily of the Bedstead from Hell in the tomb at Ek Balam. A huge mouth yawned before us, its long tongue forming a series of shallow steps. Its lips were blood red, its fangs pearly white, its bulging eyes yellow and blue. It looked like a stylized puma.

To the right of the doorway was a frieze that had been left intact. A line of five obviously male figures dominated it, and as seems common with these things, looked as if they were doing the Hokey Pokey.

"That," Revez told me, "depicts the royal succession at Yaxchilán and Bonampak. We left it intact because of the difficulty of removing it without destroying the context."

Cruz moved to stand next to me beneath the frieze. "It begins with a depiction of God K."

"That was his name?" I asked. "God K? What kind of name is that for a god?"

Cruz did not crack a smile. "Actually, his name was Ah Bolom Tzacab and he was, to all intents and purposes, the patron god of the royal house. God of agriculture and lord of rain and thunder."

"He has a leaf in his nose," I observed. "At least, I hope it's a leaf."

Revez laughed and pointed to the figures Hokey-Pokeying to God K's right. "These illustrious fellows are Shield Jaguar I, Bird Jaguar IV, and here is the god-king whose treasure house this is—Shield Jaguar II. His son, Tah-Skull III, is depicted as a child."

That accounted for the size difference between the fourth and fifth figures. "Oh. I thought he was just especially short."

Revez escorted Cruz and I to the jaguar-mouth doorway then and made us walk up the tongue and step through the jaws into a chamber as dark as the inside of a hat. Then he took the lamp and disappeared into the passage behind us. As he slid past me in the dark, he ran his fingers lightly across the nape of my neck.

I shuddered.

"What?" Cruz whispered.

"Nothing," I murmured. I mean, really, a little unwanted touching was better than having him use the cover of hat-blackness to attempt to throttle me.

Cruz shifted toward me and gave my hand a squeeze.

The lights went on. Lots of lights, strung on standards made of PVC pipe and aluminum. The place was silent as a tomb, appropriately enough, so I assumed they ran on batteries. And what they illuminated . . .

I moved down the puma's throat and into its stomach, dimly realizing that I was still holding Cruz's hand. I dropped it and kept moving, my eyes on the walls.

The murals ran down one side of the room and up the other, so vivid they seemed to stand out in 3-D. The figures were life-size and engaged in all sorts of activities from the mundane to the fantastic, from the erotic to the grotesque.

"The life of a king," said Cruz in a hushed voice. "The life of Shield Jaguar II." He pointed to a panel to the right of the doorway. "His birth here."

Hocked up like a hair ball by a dragon? I thought irreverently. This was not something Marianna Esposito would say, so instead I offered, "His mother was quite the Dragon Lady."

"Poetic license. The dragon is the portal to the Underworld, remember. You are born into this world from the Underworld; you return to it when you die."

I had a sudden, vivid image in my mind of Cruz Sacramento Veras not in jeans and khaki jacket, but in the leathery, feathery regalia of a Mayan warrior-king. He looked silly. But then anyone would look silly in that getup.

"And here," he was saying, "he learns to hunt, he plays ball, he ascends to the throne. Here, the bloodletting ceremony when he marries; again, when he fathers a child . . ." He did a slow 180, tracing the story with his finger. "He makes war and conquers, he accepts the submission of the conquered, he offers adoration to the gods, he dies."

"And is gobbled up by the dragon," I noted.

"Incredible." Cruz shook his head. "I've never seen anything like it. The scale . . ."

"Yes, the scale," echoed Revez, stepping down from the back of the puma's tongue to join us in his tummy. "And therein lies the problem. How do you remove all of this?"

I smiled and turned to face him. "With about twenty-five million dollars worth of logistical aid. But it's a bit hard to present this as a wedding gift." I waved at the murals.

Revez took my hand again and tugged me to the end of the hall. What I had taken as a little painted doorway turned out to be the real deal. When I say "little" I do not exaggerate. This was a portal even a munchkin would find constricting. Nonetheless, Revez got down and worked his way through on his elbows, dragging his legs behind. I was able to do it on hands and knees. I don't know how Cruz navigated it, but he came out covered with dust.

When I was upright once more, I thought I had passed out in the tunnel and was hallucinating. The chamber into which I had emerged was literally a treasure trove, containing a vast accumulation of artifacts stacked with seeming care—metal, stone, wood, ceramic, jeweled and carved, painted and plain. They lay on tiered shelves of stone block. They lined the steps leading up to a sarcophagus which was, itself, brimming with booty. In the lights mounted high in the corners of the room, the gold and gems boggled the eyes and the mind. I'd stepped out of reality onto a movie set.

Cruz leaned over and picked up two artifacts from the steps of the sarcophagus, holding one in each hand and turning them in the light.

"These are from two completely different eras. And this . . ." He nudged a heavy, ornate plate with one foot. ". . . this is not even of the same culture."

Even I could tell that. Like Revez and my fictional fiancé, Shield Jaguar II was apparently a connoisseur of pre-Columbian art.

We did not leave Bonampak B empty-handed. Felipe allowed me to wander the trove to find a suitable wedding present for my fabricated fiancé. My poor, not-used-to-this-kind-of-thing senses overloaded after the first ten artifacts I encountered at close range. I hadn't even seen things like this on museum tours. I was used to antiquities that looked . . . well . . . antique.

These looked as if the craftsman had just spit-polished them and set them on the shelf.

I was afraid Felipe would find my weak-kneed reaction to his largesse suspicious, but he was too busy packing up a king's ransom worth of artifacts of his own and hauling them out to the Humvee to notice my wide-eyed wonder. After herding my wits back into some semblance of order, I chose a two-foot-tall statue of gold and turquoise that reminded me strikingly of the effigies of Krishna that frequent Indian shrines.

"You don't think this might be from India, do you?" I asked Cruz, who was admiring my choice of gift as he prepared to store it in the back of the Hummer.

He gave me a look that would have driven a lesser woman to scarf an entire sixteen-ounce box of Mallomars.

"You have to admit, it really does look like Krishna," I added defensively.

He wagged his head. "Yes, it does. But it is *not* Krishna. It is Bird Jaguar IV, father of Chel-Te-Chan Ma-K'inah."

"That's got a nice rhythm to it. Again in *inglés*?"

"Shield Jaguar II. Chel-Te-Chan Ma-K'inah was his birth name. Shield Jaguar, or Itzamnaaj Balam, was his dynastic name."

"Yeah, well, his daddy looks like Krishna to me. Do you think there might have been some crossover? Trade?"

"Between India and the Yucatán?"

"Don't laugh. What about those big stone heads they found in Veracruz? The ones they thought were Olmec. Some of them look African or Asian."

The expression on his face shifted subtly. "You find these things of interest, do you?"

"Well, sure." I glanced toward the treasure temple from which Revez would soon appear after closing up shop. "'Sis' has always been into archaeology and folklore. Granted, on a different scale than this. Even as a teenager I knew more about potsherds and middens than was probably healthy."

"While as an adult you know more about choke holds and defensive blocks than a young woman should have to."

He sounded . . . rueful.

I gave him a questioning look. "Considering how we'd defend ourselves if this turned out to be a trap set for two nosy agents?"

"Most definitely. But . . ." He checked the temple again. "Revez seems to take us at face value, else . . ."

"Else, he would have shot us while we were blindfolded?"

"Morbid, aren't you? I was thinking, realistically, if he didn't trust us, and if he wasn't desperate for an immense inflow of cash, he wouldn't have brought us out here at all—blindfolds or no."

"Or let me take our little friend here." I nodded at the statue.

His eyes caressed the golden effigy. "We know a good deal about Bird Jaguar IV. After a contested accession, he had a long and apparently fortunate rule at Yaxchilán. Of his son, we know much less. There is some mention of him at Yaxchilán, some at Bonampak, but here . . ." His gaze returned unfocused to the pyramid. "This, perhaps, is where Itzamnaaj Balam is to be found at last."

Revez hove into sight around the corner of the overgrown building. I stretched up on tiptoe, put my lips to Cruz's ear, and whispered, "It belongs in a museum."

Chapter 18

An Inexhaustible
Supply of Tails

The sun was lowering itself toward the horizon when we touched down at the helipad in Palenque. The plan was to fly back to Cancún that evening—Revez was rather leery of having his pilfered haul sitting in the Raven overnight.

"Do we have time for a pit stop?" I asked brightly, as my feet touched terra firma. (There is nothing like being suspended from four way-too-thin rotor blades to make one appreciate the beauty of solid dirt.)

Revez raised an eyebrow at me. "A pit stop?"

I froze for a second, realizing that Gina had somehow poked her nose out from behind her sleek Marianna mask. Over Revez's shoulder, Cruz gave me a warning look. I felt my face flushing.

I laughed. "That's what Geoff always says. It means I need to use the ladies' room."

"If it will help you dispel some of that interminable energy you seem to have, most certainly. I feel old and decrepit just looking at you." He was smiling when he said it and I suspect he knew that even in crumpled, dirty khakis he looked neither old nor decrepit. "It will take some effort to move cargo to the jet, at any rate. I'll arrange for it."

"You intend to let the airport staff handle your crates?" Cruz asked.

"To do otherwise would invite suspicion. It will be treated like normal cargo."

And what, I wondered, constituted "normal" cargo in this neck of the rainforest?

Cruz acquiesced and expressed the need for some refreshment. When he offered to escort me to the restrooms, I smiled, tucked my arm through his, and waved a jaunty "see-ya-later" at Felipe.

The Palenque Visitor's Center was about twenty yards distant. We'd crossed less than half that when Revez shouted at us to wait. We turned to see him walking briskly toward us.

I glanced at Cruz. His jaw looked like it had steel-belted musculature under the smooth bronze skin. Revez's presence could completely jink up our data handoff.

"You're not overseeing the loading?" Cruz asked.

"I have a trusted employee assigned to it," Felipe said and appropriated my free arm.

I waltzed to the visitor's center with a handsome, if dusty, Latino on each arm. An embarrassment of riches that was wasted on someone with my emotional baggage. As we neared the modern-ancient stone-and-wood buildings (imagine Mayan art deco), I spied a couple of familiar faces in the open plaza.

"Oh, look!" I said, pointing with my chin. "It looks like they're filming something over there."

Indeed it did. Near a fountain on the rectangular plaza, a film crew of four (lights, camera, sound, action) was staging candid interviews with anyone who wandered across their path. The director and cameraman I recognized (Greg and Rodney, respectively), the audio and lighting engineers were strangers to me.

We didn't wander across their path so much as we wandered near it. I stopped to watch where we stood a pretty good chance the director would see us when he lined up the shot he was working on—a couple of college girls who looked as if they'd been hiking all day.

"My God," I said loudly, "I'd never get within twenty feet of a camera if I had leaves in my hair."

"Then you'd best not get within twenty feet of that one, *corazon*," Cruz told me. "You're wearing an entire ecosystem."

"I'm not!" I laughed.

The director looked up from checking his lighting and shushed me, a finger to his lips.

I disengaged myself from my escorts and ran my fingers through my hair. "I'm off to make repairs," I told them and headed for the visitor's center.

A glance back over my shoulder informed me that Cruz and Felipe were meandering toward the thatch-roofed open-air cantina, where a swarm of tiny white lights had just winked on against the approach of twilight.

I did a quick but thorough cleanup job, reapplied my makeup, brushed the leaves out of my hair, and dusted off the worst of Bonampak B's grime. I left the ladies' room just in time to see Cruz enter the men's facility across the way. I nodded at him and went to join Felipe at a little table in the plaza.

As I passed the film crew, the director was just thanking his last two guests for their patience and time.

He turned to his crew then and said, "Okay, guys, that's a wrap for today. We're losing the light. Time for dinner anyway." He checked his watch. "Past time. Look, you guys start packing up, I'm going to hit the john."

I slid into the chair next to Felipe and gratefully accepted the drink that awaited me—iced tea with milk, sugar, and a sprig of mint. I pretended not to watch Greg Sheffield, Director of Documentaries, cross the plaza to the men's room and wondered which of my two gentlemen friends had remembered my choice of beverage.

"Is that what you would have ordered?" Felipe asked. His tone told me that Cruz had beaten him to the punch.

"It's perfect, Felipe. Thank you. I'm parched."

He merely inclined his head and sipped his own drink—something dark and heavy with rum. I could smell the warm, coconut-y perfume from where I sat.

Cruz rejoined us a minute or two later to take up his own tall glass of iced tea—no sugar, with a twist of lemon. I, too, can pay attention to such things.

"How long do you expect the transfer to take?" Cruz asked.

"They're most likely done. We can go back any time you like." Felipe looked to me for that determination.

"If you don't mind," I said, leaning back in my chair and combing my hair back from my face with my fingers, "I'd really love to just sit here for a bit and soak up the twilight and the view."

I looked off down the gentle slope from the visitor's center where the Palenque Acropolis thrust its crown above the thick blanket of trees. It was stunning: bathed in artificial light, the mauve and violet and pewter of the twilit sky behind it, the dark, verdant forest huddled up to its flanks.

Felipe and Cruz both followed my gaze there. Cruz's lingered, but Felipe's was quickly drawn away to his watch. He rose suddenly, tossing back the remainder of his drink.

"I'll meet you back at the airport, then," he said. "I have a call I need to make."

He nodded to Cruz, gave my shoulder a swift squeeze and left us.

"He's in a big hurry all of a sudden," I said when he'd gotten out of earshot. "I could almost feel the static electricity. I wonder what's up?"

"If you had a jet full of contraband sitting on a public runway, wouldn't you be in a big hurry?"

"Maybe," I said. "But consider the position he's in. Ted Bridges is murdered and Revez has got to wonder who done it, and if they know about the connection between the two men. I think our Felipe may be scared spitless that the wrong people know where Bridges was getting his trinkets."

"The wrong people do know." He made a gesture that took in the two of us.

"That's not quite what I meant, as I think you know. How'd the data transfer go?"

He patted his pocket. "Damn. I seem to have left my PDA in the men's room." He'd started to rise when a voice arrested him.

"Excuse, me. Is this yours?" Greg Sheffield, decked out in his director's uniform of T-shirt, khaki shorts, baseball cap, and Birkenstocks stood next to our table. The "missing" PDA was in his hand. "You left it in the john."

"Ah, yes. Gracias."

Greg smiled and touched the bill of his cap. "Enjoy Palenque."

He moved to join Rodney at the cantina's long bar and ordered a bottle of *cerveza*. After a brief conversation, the two men rose and disappeared with their beers into the dark beyond the twinkle of lights.

"The transfer seems to have gone just fine," Cruz said, returning the PDA to his pocket.

I glanced in the direction Greg and Rodney had vanished. "Revez is gone, we could—"

"No. Stick to the plan. What would Revez think if he decided to return and found us engaged in conversation with strangers?"

"You're right. What next?"

In answer, Cruz fished the PDA back out and turned it on. "Next, we make a trip to Villahermosa. Details to follow. Greg says we should be out driving tomorrow morning at 10:00 A.M. with my cell phone on."

I nodded. "Cruz, about Ted Bridges—do you think it really was one of Revez's associates who killed him?"

"Revez certainly seems to think so." He sipped his tea, then said, "Aren't you really asking if that's who tried to kill Rose?"

"I guess. But look at the timeline on this. Someone—besides you—was following Rose weeks ago. Before the Blankenship looting trial. First, someone follows her—no, *stalks* her. Someone who wants to be seen. Whoever they are, they want her to back off from something. It seemed reasonable to suppose that it was the Anasazi looting—that someone didn't want her to testify. Intimidation might be expected under the circumstances, but a threat on her life was way out of keeping with the gravity of that case. No one tries to avoid a few years in prison by murdering or kidnapping a federal agent. So, after the cock-up at the headlands, we reasoned that the point of the exercise might be to keep her from leading the Bridges sting."

Cruz nodded. "And, with 20/20 hindsight, to keep her from connecting Bridges to Revez."

"Yes. But they failed to keep her away from Bridges. And when Bridges got cocky and showed her the shard of the vase, they realized he was—what did Revez call him?—reckless, unwise, and possibly in possession of too much knowledge of Revez's operation."

Cruz nodded. "So, he had to die before he could cause any more damage But it was too late. Rose had already made the connection . . . or rather, you did."

"Huh?"

"Ellen said you were the one who found the brochure connecting Bridges to Revez."

I shrugged. "Sheer dumb luck and raging curiosity. The 'hounds' did all the work—the research team," I added, at his quizzical look. "The point is: the connection was made. Rosie saw the vase. She knew what it was. And the next obvious step was for her to go to the source."

Cruz was nodding. "Which could not be allowed." His eyes shifted to mine. "Who knew the extent of her expertise?"

"Oh, anyone she's taken to court."

"Sommers. You think Sommers hired someone to keep her at bay?"

"Or pay her back."

He closed his eyes and shook his head. "God, I hate to think . . . Archaeology should be about knowledge, about finding out who we were, so we understand who we are and who we might become. Not about . . . money, investments, greed."

"Unfortunately, that's part of who we are."

"It's not worth a woman's life. Or even the life of a foolish and greedy man. None of it is worth that. I'd rather see every site in Mexico blown to rubble than have it cause people to do such things."

His eyes were on the blazing summit of the Acropolis as he said it, and I had no doubt he meant every word. I was captured by the moment, by the sheer depth of emotion I read in Cruz's eyes. If I'd met this guy before I'd known Jeremy . . .

For a split second, I felt as if Jeremy were looming over the table. *You're such a naif, little monkey.* He would have said that if he'd seen the way I was looking at Cruz Veras. I shut him out, then shook myself out of the moment.

"So let's assume for the moment that it was Sommers that wanted Rose out of the picture," I said, bringing to mind my six honest serving-men. "Why? So that they could continue to conduct business with . . . ? With who? Bridges? Revez's other operatives? We know they're not in business with Revez directly. That's what he hopes to get by doing business with my fake fiancé. You don't suppose Sommers maybe knows about Bonampak B?"

"They know of its existence if not of its location. Revez is banking on the loyalty—or perhaps the fear—of his employees to keep that secret. There's no way to know how justified his faith is in his own powers of persuasion."

"So here's some more grist for the mill," I said. "Revez has been awfully eager to do business with my 'fiancé.' Obviously, a lot of that is motivated by greed, but he's also made references to a desire to part company with his 'associates' and investors. I wonder if there's more behind that than garden-variety avarice. What if Revez isn't the one calling the shots? Or isn't the kingpin he purports to be? What if someone else is pulling his strings?"

Cruz was nodding. "Someone he'd like to be rid of?"

"I was thinking someone he's afraid of."

"If they're up for murdering a U.S. federal agent, his fears might be justified."

I leaned in closer, meeting Cruz's eyes. "You think someone is trying to kneecap him?"

"Excuse me?"

"Undermine him and his operation. Even ace him out of the picture. Maybe one of his investors or 'associates'—whatever the heck that means—has as much vested interest in obscuring the black market antiquities network as Revez does."

Cruz considered that. "You think we might have more than one actor working toward the same end? What is that aphorism—the right hand knows not what the left hand is doing?"

"Possibly. Which just muddies the hell out of the waters. More than one party may have reason to eliminate anyone who knows too much about the trafficking and is a threat to their operation. Obviously, that includes Revez. On both sides of the situation. He could be prey or predator."

Cruz shook his head. "If Revez arranged for Bridges's murder and Rose's accident, he's a pretty good actor. I think you're right. I think he's afraid, and I think Bridges's murder contributed to that fear."

"How can we get at that?" I asked rhetorically. "How can we get Revez to confide in us—tell us what he's afraid of?"

Cruz grimaced. "He trusts us to net him a source of funding. I doubt that runs to sharing a behind-the-scenes look at his operation. Look how cagey and vague he's been about everything from who his investors are to the nature of his relationship with his associates to the size of his network of loyal employees. Of the two of us, I'd say you have the best chance of getting more specifics."

I made a face and rolled my eyes. "Go, me."

Cruz stood. "We should head over to the airstrip."

I finished my tea and we set out across the darkened parkland toward the airstrip, arm in arm.

"Let's assume we can connect Revez to his associates," I said, "and that we can get even one of them to roll over on Sommers."

Cruz's laugh was mirthless. "You forget: Sommers is not really a dragon after all, but an alligator lizard. One that seems to have an inexhaustible supply of tails to sacrifice."

An inexhaustible supply of tails. In the past, sacrificing a tail had meant someone lost their job or their freedom for a time. If it was now a blood sacrifice, who had raised the stakes? And why?

Chapter 19

Associates

ere's the story." Greg's voice came through the external speaker of Cruz's cell phone, sounding as if he'd been shrunk and imprisoned in the molded plastic casing. "You're flying to meet your fiancé in Villahermosa where he will be on business. If Revez checks with the airline, that's exactly what he'll see—two fares in your names to Villahermosa."

"And my little present for you, darling?" I asked.

Greg didn't laugh, which was testament to how wound up he was about all this. "I really think you need to leave it behind, Gina. Carrying something like that could attract undue attention from the authorities."

I glanced over at Cruz, who sat next to me in the driver's seat of our rented car.

"But that's the whole point of the trip, Greg," he said. "Bringing Geoffrey Catalano proof of Revez's find. If we leave it behind, where can we hide it that Revez won't find it if he thinks to look? Besides, if we're stopped by authorities, I flash my badge."

"*No*, Cruz!" said Greg. "You can't do that. If Revez has someone tailing you or if word got back to him, your lives could be even more endangered, and the whole sting would just fold up and blow away."

"Well, not quite," I said. "We've got the GPS coordinates and physical descriptions of the site. And we've got Revez."

"But not his associates. These are dangerous people, Gina. Look what happened to Ted Bridges . . . and Rose. If we don't string Revez along far enough to get him to make some connections for us . . ."

"What happened to Ted Bridges," said Cruz, "is what's got Revez scared. He's made it clear he would very much like to part company with his so-called associates. I think the subtext is because this has now become a blood sport. Naturally, he'd like to know that his new partners in crime are heavyweight enough to shelter him from reprisal."

"Okay," I said, "so we don't use no stinking badges. In my luggage, won't Bird Jaguar look like a holiday curio?"

"Quite a curio."

"Oh, come on, Cruz! Who'd believe that anyone would try to smuggle an authentic solid gold Mayan artifact out in their carry-on? They're going to take it as a gallery reproduction."

"How can you be sure?" asked Greg.

"With a sales slip."

Cruz turned to look at me. "What?"

"There's a little gallery down on the beachfront that specializes in museum reproductions of stuff like this. All we need is a sales slip from the place to go with Bird Jaguar."

"And how are you going to get a sales slip for an authentic and unknown artifact?"

"Simple. I'll buy something. Preferably something gold with turquoise inlay."

Greg uttered a sound that could have passed for a grunt, or a chuckle, or a chuff of disbelief. "Good thinking, Gina. Really good thinking."

"Thank you!" I said brightly.

"Okay, look. Get it through airport security the best way you can. Once in Villahermosa, we can meet and plan the endgame."

Getting a sales slip was easy. The only hard part was figuring out which cute little reproduction of a "genuine" Mayan artifact would yield the best description. With Cruz's help, I finally settled on a small statuette that was sterling silver with a gold wash and some inlay. None of it was turquoise, but I figured the sales slip wasn't going to be that specific anyway.

I was right. The printed slip said, "God statue w/inlay." I wasn't sure whether "God" was a typo for "Gold" or a description of the figurine. Worked either way. I tucked the sales slip away with my copy of the Visa transaction and considered which of my carry-on bags would make the best transport for my little god-king.

Back at the hotel, there were no messages for me at the concierge and none on our room phone. I told myself that no news was good news and pumped Marianna up for lunch with Felipe.

I was positively glowing when I told him of our "glorious" good fortune. "Geoffrey is going to be in Villahermosa tomorrow morning on business, so Cruz and I are going to join him there and tell him all about the site. I know it's early, but I think I should give him his wedding present, don't you?"

Felipe smiled. "I do indeed. Do you think he will like it?"

"I think it'll be the best present he's ever gotten. The next time you see me, Felipe, I will be holding in my hands a bank draft for twenty-five million dollars and you will be the conservator of the Itzamnaaj Balam Archaeological Trust Fund."

He laughed in obvious pleasure, and it struck me that there are things even a forty-five-year-old businessman can be giddy about.

I put down my coffee cup and pulled my face into more sober lines. "Felipe," I said. "Forgive me for prying, but your associates—what sort of men are they?"

The laughter faded from his eyes. "What sort of men . . . ?"

"Politicians, businessmen, drug-runners, what?"

He twitched slightly and shook his head. "Why do you ask?"

"Because Geoffrey will ask. He's going to want to know what sort of men may be vying with him for the proceeds from this venture."

I studiously avoided looking at Cruz, whose eyes I could feel boring into the side of my head. We had not discussed this line of questioning; it was something that had come to me during a long, mostly sleepless night.

"Politicians, yes. Of a sort. Businessmen too."

"Of a sort?" repeated Cruz.

Revez studied the abstract pattern on his plate, as if weighing his next words. "Have you heard the name Mario Torres?"

I shook my head, but Cruz was nodding.

"He," said Revez, "is one who benefits from the work at the site."

I searched Cruz's face for an indication of whether this was a Good Thing or a Bad Thing, but came up snake eyes. His face was completely opaque—which I suppose should have told me everything I needed to know. He set his coffee cup down with such studied delicacy that it raised hairs on the back of my arms.

"I take it then," he said too carefully, "that his chief interest in the treasure is how many weapons it will buy?"

"His men are well armed," said Felipe. "Some of them have served as guards at the site. To ensure that he receives his just share."

"And how did you fall into bed with Mario Torres?" asked Cruz baldly.

"The man who found the site was my employee. But he was Torres's devotee."

"I see."

"I don't," I said. "What are you two talking about? Who's Mario Torres?"

Cruz pointedly picked up his coffee cup and raised it to his lips, leaving Revez to do the explaining.

"Mario Torres is the very popular leader of a citizens' group—"

"A paramilitary organization," Cruz corrected.

"Yes, a group that came into being during the . . . difficulties in Chiapas some years ago. He wields considerable command in the region, but not much in the way of financial resources. For that he looks to many sources, this enterprise among them."

"Are you telling me," I asked, "that you expect your association with Geoffrey to protect you from a local warlord?" I looked at Cruz. "Geoffrey isn't going to like that."

"Nor will he like that Torres's men know where the site is," Cruz added.

Revez shook his head vehemently. "No. They were brought in blindfolded, just as you were. The only men who know where that site is are completely loyal to me."

"Pardon," said Cruz, "but wasn't it one of your employees who told Torres about the site?"

"No, he did not. He did, however, suggest that Mr. Torres and I might have a mutually beneficial relationship because of his find. He was right, of course. He facilitated that relationship, in fact. Torres's men have no idea where the site is. Nor have they been allowed into the Treasure Room. They helped us clear the outer gallery, that's all. And they stood guard during the early excavations—until Torres was comfortable with the quantity and quality of items he received."

"Which he deals to private buyers," I guessed. "How does he know where to set the price?"

"He doesn't. He is, as you said, a 'warlord.' He sends his trophies to the United States where they are privately auctioned to the highest bidder at prices set by experts at that end." He leaned forward across the table, his eyes sharp, desperate. "With your fiancé's backing, Marianna, we will be able to greatly increase the amount of antiquities we can remove from the site. There is no reason for Mario Torres to know anything has changed. He can still receive his share, divest it as he pleases—"

"He'll know," I said, "when the treasure trove dries up."

Revez shrugged. "And so? He knows it must dry up, as you put it, some day. As it is, I showed you only one of three temples at the site. We have yet to do more than peek into the others. He knows of only the one."

"You hope. What if he suspects he's being cheated?"

"You will be safely in the States, and I will have the means to simply disappear."

"How does he take delivery of his share?" asked Cruz.

"Does it matter?"

"It may. We don't want to accidentally cross his path."

Revez looked from one of us to the other. I knew he was feeling the thin paper of that twenty-five million dollar bank draft slipping from between his fingers.

I gave it a little extra tug. "I don't like this, Felipe. This is beginning to sound dangerous—"

"There is a village called Sival southeast of Bonampak. It has an airstrip that is little more than a clear patch of earth, and a warehouse. When we have been able to dig, I take the helicopter there and leave my cargo in that warehouse."

"How is it he has allowed you to maintain the secrecy of the site?" Cruz asked. "Why has he not sought to exploit it himself?"

"He is not an archaeologist. He's an ideologue. A 'warlord', as Marianna styled him. This world is as alien to him as his is to you."

Cruz twitched as if something unpleasant had just scurried up his spine and I wondered what other worlds he might have lived in before going into the service of the Mexican government.

"Mario Torres," Revez continued, "does not want antiquities for their own sake. He doesn't want to have to maintain a dig, or guard a treasure, or run a business. He wants only to receive the money those things produce so that he can arm his followers."

But that was only part of the puzzle, I mused, when we had left the penthouse. If Revez dug the treasure up and ferried it to Torres, and Sommers sold it to buyers at the other end, who were the matchmakers? Who connected the Mexican warlord to the crooked American auction house?

Chapter 20
Tink Goes Rogue

I t occurred to me to wonder how Felipe Revez had come to recruit Ted Bridges, but that was one question I wasn't sure how to put into Marianna's mouth. That is, I wasn't sure until late that night as I was sitting on the balcony soaking up the light pollution and distant, discordant strains of warring street bands.

I got suddenly to my feet on a rush of adrenaline and slipped back into the suite. Cruz had disappeared into his bedroom and the door was closed. I started to knock on it, but heard his voice carrying on one side of a phone conversation in Spanish.

I hesitated momentarily, then went to the room phone and dialed Revez's private number. I'd decided he wasn't there and started to hang up when I heard his voice come on the line.

"Felipe? This is Marianna. I'm . . . I'm a little concerned about a few things."

"Marianna, I told you, there's no reason for concern—"

"Felipe, can I come up and talk to you about it?"

There was a moment of silence at his end, then he said, "And Cruz?"

"Cruz doesn't know I'm calling. He'd think I was being a coward. I think he's already asleep anyway. I need to talk this out."

"Yes, of course. Come right up."

He was waiting for me at the front doors to usher me in. I had taken great care with my wardrobe. I didn't want to look like I was either baiting him or blocking him, so I chose a pair of full-length gauze pants and a long-sleeved wraparound shirt that tied snugly in back. Front buttoning garments might send the wrong message, I figured.

I was also careful not to overdo my angst. I didn't wring my hands, but I came into the room playing with my engagement ring, which had the advantage of reminding him that I wore it.

He led me into the living room where a pot of coffee had been set out, and poured me a cup before sitting me down in a huge, masculine chair that practically engulfed me. He perched on the edge of the coffee table facing me, our knees nearly touching.

"What can I say to you that will calm your fears?" he asked softly.

"The operative who was killed. Cruz got the feeling you thought your associate had done that. Is that true? Is this Torres capable of . . ."

Shaking his head, he took the coffee cup from my hands, and wrapped them with his own.

"Capable, yes. And Cruz was right—that thought had occurred to me. But the more I thought about it, the less credible the idea seemed for the very same reasons that have kept Torres from involving himself intimately at the site. Mario Torres is focused on his cause and whatever will further it. He is a powerful man in Chiapas, *amor*, but I don't believe he has the resources to strike at someone in the United States. And that is where my operative died—in Phoenix, Arizona, far from Torres's home ground. I feared Torres had done it simply because I could think of no one else who would wish to. And frankly, if Torres was behind the death of this man, I would have expected him to deliver a warning to me at the very least."

"The murder wasn't warning enough?"

"No. It is not like Torres to be even that subtle. Someone else is responsible for that man's death, I think."

I felt as if someone had just pulled the plug on my higher faculties. If not the vicious warlord, then who?

"What about your other associates?"

"There are none of any account," he admitted, wagging his head contritely. "I puffed myself up, you might say. To look bigger. My other associates are local businessmen who like to collect pretty baubles. They know nothing of where those baubles come from and nothing of my connection to Mario Torres."

Truth or soothing lie? Only Felipe Revez knew and I had no way to be certain. "Then what about the people who smuggle Torres's antiquities into the U.S.? Do you suppose they might have killed that man? Maybe they thought he was—I don't know—moving in on their territory."

"That," he said, "is a distinct possibility. But with your Geoffrey involved, we will not have to rely upon small-time smugglers to connect us to the market, will we? And so, we may never run afoul of those people."

"How did you come to recruit this operative? Or any of your operatives?" There, I'd asked the question. I'd tried to set it up, but it still sounded bald, jarring.

His eyes narrowed. "Is that important? He's dead. And I suspect he was killed because he drew attention to himself."

"Whoever introduced you to him knew you two were connected. It seems to me that makes that person dangerous."

To my surprise, he chuckled. "Hardly. That person was a poorly paid and disgruntled museum employee whom I recruited personally at an antiquities show. He is of no importance." He was smiling, and his eyes said, *There, there. You see, I have put all the bogeymen to rest.*

If I were Marianna Esposito and there really were a rich and powerful Geoffrey Catalano in the wings, that would have been so. And my proper response would have been a demonstration of my relief. But I could not disengage from Gina Miyoko, who had just seen her best friend's would-be murderer slip on another mask and fade into the shadows.

Hence, I was staring somewhere over his left shoulder and trying to wrap my mind around this new information when Revez went to his knees in front of my chair and slid his hands up my thighs, bringing our faces close together.

"Now, have I put your mind at rest?"

Not even close.

"I . . . I feel a little better. Yes," I lied.

He smiled into my eyes and moved his hands caressingly to my waist. "Only a little? I must try harder then."

He kissed me, pushing me back into the overwhelming chair and pinning me there. My legs were trapped between him and the chair, so I put my hands on his shoulders and pushed. He didn't seem to notice. The kiss deepened and I pushed harder, digging in with my fingernails. This did not have the intended effect. Instead of discouraging him, it seemed to add fuel to the fire. He made a growling noise deep in his throat and pressed harder, crushing my lips and digging his fingers into my stomach.

My cry of panic and pain sounded like the mew of an outraged kitten, but he released my lips at last and rocked backward. I shot straight up out of the chair like a jack-in-the-box, a move he mistook for enthusiasm. He wrapped his arms around me, burrowing his face into my stomach.

My *bare* stomach. During the clinch, he'd untied the sash of my wrap-around shirt.

Note to self: From now on buy nothing but pullovers.

"Ah, Marianna," he murmured and licked my navel.

That was it. That was absolutely it.

I collected my breath, grabbed the hair on both sides of his head and said, "Felipe, *please!*" It came out in a throaty gasp.

"Yes . . ." he murmured. He caught the waist of my pants and dragged it downward.

I pulled his hair as hard as I could. "NO!"

He rocked back on his heels and looked up at me, seemingly dazed. Which gave me a window of opportunity to disconnect his hands from my pants and do a half-assed backward roll over the arm of the chair. I landed shakily on my feet and quickly put the chair between us.

"Marianna, I don't understand—"

"I can't, Felipe," I mumbled, trying to cover my swollen lips, pull up my pants, and catch the loose edges of my shirt all at the same time. "I just can't."

"Why, *amor*?"

"He'll know."

"Who will know? Geoffrey? Cruz?"

I shook my head. "Both. Either. It—it doesn't matter. If one of them knows, the other will. Either way, this deal will be blown. You don't want that."

He got to his feet, face flushed, eyes bright. "I want *you*, Marianna."

"Not that much. Not twenty-five million dollars worth."

The light faded from his eyes and he sagged back against the coffee table.

"Good night, Felipe," I said, and fled as fast as my strappy little sandals would carry me.

As I went, I tried desperately to rewrap and retie my shirt, but my hands fumbled with the cloth, unable to draw it together. It was only when I was waiting for the elevator that I looked down and realized why. During his amorous foreplay, Felipe had pulled the sash completely out of its tunnel.

I pressed one hand to my swollen lips and the other to my bruised stomach. Tears pressed for release. The capable, police-trained private detective was getting ready to melt down, and I could only pray that the elevator would get here before that happened.

It did. Cruz was in it.

I'd taken one step forward before I realized this and stopped in confusion. We stared at each other—me in complete mortification, he in I have no idea what—then he reached out and yanked me into the car.

Well, I couldn't cry now. Not with him looking at me. So I swallowed and tried to meet his eyes. That's when I caught sight of myself in the mirrored back panel of the elevator. I was already crying. I was just too damn numb to feel the tears sliding down my cheeks.

Cruz started to say something, then pulled me into his arms and held me until the doors opened on the fifth floor.

I don't drink, but the thimbleful of brandy he gave me put some of the sensation back into my face and limbs. He'd sat me down in front of the hearth and started the gas fire since I was shivering as if he'd just fished me out of a snowbank. Then he pulled his own chair up next to mine so that he could watch my face. He was careful, I thought, not to cut off my line of retreat.

"Gina, what happened?" he asked at length. "Can you talk about it?"

I listened hard for accusation in his voice, but heard none.

"I wanted to . . . find out who . . . I wanted to know if he really thought Torres . . ."

He read my face. "Killed Bridges? Maybe tried to kill Rose?"

I nodded.

"And?"

I shook my head. "He didn't think so. He didn't think Torres had that kind of-of reach."

"I wondered about that, myself. And so . . . things got out of hand?"

"I didn't go there to seduce him," I blurted. "I didn't try to—to . . ."

"I know. You just wanted to press for more information."

I met his eyes then and tried not to see my sorry state reflected in them. "How did I blow it, Cruz? What did I do wrong? I didn't dress like a vamp. I didn't come on to him. I didn't even wear perfume, for God's sake."

"But you let him think you were afraid, didn't you?"

"Well . . . yeah. I wanted to make him think I was worried about Torres."

"You gave him a vulnerable moment, Gina. You can't do that with men like Revez."

Was he accusing me or just explaining what had gone wrong with my calculations?

"You think I should have asked him to meet me someplace public."

"Well, that would have been a good start."

"But Cruz, I was afraid he wouldn't level with me if he thought I didn't trust him. That's why I deliberately left you out of it. It was my way of showing him trust."

"That's not quite the way he read it, unfortunately."

"Tell me something I don't know."

He put his hand on my arm. Lightly, like a bird that would fly away at the slightest twitch. I held perfectly still.

"He didn't hurt you?"

"No. Well, except for my lips." I touched them with the tips of my fingers. They were still throbbing. "Grossed me out pretty badly though—he licked my navel."

Oh, night of nights. I seemed to have succeeded in humiliating myself not once, but twice. And with two different men. I watched Cruz silently for a moment as he lay back in his chair, shaking with helpless laughter, then said, "You can stop any time now."

He sat up, shaking his head and making vague, *I'm okay* gestures with his hands. "It's just . . ."

A flash flood of cold fury hit me out of nowhere.

"It's just what, Joe Cool? It's just funny to see the cocky little PI get what she deserved? I suppose you think I should have just screwed him and gotten it over with."

I started to rise. Cruz sobered very quickly and stopped me. This time the hand on my arm was not in the least birdlike. Unless the bird had pumped a lot of iron.

"Stop talking garbage, Gina. I was going to say, 'It's just relief.' When I came out of my room and found you gone, I was pretty sure I knew where you'd gone and why. I was afraid it would get unpleasant. That's why I went up there after you, prepared to play the outraged lover. When I saw you standing in the hallway like that . . ."

I clutched my shirt together over my breasts and sat back in the chair. "I'm sorry. I've still got too much adrenaline surging through my veins. I was scared," I admitted. "I was terrified. The black belt didn't mean a damn thing in that situation. He had me trapped, physically and mentally. The only moves I had open to me were pretty dire and I didn't want to really hurt him. I didn't want to take a chance on screwing the sting."

"Screw the sting," Cruz said.

"Oh, now who's talking garbage?"

He smiled wryly, then looked at me through his lashes. "You didn't, did you?"

"Nope. Felipe is under the impression that I'm hot for his body, but afraid you and/or Geoffrey will find out about our grand passion. We came to the reasonable conclusion that I'm not worth twenty-five mil."

"Really? I would have said you were worth at least twice that much."

"Why, thank you. You got Visa? I don't take American Express."

He stood and drew me to my feet. "You joke, but if it comes back to haunt you later, don't be macho about it, okay? I'm here if you need me."

"I think I'm okay now. Really."

"Except for your lips, of course."

"Yeah, I look like I'm on collagen, don't I?"

He put a hand to my face and brushed my lips with his thumb. "They'll be fine," he said and pushed me toward my room.

"Don't tell me you're a practicing lip doctor, too?" I said over my shoulder.

I think he said, "I don't get enough practice," but I couldn't be sure.

He meant what he said about being there if I needed him. When I left my room later to get a bottle of orange juice from the wet bar, he was asleep on the sofa just outside my door.

Chapter 21

Where On Earth is Itzamnaaj Balam?

The sales slip turned out to be unnecessary. We didn't take a commercial jet to Villahermosa, but instead flew in the charter Beechjet in which Revez had taken us to Palenque. It turned out that one of his "no-account" business associates owned the charter service. For providing the gentleman with the occasional eye-catching antiquity, our host had a jet pretty much at his beck and call.

The flight was uneventful, and I was able to get back a little of the sleep I'd lost the night before. My encounter with Revez didn't inspire nightmares, but I had trouble shaking the feeling of suffocation that had enveloped me when he'd crushed me into the fine leather of that monstrous chair. It was as if the flesh he'd touched was remembering the moment repeatedly, obsessively, whether I was consciously thinking about it or not.

Haunting was a damn good word for it.

"You okay?"

I looked up from the magazine I hadn't been reading and found Cruz looking at me, his expression noncommittal.

"Why?"

"You're not talking."

"I'm *reading*. Honestly, Cruz, I don't talk *all* the time."

"You were not reading. You were staring through the magazine into another dimension."

"I was not—"

He grabbed the magazine and closed it. "What was the article about?"

"What?"

"The article you were allegedly reading. What was it about?"

When in doubt, bunt. "Island getaways."

"A fascinating subject, but no."

He opened the magazine to a piece on New Age medicine. It wasn't even a travel magazine. He tossed it into the seat across the aisle and turned back to me.

"You promised me you wouldn't be macho. That's my job."

"Well, you're not very good at it," I told him. "A truly macho guy would slap me and say, 'Snap out of it.'"

"You didn't sleep well."

"No."

He just looked at me until I capitulated.

"Okay, it's . . . I've never had anything like that happen before. I mean, yeah, I've had guys try to pick me up in bars or at the fitness club. Insistent guys, even. But nothing like that. I don't think he would have raped me or anything. I mean, look how easily he folded when I played the money card. But the feeling of being trapped . . ."

I tried to describe to him the way my skin felt—the way it echoed the event over and over like a scratched CD. It occurred to me, in one of those random flashes of insight, that this was very much like the aftermath of Jeremy. In that case, the echoes were from willing kisses and longed-for touches that had been twisted into little nightmares by a single, horrific, unforgivable act of betrayal. In this case, the haunting event was intense but brief. I had every hope that the aftereffects would be brief as well.

I looked down and realized that Cruz had woven his fingers through mine.

"I'm not sure you want to do that," I said. "My ghosts might jump ship."

He smiled. "The haunted girl?" He gave my captured hand a squeeze, then let go of it. "Maybe you should have your inestimable mother perform an exorcism."

"Don't think she hasn't tried."

He studied me a moment more, then said, "I want to ask you about that ghost, you know. The big one. The bad one."

I shook my head.

"I'm *not* asking. I just want to."

"Speaking of asking," I said, eager to move along to another subject, "I forgot to tell you something about last night. I asked Revez how he'd gotten set up with his deceased operative. He said he was introduced to him by one of his earlier recruits, a—how did he put it?—an 'underpaid, disgruntled museum employee' who was apparently looking to make some extra money."

Cruz sat back and thought about that for a moment. "How does an 'underpaid, disgruntled museum employee' come to know how to smuggle antiquities into the U.S., much less get them to prospective buyers?"

I wished heartily that I'd gotten more sleep. In the adrenaline-charged aftermath of my fight-or-flight moment with Felipe, I hadn't thought to ask myself that simple question. Now I struggled to come up with a simple answer.

The one that fell off the tip of my tongue sounded less simple to me than stupid. "He's acquainted with other smugglers?"

Cruz was nodding. "Maybe he handles shipments, deals with auction house personnel . . ."

"And attends antiquities shows. Revez said he met this guy at an antiquities show. Same place Rose and her team shop for pothunters. Same place they found Bridges."

Cruz tilted his head back and covered his eyes with his hands, pressing his palms into his eyelids. "Too many connections. How to know which ones are critical? Ah, my head hurts."

"I'll bet. I can't imagine that sofa was too comfy."

He pulled his hands down and looked at me.

"I kind of figured I wasn't supposed to know about that, seeing as how you were gone within five seconds of my alarm going off. Thanks, though."

He shrugged. "*Por nada*. All part of the Gutierrez bodyguard service."

We took a cab from the airport to the hotel where Greg was registered as Geoffrey Catalano. I took the opportunity to call home. Rose was still in flux—here one moment, gone the next. The doctor had told Dave this was a positive development. Dave told me this was a positive development. I told myself it was a positive development. Then, for good measure, I told Cruz it was a positive development.

Greg was waiting for us in his suite, looking nothing like the erstwhile documentary director, and very little like the Greg Sheffield I knew. He was wearing a very good wig of curly brunette hair and a neatly trimmed beard and mustache, and he was dressed impeccably in a suit of raw taupe silk. He wore the jacket open over a sand-washed silk shirt of creamy terra cotta. No tie. The epitome of the well-heeled entrepreneur.

The first thing I did upon entering the room was give him a peck on the cheek. Then I wheeled my little bit of baggage over to a nearby table, opened it, and lifted Bird Jaguar IV to the tabletop. Sunlight gleamed from the freshly cleaned gold and sparked the chips of turquoise to the brilliance of a summer sky.

"Ta-da!" I said. "Happy wedding, Geoff. You can thank me later."

Greg gaped at the statue speechlessly for ever so long. Then he circled the table, finally stopping in front of the god-king and touching it gingerly.

"My God," he said. "It looks brand new."

I nodded. "Yeah. I had the same reaction. Doesn't look as if it's been lying under a manmade hill for centuries, does it?"

"And there's really more?"

"At least one chamber full," Cruz told him. "Revez says there are more. He's right about this not being a tomb. It was built for that purpose, but ended up being used as a literal treasure house in which Shield Jaguar collected a lifetime of souvenirs. There are artifacts in that cache from a half-dozen other cultures. Some unlike any I've ever seen."

"It's like a holographic scrapbook," I added. "*My Conquests*, by Itzamnaaj Balam."

"And you're sure they're real? This isn't a scam?"

"No, they're real," Cruz said. "I was able to handle anything I wished. No matter where in the room I went, no matter how far under a stack I reached, every artifact I laid my hands on was authentic."

"This is . . . amazing," Greg said inadequately.

"So," I said. "What's our next move? Call in the cavalry, secure the site, grab Revez?"

"What about his associates?" Greg asked.

"Ah," said Cruz. "Now that's more complicated. You see, there is really only one 'associate' of any importance. The others are little more than collectors who pay Revez or do him favors for the occasional new toy. Or so he says."

"And this associate is?"

"Mario Torres."

Greg's hands dropped away from the statue. "Mario Torres of the Amity and Truth Brigade?"

"The very same."

"No-no-no-no." Greg moved away from Bird Jaguar as if in a trance. "He's partners with a damned terrorist?"

"Torres's only interest in the site, according to Revez, is the money he makes from the sale of the artifacts it supplies him. He has no direct connection with the ruin. He doesn't even care to know where it is. He only wants his share."

Greg glanced at him sharply. "And you believe this?"

"Yes, I do actually. I don't see any reason Torres will notice anything is amiss until Revez's shipments stop. By then, the NPS and the INAH will have made a clean sweep of things. What I do not necessarily believe is that the other associates and investors are as insignificant as he makes it sound. I think he wants you—or rather, Geoffrey Catalano—to believe he will be king of the hill."

Greg nodded. "All right. Here's how we proceed. I want you two to return to the site—you should be able to hop a plane to Palenque and drive down using the GPS data. You can take Highway 199 as far south as Ocosingo, then head east. It may get tricky once you're off the government-maintained fire roads, but the weather's been good, so you should be fine. You could be there by late this afternoon."

"And once we're there?" asked Cruz.

"Take pictures. Document where the cache is and the extent of its contents. And look for any physical evidence that will connect Revez and/or Torres to the site. Meanwhile, I'll report in with Ellen and mobilize the troops. We'll join you there ASAP."

Cruz nodded. "If we're going to get out there by sunset, we'd better get moving."

I went to give Bird Jaguar a pat on his gold-and-turquoise headdress. "Bye-bye, Bird Jag. I'm gonna miss you. See you in Bonampak B," I told Greg and followed Cruz into the hallway.

Cruz had taken a room under his nom de guerre and it was here we went to change clothes and disguise ourselves just a bit. In the lobby of the hotel, I spotted an American tourist who looked suspiciously like Rodney Hammermill. Then we hopped a cab and drove around a few sightseeing centers before heading to the small executive airport from which Cruz had arranged a plane to take us to Palenque.

In Palenque, we found a rental service from which we selected a dark green Humvee. Cruz was leaning toward a jeep, but I explained that as I had some experience dealing with a Hummer's autovoi, we'd be better off with that.

"Is it okay to laugh at you when you say things like that?" he asked as we drove off down Highway 199.

"Feel free," I said. "I laugh at myself when I say things like that."

"You weren't serious though—about the Humvoi, I mean."

"I'm not sure, to tell you the truth."

He did laugh at me then. I was okay with that.

It was a long and bumpy ride. Once we left the main road at Ocosingo, conversation became practically impossible, punctuated as it was with *whoa!* and *ow!* and *sonuvabitch!* The last several miles we took slowly, carefully working our way toward the coordinates displayed on the GPS module's digital map.

"You know we can't just keep calling it Bonampak B," I shouted over the revving of our oversize engine.

"What did you have in mind?" he shouted back.

"What about Itzamnaaj Balam?"

His answer was lost in a precipitous drop followed by a stream of abuse delivered in a medley of English and Spanish. I speak Spanish, as it happens, but there were a number of words I didn't recognize.

Going was smoother once we connected with the track Revez had taken from his woodsy garage, and we were able to speak in reasonably normal voices. So it was that when Cruz's cell phone rang, we actually heard it. Cruz gestured at his shirt pocket with his chin, clearly intending me to pick up.

"Hello?" I said noncommittally, expecting to hear Greg's voice.

It wasn't Greg; it was Felipe. And he didn't sound good.

"Felipe?" I said and Cruz cut the engine. The silence, as they say, was deafening. "Felipe, what is it?"

"Where are you?" he asked me, his voice sounding tight and fierce.

"We're in Villahermosa. Where else would we be?" I met Cruz's eyes, grimacing to indicate something was off-kilter.

"Where in Villahermosa? What was that engine noise?"

"It was a sports car driving by. We're having a late lunch in an outdoor—"

"What's the name of the restaurant?"

The name of the restaurant at which we'd grabbed our lamentably early lunch was *El Plata Calienté*, so I gave that one. It had actually had an outdoor dining area.

"Why are you asking me all these odd questions, Felipe? What's going on?"

"Have you delivered the gift yet?"

"Yes. I did it the moment we arrived. Geoffrey was stunned speechless. And that's no mean feat. There are very few things that catch that man by surprise."

I heard him take a deep breath. When he spoke again, he sounded more relaxed. "Then everything is as we hoped?"

"Well, I should say so. Geoffrey is a very happy man. In fact," I added in a teasing voice, "he says the next time I see you I should give you a kiss since you most likely won't be at our wedding to get one. He wanted to make sure I thanked you properly and sincerely."

I swear to God and Saint Boris, I could feel my lips burning even as I said the words. And my skin was suddenly two sizes too tight. Cruz's fingers touched my arm and lingered.

"I will look forward to that," Revez said. But this was not the lusty purr he usually used with me. There was still something. "May I speak to Mr. Catalano personally? I want to thank him."

"He's not here, darling. I told you he was in Villahermosa on business. He's in meetings at the Hyatt all day. You might be able to reach him there, or at least leave a message on his room phone. He's in suite 501. But I'll be bringing you the money, so save a few thank-yous for me, okay?"

"When? When will you bring the money?"

"Tomorrow morning. Geoffrey's only in town for one night. Naturally, I'm going to spend it with him. Felipe, what's gotten into you? You sound worried. What's happened?"

Again, the deep breath of a man pulling himself together. "I received an anonymous message saying that you and your . . . bodyguard have left Villahermosa for other attractions."

"Felipe, that's absurd. Who'd even suggest such a thing? . . . Felipe?"

"I'll see you tomorrow," he said, and hung up.

"Well, that was weird." I stared at the cell phone as if it were somehow responsible for the weirdness.

Cruz's face looked as if it had been chipped out of stone. "How weird?"

I outlined the gist of Revez's questions, then delivered the punch line: "Someone has given Revez an anonymous tip that we're . . . doing pretty much what we're doing, I think. Visiting the site behind his back."

Cruz checked the time. It was about 3:30 in the afternoon. "Do you think he believed what you told him?"

"I don't know. He sounded *muy* jinky. I'm pretty sure he'll try to get hold of Greg—or rather, Geoffrey."

"Then he'll find there is a Geoffrey Catalano registered at the Hyatt. Perhaps leave a message on his room phone as you suggested. If Greg gets the call, he should be able to allay Revez's fears."

"And if he doesn't?"

He started the Humvee up again. "Perhaps we should call him—warn him."

I was already dialing Greg's mobile phone. "That'll only work if Revez actually leaves a message for him. What would Revez think if he gets a call from someone claiming to be Geoffrey Catalano out of the clear blue sky?"

"That we were covering our asses."

"Precisely. Greg!" I'd gotten his message box. "Damn . . . Okay. This is Gina. Check your phone messages at the hotel. Revez may call to make sure you're registered. If he leaves a message, call him back. Someone's trying to spook him." I texted him with the same message then handed the phone back to Cruz. "If someone knows we've left Villahermosa, we most likely have been followed."

Cruz's answer to that was to reach beneath the front seat and pull out his Glock in its well-worn shoulder holster. "You have your gun?"

"Is Saint Boris Orthodox?"

He smiled, pausing to strap on the gun before putting the Humvee back in motion. "Thank you, Gina Miyoko. I was getting ready to take all of this seriously. Once again, you have saved me from indulging my penchant for melodrama."

We reached the site a little after 4:00 P.M. Cruz figured we should make a quick recon of the two smaller pyramids while we still had the light. They had, as Revez noted, barely been poked.

It was impossible to tell what was in the larger of the two, but someone had clearly entered the smaller one.

They'd had help from Mother Nature. About twenty feet up the steep side of the temple, plant roots had broken through the stonework and created a crude natural skylight. It was visible from the bottom of the pyramid at the end of a macheted trail.

We climbed to give this a closer inspection, which revealed a long, broad hallway not unlike the one through which we'd entered the largest structure. Below in the semi-gloom we could see little more than sun-dappled tumbles of debris from the broken roof.

Cruz looked at that root-bound hole as if it were a long-lost lover. I knew he was just dying to climb down into it, to intimately explore the insides of the temple. I felt like a third wheel.

"Should I give you two a moment alone together?" I asked.

"Ha. Funny."

He turned away from the enchanted skylight and we descended to the overgrown plaza. After we'd inspected the greenery around the buildings about as thoroughly as we could, finding various candy and cigarette wrappers, we headed back to the main temple. There were also some spent shell casings that made us wonder who'd been shooting and what they'd been shooting at. Cruz settled that by pointing out a number of trees that looked as if they'd been mobbed by big angry woodpeckers.

"Boredom and machine guns," I said as we entered the Vestibule. "Not a healthy combination. At least not for the local flora."

In the Vestibule, we were met with our first major roadblock in the form of Revez's drawbridge. It was closed up like a giant clam and we had no way to open it.

Chapter 22

Labyrinth

In the end it took both of us, tools cobbled together from the Hummer and the chest in the Vestibule, and two hours of very slow-moving time to force the drawbridge to lower. We pretty thoroughly wrecked the motor in doing it and I doubted Felipe's little garage-door opener would ever work on it again—which hardly mattered at this point in the game.

The Vestibule stash had provided us with a couple of military-grade flashlights that cast a wide circle of illumination perfect for spelunking or tomb raiding. I set them out on the floor and took pictures of the drawbridge and its mechanism and the walls of the entrance hall. Then we set off to retrace our steps to the Treasure Room. At the entrance to the maze it hit me: Revez had clearly navigated these passages countless times. We'd been through exactly once. I stared at the narrow black slit in the stone wall and drew a complete blank.

Cruz merely handed me his flashlight and said, "Hold this, please," then whipped out his PDA.

"GPS isn't going to do diddly down here, you know," I told him.

He gave me a wry sideways glance, performed a series of taps, then held out his hand for his flashlight. He started forward and down, one eye on the softly glowing little screen. In about five yards, we came to a junction that offered three options: left, straight, right—four, if you count "U-turn."

Cruz didn't hesitate. He went straight.

"I thought it was a right on the first turn," I whispered.

"Straight. I suspect you were distracted by Felipe blowing in your shell-like ear."

I did recall that something had made me kvitch right about here.

"He didn't blow in my ear. I walked into a cobweb or something."

"Ah. Why are you whispering?"

"I dunno. It just feels like a whispery sort of place."

We'd reached a second junction. Same three (or four) options. This time we turned right. Three yards later we turned left. Then we went straight for a good ten yards, then left again, then right, then left. Fifteen yards later we were presented with a "T." We turned left yet again.

"Must be the south wall of the temple," I guessed. "So when did you have the opportunity to get all this down? Don't tell me you memorized his moves?"

"The advantages of being left to bring up the rear. While you kept Felipe chatting, I kept track of the turns. It only took three keys: S, L, R. Pretty simple, really." He paused to show me. Sure enough, the little notepad window revealed an unbroken line of letters: SRLLRLLLRL(P) RRRRSLRSLR

"What's P?" I asked.

"That odd and rather steep descent—the corkscrew switchback. Reminded me of a pig tail."

"P is for pig tail?"

"Precisely."

That weird, steep pig tail stair was the one place in our tortuous path that descended precipitously, but I was aware of a leisurely downward slope to a number of the passages. I'd gotten out my pocket compass by now and was trying to calculate how much distance we'd covered in each direction.

"I'd be willing to bet we're directly under the main entrance to this labyrinth," I said when we'd negotiated the steep ramp followed by a series of quick right-hand turns. "We were probably right up there not twenty minutes ago."

I narrowed the beam of my flashlight and flicked it up toward the ceiling.

"You're whispering again," Cruz said.

Then he stopped.

"Are we there yet?" I asked.

"Funny. No. Right about here, Revez turned back to say something to me. I had to stop taking notes. I may have missed one."

I thought, suddenly, of the thousands of tons of earth and rock over our heads, which, to its credit, had been holding its own for centuries.

"*Now* you think of this?"

He consulted the PDA. "It says left, but . . . No, I missed one. He went straight here. Left at the next junction."

"Please be sure about this, okay? I don't really want to become part of the ruin. And I'm not sure I'm carrying an obereg for getting buried alive. I think that's Saint Damasus."

"Damasus is the patron saint of archaeologists."

"What did I just say?"

He laughed, the sound echoing oddly on the rock around us. "Gina, where's your spirit of romance? Chances are we'd find the trove by trial and error anyway. And if not, then we die in each other's arms." He uttered an exaggerated sigh.

"Cruz, I appreciate your trying to soften the peril of creeping through dark underground tunnels beneath tons of earth and rock, possibly getting lost and falling into God knows what booby traps, but I'm not claustrophobic or anything like that. You don't have to play class clown on my account."

He glanced down the passage to our left. "I was playing class clown, as you put it, on my own account, thank you. As it happens *I* am a bit claustrophobic."

I honestly couldn't tell if he was serious or razzing me.

"Then again," he said, putting his hand to the left-hand wall, "if worse comes to worst, we could just reverse the directions in the PDA and follow them out of here." He ran his hand up and down the angle of the corner as if searching for something. After a moment, he grunted and moved to the straight right-hand wall to repeat the exercise.

"Ah," he said finally.

"What are you doing?"

"Come here. Look." He shone his light on the wall where his hand rested.

I moved a bit closer and peered around him. Just above his fingertips at about the height of his shoulder, there seemed to be a vertical groove in the wall. It wasn't much—the width of two fingers and only about three inches long.

Cruz took my hand and pressed my fingers to the smooth slot.

"The ancients weren't dummies," he said. "Weren't you the least bit curious about how the king's men found their way around down here? They notched the walls. Vertical slot for straight ahead, vertical and horizontal for left or right. Horizontal then vertical is left—"

"Vertical then horizontal is right," I guessed. "Go, ancients."

He was right about the missed letter and, in due course, we found ourselves in the transverse corridor that ran along the front of the Mural Gallery. He immediately started prowling toward the end of the long anteroom.

"The controls for the lights must be here somewhere. Revez turned left out of the Gallery and went along here . . ."

He found what he was looking for at the far end of the hall—a narrow access corridor that cut left. It required one to turn sideways to slip in, but inside, where it widened just a bit, there were a couple of huge, heavy-duty marine batteries hooked up to a set of cables. The cables did not—I noticed as Cruz flipped the switch that would shunt power to them—run back into the hall the way we'd come.

"Where are you going?" Cruz asked me as I slipped past him in the narrow slot, following the wires away from the battery.

The cabling ran back along the floor for a while, then went up the wall to disappear over the top of a pile of fill. It seemed like an odd place for fill, the usual intent of which is to foil further exploration of a tomb. I panned my flashlight up toward the ceiling, expecting to see a hole where the roof had caved in. The rock overhead looked seamless. This was deliberate, then.

"What do you make of this?" I asked Cruz as he sidled up behind me.

"Looks as if they've taken the wires in through the rear of the gallery. In fact," he added, training his own light over the place where the wires ducked through a raccoon-sized hole in the top of the debris, "I'd be willing to bet that the ancients brought their booty in this way, then sealed up the corridor when the treasury was nearing capacity. It was hard to imagine them shoving some of those objects through that little access way in the Mural Gallery. This makes a lot more sense. A properly outfitted excavation team could probably clear this fairly easily and use this passage to remove the artifacts."

The Mural Gallery was just as impressive the second time around. I stepped over the threshold, wondering if this—this quickened breath, haring heart, and flushed skin—was even a tenth of what Cruz Veras was feeling. This was, after all, his *thing*. These vivid pictures, that room full of artifacts, were stunning to me in a *Holy Mother of Pearl!* sort of way. To Cruz, they were a life's work, a calling, a cause.

I watched him move down the length of the hall, his eyes on the bright and fantastic figures.

"A penny for them," I said, shutting off my flashlight and following him.

He laughed. "I'm—what do you call it?—'geeking out,' aren't I?"

"A little. Justifiably so, I might add. What *were* you thinking?"

"That I would love the opportunity to excavate the rest of this site. I wish there *were* a Geoffrey Catalano waiting in the wings to fund the venture—legally, of course. I doubt my government has the resources for this big an undertaking."

"Speaking of which . . ." I unpocketed my digital camera. "We should probably start photographing in here."

He nodded toward my camera as he pulled out his own. "You know how to shoot panoramas with that?"

"Yeah. Is that what you want?" I made a sweeping birth-to-death gesture.

"*Exactamente.* I'll start in the Treasure Room."

"Don't space out in there."

He disappeared through the little crawlway into the inner sanctum while I started photographing the murals. I'd gotten to about the bloodletting ceremony that accompanied Shield Jaguar's nuptials (which I find preferable in some ways to the production numbers people stage these days) when I felt a peculiar trembling in the air—maybe even in the stone and earth around me. It was almost, but not quite, a sound. A mere blip on my radar.

I paused to focus on it, but it was gone, fading like the flutter of dragonfly wings on a lazy day at the beach. I shrugged it off as low blood sugar and went back to my work.

When I was done, I crawled through to join Cruz in the tomb. He was sitting on the ledge that ran around the base of the corpseless sarcophagus, turning a large disk of beaten metal in his hands—a stylized mask made to look like the disk of the Sun. His camera sat on the step nearby.

I took a seat next to him. He didn't seem to notice.

"You're doing it again," I told him after a moment.

He shook his head and chuckled. "Hard habit to break. I was just getting ready to photograph it, I promise you. What have you got?"

I handed him my camera, then sat back as he checked my work with a professional eye. He seemed pleased.

Something tugged at the periphery of my hearing.

"What was that?" I asked.

He paused to listen. There it was again: a faint wisp of sound like a birdcall—high, thin, muted—then a sharp but muffled report.

"That's gunfire," Cruz said, and shoved the camera back into my hands.

We wiggled our way out of the Treasure Room and slipped back into the tunnels with weapons drawn, moving as swiftly and quietly as possible, not sure what we'd be facing or when. Cruz had left his military torch behind in the Treasure Room, in favor of a pocket flashlight, which he Velcroed to his left wrist. The guy was a regular Inspector Gadget.

"Is there anything you *don't* have in your pockets?" I murmured.

"Right turn," he said, ignoring me. "Kill your flash."

I did, and visibility was suddenly limited to the small pool of light cast by Cruz's flash.

"You've done this sort of thing before, haven't you?" I said.

"Actually, no. But I was a Boy Scout."

"You're not really claustrophobic."

"I'll never tell. Left."

I put my hand to the wall as we oozed around the corner, somehow comforted by the markings. If I had to, I told myself, I could find my way around down here in complete darkness.

The sound of sporadic gunfire became clearer the closer we moved to the entrance. We'd just climbed the pig tail and were making our way along the south wall of the temple when we heard a shot that echoed sharply and clearly down the stone corridors as if . . .

I caught at the belt of Cruz's jeans to slow him down.

"Cruz, that's awful loud. I think the shooter might be in the temple. Maybe even in the Vestibule."

He turned to look at me in the chaotic dance of shadow and light from his flashlight. "In that last straight passage . . ."

"Fish in a barrel comes to mind," I said.

He turned off his flashlight, plunging us into complete darkness. I was suddenly hyper-aware of the presence of gravity and oxygen.

"Three right turns coming up," he told me. "Then a left into the last leg."

"What do we do when we get there?"

"Pray no one is watching for us."

"Oh. Great plan."

We were approaching the last right turn when my cell phone beeped. The sound was so shocking in this context, at first I wasn't sure what it was or what to do about it.

"Answer!" Cruz hissed.

"Hello?" I said tentatively.

"Gina?"

"Greg?"

A hiss of expelled breath rasped in my ear. "Thank God. I had visions of you buried under tons of rock or lost in the bowels of the Earth."

"Funny, same visions I was having. Where are you?"

"Just inside the—uh—the upside-down garage door. Where are you?"

"In the labyrinth. Maybe fifty, sixty yards from your location. What the hell is going on up there? Are you under attack?"

He laughed. "No! No, that was me. Hoping just maybe you'd be able to hear me from wherever the hell you were and would come out to get me."

I sagged against the wall of the corridor, keenly aware of Cruz's eyes on my face.

"Sorry. Didn't mean to leave you stranded. We were getting into our work."

"No problem. Is Cruz with you?"

"Yeah. He's right here."

"Great. Good. Come on up and rescue me."

I pocketed the phone. "Greg's waiting for us in the lobby."

"The shooting?"

"He was trying to get our attention. He couldn't raise our cell phones. And we got so carried away with our archaeological zeal we forgot he'd need directions to the party."

I holstered my gun and started for the last turn.

Cruz laid a hand on my arm. "Just in case," he said, "keep the lamps off and hug the wall."

I started to protest, then realized he was right. If we'd been followed by Revez or whoever was messing with his head, there was at least a small chance that someone might have shown up to keep our guys company. For all we knew, Greg had placed that call with a gun to his head.

That thought made it hard to relax even when we saw Greg squatting opposite the entrance to the maze in the wash of his flashlight beam. Cruz stepped into the entrance hall quickly, back to the wall, gun raised in a two-handed grip.

Greg blinked and stood slowly, eyes wide and watchful, hands clear of his body. I waited just inside the opening to the labyrinth with my gun aimed at the drawbridge while Cruz scanned the nether shadows.

"What?" Greg asked, his eyes on my partner.

Cruz turned back to us and holstered the Glock. "I just wanted to make sure you were really alone up here. Dropping in by helicopter might have drawn unwelcome attention. And there is a possibility we were followed."

Well, duh. A helicopter. That explained the subtle fluttering I'd felt down in the Mural Gallery.

Greg nodded. "So your message said. We need to move quickly. Secure the evidence and get Revez and his crew before he has a chance to move." He picked up his flash. "Let's go."

"You're alone?" I asked. "I thought you were going to roll in with the whole support team."

"By chopper? If you think one little black helicopter might draw attention, imagine what three or four would do. The rest of the team's coming in by ground from Bonampak. It made the best staging area, but it'll take them a while to get here in the dark."

We made our way back through the knot of narrow passages and I couldn't help but notice that, after a quick glance at his PDA, Cruz pocketed it and navigated without. I slid along behind him, trying to memorize the turns and using the wall notches for confirmation.

"Road signs?" asked Greg from behind me.

I turned to see him fingering the groove my hand had just abandoned.

"Pretty clever of those old Mayans, huh?"

"Yeah. Pretty clever. Not real obvious though."

"You have to know they're there," Cruz said over his shoulder. "Unfortunately, Revez's first exploratory team didn't. I understand one of his men lost a foot in a booby trap down below. Taking a wrong turn in here can be very costly."

A chill raced up my spine. I was damn glad I hadn't heard Revez say that. While it's true that I'm neither afraid of the dark nor claustrophobic, the thought of falling down a deep pit in the dark made my stomach turn flip-flops.

"I should warn you," Cruz continued as if he hadn't just wrinkled my reality, "that the notches can be unreliable as well. Some of them may be intended to deceive."

I pulled my hands away from the wall. "Thanks for the safety tip."

Cruz kept up a brisk pace. Our return took about half the time it had taken us to navigate the King's Maze in the first place. On the way, I found my eyes drawn down every false corridor, peering as far as the beams of our flashlights would reach, and wondering what nifty surprises the ancients had crafted for the unwary.

Cruz noticed my morbid obsession. "Some of them are just plugged with fill," he told me. "But I wouldn't be surprised to find some drops that go through to the sublevels."

"Nice."

When we reached the Hall of the Puma Head, Greg exclaimed over the desecrated walls. "I suppose the friezes are already in private collections all over the globe. What a shame."

"I wouldn't be surprised to find some of them in public collections," Cruz said. "The cache is unknown. Provenance for such a find can easily be fabricated."

He led the way into the Mural Gallery and I followed him, turning to watch Greg Sheffield's face as he stepped over the eccentric threshold and saw what the walls contained.

"My God." Those were the only words he spoke during his entire circuit of the room.

His reaction wasn't nearly as gratifying as I'd expected, and I knew why. Rose should have been here to see this. I realized as soon as I had the thought that if Rose were here, I probably wouldn't be. I'd be sitting on the patio at the Pavo, sipping virgin piña coladas and fighting boredom. Or worse, back in San Francisco spying on middle-aged joggers.

Greg turned to me, shaking his head in awe. "This is beyond amazing. Where's the hoard?"

I pointed at the little doorway that formed a brief pause in Shield Jaguar's busy life. Cruz had already gone on through.

Greg bowed. "Ladies first."

I got down on my hands and knees and, pushing my flashlight ahead of me, crawled to the Treasure Room with Greg scraping along behind. Oddly, when I got to the far side, the room beyond was dark. I scooted my light out onto the floor and had just followed it with my head and shoulders when it winked out.

"Cruz?"

The darkness didn't answer, but only pressed coolly against my face. I crawled out into the room and stood, the radiance of Greg's flashlight leaking out of the crawlway to lap around my ankles. My skin tingled.

"Cruz?" I repeated. "Cruz, for God's sake—"

"Gina?" Greg's voice came from the tunnel unnaturally loud. "Gina, what's wrong?"

I stepped reflexively to the right, away from the low opening. "I don't know. My light went out. Cruz! Where the hell are you?"

The darkness was slashed by the wide beam from Greg's flashlight as he pushed it out into the room. His head and shoulders emerged behind it. In the split second it took me to realize he'd drawn his gun (as I should have done) a shot blew the flashlight to shrapnel. I yelped in pain and surprise, my ears ringing.

There was a moment of intense silence in which I could hear myself breathing above the air-raid siren in my head.

Then Greg said, "All right, Cruz. You want to explain the game?" When there was no answer, he asked, "Gina, you okay?"

My weak "Okay" sounded in stereo with Cruz's sharp "Don't answer!" which came from so close to my right ear, I literally leapt forward, away from the wall I'd been hugging.

There was a rush of movement and an arm went around me just below my shoulders, pinning my arms to my sides and forcing me tight against a hard, trembling body. Instinctively, I raised my foot, intending to take out his knee, when cold steel bored up under my jaw, the sharp protrusion of a gun sight biting into my skin. The snick of a revolver's hammer being cocked sounded as loud in my ears as the earlier gunshot.

No, whimpered the stunned voice of Denial. *How could this be? How?*

My heart wasn't sure whether it wanted to leap to my throat or sink to my soles. It settled for beating wildly in my chest.

A slender beam of light hit my face, blinding me.

"That's right, Cruz," Greg said. "We have an impasse. Drop your weapon."

"I can't do that."

"You won't fire. You might hit Gina."

The flashlight beam wavered slightly. "And you," Cruz said from about eight feet straight away, "won't fire for the same reason. Shoot her and you'll be dead before she hits the floor."

"Let's try this then," Greg countered, shifting his hold on me slightly. "I'll shoot her someplace that won't be immediately fatal. She's light, so I'll still have a shield. Until she bleeds out."

The muzzle of his gun crept down to burrow into my lower back.

Terror, in case you didn't know, has a color. The color is blue. The color of glacial ice. The color of an empty sky. The color of the holstered gun that was pinned to my ribs beneath Greg Sheffield's encircling arm. Terror has a smell too—a metallic smell with a breath of cordite and sweat.

"Drop your gun, Cruz," Greg commanded.

After a mere instant of hesitation, I heard Cruz's gun hit the hard pack floor and skitter away to my left.

"Good. Now, your PDA. Turn it on so I can see it."

"What about the rest of your team?" asked Cruz. "Aren't you afraid they'll blunder into the middle of this?"

"Considering that they have no idea where we are—no. They really are at Bonampak, by the way, but they're waiting for instructions . . . and directions."

"But the GPS data—"

"They never got the GPS data. You have it and I have it. I told them the GPS plan failed. As far as they know, what you told me at Palenque was that Revez had gotten suspicious and you were forced to leave the GPS module and the wire behind on your first trip out here. My team was counting on you two being able to find your way back here by sheer cunning. But unfortunately, Revez got wind of what you were doing and got here before I could bring in the cavalry and perform a rescue. . . . The PDA, Cruz."

He dug the Ruger GP100's sharp, nasty little muzzle sight into my kidneys. I tried not to, but I gasped out loud.

The PDA scooted toward me across the floor, its screen a rectangle of eye-piercing white.

"Now your phone."

The phone skittered almost to my toes.

"Why are you doing this?" Cruz asked.

"Do you really need to know that? It won't matter in the final analysis."

"I'd just like to understand why a veteran Park Service agent sells out to the pirates. You have a lot of years of outstanding service to the NPS. Why this?"

"Because all I got for my 'years of outstanding service' was a kick in the teeth and a cost-of-living raise. I've read your CV, Dr. Veras. You have no idea what it's like to work your ass off in the field only to have someone else get the credit . . . and the promotion."

It was so absurd, I almost laughed. "You went to the Dark Side because Ellen Robb got the job you wanted?"

"The straw, Gina. The camel's back was already sagging. Did you know that Sommers has what they call 'special acquisitions clerks'? On paper they look like any other clerk in the organization. Paper-pushers. Little better than accountants who get the added perk of handling acquisitions. And on paper, they're paid like any other clerk. Do you know what one of those people really earns?"

"No."

"At least twice as much I do. Plus bonuses for locating and facilitating the purchase of especially good lots. They troll for NPS agents, Gina. They poke and they prod and they sniff anonymously around. Rose could tell you. They've been sniffing around me for years, and I've been shutting them down. Going so far as to report them so our people can follow their back trail. That all stopped when I got passed over. I thought I'd see what they had to say. If I didn't like it, I could still turn on them, make a good bust, look like a hero. Maybe even prove myself to whoever the hell needed more proof."

"But?" prompted Cruz when Greg lapsed into ruminative silence.

"But, I liked it. And all they wanted was a shill and a dodger. Someone who could play both sides against the middle, keep their guys out of serious trouble, make sure we never got too close to anything important."

My stomach lurched. "Did you make sure *Rose* didn't get too close?"

He jerked as if I'd hit him with a cattle prod.

"I didn't shoot Rose." He said it directly into my ear, biting off each word as if it were foul-tasting.

"But you know who did," Cruz guessed.

"Yes."

"An *associate?*"

"Only in the sense that he was paid by the same people who pay me. They were protecting their Central American interests. I had nothing—" He swallowed convulsively. "I had *nothing* to do with that."

"Nothing?" repeated Cruz. "Not even looking the other way during that cocked-up operation at the headlands?"

I gasped aloud, only now making the connection.

Greg's grip tightened. "It was meant to scare her. To warn her off," he growled, his voice sounding strangled.

"And Ted Bridges? Did you have nothing to do with that?"

Greg was trembling again, as if all this Q and A was really getting to him. The gun pulled back marginally, its muzzle quivering.

"I told them what happened . . . at the sting. That he'd brought an item from the new site, that Rose Delgado had seen it and known it for what it was. I thought they were only going to get the stuff away from him so we couldn't trace it. I didn't know they were going to kill him."

Cruz gave a short, mirthless laugh. "I find that hard to believe. You seem more than willing to kill us."

"Willing? I seem *willing*? Believe me, I'd do just about anything to not—" He took a deep breath. "I don't have a choice."

"You always have a choice."

"No. They made it very clear after Bridges. He was my first screwup, you see. I recruited him and he turned out to be a renegade and an idiot. If I could have controlled him, I'd have earned their trust. But I couldn't. I failed to reel him in when he first hooked up with Revez. Hell, I couldn't even get him to tell me who his source was. That was my first strike. Then I failed to keep Rose away from him. You know how that turned out. Strike two. Then I botched cleanly cutting the connection to Revez." He laughed harshly. "I completely purged the files in Bridges's office. But you, Gina, had to go and find that brochure. And here you are. Letting you get this far is just one more failure."

"Turn yourself in," Cruz told him. "Turn your contacts in. You'll get protection. Provide the evidence that will bring these people down and you could certainly cut a deal . . . with both our governments."

"Then what? I go to prison? Someday I get out? And do what for a living? Become a rent-a-cop? The location of this site is a treasure in and of itself. Sommers doesn't know where it is. The NPS doesn't know where it is. When this is over, Revez and his most loyal men will be the only other people who know, and I'm betting he can be convinced to work with me. That's a big deal. That's more control than I've ever had over *anything* in my life to date. What's your alternative? *No* control. My life goes on permanent hold . . . or worse. You think I'll get protection? How well protected was Rose?"

The tears were so swift I had no way to stop them. At least no one knew they were there but me.

"And this is worth our lives?" Cruz asked softly.

The muzzle of the Ruger answered emphatically. I bit my lip and tried not to sob aloud.

"End of psych session," Greg said. "Cruz, I want you to put the flashlight down and move away from it. Don't think about trying to blind me. I'll shoot her. Don't doubt it for a minute."

The flash beam lowered as Cruz moved to obey.

"Just out of curiosity," Greg said, his breath fanning my ear, "how did you know . . . about me?"

I didn't, I thought wildly. *I didn't know about you.* Not until I felt that gunsight biting into my neck and heard the revolver being cocked. Cruz's Glock was a semi-automatic with a smooth, square muzzle.

"The tip to Revez," Cruz answered. "The most likely candidate was an NPS agent well on the inside of the sting."

Cruz's voice moved, but the flashlight remained stationary, apparently where he'd set it down as Greg had ordered.

"It could have been one of Revez's people. In Villahermosa, at the airport . . . Someone assigned to follow you."

"One of Revez's people would have wanted to be recognized and rewarded," Cruz said from a point to my far left. "That the tip was anonymous, seemed significant to me."

"That's all?"

Cruz didn't answer.

"Cruz!" Greg said sharply. The gunsight bit further into my back just below my shoulder.

"You were alone," I said, on a wave of epiphany. "No backup. An agent never goes into the field without backup. Especially an agent who's been warned of a possible hostile presence."

I felt Greg's attention shift to me, felt him adjust his grasp. His right hand gave up its bruising grip on my upper arm, moving to lift the Taurus out of my shoulder holster. It wasn't much, but it might be the only opportunity I got.

I let my body go limp, dropping to a crouch on the sandy floor. The moment I hit bottom, a camera flashed, flooding the small chamber with dazzling white light.

Greg swore and fired wildly. I brought one leg around in a sweep, catching the side of his left knee. The joint didn't buckle, so it wasn't enough to bring him down, but he grunted in pain and staggered back against the wall, off-balance. I dove toward the center of the room, then rolled up like a pill bug. The flashlight blinked out and I ended my tumble in darkness, colliding with a clutter of objects that tumbled noisily around and over me like mismatched bowling pins.

Hands gripped my shirt, pulling me forward and up, then lifted me bodily and shoved me into a narrow stone slot. Before I could orient myself, Cruz wedged in behind me. His hands found my waist and lifted me again, straight up.

Reflexively, I stretched out my arms and found what amounted to a window cut into the rock nearly six feet from the floor. My flailing hands found the electrical cabling draped over the sill.

I knew where I was now, and scrambled to gain purchase on the window ledge. A shove from behind put me up and in. I wriggled away on my belly toward the nether end of the shaft, following the cables. Faint light from the antechamber filtered through the hole through which they connected to Revez's batteries. I prayed to Saint Damasus and anyone else who was listening that the shaft didn't dead-end there.

It didn't. It ended abruptly about five feet from the pile of fill. I sat on the ledge listening to the sounds from behind me—Cruz dragging himself through the shaft and Greg swearing imaginatively while he no doubt searched for a working flashlight.

Cruz reached me as I was discovering that my gun was gone, lost when I dropped from Greg's grasp. He wordlessly clicked on his flashlight and aimed the beam at the floor below my dangling feet. I took the six-foot drop, landing lightly on the uneven floor below. Cruz followed, shining his flashlight around the small space. It was no bigger than an elevator, but it did have one important feature. There was a narrow doorway cut into its eastern wall.

Cruz crossed to the doorway and aimed the flashlight beam into it. "Tunnel," he murmured, then shot a glance back over his shoulder at the raccoon hole. "Could you squeeze through there?"

"Maybe. But you couldn't." I breathed the words so softly even I barely heard them.

He turned and took a step toward the pile of debris. I knew he was going to suggest I escape without him.

I stopped him with a lie. "Joking. I'm small, but not that small."

"No choice, then. The tunnel. Hold onto my belt. I don't want to lose you."

I uncrossed my fingers. "Don't want to be lost, thanks."

We moved into the tunnel following the narrow beam of yellow light, defenseless and clueless. I glanced back at the shaft we'd just exited as I stepped into (or under) terra incognita. In the otherwise stygian gloom, I could just make out the shape of the window, softly illumined by light coming from the Treasure Room.

Chapter 23

A Night Trip into the Underworld

The corridor was unusually constant. We'd gone thirty or forty yards before we found its first branch. The notches indicated we should go straight. Well, straight isn't exactly right, because the tunnel seemed to veer slightly to the right—south, on my handy compass.

"Where do you think this goes?" I asked.

"On a wild guess, I'd say to the second pyramid."

"The Mama Bear one?"

"What?"

"The medium-sized one."

"Ah. Yes."

"That one hasn't been excavated at all. What are we likely to find when we get there?"

"At this point, Gina, your guess is as good as mine."

My guess wasn't good. It was depressing. It was also right. Notches notwithstanding, the first southern passage we tried to take ended in a solid pile of rock and dirt. There wasn't a hole even a mouse could squeak through.

We moved on with more care, veering southwest down a tunnel we guessed ran beneath the face of Pyramid Two, not knowing if the path ahead would be booby-trapped or not. At least I didn't know.

"Cruz," I asked at length, "all that stuff about Revez's man losing a foot in a booby trap and the notches being unreliable. Was that all for Greg's benefit?"

"Mostly. I wanted to make sure we made it all the way to the Treasure Room. We were more likely to do that the stronger his incentive was for keeping us alive."

"He could have shot us both and taken your PDA," I observed.

"At that point," Cruz admitted, "I was hoping he hadn't noticed my PDA."

"He noticed," I said. "Now he can come and go at will . . . or can he?"

Cruz stopped at another left-or-straight "T" junction, and looked back at me. "What do you mean?"

"Did you ever fill in that missing turn? The one after pig tail stair?"

The smile he gave me was slow and utterly evil. "Alas, I never had the time." He looked up at the stone ceiling. "We need to get back to the surface. Do you still have your phone?"

I patted my pockets and came up with it. The so-called high-impact case was cracked, but the touch screen was functioning.

"No signal though," I said. "We're in too deep."

"Please, no puns."

He slipped around the corner to the left, moving as quickly as he dared, flashing his light ahead of us.

We were met by another pile of fill. I climbed to the top of this one and poked around. The earth near the top was loose and I was able to roll a few chunks of rock down the other side. Dust rose up to make me sneeze.

"It's possible we could dig through here," I told him, lying back on the steep, uneven slope. "But do we want to?"

"Assuming that the corridor we've been following connects all three pyramids, the answer is probably no. Let's go."

He pulled me off the pile and hurried me back out to the tunnel. We turned left and began moving again more briskly than before, reasoning that if the intent of the passage were to link the three temples, it was unlikely to contain any booby traps along the main thoroughfare. We stopped to listen occasionally and to peer down our back trail.

We had gone some distance without encountering any side tracks at all when we first heard sounds of pursuit. They were subtle—Greg wasn't likely to come screaming after us like a demented ax murderer—but they were there: something scraping stone, a heavy footfall.

When the gloom behind us went from darkest night to a flickering twilight, I started to get really and truly scared. We were heading due west in the no-man's-land between Pyramids Two and Three. And there were no alternate routes to be had. We began to run. Unsafe, but considering the alternative, prudent.

Right about the time I decided that I wasn't imagining that Cruz's flashlight was starting to wane, we almost literally ran into a peculiar feature. A log as big around as a man's thigh stuck out across the tunnel from left to right. It did not completely bisect the passage; it stopped shy of the outer wall by about six inches. The other end of the log was buried in an oddly uneven patch of masonry.

Cruz stopped and stared at it momentarily, then put his hand on the rough patch of wall, studying where the smooth planes of the surrounding stonework met it. He wiggled the rock beneath his hand—a big, melon-sized thing. It scraped against its fellows. Then he ducked under the obstruction, motioning for me to follow.

Once on the other side, he turned and threw his entire weight onto the log. The wall it impaled, now to our right, made a funny crunching sound. It was a booby trap, I realized, made just for this sort of situation. "Good guys" being pursued by "bad guys" had a way to keep said "bad guys" from getting to whichever temple they were trying to crack.

I sent up a prayer to the thoughtful builders of Mama Bear and threw myself onto the log beside him, watching the corridor beyond. It was no longer unrelieved black.

"Cruz . . ." I murmured.

His response was to douse his flashlight beam. The passage beyond seemed to pulse and quiver in the fitful glow from Greg's flashlight. We threw ourselves at the log again, making the wall of mismatched stones creak and complain. A sound that was equal parts slither and rumble issued from behind the wall.

The passage here was long and fairly straight. Greg must have been a good thirty yards away when I caught sight of his flashlight beam.

Cruz had seen it too. He shoved the flashlight into my hand. "Run," he told me.

I ignored him, throwing my body onto the log again.

"Gina, *now!*"

The rumble was louder, but not as loud as the shot Greg fired. I swear I felt the air of its passing. I know I heard it ricochet off the walls behind us.

A couple of good-sized rocks hit the floor, followed by a spill of gravel. Dust billowed upward. Cruz grabbed my arm and dragged me backwards, then turned me around and shoved me down the passage. Light licked around us as we ran.

I counted two more gunshots. The third one, I felt. It sent a burning pain along the outside of my right hip. Maybe a bullet, maybe splinters of rock blasted from the wall. I for sure didn't have time to stop and check it out. I could only keep running pell-mell into the dark underground, hearing behind me the sounds of Cruz's breathing and the roar of loose rock.

Like Orpheus, I was terrified of looking back.

I don't know how far we'd gone when my hand encountered a break in the left-hand wall. I didn't realize I'd been using it to support myself until I staggered and went down, pitching up against the wall of the cross corridor.

Cruz landed almost on top of me, making my hip scream for mercy. His lips were against my ear. "The flashlight. You still have it?"

"Yeah. Here." I pressed it into his hand, then tried to sit up. My hip burned like hell.

He flipped the light on, aiming it down the side route. Then he reattached the thing to the Velcro band at his wrist and scooped me up off the ground, dragging me bodily into the narrow tunnel.

He let go of me after a moment and moved down the passageway several yards while I sagged against the wall. Warm liquid seeped down my thigh.

It's gotta be just a cut, I reasoned. If it were more than that I wouldn't be able to walk.

I turned my head and listened for sounds of pursuit, scanned for light in the outer passage. I heard and saw nothing.

Cruz grunted in approval at something and came back to me. "There's another turn just ahead. If he's still in pursuit maybe we can—*Dios*!"

I squinted up at him in the half-light. He was standing in the middle of the passage, staring at his left hand. Even in the weakening flashlight beam, it looked vibrantly red. There was more red on his shirt.

I was overcome with the irrational fear that he'd been wounded too. "Cruz, are you all—"

He was on me before the words were out of my mouth, lifting me off my feet and carrying me around the turn in the tunnel, where he deposited me gently on the hard floor.

"I'm okay," I protested. "Really."

"The hell you are. My God, your pants are soaked with blood. How badly does it hurt?" He was unbuttoning my khakis.

"It burns a little, that's all."

He raised his eyes to mine.

"Okay, dammit, it burns a lot. But I can walk."

"We've got to staunch this." He'd gotten the zipper down and was peeling the pants off my hip.

I gasped as the fabric dragged over the wound. "Cruz, we don't have time—"

"Shut up, Gina."

"We need to keep moving. We're sitting ducks here."

He made a hissing sound between his teeth, then said, "Only if he's still following us."

"Well, what if he is?"

He got up and moved back toward the main corridor, flicking off the flashlight as he went. I listened for the sounds of his passing, but lost them in the oppressive gloom.

Well, I thought, *if ever anyone were going to develop claustrophobia this would be a good way to go about it.*

I heard sounds of movement again and held my breath. The light popped back on.

"There's no sign of him," Cruz said, stepping over me.

When he squatted next to me again, he had a knife. It was only about a four-inch-long pocket knife, but at that moment, the blade looked about a foot long. I recalled all those old Westerns I'd watched in which the hero was required to dig the bullet out of his buddy or his lady love with his bowie knife. In this case, Cruz simply cut open the side seam of my panties.

"Why'd you do that?"

"They were stuck in the wound. Hold this."

He handed me the flashlight, aimed it, and bent to inspect the damage. He shook his head, then murmured something under his breath. When he wielded the knife again, it was to cut the sleeves from his shirt. He turned them inside out, then wadded one up and daubed at me with it while I bit my lip and clutched at Saint Boris with my free hand.

Cruz finally seemed to be satisfied with the results of his labor, stopped daubing, and studied the wound. "It's shallow, but ragged. I'd kill for a proper bandage, but this will have to do."

The sleeves came back into play then—one to serve as wadding, the other to help hold the wadding in place. Then he pulled my pants gingerly back up to my waist and zipped them.

"I forgot you were a paramedic."

"I did too for a moment," he said, enigmatically. "Can you stand?"

I held my hand out to him and he hoisted me up. I was dizzy, but tried not to show it. "I'm okay," I said firmly. I hoped.

"Really? Or are you just being macho? If you're being macho, we're about to have a 'snap out of it' moment."

I laughed. "I'm a little woozy. But I can move."

Move we did, back out to the main corridor and left, seeking a passage into the pyramid, up to the surface, anything. We encountered another of the log-lever booby traps, this time carefully avoiding contact with it.

At the junction after, Cruz flicked his light up to read the notches. They told us to go straight ahead. Cruz started down that way, but I tugged him back.

"What?" he asked, eyes intent on my face. "Your hip?"

I pointed up at the notches. "Those say go straight?"

"Yes."

"What would it take to make them say, 'Go left'?"

Cruz grinned. "Oh, you clever woman."

Well, didn't that just beat the what-all out of being a clever monkey?

Cruz stuck his flashlight into his mouth and aimed it up at the notches. Then he flicked out his pocket knife and used the knife to chip a hole in the stone just to the left of the vertical notch. In a matter of moments, the steel blade had dug a trench roughly the width of a man's thumb into the rock. It was just deep enough to catch the light and turned a "go straight" rune into a "go left" rune.

"Looks really new," I opined. "D'you think he'll buy it?"

Cruz put the knife away, scooped up a handful of dirt and patted it around the new notch. "Better?"

He didn't wait for me to reply, but grabbed my hand and moved swiftly down the corridor. Refreshingly, it had not been sabotaged. It led us south thirty yards or so, then deposited us at the bottom of what looked like another pig tail switch-back. Man, those Mayans loved their switchbacks.

I admit, I am not a fan. The upside was that it meant we were beneath and within the third temple.

I required assistance to make it up the stairs. Walking I could get away with, climbing not so much. At the top, we reoriented ourselves and began notch-hunting. It was a laborious process, one that severely taxed my strength and our flashlight's failing batteries. I was dragging my right leg by the time Cruz finally stopped in the middle of an intersection and helped me to sit down against the cool wall.

He slid down the wall next to me and said, "We've risen hundreds of feet in the last half-hour. Let's try your cell phone."

I pulled it out of my shirt pocket and turned it on. "No signal."

"Are you sure?"

I handed it to him and he checked it himself. "I would have thought we were very near the surface now." He looked the thing over suspiciously, using the flashlight as sparingly as possible. Finally, he shook it. It rattled in a most disconcerting way.

"Oh," I said. "But 'lectronics is your hobby, right?"

Cruz got out his knife again and pried off the back plate. "One of them, but the receiver is in pieces—wires are disconnected. There's not much I can do about that without a toolkit."

He handed me back the useless phone.

"No toolkit?" I whined.

"I left it in my other pants. You still have your camera?"

"Yeah, why?"

He held out his hand and I fished the camera out of my pocket. He extracted two of its AA lithium batteries and exchanged them for the ones in the flashlight. The flashlight came back to full brilliance in a way that I found absurdly cheering.

He turned it off.

"Oh," I whimpered. *"Why?"*

"I want you to try to rest for a while. That's why."

"But we should keep moving."

I realized suddenly that I couldn't tell whether my eyes were opened or closed. A few seconds later, I didn't care.

"Gina. Gina, wake up . . . Wake up, *querida*."

I stirred, opened my eyes and saw light. I found the thought of light exhilarating, exciting, awesome. I sat up. It was only Cruz's flashlight. I was ridiculously deflated. I'd hoped for sunlight pouring through a Mayan skylight. No such luck.

"How long was I out?"

I saw his watch dial light up. "About forty-five minutes. Not nearly long enough. But I've found something. We need to go."

"Any sign of Greg?"

"None. I hope we left his lifeless body behind us under a ton of rubble, but I'll settle for having cut him off and forced him to retrace his steps . . . or at least some of them."

"You don't mean that," I said. "About Greg being crushed by tons of rubble."

He studied my face. Apparently, I looked disturbed by the thought, because he said, "No, of course not." He held out his hand to me. "Can you get up?"

It took more than just a hand up to get me to my feet, but once I was there, I found the pain of movement tolerable. Cruz took off toward the west, leading me by the wrist as if I were a recalcitrant child.

"Gina," he said, when we'd gone about five yards. "Have you ever shot anyone?"

"You mean a real someone? A criminal? No. No, I haven't."

"If it was Greg Sheffield or you, would you be able to pull the trigger?"

"If this is because I didn't want him squashed like a bug under a ton of rubble—"

"Could you pull the trigger, Gina? Because you know you might have to before the night is over."

"I don't have a trigger to pull at the moment."

"Gina, stop playing dodgeball with me."

"I don't know," I answered truthfully. "I guess I have to hope I would."

I felt what Cruz had to show me before I saw it. I was plodding along, working on my twentieth refrain of "Ten Little Monkeys," when I had the most incredible sensation of having walked into an air current.

I stopped dead in my tracks and sniffed. I smelled something besides damp earth. I smelled jungle. Dark, lush, damp, green jungle.

Cruz tugged me forward again, and I went eagerly, following him into a broader corridor that reminded me of the entry hall to the maze in Pyramid One. Suddenly, I knew where we were. This was the sun-dappled hall we'd peered into earlier in the day. The one with the well-ventilated roof. And through that roof moonlight, beautiful, blessed moonlight was spilling down into the gloom, creating a bizarre topographical map, its hills and valleys awash in pale glory.

Cruz turned off the flashlight again and pointed toward one of the larger holes. It was about fifteen feet from the floor of the room. "We have to climb. Do you think you can climb?"

"To get outside, I'll levitate if I have to."

"That's the spirit."

He led me to the bottom of a nice big pile of rocks and dirt and plant fiber.

"Okay, you go up first, I'll be right behind you. When you get to the top, climb out on your hands and knees, move to your left, and sit. Do you understand?"

I figured I must look really awful to have him talking to me like that. "Me climb, get out, go left, sit," I said.

I saw his teeth flash white in the moonlight. "And no makee sounds, okay?"

I tensed. "Is he out there? Did you see him?"

"No. I haven't seen anything or anyone. I just don't want to take a chance. If that booby trap cut him off, he might've had to go back. Ready?"

I wasn't, but I climbed anyway. Slowly, excruciatingly, dizzyingly. I put one hand, one knee, one foot in front of the other, moving ever upward toward that growing patch of starlit sky. I wanted that sky more than I recalled having ever wanted anything, and I willed that wanting to overwhelm the growing agony that was running up and down my right side.

I climbed out onto the overgrown ledge, achingly aware of the endless vault of the night sky overhead, and sidled to my left, just as Cruz had instructed. I sat and looked up at the star-spangled darkness in silence, not *oohing* or *aahing* or praising Brahman as would have been appropriate.

A moment later Cruz was sitting beside me. We spent a few moments letting our eyes grow accustomed to the different quality of light and taking deep, delicious breaths of fresh air that was warm to the touch and honey on the tongue.

Across from us on the other side of the clearing was Pyramid One. It looked like nothing so much as a sleeping dromedary. Rose was right, I have no sense of romance. We'd just Indiana Jonesed our way out of there; I knew what danger it contained, but I couldn't force it to be a lion or a dragon or even a malevolent volcano.

Cruz and I watched it for a while to see if there was any movement around the entrance. There was none.

How long should we sit here, I wondered. I turned to ask Cruz. He was looking at me solemnly, his eyes glinting in the moonlight. Before I could say anything, he caught my face between his hands and made me meet his gaze.

"He could be coming through the temple underneath us, or he could have doubled back to Pyramid One."

"Or he could've died in the rock fall," I murmured.

"We can't assume that, Gina. I need to know that if he catches us—if he catches you—you'll be willing to defend yourself."

"I can't know that," I said truthfully. "There's no way for me to know that."

"Gina—"

"Look, I could say 'yes,' but I don't know if I really could . . . pull the trigger. Would it make you feel better if I lied?"

He pressed his forehead against mine and shook his head, sighing. "How is your hip?"

"Okay." My pants weren't quite on fire, but they were very warm.

"Are you all right? Really?"

Well, other than a sudden reluctance to move, yeah. I nodded, rocking both our heads.

Cruz rose wordlessly then, and led me carefully down the tumbled slope.

Chapter 24
Hide and Seek

We made it back to the entrance of Pyramid One without incident. I regretted my bum hip, my broken phone, and my missing gun, but as they say: *No matter where you go, there you are.* Which I figure is a more esoteric rendering of *Work with what you got.*

The Vestibule was dark and there were no more flashlights in Revez's steamer trunk. Greg must have searched it and found the ones Cruz left behind. The maze was silent, giving up nothing. Greg could be anywhere. Lying under the rubble between Pyramids Two and Three, lying at the bottom of a pit in Pyramid One, or happily filling duffel bags with buried swag, singing, *"Yo-ho, me hardies. Yo-ho!"*

Or he could be wandering, lost but well-armed, mere yards away from where we stood listening to the maze.

Cruz took a long, slow breath as if he were getting ready to dive into a pool. "You wouldn't stay here if I . . . asked you to."

It was not so much a question as a statement of fact, so I saw no reason to answer.

"*Por supuesto*," he said, then placed a hand on either wall. "Like this."

I followed suit and we moved off into the Underworld.

If Greg had survived the rockslide and had found a way through, I reasoned, he would likely have taken a wrong turn and be lost somewhere in Mama Bear. If he'd doubled back, he would have taken his wrong turn just before the pig tail. *If* he had used the PDA to navigate. If he was also using the notches, that turn would at least slow him down. Cruz had told him the notches were unreliable, which might incline him to trust the PDA. Cruz had been lying, of course, but then so was the PDA he'd tried to hide from Greg's notice.

Cruz, I realized, had presented our adversary with the classic conundrum: *Don't trust me. Everything I say is a lie.*

At the top of pig tail stair, we stood and listened anew, trying to think like Greg Sheffield. He wanted to keep the site to himself, but he was scared. Would greed drive him to seek us out to finish the job, or would fear incline him to cut his losses and flee with whatever he could carry? He had a helicopter after all.

I felt Cruz's arm go around me, jerking me upright. "*Caray!* Gina, sit down before you fall down."

I hadn't realized I *was* falling down. I let him lower me to the top step of the pig tail so that my back was propped against the wall.

He put his forehead against mine again and murmured, "Two tunnels converge on either side of this landing. Either will offer you places to hide."

I saw where this was going and didn't like it one damn bit.

"No," I whispered.

"You can't continue. Not like this." He pushed something into my hands. "I'll leave you the flashlight."

"No."

"Gina, you're no good to either of us in this condition."

"No."

"If he finds us, you would not be quick enough to get out of his way." I felt his head tip from side to side. "I would have to rescue you again. Very tedious."

"Get over yourself," I said, then, "*You* take the flashlight."

This was the worst kind of fear—the slow, agonizing, impotent kind. It was the fear that visited me in my dreams. The fear of walking inexorably into the ocean, of watching my best friend's car flip like a hooked fish, of watching her be wheeled into an operating room with no guarantees she'd ever come out again, of losing this man to the darkness of the Underworld.

I realized I had not let go of the flashlight; I was clinging to it and had captured his fingers as well. He carefully extricated them from mine.

"I'll be back for you," he whispered.

I felt his breath against my lips in the moment before he kissed them. Softly. Quickly. A strange, quivering warmth spread through me.

Listening to the sound of Cruz's footfalls moving away from me down that wretched stair is one of the hardest things I'd ever done. I am not a person who takes well to being deposited on the sidelines, but here I was, alone with myself, exhausted, hurting, hungry, dizzy, and scared.

"Oh, snap out of it," I murmured.

When you are sitting alone in the dark, frightened—no, terrified—that the next sound you hear is going to be the dying scream of a friend or the hammer of a Ruger GP100 being cocked, you find things to do with yourself.

I prayed. I held imaginary conversation with Saint Boris. I checked my watch. It was 2:08 A.M. How time flies.

I checked my pockets. I had a little pack of Kleenex (might have been useful during triage), my compass, my camera, and a hair clip. That was on the practical side. On the arcane side, in addition to Saint Boris, I had Rosie's tinu, an obereg, and—lo and behold!—my old Caddie wire, which I thought I'd ditched. And then, firmly in a class of its own—Things That Were Once Practical But Are Now Junk—was the cell phone that was no longer a cell phone.

I turned it on and was immediately mesmerized by the pale luminescence of the little screen. I hoped there was enough kick left in its battery to light my tiny world for a while. The screen was shot, so I couldn't turn on the little flashlight, so I used the wan light to check my bandages. They were fairly dry.

Mercy.

I shut off the cell phone-cum-flashlight and checked the rest of my personal inventory. I was wearing a pair of sterling silver hoop earrings studded with tiny topazes (not real). The ersatz engagement ring was still on my finger. My watch still ran. Saint Boris still hung around my neck. I still had a secret Russian Orthodox Buddha tattooed on my right hip. Or at least I had before tonight. For all I knew, Greg Sheffield's bullet had put a bypass through that neighborhood.

I prayed not. I was a bit superstitious about that tattoo. I wondered, sleepily, if Cruz had seen it. Probably not, I reasoned, given that it was covered with gore at the time.

A jolt of raw terror shot from one end of my body to the other.

I was falling asleep.

I *couldn't* fall asleep.

I thought of the Wicked Witch of the West with her infernal poppy fields. I thought of snow. I pulled myself up off the stairs and stretched. I'd've done calisthenics if I could. Instead I took deep breaths and held them for three seconds, then let them out . . . quietly.

I was in my fifth rep when I heard something that woke me utterly: a gunshot.

A gunshot.

I plastered myself to the wall and moved down the stairs one shallow tread at a time. At the first switchback, I paused and listened again. Other sounds found my ears—movement, shoes on stone. I descended to the next level.

Quiet again.

Trying not to make a sound, I reached the bottom of the pig tail and moved to the Questionable Intersection. The notches still said, *Go straight, young woman*, the PDA would have sent Greg Sheffield (and now Cruz?) down the passage to my left.

I moved to the verge of the false trail, put my head against the cool stone, and listened. Sounds came back to me from below, sounds that might have been taken for the scurrying of mice. But there were no mice down here.

I peered down the passage, my eyes hungry for light, yet dreading to see it. Was there a slight paling of the darkness ahead?

I heard a shout. Inarticulate by the time it reached my ears. Then another gunshot.

I pulled the cell phone from my pocket and turned it on. Waxy bluish light created a soft glow around my hand. I held it out to one side and could dimly make out the corridor ahead. I shot a prayer toward heaven and stepped into it.

There were no notches here, but there were still corners and intersections, all terrifying in their prospects. At each one, I turned on my phone and shone the meager light down the various paths. Sometimes there was a wall of mute stone or a pile of debris; sometimes there was only more darkness and I would hesitate for a moment, weighing ridiculous options, then turn off the phone and move on.

I had fallen into a sort of stupor, shuffling through the shadow lands, listening and watching. So when my eyes saw light, the significance of it didn't immediately register with my brain. I was standing in a straightaway when I found myself being drawn toward a strange, faded spot on the left-hand wall of the corridor ahead. I was nearly upon it when I realized that it was the reflected light issuing from a cross-passage to my right.

I flattened myself to the near wall and peered around the corner. Ambient light washed out of everywhere and nowhere to light the narrow way. I could see clear through to its nether end, where there was a wall as solid and opaque as the one behind me.

Where was the light coming from? Curiouser and curiouser.

I stepped cautiously out into the junction. And was turned to stone by the sight of Greg Sheffield seemingly emerging from the very wall of the maze not four yards distant, a flashlight in one hand, his revolver in the other.

He hadn't seen me; he seemed intent on the path ahead. I took in the nature of the trompe l'oeil in a chaotic glance: it was a Russian Orthodox Cross—one vertical, three crosspieces. I was standing in the foot bar, Greg was in the main cross piece, and as I stood transfixed, Cruz stepped across the top bar and out of sight.

Greg's head came up and turned in that direction, as if he'd caught the movement from the corner of his eye.

I gasped.

Greg swung slowly toward me, bringing the muzzle of his gun to bear. I stood and clutched my useless cell phone and waited for him to shoot me. He didn't.

"Hello, Gina," he said, sounding like Eeyore—relieved to have found me, but depressed as hell. "You don't look so good. I guess I'm a better shot than I thought. Come closer."

"I'm sure you can hit me even at this range," I told him.

"Come here," he repeated. "You're going to lead me out of here first."

"Why would I do that? You're going to kill us anyway."

"Oh, but there's many a slip between the cup and the lip. The longer you're alive the more chances you have of escaping, right? Now come closer."

I stumbled toward him, deliberately making myself look more unsteady than I was. In the light from his flashlight I noticed that the floor behind him looked funny. It didn't reflect light the way the rest of the stonework did. As I drew near, I realized that was because it wasn't stonework. It was dirt.

"Stop right there, please," Greg said politely when I was still over two yards away. "Now, tell me: Where's Cruz?"

"I don't know. He left me behind."

"I don't believe that. He'd never abandon you down here."

"He wanted to go after you. He didn't want me to get hurt. He left me at the top of the stairs." I gestured with my head.

"And you came down here because?"

"I heard you shooting at him. You don't want to kill Cruz, Greg. He's the one that really knows how to get out of here. I don't."

"Why'd you tell me that? That makes you pretty useless, doesn't it?" He raised the muzzle of the gun again.

"I guess it does."

He cocked the Ruger. "I'll ask you one more time: Where's Cruz?"

"Here."

He stepped out into the far cross-corridor behind Greg. If he'd been armed this would've been all but over. But he wasn't.

Greg spun away from me and took two steps toward Cruz, before stopping to look down at the footing. He apparently didn't like what he saw, because he stepped back from the edge of the funny patch of floor.

"You know, Veras," he said, "if you hadn't gotten involved in this, none of us would be here right now. Gina would be safe and sound in San Francisco; you'd be writing articles on pre-Columbian art; I'd be running Revez; and Rose might never have gotten shot."

"Always someone else's fault, isn't it?" Cruz said.

Greg swung the gun back toward me. "If you don't get your ass over here right now, Gina dies. It's that simple."

As I saw it, I had one option. It was a stupid option, but I took it. I threw the cell phone at Greg's head.

He was only half-watching me, and reacted late. The phone clipped his ear and bounced aside, his shot went wild, and he dropped the flashlight. It fell onto the suspicious patch of earth and kept right on going.

Darkness was swift and complete. None of us moved for a moment. Then I heard the hammer of Greg's gun click.

"These corridors are awfully narrow. My chances of missing whoever I'm aiming at are pretty slim. Gina, come here."

I took a shuffling step forward. Cruz's camera flash exploded into the gloom, backlighting Greg. He was standing in profile to me, the Ruger aimed at Cruz.

In the psychedelic darkness after the flash I screamed and dove for Greg's legs. I hit him just below the knees. Caught off balance, he toppled. The muzzle of his gun flashed, the report echoing off the walls, mingled with our screams and shouts.

My scream cut off when I hit the floor. The breath was forced from my lungs and my left arm flailed empty air. Greg's scream continued for several long moments before coming to a sudden stop somewhere far below. I pulled myself back from the edge of the pit and rolled up against the wall.

The beam of Cruz's flashlight swept over me.

"Gina!"

I suddenly lacked the ability to answer. I'd swear that every drop of adrenaline in my body had been utterly spent. I could only lie curled up on the cold stone next to the pit and fight off the equally strong urges to sleep or retch.

I heard the sound of running feet and looked up in time to see Cruz sail over the booby trap and touch down on my side of it. He skidded to a stop and came back to join me on the floor, his arms going around me.

"He didn't get you, did he?"

I shook my head.

Cruz leaned over the edge of the false floor and shone his flashlight down.

"Some kind of woven matting. They put dirt and gravel on top of it and it looks like an earthen floor."

"Can you see him?" I asked. "Do you think he's dead?"

"I don't see him," Cruz told me. "I don't hear him either. I think the best thing we can do is get out of here and try to find the helicopter." He checked his watch. "The sun should be coming up in a couple of hours. Until then, I think we should go back to the Humvee. There's water there. Food. Some proper bandages."

He helped me into a sitting position, propped against the wall. "Do you want to rest for a while down here?" he asked.

"No, thank you. I think I'd really like to take a walk. Stretch my legs. Do a little sight-seeing." At that point, I ran clean out of sass. "I really want out of here, Cruz. Please."

There were no shortcuts out of the King's Treasure Pyramid. With my lumbering gait it took us a good twenty minutes to navigate our way to the surface. I was shivering so hard my teeth were chattering. The warm, humid jungle air helped, but even with that, Cruz had to break a blanket out of the back of the Hummer to wrap around me. He found the first aid kit and some water and alcohol, cleaned me up, rebandaged me, and helped me into the mandatory spare set of clothing one packs for these little day trips.

Afterward, I lay on the back seat of the Hummer beneath my blanket, waiting for the sun to rise and reflecting on pulling the trigger.

Cruz woke me at dawn. I had slept for over two hours; he had slept not at all. Instead, he'd taken his flashlight, gone back down to the Treasure Room, and retrieved our gear. His PDA and cell phone had gone down with Greg.

And he'd found the helicopter. It was set down in a clearing just west of Pyramid Three.

"I'm honestly surprised we didn't see it when we were descending the pyramid," he told me.

"Great," I said. "That means you can fly us out of here, right?"

"Sorry, no. But I did radio for help. The team may already be leaving Bonampak. I found food."

He held out a Snickers bar and a bag of Corn Nuts. I took the Snickers. Stress always makes me crave chocolate and peanuts.

"You can't fly a helicopter?"

"Alas, that is not among my copious talents."

He sat down on the seat next to me, intent on opening the bag of Corn Nuts.

"No, really. You're kidding me, right? I mean, journalist, archaeologist, paramedic, bodyguard, Boy Scout—no helicopter pilot?"

"You're feeling much better."

I smiled. "Yeah, I guess I am." I munched on the chocolaty treat for a moment. "Greg . . . he's . . ."

"Dead, I'm afraid. I could see his body with the flashlight. I saw no way to reach it. When help comes . . ."

I nodded. "So . . . Cross Sacred True, did you ever get any cute nicknames in school?"

He crunched a handful of kernels. "In Mexico, no nicknames. In the U.S. during my postgrad work, 'Cruiser,' 'Sacra-tomato,' 'Sacre Bleu,' 'Right-Cross.' Stuff like that. Nothing as musical as 'Tinkerbell' or as whimsical as 'Tink.'"

"Whimsical? Is that what you call it?"

"People give and use nicknames because they either like you very much, or dislike you very much. I doubt the boy who gave you that name disliked you. And I'm damn sure the friends who use it now like you *very* much."

He didn't give me any time to get all bashful on him, but reached into his pocket and took out my much-abused cell phone. It didn't look good. He pulled off the back panels and peered at the innards. "You know if I had the right tools, I might be able to fix this. Hell, if I even had a stout piece of wire . . ."

"Like this one?" I fished my once-lucky Caddie wire out of my shirt pocket. (Yes, I know the fact that I continually move it from one set of clothes to another is telling.)

"Exactly like that one. You never cease to amaze me. Is there anything you don't have in your pockets?"

"A ring of power? A three-course meal? A big, tall frosty glass of milk to go with my candy bar?"

"It was a rhetorical question."

I shut up and watched him put the Caddie wire to good use. Perhaps there was still some luck in it after all.

Chapter 25

A God's-Eye View

They caught up with Revez in Palenque as he was prepping his helicopter for a trip to parts unknown. He gave up quickly and easily, his attitude—or so I was told—was one of obvious relief. I didn't doubt it. He was probably imagining what would happen to him if he chose the wrong place to hide out and his old buddy Mario decided to look him up for old times' sake.

Nor was it difficult to get him to roll over on his "associates"—collectors and warlords alike, although I didn't expect anything earthshaking would happen to Mario Torres—other than him having to find another way of financing his little war. If the Mexican government had the wherewithal or maybe the desire to deal with him, they would have already done it. On the other hand, the collectors Felipe had been supplying with pretty baubles were forced to cough them up. The INAH was ecstatic.

Revez also pointed the NPS at his two remaining operatives—both American citizens—and confirmed Greg's connection to Ted Bridges, if obliquely. Bridges, he said, had bragged of having a "pet" NPS agent.

Greg's worldly goods and financial records were a bit less revealing. There was an unusual and steady influx of money to a bank account he held under an assumed name in a separate institution from his normal transactions. As he'd said, the deposits from his netherworldly connections outweighed his paychecks about two-to-one.

But he had been careful, as had his contacts at Sommers.

Take phone numbers for example: his phone records revealed calls to several disposable cell phones (virtually untraceable), and to an extension in a supply warehouse that was only loosely associated with Sommers (and with a host of other customers) and which had not been assigned to an employee since a round of layoffs the previous year.

His computer files were equally tidy. The only corroboration for what he'd told us in the King's Treasure Room came in the form of a single email from a now-defunct address that indicated he had fallen out of favor with his client (who had dealt with him in "good faith" according to the message), and would find it in his best interests to do everything necessary to redeem himself.

Like killing a couple of fellow field agents, for instance.

"But surely we have enough," I begged Ellen Robb during our debriefing, "to go after Sommers. Greg gave us everything but the name of his contact. There's got to be enough there to go with."

She did not look encouraging. "As you might suspect, Sommers can field some pretty heavyweight attorneys. They'll make this a case of 'he said, she said.'"

"He told us he'd been recruited by Sommers's people. The email you found on his laptop—"

"Doesn't mention Sommers by name. And it's from a dead account under a name that traces to dozens of people. None of whom have any connections to Sommers whatsoever. And trust me, Gina, their lawyers will use the circumstances of Greg's confession to their advantage." She shook her head. "God, I still can't believe it myself. Greg Sheffield . . . I thought he was incorruptible. I would have staked my life on it. I did stake *your* lives on it."

"How will they be able to use this to their advantage?" asked Cruz.

She shrugged, coming back to the here and now from her trip up Recrimination Row. "You were under duress. Literally in the dark. Gina indicated there was a moment when she wasn't sure which one of you was the turncoat."

"A split second," I corrected, my face flushing. "Less than that—a nanosecond."

Cruz smiled slightly as he no doubt added this to the List of Things to Hold Over Gina's Head.

"You might have misunderstood what he said. He did, by your own admission, make an allusion to conning his alleged contact at Sommers into trusting him. Maybe what he described to you was a sting within a sting, and you misunderstood who the target was." She glanced over at Cruz.

"Of course," he said. "Greg Sheffield was a longtime agent, an *American* agent. I am a foreigner. Who knows if I can really be trusted?"

"No way!" I protested. "They wouldn't make citizenship an issue, would they?"

"Race," said Cruz softly.

"They *wouldn't*," I repeated. "We know what we heard. And saw. The photographs—"

"Are inconclusive," Ellen said, spearing me with her impossibly green eyes. "They show a startled agent holding a gun. Even the one taken in the tomb shows you crouched on the floor at Greg's feet. His stance could easily suggest he's protecting you. As awful as it sounds, Gina, Cruz is right: his testimony may not carry that much weight if Sommers's attorneys decide to play the xenophobia card and twist things around a bit."

"But either way, Sommers is implicated as an organization. If Greg was running a sting—"

"They might maintain they were cooperating in a plan to root out dishonest employees. Greg's dead. Who's to know?"

Cruz shook his head, dug into his pocket, and placed a microcassette on the table in front of Ellen.

She picked it up, raising an eyebrow. "Please tell me this is what I think it is."

"It is a complete recording of everything that transpired from the time Greg Sheffield entered the Treasure Room."

"You were wired?" I asked incredulously.

He shrugged. "I thought merely to record the directions to the cache in case something happened to my PDA. When things took a turn for the treacherous, I thought . . . if our bodies were ever found . . ."

I shivered. "I love your sense of optimism."

"This," said Ellen, "changes things."

I left the debriefing praying she was right, and praying, too, that Dave had left a message on my cell phone. The comfort afforded by that old no-news-is-good-news saw has a shorter shelf life than yak butter.

There was no message.

"Anything?" Cruz slipped up beside me in the lobby of the Park Service offices.

I shook my head. "How long can she do this? Duck in and out of consciousness?"

"I've seen people go weeks that way. It *is* a good sign. Trust me."

I did trust him, I realized, when it came to this.

"I knew a man once," he said, "who went into a coma for years, then just spontaneously came out of it. At the end, he was in and out for about a week. Then one day. Bang—he just woke up. Funny thing, though, he went into the coma as a teenager—barely sixteen—and came out of it as an adult of twenty-three. But inside—" He tapped his breast. "Still a kid. The only thing that seemed real to him was a TV show he had loved. So for a while, he lived in that world instead of this one, until he caught up."

"And this is supposed to comfort me?"

He laughed. "What I'm trying to tell you, and doing it poorly, is that even in much more extreme cases, a complete recovery is possible."

My new cell phone chose that moment to massage my hand. I yipped and fumbled it; Cruz fielded it neatly and put it to his ear.

"Cruz Veras. Gina's right—" He broke off, his eyes meeting mine while he listened to whoever was on the other end. "We'll be there in ten. How's R—" He blinked. Apparently the speaker had hung up.

"What?" I said.

His answer was a swift hustle toward the parking garage.

"You're going to the hospital. You can drive yourself or you can leave Boris in the garage and I'll drive you. Your call."

"But why am I going to the hospital?" I asked. "Is it good, bad—what?"

He shook his head. "I don't know. It was Dave. He sounded . . . excited. He might've been laughing or crying or both. I honestly couldn't tell. Who's driving?"

I started to say that I'd get myself there, then gave it up as a bad deal. I wouldn't be safe, driving. My hands were shaking, my legs felt like Silly Putty, and my brain had shut down all sensory input.

We were there in less than ten minutes, something I attributed to the fact that Cruz had probably learned to drive in Mexico City. We checked in at the nurse's station and were sent directly to Rose's room in the ICU.

I swear when we came through her door, I couldn't tell what state Dave was in. His face was haggard, his eyes were red and teary, his mouth was doing mysterious things behind his new beard and mustache. If he hadn't left her side even to shave, I didn't want to ask what else he'd forgone.

My eyes were on him, trying to read the news in his ambiguous expressions, when a raspy voice said: "Hey, what year is it?"

I pivoted toward the bed.

Her eyes were open, dark with overmedication, but open. She smiled.

Dave beamed at me and hiccupped. I threw my arms around him and squeezed hard enough to knock the stuffing out of him.

"Don't I get one?" Rose complained. "*I'm* the invalid here."

I gave her a gentle, tremulous hug.

"I'm not made of glass, Tink," she whispered, and squeezed *my* stuffing.

I responded in kind. I hiccupped. I wept. I made a mess of the more-than-Gina-but-not-quite-Marianna makeup I'd put on that morning. I felt Dave's arms go around both of us.

"Hey," said Rose, into the middle of our group hug. "What the hell's *he* doing here?"

Dave and I straightened and followed Rose's eyes to the end of the bed where Cruz Veras lounged, looking singularly at ease with our display of emotion.

"That's a long story, Rose," he said. "You have time to hear it?"

"Time, I got lots of," she said. "Pull up some chairs."

Time was something Sommers auction house did not have. The Department of Justice and the NPS moved more swiftly than I could have possibly imagined and, within three short weeks, Sommers had to deal directly with Greg's taped confession. They dealt with it by selecting one of their "special acquisitions clerks" to be the ritual sacrifice—trotting him out in a closed-door hearing at which Greg's taped testimony was one of the star witnesses. The other was Rose Delgado, out of ICU and well enough to give video testimony from her hospital bed in regards to her two run-ins with the hit man Greg had suspected was in Sommers's employ.

It was at this hearing that Ellen Robb played her own trump card. The NPS, in cooperation with the INAH, had run Revez's remaining two operatives to ground (quite literally, in one case) and had jogged loose a couple of names. Neither was the name of the sacrificial goat, and Sommers was forced to give up not one, but three of its high-level employees for federal prosecution.

It was gratifying, I have to say, to be sitting on the prosecution side at the point Ellen was asked about the confessions of Revez's runners (which

I think is a great name for a soccer team). I don't believe I'd ever seen faces quite so red as the ones on Sommers's legal team as Ellen recited the names.

Now, one bad egg might be chalked up to . . . well, one bad egg. But *three* bad eggs indicates a systemic problem. Sommers gave up a supervisor. Who, under questioning, inadvertently gave up *his* supervisor.

PROSECUTOR: "So, rather than labeling the shipment as instructed, you chose to divert it to this 'special holding area' you mentioned?"

SUPERVISOR: "Oh, *no* sir. I labeled the shipment as instructed."

PROSECUTOR: "Excuse me?"

SUPERVISOR: (*Oops.*) "I'm sorry, could you repeat the question?"

PROSECUTOR: "Did you label the shipment as instructed by your superior? Please remember that you are under oath."

And so on and so forth.

In the end, a total of five Sommers employees were indicted—including an acquisitions director and a senior vice president—and the auction house's accounting, shipping, receiving, human resources, and data entry practices came under scrutiny by a hydra with heads from the NPS, the FBI, the SEC, InterPol and other acronyms.

The most serious charges—murder in the first degree and conspiracy to commit murder—were spread about in such a way that the prosecutors were fairly confident that *this* time fingers would be pointed and heads would roll. There is no amount of money that can compensate a sacrificial goat for a life sentence without hope of parole.

Oddly, when the aforementioned finger-pointing was over, not one member of Sommers's board of directors ended up in court. Go figure.

The major San Francisco museum in which Cruz had first seen artifacts from Bonampak and Itzamnaaj Balam (a name that stuck, by the way) immediately and very publicly released every last artifact of questionable provenance to the Mexican government. Others, Cruz assured me, would follow as they determined it best to cut their losses.

And as for us, the intrepid field agents (tongue very firmly in cheek), we got to see ourselves on TV and in the newspaper; we were interviewed on National Public Radio. The government commended us, the NPS tried to recruit us, and friends wanted to throw us parties. I cheerfully accepted the first, gave the second serious consideration, and skillfully wiggled out of the third. I am not and never have been a party animal.

The only party I was interested in attending involved a whole and healthy Rose Delgado coming home from the hospital to her family. This was the occasion of much subdued festing and feasting at which the inevitable happened: Cruz found himself in a room with my mother and father. Dad was happy to talk shop (law enforcement and antiquities of the Japanese variety). Mom had a whole other agenda which involved, as I had feared, procuring samples of Cruz's jet-black locks.

There was not a court attorney born who could grill a witness in quite the way Mom could.

"You are not married? But then you travel so much, eh? But a good-looking young man like you must have a girlfriend, yes? Or perhaps many girlfriends? No? But then what woman could contemplate such a life—crawling through ruins, toting guns through jungles?" A pointed glance at me. "A very hard life to share, this archaeology. Not very many women are robust enough for such a life. I imagine you would be pleased to find such a woman, yes?"

And so it went.

As for Cruz, he was neither standoffish nor overly intimate with me, but struck a balance somewhere just to the left of friendship—a step, maybe two. It was enough to make Mom's lips curl and Dad's eyes sparkle, and Alvie's eyebrows draw into an uneasy inverted V.

And what did it make me do? It made me warmly aware of him . . . and of myself. It made me pray to keep my head on straight.

When Cruz left the Delgado's sometime around 9:00 P.M., I walked him out to his car and apologized profusely for the grilling he'd taken from Mom.

"No need to apologize," he assured me, leaning against the flank of his Honda. "She was charming in every sense of the word. In fact, she reminded me very much of my own mother. Right down to the grueling interrogation."

I laughed. "It would be fun to get them into a room together just to see what happens."

"They would either become the best of friends or end up hurling spells at each other."

"Oh? Is your mommy a witch, too?" I asked in my best little girl voice.

"Oh, powerful. A most prodigious bruja."

"What does she do, your mom?" I asked, picturing some cute little, roly-poly Mexican señora in a bright smock dress.

"She's head curator at the Mexican Anthropological Museum."

I smiled. "Of course she is."

He leaned toward me conspiratorially. "When you meet her, be prepared to give up a lock of your hair."

I blushed. "I'm really sorry about that. God, could she be any less subtle? 'Oh, look, Dr. Veras, there's this tiny too-long piece of hair hanging over your collar. If you want I could trim that for you.'"

He grinned at me and slipped something out of his pocket. "Here, give this to her with my compliments."

I took it. It was a tiny zip-up plastic baggie with a lock of black hair in it. "Cruz, why? You'll only encourage her."

"Your choice," he told me. "Give it to her or not." He gave me a swift kiss on the cheek and slid into his car. "Take care of the hip."

"Sure," I said, and watched him drive off before going back into the house.

I put the baggie in my pocket.

The Haunted Girl

The room was large, well-lit, and crowded with boxes and crates full of antiquities. On the ample work surface at the center of the room, Rose had laid out the most exquisite and delicate of the finds from Itzamnaaj Balam. They included the museum acquisitions, the lots uncovered in an out-of-the-way warehouse that may or may not have been used by Sommers, my "wedding present" for my fictional bridegroom, and what had come to be known as the Peacock Hoard (Felipe Revez's private stash).

Front and center in our gathering of gods and great men were the mask of Shield Jaguar II and the statue of his daddy, Bird Jaguar IV.

Rose had been granted (the official term was "assigned" but I suspect there was some begging involved on her part) the privilege of overseeing the cataloguing, describing, and packing of each incredible piece of Mexico's past. And I had been granted the privilege of assisting her. To Rose, and therefore to me, this was something in the nature of a ritual. A setting to rights and redressing of wrongs.

Most of the swag would be crated oh-so-carefully and flown to Mexico City, but the two pieces at the center of our collection were to be hand-carried by one Dr. Cruz Veras, PhD, of the *Instituto Nacional de Antropología e Historia*. They would be presented by that institution to the President of Mexico in a special ceremony that was part political haymaking and part fund-raiser. If Itzamnaaj Balam was going to be excavated, monies would have to be set aside, and if monies were to be set aside, they had to come from somewhere. A nice big meet 'n' greet photo op with international media attention was just the thing.

Cruz would be the focus of much of the hoopla, of course. Not only was he a person to whom the INAH and the Mexican government owed a debt for the restoration of their national treasures (and who'd helped the U.S. government put a good-sized hurt on the illicit antiquities trade), but he was a well-known and eloquent science journalist, a legitimate (and dashing) archaeologist, and he photographed well. He was the sort of character they made movies about. Or at least they might if he learned how to fly a helicopter.

I'd made that observation to him before he'd taken off with a survey team to Itzamnaaj Balam for a week of mapmaking.

"No matter," he'd told me. "Whether or not I fly a helicopter in real life, I'm sure I will fly one in the movie. And of course, there must be at least one scene with me hanging from the landing struts, fighting off the villain."

"Oh, while I try to fly the damn thing I suppose," I'd said.

He had laughed. "No, no. In my movie, I fly the copter while *you* fight off the villain. A team effort."

"Earth to Gina. Earth to Gina."

I looked up from the statue I'd been absently stroking to see Rose regarding me with raised eyebrows from about three feet away. She had a cardboard box in her arms.

"Where were you?" she asked me, setting the box down on the table.

"In a helicopter teetering dangerously over Itzamnaaj Balam."

"Uh-*huh*. Well, bring it in for a landing. We've got artifacts to pack."

I looked dubiously at the box. "We're not going to pack these in cardboard."

"No, silly, of course not. We're going to pack them in these. Or at least most of them." She lifted a stack of plastic containers out of the box.

I was stupefied. "Tupperware? You're going to put a thousand-year-old Mayan mask in Tupperware?"

Rose laid a piece of bubble wrap on the bottom of the container, then set Shield Jaguar's life mask on top of it. "Grampa told me that the eyes of the spirits must be always able to look up at the sky. So, the mask will be stored like this—face up, with a clear plastic cover so that the spirit of Shield Jaguar can see the heavens. Hey, it's not romantic, but it keeps the spirits happy."

"Oh, well, if it keeps the spirits happy, then by all means. What about daddy-o here? You have a piece of Tupperware that'll fit him?"

She crossed to a gunmetal gray shelf and returned with a container that was, indeed, large enough to transport a statue of Bird Jaguar's approximate dimensions. I recognized the thing—Mom had one just like it that she used to transport watermelon halves, large batches of galobki, and garlic baguettes. It even came with a nifty, insulated jacket.

I lined the casserole keeper with bubble wrap and laid my statue in it. I suppose I'll always think of Bird Jaguar as "my statue." I already had an invitation to join him for his royal reception in Mexico City in two weeks. After all the literal blood, sweat, and tears Cruz and I had put in—not to mention the danger we'd faced—I found seeing these two particular pieces crated in this routine way a bit disturbing.

I remembered what both Cruz and Rose had told me about the disposition of many of the artifacts collected during busts. They didn't end up in museums. They ended up sitting on dusty, fusty old shelves in the *basements* of museums.

"Please tell me this thing isn't going to stay in this box for the next millennium," I begged, caressing Bird Jaguar's gleaming cheek.

"No, it isn't. Thanks to Cruz the Jaguar boys and the other remnants of Revez's hoard will be studied by experts before going to a permanent home in the Mexican National Museum."

Cruz, of course, was the lead expert. And if things went the way he hoped, he would be taking an internationally sponsored team of archaeologists to the site to begin excavation by the end of the year.

And that, as they say, was the good news . . . and the bad news. I was happy for Cruz and for Itzamnaaj Balam, but less than thrilled on my own account. I had tried (I thought I had, anyway) to keep Cruz at a distance. I'd tried to ignore the fact that while I was with him in the dark, under tons of earth and stone, playing hide-and-seek with Greg, wounded, exhausted, and scared spitless, some part of my internal landscape had shifted.

In my heart of hearts I knew that the time during which I was uncertain who held me captive in the Treasure Room could have been counted in a thousandth of a heartbeat. I didn't need the sound of a revolver being cocked to know who the betrayer was and who the friend. Not by then.

It made seeing Cruz off at the airport especially hard. It wasn't as if we were saying "goodbye" forever, but I was just getting the hang of that whole suspension-of-disbelief thing, and I'd kind of hoped I'd have time to explore . . .

"A penny for them."

I pulled my eyes from the two insulated casserole keepers on the institutional blue carpet near Cruz's feet and met his gaze. We stood just outside the security checkpoint in the charter terminal at SFO, waiting to hear his flight's boarding announcement.

"Actually," I said, "I think they may be worth more than that. I was thinking about trust. Loyalty. Esoteric stuff like that."

"Ah, the deeper questions of life. Which reminds me that I still have questions for *you*, Tinkerbell. I hope someday you'll answer them."

"I told you how I got my nickname." Dodge.

"That was not one of the questions. I meant the man who was not what he seemed to be. The man who made you afraid."

"I'm not . . ." I'd been going to say, "I'm not afraid," but that would be a lie. I was afraid. Of Cruz. Of trust. Of betrayal. "I'm not sure—"

"Then, I'll ask again, next time I see you."

Next time I see you. "If you still care."

"Of course, I will still care," he said gently. "Why would I not?"

I took a deep breath, like a swimmer getting ready to dive into a pool. I dove. "His name was Jeremy. Jeremy Augustine. He was a cop—Dad's partner, in fact. A rising star in the SFPD. Young. Savvy. Charismatic. He had been the perfect cadet. He'd matured into the perfect cop. He was the perfect fiancé. He'd be the perfect son-in-law."

I closed my eyes and envisioned him: tall, with chestnut hair woven with copper, a smile that lit up the world. Jeremy had pale blue eyes that nothing escaped. He had a way of looking at me that made me feel as if I'd just done something clever to surprise and amuse him. I'd liked it, until I recognized it for what it was—a patronizing smirk, a pat on the head. *Well done, little monkey. How amusing you are.* He even called me that on occasion: little monkey.

"Jeremy Augustine," I said, "could charm the stars out of the sky. He certainly charmed me. He inspired trust. So, I trusted him. Dad trusted him. Until he began to uncover evidence that Jeremy was involved in dealing illicit drugs—often right out of the evidence locker."

I swallowed and opened my eyes, glancing up into Cruz's face. It was solemn, watchful.

"I think Dad still wanted to trust him right up until the moment a drug bust went bad and he realized that Jeremy—his partner, his future son-in-law—had set him up to be killed, leaving him at the mercy of a pack of enraged and frightened crackheads."

"Dios mio." Cruz's gaze shifted to something outside the tall plate-glass windows. His narrowed eyes glittered in the glare of the sun.

I went on, suddenly needing to cauterize the wound I'd opened up. "Dad wasn't killed. But he did sustain the injury that ended his career. And Jeremy, instead of playing the bereft son-in-law-to-be, ended up serving fifteen to twenty on a litany of charges, including conspiracy to commit first degree murder. *That* was the man," I added.

A moment of leaden silence settled between us, then Cruz cleared his throat and said, "Thank you, Gina, for telling me this. For trusting me enough to tell me this. I . . . can't begin to imagine what that betrayal cost you. I would like you to understand one thing: I am *not* that man."

I met his gaze head on. "In the Treasure Room, Cruz, there was no moment, no second, no heartbeat in which I thought you'd betrayed me."

He took a half step toward me and took my hands in his. "Thank you, for that too."

I didn't know what else to say. "You said you had questions—plural."

"Ah, yes." He put his lips to my ear and murmured, "Someday I would like to hear the story behind that extraordinary tattoo."

I smiled down at the floor, blushing like a schoolgirl. "Someday you will."

They announced his flight then, and we shared a long awkward moment. Stupid, in view of all we'd been through together. Then he kissed me.

No, we kissed each other. I'd be lying if I said otherwise. I'd also be lying if I were to describe that kiss as being gentle or passionate or longing. It was any and all of the above. And while we kissed, I thought about that shift in my internal landscape—a shadow that had begun to fade. Jeremy's ghost was still there, but his sheet was getting threadbare.

I looked up at Cruz as we pulled reluctantly apart, and wished I were someone else. Someone who had never known and trusted Jeremy Augustine, or who had trusted him, but gotten over it or past it or whatever one is supposed to do with life-changing crap like that.

Still, as I watched Cruz stride away down the concourse carrying the "Jaguar boys" in their Tupperware cases, I was hopeful for the first time in three years. Cruz Sacramento Veras had seen the Russian Orthodox Buddha—the one obereg-mingei I carried with me everywhere. He knew a secret thing about me.

Of course, I'd have to be superstitious to believe that meant anything.

Acknowledgments

Long ago, it seems, when I first conceived of my diminutive Japanese-Russo-American detective, I braved several law enforcement news-groups seeking to understand how police departments worked. I am indebted to officers of the San Francisco and San Diego PDs for their invaluable (and cheerful) role in my education.

Many thanks to Sandy and Gerry Tyra, the dearest of friends, who turned me and my daughter Kristine loose on the shooting range and let us load and fire a case full o' guns in our search for Tink's perfect weapon . . . and then made us disassemble, clean, and reassemble every last one of them.

I'd also like to thank my husband, Jeff, and my offspring, Alex, Kristine and Amanda, for putting up with my non compos mentis-ness as I wandered through fictional worlds, and who only occasionally laughed at me when they caught me talking to my characters.

Special thanks goes to my wonderful editor, Merritt Small, for her sharp eye, great instincts and questions that encouraged me to dig more deeply into my character's inner landscapes.

ACKNOWLEDGMENTS

A shout out to my Muses: Ray Bradbury for instilling in me a love of words, Edgar Allan Poe—father of modern detective fiction—for inspiring my first ink tracks across the blank page and Tim Powers for opening my eyes to the fine line between mundane reality and magic.

Last, but in no way least, I thank my amazing agenting team, Trodayne Northern and Leslie Varney, who have been so very supportive, positive and just plain awesome.

About the Author

Maya's fascination with speculative fiction dates from the night her dad let her stay up late to watch *The Day the Earth Stood Still*. Mom was furious. Dad was unrepentant. Maya slept with a night-lite until she was fifteen and developed a passion for mysterious things that went bump in the night.

Maya started her eclectic writing career sketching science fiction comic books in the last row of her fifth grade classroom. Since then her short fiction has been published in *Analog, Amazing Stories, Century, Realms of Fantasy, Paradox, Interzone, Jim Baen's Universe*, and a raft of anthologies. Her magical realism novelette "The White Dog" (*Interzone* #142) was a finalist for the British Science Fiction Award; her alternate history novelette "O, Pioneer" (*Paradox*) was a finalist for the Sideways Award. Her debut fantasy novel, *The Meri*, was a *Locus* Magazine Best First Novel nominee, and *Star Wars Legends: The Last Jedi*—her 2013 foray into the Galaxy Far, Far Away with co-author Michael Reaves—was a *New York Times* bestseller.

The Antiquities Hunter is Maya's first novel of mystery/detective fiction.

Maya lives in San Jose where she writes, performs, and records original and parody (filk) music with her husband Chef Jeff Vader, All-Powerful God of Biscuits. The couple has three children who have been known to perform with them.

Maya's very own website: mayabohnhoff.com

Jeff & Maya's music site: jeffandmaya.com

Parody music videos: https://www.youtube.com/user/mysticfig/videos).

20x